KNIFE EDGE

A ZEE & RICO MYSTERY: BOOK 1

TERRI MAUE

CAVEL
PRESS

Kenmore, WA

A Camel Press book published by Epicenter Press

Epicenter Press
6524 NE 181st St.
Suite 2
Kenmore, WA 98028

For more information go to:
www.Camelpress.com
www.Coffeetownpress.com
www.Epicenterpress.com

Cover design by Scott Book
Design by Melissa Vail Coffman

Library of Congress Control Number: 2022946239

ISBN: 978-1-68492-200-0 (Trade Paper)
ISBN: 978-1-68492-201-7 (eBook)

Printed in the United States of America

To everyone who has a dream,
especially those who think they're too old to achieve it.
Also, to Dad and Mom, with all my love.

ACKNOWLEDGMENTS

WHERE TO START? I owe so much to so many. Thanks to Toni Pacini and Sin City Writers, who welcomed and encouraged me when I moved to Las Vegas. Thanks to Tonya Todd and Ron Fink, my deep critique partners, who pushed and prodded me to keep making the work better. I sometimes described our critique sessions as akin to sticking my hand in a blender, but they invariably improved my storytelling. Thanks to all my writer friends in the Las Vegas-based Henderson Writers Group and in the online group, The Writer Workshop. Thanks to my Cincinnati writer friends, who heard this story over a decade ago and enjoyed it so much that I kept writing. Thanks to my husband Eddie, who brainstorms with me and puts up with my writing obsession, and who took my fantastic author photo. Thanks to my parents, who valued reading, especially my dad, who gave me my love of the mystery genre. Thanks to Jennifer McCord at Epicenter Press, who saw the potential in my writing and guided me to bring the story to fruition. I know there are countless others. I stand on their shoulders, and any sun that shines on my face, shines because of them.

CHAPTER 1

ZEE MORANI EMERGED FROM HER Mini Cooper and inhaled humid September air. A favorite saying of her navy veteran grandfather floated through her mind. *Red sky at morning, sailors take warning.* She never could figure out how that bit of nautical lore pertained to landlocked Valerian, Ohio. Not that it mattered today. This morning, the flame-limned clouds fired her spirits.

Today she would grab her chance, take the tide at the flood, as her grandfather would say. She would nail this interview, explode across the Metro section front page with the next chapter in the saga of disgraced Dr. Ian McNeary, and transform her professional identity from syndicated opinion columnist to serious journalist.

As she set out across the parking lot, her gaze lifted to the top floor of the building across the street: McNeary's lab. A smile eased onto her face. She could hear the reporters at the *Valerian Tribune*, showering her with praise. Maybe she'd even get a few semi-appreciative words from cranky old Karl.

Stop calling him that, she reminded herself. As senior editor, he would be her boss if she succeeded as she planned.

Her foot sank with a sickening squish, and she jerked her head. Focused on the gray brick building, she'd missed the puddle of sludge leaking from the dumpster. The soupy mess seeped over one toe of her favorite pair of heels, spreading into the crevices of tan leather. She groaned. Just Jimmy Choo knockoffs, but still . . . damn trash collectors' strike.

A trail of *eau de garbage* would not make for an optimal first impression. Trying to tread lightly, she hurried back to her car and swapped the offensive footwear for her driving flats.

On her way again, she caught a blurred figure moving in one of the tinted, top-floor windows. Her pulse quickened—show time.

She slowed as she approached the building's heavy glass doors, belatedly checking her reflection for other "gifts" from the dumpster. To her relief, the trousers appeared pristine. The navy pantsuit was one of her best, confidence-boosting outfits. Its tailored lines exuded power and hid her figure flaws.

A gust of moisture-laden wind whipped her ivory scarf and caught the end in a thicket of her curls. She pulled the filmy fabric free, lifting her brows in resignation. Not much she could do about the rebellious brown halo, exacerbated by the worsening damp.

She pushed through the doors, skirted the morning zombies straggling into the coffee bar, and hustled toward the elevators. As she neared them, the doors to one car creaked apart. A man lurched out, his head down, and shoved through the cluster waiting to board. She sidestepped to avoid him, but his shoulder bag swung loose and struck her arm.

"Hey!" She grabbed the tender area above her elbow. The bullet wound had scarred over in the last two months, but not fully healed. The ever-present dull ache sharpened.

The man spun. His watery pale eyes squinted at her. He grunted, ran a hand through stringy gray hair, then staggered toward the exit.

"You have a nice day too," she muttered. Then pricked by conscience, her heart softened. Who knew what he endured in his life? Not everyone stood on the brink of a dream, like she did.

Still clutching her throbbing arm, she rushed to squeeze into the elevator before the doors shut.

The car rumbled upward until a gentle chime announced the second floor. One rider departed, leaving a silken thread of jasmine in her wake. The car crept on.

At the third floor, the remaining passengers unloaded. Zee tamped her rising excitement by forcing herself to review her plan for the interview. She'd avoid rehashing the already well documented human misery brought about when the doctor's earlier drug failed. Her focus would be on his long struggle to get to where he stood now, on the edge of redemption.

The elevator glided to a stop.

The door opened onto a view of scuffed beige walls and a featureless door sans knob or window. To her left, at the end of the hallway, a darker door gaped half-open.

The pain from the wound drummed in her arm. This top-floor corridor was isolated, ill-lit, quiet, like that rain-slicked street before—

Movement flickered at the edge of her vision.

She whirled.

The corridor was empty.

She sucked in a breath, re-orienting herself.

The dull gleam beneath her feet was flooring, not asphalt. No cocky young would-be gangster strode down it, on his way to make a drug deal, hand thrust meaningfully into his bulging jacket pocket. No foolish girl ran to meet him.

That night, Zee had hissed her name in warning, had run to save the girl when the guns erupted. And Zee had fallen, fire detonating in her arm, the bullet tossing her body to the ground like a rag doll. Before her helpless eyes, an orange rolled past, leaving a pockmarked trail of blood.

Stop.

Anchoring her feet on the cracked vinyl floor, she recalled Fontina's instruction from yoga class: *Follow your breath. Ground yourself in your body.* She inhaled and swept awareness through her five-foot-six-inch frame. Her attention snagged on her snug belt. She'd have to do something about getting more fit. Her thirty-nine-year-old body no longer easily forgave her laissez faire approach to health.

She pushed aside the thought, food for later consideration.

She blew out a quiet breath, her pulse slowed, and her brain kicked into gear. McNeary had said his assistant would not be there. Likely, the doctor left the door open for her. She relaxed her jaw. The frost between her shoulder blades dried. Straightening, she stepped across the threshold and scanned the room.

A worn path crept across gray-brown institutional carpet. Along the wall to the left sat a pair of standard-issue, chrome and plastic reception area chairs. The center of the room hosted a typical secretary desk, neat and tidy, fronting a partially open door to an inner office. Saving the room from complete banality, a rubber tree sprawled in the right corner, so tall its topmost branches bent sideways against the ceiling, huge glossy leaves drooping like fat spearheads. The effect was vulture-like, as though the plant silently awaited its chance to sweep away the puny civilization at its feet.

Zee blinked. Since when did a houseplant pose an existential threat? With brisk steps, she crossed to the desk. "Doctor McNeary?"

A minute dragged by. Only her breathing replied.

In the room beyond, a phone rang. The bell echoed and faded.

It rang a second time.

No footsteps or voice broke the ensuing stillness.

It rang a third.

The hair on Zee's neck prickled. Perhaps he hadn't arrived yet.

The shadow in the window belied that.

Then he should answer that damn phone.

The fourth ring's siren call pulled her closer. She circled the desk, hesitated steps from the inner door. McNeary hadn't spoken publicly in years. She didn't want to sabotage her chance.

The ring died. Zee strained forward, listening, willing the space beyond the door to yield a sound.

The silence lengthened.

Gritting her teeth, she inched to the doorway and peered through the gap. Her eye swept across folders on the corner of a worktable, an open drawer in a file cabinet, the paper-strewn edge of a desk . . .

. . . and a body on the floor.

The walls swayed. This couldn't be happening again. Blackness crowded the edges of her vision. She hissed air between her teeth, waited until the starbursts faded, then forced a second look. Dark stains glistened on the carpet near the motionless form.

She'd heard enough from Rico, his cop friends, and his fellow reporters on the newspaper crime beat to know not to touch anything. But she needed to make sure the man was . . . no longer alive. She couldn't bring herself to form even silently the other word. Turning sideways, she pulled in her stomach and squeezed through the opening.

A closer view confirmed her fear. Blood. Wet pools of it dribbled across the lapels of his rumpled lab coat. The soft bursting bubbles sickened her.

She forced herself to stare down at the carnage. Ian McNeary had been tall, probably handsome once. Time and struggle had etched the broad planes of his face and stolen most of the color from his mussed mop of hair. His round-lensed glasses lay askew on his nose, but his eyes, steel-blue and frozen wide, would never again have need of them.

Almost tenderly, she crouched. She was near enough to smell the metallic sweetness, near enough to sense the hatred that drove the knife.

She jerked back, stunned as if she herself had been stabbed. Nausea rose in her throat, but she forced it down. She should check. If there was a chance . . . She leaned forward, trembling, and touched her fingers above the wound on his neck. No pulse stirred beneath his still-warm skin.

Terror slammed her chest. Eyes darting, she fled the room, called 9-1-1, and then gave up her breakfast in the assistant's wastebasket.

CHAPTER 2

In McNeary's reception area, Zee huddled in a plastic chair. In contrast to the deathly silence an hour ago, muffled bumps, scrapes, and comments spilled from the inner office.

Where the body lay.

Zee shivered, despite the irritation radiating like coals from the large man crammed into the seat beside her. She pulled her jacket tighter and clenched her jaw to stop her teeth from chattering.

Shifting in the adjacent seat, Detective Larry Bernstow flipped his notebook shut. "That'll do. For now."

Zee hid a grimace. He *would* get the case. After the summer's gang shooting, she'd hoped never to see him again. Nestled in the hills of Southwest Ohio, Valerian didn't merit the law enforcement strength of Cincinnati or Cleveland, but surely a city of 155,000 boasted more than one detective in its police department.

As she swallowed the tepid remnants of a bottle of water, a commotion erupted across the room. A short, buxom woman tried to push past the uniformed cop guarding the hallway door. "What's going on?" Fear laced her voice.

"You can't go in there." The cop's slender body, not much taller than the woman's, barricaded the way.

"Why? What's wrong?" The woman's voice rose. "What's happened?"

"Take it easy, miss." The officer gripped the woman's shoulders. "What's your name?"

"Janece. I'm Doctor McNeary's assistant." She craned to see into the room.

The cop shifted stance but kept a hold on her. "I think you'd better sit down."

Detective Bernstow shoved to his feet and dragged his chair across the worn carpet. "Take this." He set it just inside the doorway.

Janece sank onto the seat, her round body quivering. Arms wrapped across her chest, she tugged her sweater tight as a second skin. Her eyes, huge behind tortoiseshell glasses, darted around the room.

A white-suited crime scene tech stuck her head through the doorway from McNeary's office and beckoned. Two others entered from the hallway, rolling a gurney on top of which lay a folded body bag. Janece whimpered.

Zee wished she had words of comfort to offer, but before she could think what to say, Detective Bernstow planted his solid torso in front of her. Sandy hair, ruddy face, tan blazer, beige shirt—a monotone brick wall, he blocked her view. "You can leave now. Go home."

"What?" Zee bolted upright, an unwise move, considering her shaky state. She tottered, but bulled onward. "You can't just dismiss—"

"This is an active investigation." Hard bronze eyes skewered her.

"I'm on assignment." Not exactly accurate but close enough.

Bernstow clenched his meaty jaw. "All the more reason. No place here for clever writers."

There it was. No matter the success of her syndicated column, witty satire would never earn her the respect afforded serious journalists.

She clenched her fists. No way Detective Bernstow was keeping her from this story. He couldn't treat her like some fresh-faced neophyte. It took discipline and skill to successfully skewer human idiocy and bureaucratic hypocrisy, twice a week, week after week, year after year, at a thousand words a crack.

She stepped sideways. Bernstow barred her way and barked over his shoulder. "Sergeant Jones, escort this witness out of here."

The cop who'd been guarding the door hurried toward her. Zee glared at her and pushed past Bernstow's bulk. Chin up and spine straight, she strode across the room, ignoring the glower that burned like a brand on her back.

Janece's brown ringlets shook with her sobs, and Zee stopped to touch the slumped woman's shoulder. "I'm sorry for your loss."

McNeary's assistant wiped her eyes with her sweater sleeve. "What happened to him?"

Zee opened her mouth to answer, but a firm voice cut in. "You heard the lieutenant." With a vise-grip on Zee's elbow, Sgt. Jones propelled her through the door. "Go home."

Zee winced when Jones released her. They must teach that pincer move in cop school. She glanced back toward Janece, striving to convey sympathy while complying with official instructions. Janece met her gaze, then dropped her eyes.

In mid-stride, Zee turned and bumped against something solid, warm, and uncomfortably familiar. Her hands flew to brace themselves on a broad, leather-jacketed chest. Knowing what she'd see, she angled her head upward—and dove straight into a pair of cobalt eyes. "Rico."

He grasped her forearms, steadying her. Electricity zinged from his fingers. She bit her lip and tried to ignore the heat that flushed her cheeks. How long before she would stop having that reaction to his touch?

"What are you doing here?" he said.

Typical of him to go right to the point, but concern softened his blunt question.

"I found . . . the body." Her knees threatened to give way at the memory. She locked them.

He loosened his grip. For a moment, she thought he'd wrap his arms around her. Wished he would. Hoped he wouldn't.

She should have felt the warning four months ago at the first sight of him, roaring into the parking lot on his Harley Road King: the tough reporter all in black. Leather jacket, snug jeans, and tight t-shirt—he wore the inky color like armor. Thick dark hair, five o'clock shadow, deep blue eyes, mesmerizing smile, and on top of all that, he worked the crime beat.

Everything about him said *danger*. And she spiraled to him like a moth to the devouring flame. She just wasn't supposed to get burned.

He was meant to be just another guy, someone to date, have fun with for a while, then let go. Her feelings for him snuck up on her, but she had too much baggage for love. She told him so—awkwardly, painfully. She implored him to be a friend, nothing more.

Outside McNeary's door, his gaze searched her face. "Wait here. I want to talk to you."

She stiffened at the order and dogged his steps.

"What's the story here?" he asked Sgt. Jones.

"It's early," she said, her chiseled face impassive.

"I heard he was stabbed."

The faintest humor crinkled her hazel eyes. "Nice try."

"No reporters. I told your girlfriend," yelled Bernstow from somewhere inside the room. "You'll get a statement later."

Zee flinched at the comment.

If Rico heard, he ignored it. He gestured toward Janece. "Is she a witness?"

"No comment," said Sgt. Jones. The gurney appeared at the exit from McNeary's inner office. Jones swept out an arm. "Clear the door please."

Zee averted her eyes at the lumps under the dark plastic and concentrated on staying vertical while wheels squeaked over the carpet and clattered across the threshold. A whiff of something rotten-sweet brushed her nostrils. She swayed.

"You can't drive." Rico's fingers brushed her arm.

Her vision blurred at the kindness in his voice. She turned from him. Now was not the time. She could fall apart later.

"Give me your car key." He held out his hand.

"I'm okay." She had to be. Marshalling strength, she sidestepped to pass him. As if to defy her, the toe of her shoe snagged on the floor. She tripped into his arms.

Pride goeth.

"Damn." Leaning on him, she tested her ankle and fought not to notice her heart thrumming. The rip in the vinyl flooring grinned at her.

"You're not okay."

She grit her teeth. First Bernstow, now him. This was not her day for avoiding troublesome men.

"I'll drive you . . . to my office." He softened his tone. "We can talk there."

It would be a safer environment than her apartment—for both of them.

Her spaghetti-for-bones told her he was right about driving. And her stomach threatened another revolt if she didn't put some distance between it and the plastic-shrouded horror in front of the elevator.

She nodded, fumbled in her purse, and located the Mini Cooper's fob. His warm hand cradled hers as he lifted the key from her grasp. The vibration beneath her ribcage jumped a register.

"Can you do the stairs?" He pointed toward the fire door.

"Better than the elevator."

She forced her feet down three flights, through a maze of blurred faces in the lobby, and across the cloud-darkened street to the sanctuary of her car.

The Mini proved no haven, though. From the moment she slid into the passenger seat, her brain contested her decision to go with him. Her body protested in return, quaking with every dip and bounce in the road. She should have taken the wheel, argued her brain, if for no other reason than she was familiar with the sporty car's go-kart handling. Surely, she could maintain control long enough to get home. When they got to the paper, she'd tell him that.

A sigh of relief puffed from her lips when they left the teeth-jarring potholes of struggling southcentral Valerian. Rico's driving wasn't at fault. Weather in the Midwest was an equal-opportunity destructive force.

After another stretch of rough temporary patching, he swung the car between two faded lines in the *Tribune* lot. She faced him. "I'm going home."

"You can't." Apprehension shadowed the blue in his eyes. "It hasn't sunk in yet."

"I'll get home before it does." She pulled free of his gaze, pushed open the door, and heaved herself into the charged air of the impending storm. A wave of dizziness rocked her against the car.

Rico appeared at her side. "No, you won't."

She rested her head against the Mini and stared up at a sky so low it seemed to touch the granite upswept wings of the art deco angels, eight stories above. Four of them guarded the central tower of the *Tribune* building, their wings arrowing to the rooftop, their draped robes tapering in elongated geometric blocks to vanish four floors below.

As a college intern, she'd fallen in love with these sentinels. They stood for rigorous pursuit of truth, high ideals, and steadfast courage. She imagined reproach from their disciplined faces today.

A shiver spasmed through her body. Rico was right, and she was acting like a fool.

He steered her to a side entrance, where Newsboys was chiseled into the lintel. Inside the historic building, the vintage aura disappeared, replaced by the mechanisms of a modern publication, cubicles, computers, clicking keys.

As they hurried through the newsroom, the undertone of noise clawed at her skin. A phone rang. She jumped, let out an involuntary squeak, tripped against a chair.

Karl stuck his head out of his office. His iron-gray eyes pinned Zee. "What's your problem?" Then to Rico, "What's she doing here?"

"She found the body this morning. McNeary," said Rico.

Zee wished she could will some color into her pasty cheeks. She straightened as much as she could on wobbly knees.

Karl's sharp eyes dissected her. "Said you couldn't cut it out there in the real world. Stick to poking fun from a nice, safe distance." He turned on his heel. Silently, Zee cursed her luck.

"Steady." Warm hand on the small of her back, Rico shepherded her into his cubicle. "Have a seat. Be back with coffee."

She slumped in a chair, icy hands tucked beneath her.

Of all the days to run into him.

She dashed at tears. Pigeonholed by the twice-a-week social commentary of *Z Beats,* syndicated in forty-seven Midwest newspapers. Further trapped by the top-selling compilation of her columns, *You Can't Make This Up.* And nailed like a bug in an exhibit by the TV interview last month, a segment of *18 to Watch in 2018.*

She quirked her lips. The more success she earned in her niche, the more her options shrank.

Rico returned with a steaming mug. She wrapped her fingers around it, and even knowing better, was tempted to swallow the notorious sludge-like brew. Instead, she closed her eyes and let its heat sink into her frigid flesh.

He rolled his chair to sit across from her. "You need to talk."

She stared beyond him, seeing the scene again. "It was terrible. He was sprawled on his back. His eyes . . ." Her voice cracked. She dropped her head and hid her face behind matted curls.

He raised a hand toward her, paused, then let it fall.

For a moment, she wished he hadn't pulled back. Smothering the thought, she set the coffee on his beat-up steel desk. Her knees grazed his, silky trousers against rough denim.

He inched his chair back and laid his hand on the arm of her chair. "You need to get it out. Otherwise, you'll have nightmares."

"I'll have nightmares anyway." She leaned forward, conscious of the hints of leather and motor oil that clung to him, the faint tang of hot metal. She tore her attention from the seductive scent, only to have her mind careen to the murder scene and a less pleasant odor: sharp, metallic, fecund with death.

"Zee, talk to me."

His command snapped the paralytic hold on her vocal cords, and the words tumbled out.

"The blood, Rico. His neck. Horrible, gaping." She clenched her arms across her belly, fingers digging into her elbows. "I feel like someone jabbed a stick in my gut and wrenched it around."

"That's shock. You need a drink."

"It's ten in the morning."

"Ten-forty. And not a normal morning."

He moved to stand, but Zee held up her hand. "Wait. I haven't told you the worst. The rage." She shuddered. "I swear, if the knife hadn't killed him, the pure venom would have."

He drew closer and captured her eyes. "Don't. Don't add anything that's not there."

"But you weren't—" Zee stopped, too drained to argue.

He rubbed a suntanned hand along the perpetual dark stubble on his jaw. "If it'll make you feel better, I'll keep you informed."

"No. I don't want . . ." She buried her face in her hands, clamping her teeth as if she could dam the wail rising in her throat.

She failed.

"It's all right." Rico pulled her to her feet and gathered her to him.

It wasn't all right, but she let him cradle her anyway. Surrendered her trembling body to the shelter of his tall, well-muscled frame and protective arms.

"It's not your fault," he murmured.

Muffling her sobs against his shoulder, she allowed him to hold her until her ragged breathing slowed and her apprehension surfaced. She loosened from his embrace and brushed her fingers at the wet spot on his broad chest. "I messed up your shirt."

"It'll dry." He smiled—the smile that so easily disarmed her.

Needing to break contact, she bent to rummage in her purse. "I'll drive you back to get your bike."

"Jake'll give me a ride. And here, I still have your car key." He pulled the fob from his jacket, hesitated, then dug into his jeans pocket. "Might not be the right time. Might never be." He dropped her apartment key next to the fob in his palm.

Zee reached for them, wobbled.

"You okay alone?"

The soft concern in his cobalt eyes nearly undid her resolve. Heat from their embrace lingered. She could cling to this rock until her roiling emotions calmed, but that wasn't fair to him. She'd made herself clear, though not with great skill.

She fought the pounding of her heart and forced her expression to relax into the half-lie. "Alone is exactly what I need to be."

CHAPTER 3

THE STORM HAD NOT YET BROKEN when Zee pulled the Mini from the shadow of the *Tribune* building's stern-faced art deco guardians. She glared at the swollen sky. She could use a raging, cleansing tempest to wash away the morning. McNeary's glistening blood. Rico's electrifying touch.

Her route home forced her to clank over a long series of metal plates, bulky scabs covering street excavation. She snatched at the distraction. Hadn't that stretch been dug up just a couple of months ago? Were the work crews that incompetent? Or were they guaranteeing themselves ongoing employment? Her thoughts piled atop each other. She should check the frequency of repairs. Get a map. This could be a topic ripe for satirizing in *Z Beats*.

Aware that the diversion was losing its power, she spared a glance as she passed a toga-draped, laurel-crowned statue. The Emperor Valerian.

Bad move.

Most days she enjoyed the joke. Many a visitor, drawn here for hiking and canoeing along the Great Miami River, expected pastoral ambiance. Why else name a place after a root that induced sleep? What they got was a town founded by lovers of all things Roman and inexplicably named for a murderous emperor.

And while the original settlement was laid out neatly around a central square, instead of a rustic, white-painted gazebo, it hosted the Forum Pavilion, complete with Corinthian columns and statues of Roman deities. Visitors found no street names as prosaic as Apple or Sunnydale. Instead, roads were numbered and named for their direction: cardo for north-south, decumanus for east-west— although the countryside's rolling hills sometimes strained credulity in that respect.

Heading roughly west, Zee jolted past the emperor's proud form, the Mini's low-slung suspension and her exhausted body paying the required eyeball-rattling tribute. No smile today. The metaphorical blood that stained Valerian's robes was no longer an abstraction, far removed in history. It was tangible, fouling her nostrils, clogging her throat, trickling like a nightmarish stream in her ears. Real human beings had spilled it, people with hopes and dreams, people like Ian McNeary.

She drove the rest of the way white-knuckled, a band of tension tight across her forehead.

The deepening gloom cast the parking lot at the rear of her apartment building in cave-like shadow. Or maybe it was the darkness in her mind. Feeling disoriented, she squinted through bleary eyes to be sure the sign read *Legate I*: her building.

Her lips twisted in a wry smile. The name indicated a Roman military officer of high rank, commander of a legion. A rather lofty appellation for a plain-fronted, three-story, six-unit block of apartments. Even on the newer west side, it seemed builders couldn't resist the lure of Roman inspiration.

Maybe they got tax breaks. The idea snagged her addled brain and sent it spinning. She should delve into the mystery of the missing *Legate II*. Next door, separated by forty feet of green space, stood *Legate III*. Maybe the missing Legate was the victim of an internecine imperial plot. A giggle bubbled in her throat. She clamped her teeth.

Corralling her wandering mind, she headed for the stairs to her third-floor refuge. Her leaden legs protested. Surely her fitness resolution could survive an exception today.

She shook her head. That way lay the graveyard of good intentions. Gritting her teeth, she plodded floor by floor until she reached her apartment. Too exhausted to shower, she plopped her purse on the coffee table and fell supine onto the couch.

On silent paws, her cat jumped to join her. With that sixth sense that animal companions seem to have, Candy kneaded Zee's midsection, the universal feline remedy for a distraught human.

"Mmm," Zee murmured. "Thanks."

Candy stretched out all ten pounds of her orange-and-cream-striped body and nuzzled Zee's chin. Her low, rumbling purr smoothed the raw edges of Zee's nerves. Lulled, she relaxed. Her furrowed brow eased. Taut cords in her neck unwound. She slid toward oblivion.

The three-note trill of an electronic bird interrupted: the notification alert on her cellphone. She willed herself to ignore it and focused on the radiating feline warmth. Amazing how such a small body generated that much comfort.

The summons faded, and quiet settled over the apartment. But Zee's respite had been breached. Curiosity prodded her eyelids open. Grumbling, she eased aside her languid furry friend, and heaved her own body upright.

A new email:

I know you saw me, but I didn't do it. No matter what you think. Please just keep your mouth shut.

What? She checked the sender address, already knowing she wouldn't recognize it.

"Damn." She reread the message. *I know you saw me.*

Her pulse thudded in her ears. She hadn't seen anyone. No problem, she could ignore this.

Except she couldn't.

It was her duty to report it to the police. Her listless fingers slid the phone onto the coffee table. She was tired, worn out, *half-dead*, she nearly said aloud, and at those words, the whole horrifying scenario in McNeary's office flooded her mind again.

She pressed the heels of her hands to her eyes as if to stifle the bloody images. Like rewinding a tape, she backed through the events: no one in his office, no one in that deserted hallway, a handful of people in the elevator. She hadn't looked at any of them.

Her head jerked. *The man who shoved her aside in the lobby.*

Their eyes had locked. He must have recognized her.

Her photo with *Z Beats*, her popular book, that television program. Fame was a two-edged sword and she'd just been cut.

Cut. The gruesome stab wound hijacked her vision. She squeezed her eyes shut.

Her head throbbed at the thought of another session with Bernstow. He would demand a description. She hadn't paid attention until the guy's bag hit her. On cue, the ache in her arm flared.

Her cell vibrated against the coffee table, and the deep tones of a Tibetan singing bowl reverberated, floating like waves through the apartment. Fontina's ring.

Zee snatched the phone.

"I just heard from Rico." Concern pitched Fontina's voice high. "Are you okay?"

"I'm . . . I don't know. I—"

"I'll be right over." The line went dead.

Zee gaped at the device, whipsawed by its transformation from agent of alarm to messenger of mercy. Candy twitched her ears as if interrogating her, then apparently satisfied, curled into a ball and began to clean her front paw. Zee stroked the velvet fur. "Big sister is coming."

The sibling title coaxed a weak smile from Zee's lips. From their first meeting, Fontina had been a source of comfort. A self-assured little girl, she had scanned their first-grade story circle, nudged aside a round-faced boy, and sat down next to shy, quiet Zee. While Zee admired her new friend's coronet of braided black hair—even then Zee's wild curls resisted taming—Fontina stuck out a hand, introduced herself, and asked Zee if she liked "mysterious stuff."

Six-year-old Zee's lonely soul leapt.

That had been the beginning. She leaned against the couch cushions, warmed by the strength of Fontina's presence in her life, no longer questioning their intuitive connection. Zee would have called it psychic, but Fontina disliked the term, said it gave the wrong impression.

Zee's smile grew. Whatever Fontina called it, throughout their long friendship, her sister of the heart had demonstrated uncanny skill in reading Zee's thoughts and feelings. It was almost as if she could inhabit Zee's mind and heart.

Did Fontina feel the touch of that email message's icy fingers?

The caller thought Zee believed he was the killer. He said he wasn't, but she had only his word. She folded her arms across the ball of ice in her stomach and rocked on the couch. She not only should go to the police, she needed to for her own sake.

Only moments later, Fontina's key clicked in the lock and her tall, lithe friend settled next to her on the couch. A reassuring image of normalcy, she was dressed in her usual form-fitting yoga wear, in hues that accented her cashew-colored skin. Today's outfit featured swirls of yellow and orange that climbed her leggings and cascaded down her arms. As usual, her thick, jet-black braids were twisted up and clipped at the crown of her head.

"How are you?" she asked, as Candy abandoned Zee's lap and began investigating her visitor's soft multi-colored striped shawl, obviously, a new toy.

Zee stared into the liquid brown eyes so like her own. "It's a nightmare." She shuddered.

Fontina wrapped her in a subtly lime-scented hug. "I'm sorry, Zee-zee." She dipped into her woven shoulder bag and held out a small brown bottle. "Perhaps you'd like to try this? Vetiver, lavender, and ylang-ylang. The combination calms emotions and eases stress."

Sounded perfect. Zee held out her hand.

"Two sprays on your tongue," said Fontina.

The sweet buttery flavor surprised Zee. Fontina's herbal concoctions tended toward the tart end of the spectrum.

"Rest now." Fontina extricated Candy from the folds of her shawl and handed the wrap to Zee. "It'll help if you stay warm. And I brought something for you to eat. I'll heat it while you nap." She scratched Candy behind her ears. "I'll take care of you, too."

Zee stretched full-length on the couch. Maybe it was Fontina's calm presence, maybe it was the placebo effect, maybe the potion in the bottle had actual therapeutic value; she didn't care. She wriggled more deeply into the suede-like microfiber cushions. Tension drained from her muscles. Her mind quieted.

ZEE OPENED HER EYES to a dark apartment. Not night, it was a strange, midday shadowing, pierced by light from the pendant lamp over the kitchen counter. Thunder rumbled. Rain pattered against the French doors to the corner balcony.

"Welcome back." Fontina laid aside her e-reader and rose from the easy chair. "Feel better?"

"Like I slept for hours."

"Actually, about forty-five minutes."

The edges of Zee's tranquility began to fray as the memory of the morning returned. "Fontina, I need—"

"Hold up a moment." Hands swathed in worn blue oven mitts, Fontina lifted a small casserole dish from the oven. "Eat first. It will clear your mind."

Her friend's unflappable patience could be annoying at times, but the savory aroma of chicken and noodles demolished any thought of argument. "Sweet heaven, that smells good."

"Emilio's special recipe." Fontina spoke over a metallic clatter. "Ah, there it is."

Zee cringed. "I really need to clean out my utensil drawer." It would be a great day again when that was her biggest problem.

Serving spoon tucked in one hand, Fontina carried the dish to the coffee table and set it atop a trivet on the inlaid tiles. Zee snagged a mitt, lifted the lid of the casserole, and spooned a fragrant serving onto her plate. "Are these noodles home-made?"

Fontina smiled. "My partner the chef. These leftovers were supposed to be our lunch, but I appropriated them."

Mouth full, Zee nodded her gratitude and an apology. Emilio's deft touch had produced tender yet firm pasta and succulent chicken chunks, but it was the creamy sauce that sent the dish into gastronomic heaven. Satiny on her tongue, it rewarded her taste buds with evocative hints of onion and garlic, and a generous smattering of chopped artichokes.

For a fleeting moment, she was tempted to ask for the recipe, but then she'd feel obligated to make it, and she knew where that would lead.

She didn't cook food, she ate it.

Revived, she set her empty plate on the coffee table. From her perch on the arm of the couch, Candy stretched toward it, ears up, nose twitching. Zee patted the soft fur. "Okay, you can have some." Under watchful yellow eyes, she moved the plate to the floor. Candy leapt, sniffed, and flicked a tiny pink tongue, then settled on her haunches to enjoy her repast.

Zee shifted her gaze to Fontina. "That was fantastic. You really need to marry the guy while you have the chance."

Fontina laughed. "Why get into that sinking boat? Our spirits are joined. That's enough."

Zee mock-slapped her forehead. "Sorry. What was I thinking? Your Flower Child roots run deep." Fontina's parents, unlike Zee's, chose to distance themselves from society rather than become immersed in the racial and political tumult of the '60s. Fontina lived on a farm until moving next door. Even after that, her parents grew their own food and made the rounds of craft fairs to support their family.

The contrast with Zee's parents couldn't be starker. She flinched at the painful reminder of loss: her deceitful mother, dead for decades but still haunting her; her dad already sliding into dementia, and now recently felled by a stroke.

"And I'm grateful." Fontina's voice pulled Zee into the present.

"My parents gave me freedom, the courage to follow my heart and chart my own path." She poured a cup of tea and settled on the couch beside Zee. "Now, tell me about your morning."

Zee blinked, banishing her distress, then launched into the story. At the end, she gestured to the phone. "I have to take it to the police, but I can handle it now. You and Emilio are a godsend."

Fontina rubbed her thumb across the golden topaz dangling from her ear. "Maybe we should ask Rico to come with us." She held up a restraining hand as Zee opened her mouth to protest. "I know the . . . distance . . . has been hard, and it's only been three weeks."

Twenty-three days.

"I wouldn't suggest this if I didn't think—"

"I shouldn't have gone to his office with him." Zee struggled to keep frustration from her voice. "It was just. Another body. I can't believe this happened again."

Fontina grabbed her hands. "This is different. You know that, don't you?"

"Rico said that, too." Zee shifted her gaze, seeking nourishment from the scene outside the balcony doors. This view fed her soul. In fact, the moment she saw it, she knew she'd found her home.

The French doors sliced diagonally across the south corner of the room, flooding it most days with light and warmth. In the morning, she could step onto the wide triangular balcony as the sun, rising behind her, brushed gold along poplar trees shielding the parking lot.

The planet turning.

In the evening, she could sink into her lounge chair and watch the sun draw a curtain of shadow across the lawn between the Legate buildings.

A good-night kiss.

No such solace was afforded her today. In the southwest sky, lightning burned a path through a dark bank of clouds. Like Rico's touch. "So much for boundaries," she muttered.

"Don't be so hard on yourself," Fontina said gently.

Facing her friend, Zee squared her shoulders. "I have to keep the lines clear. It's the only way I can keep his friendship." She slumped. "It feels cruel, though. I know he wants more."

"You're both finding your way. You'll make it work." Fontina swept a hand around the room. "You went to the newspaper, not here. You kept this boundary."

That had been his idea. Worse, if he'd offered to take her home, Zee didn't know if she would have refused. Her resolve had melted in his embrace, despite the fact that she swore off any entanglement with love after Jeff's betrayal.

Her ex-fiancé rose like a third presence in the living room. Jeff, with his shock of black hair falling over his wide, green eyes, his infectious laugh.

She'd felt like a feather in his arms when they danced that night at the Norman State homecoming. The night he proposed. All her post-graduation plans melted in his embrace, dissolved in the sparkle of the diamond he'd slipped on her finger.

How long had the euphoria lasted? Weeks? Months? She only knew when it ended—at the sight of him with another woman in a dingy motel room.

"Rico isn't Jeff," Fontina said.

Zee snapped her head up. Damn her friend's intuition. "Am I that transparent?"

Fontina squeezed Zee's hands and released them. "To me."

Zee could not doubt that. Fontina had been at a Buddhist monastery in Thailand when Zee's world fell apart. She'd called Zee on a premonition and flown home at the first opportunity, to offer comfort and strength. And even after she'd gone back to resume her studies, Fontina's presence remained as Zee put her life back together, re-enrolled in school, and completed her degree.

Zee huffed in exasperation. "I know Rico's nothing like Jeff. I just can't go there in a relationship right now, with everything else that's going on. It's safer to be just friends. Isn't it?"

"In a way, yes." Over the rim of her teacup, Fontina met Zee's eyes. "But maybe you're tiring of what is ultimately a more restrictive life. It might be time to lay this ghost to rest."

A wave of relief swept through Zee. What would it be like to live unchained from the past? But that was too big a leap right now. She dug fingers into her curls and massaged her scalp. "I wish I could be sure Rico didn't misread my behavior this morning."

"Give yourself a break." Fontina patted Zee's hand. "Even Shelby couldn't read minds."

A smile crept over Zee's lips at the thought of her childhood imaginary detective. "That wouldn't be playing fair," she said.

Shelby was modeled after her idol, Sherlock Holmes. In the early years, Shelby focused on solving the intellectual puzzle of a murder, a trait Zee's cerebrally oriented dad valued. Later, Shelby's values shifted to include doing what's right for the person or people involved.

Zee's eyes misted. As Shelby, she had learned to look for the telling detail and to identify the pattern in events, skills that she used to her advantage in *Z Beats* and that would serve her as well in writing in-depth features—like the one she'd planned for McNeary.

"Sorry," she said. "I argue enough with myself. I don't mean to drag you into it."

"Over and gone," Fontina said.

"Over and gone." Zee echoed the code phrase from their teen years. It had banished many a blunder that might have derailed their friendship.

Fontina gathered an armload of dishes. "So, shall we call him? I have a feeling that his presence may be useful."

Useful. An interesting choice of words. Zee cocked her head, studying her friend as she carried dishes to the kitchen. Fontina moved with grace like water flowing, but in truth, her energy was more akin to banked fire, ready to sprinkle sparks or pile on coals as the situation warranted. Was she trying to get Zee and Rico back together? Or was she simply suggesting a better way to deal with the police?

Rico enjoyed a decent working relationship with Bernstow, as much as natural antagonists could. Zee thought back to her earlier acerbic clash with the police lieutenant. Rico might exert a calming influence . . . on Bernstow, anyway. She would need to keep her own feelings in check.

"You're looking sideways at the world again," teased Fontina.

"It's Shelby's superpower," said Zee. "How else can she see things others don't?" She glanced at her rumpled suit. "You call him. I need to change."

Fontina didn't quite suppress her chuckle.

CHAPTER 4

B Y DINT OF WILL, ZEE FORCED HERSELF to sit upright in the Valerian police station conference room. Was it still Tuesday? Had she discovered McNeary's body only this morning?

Mustard yellow walls pressed in on her. The burnt odor of overcooked coffee drifted from a battered pot and wafted across a clouded plasticized poster listing the steps for a choking emergency. Next to it, a dusty photo of Ohio Governor John Kasich flickered in the sputtering fluorescent light.

If this was a conference room, Zee didn't want to see what the police used for interrogation.

Not that this didn't feel like an interrogation to her, Detective Bernstow tearing at her story while Sgt. Jones captured every word on her laptop. The sweat of decades of adrenaline-soaked bodies leached from the stuffy air and crawled across Zee's skin.

At the far end of the pitted gray table, Fontina offered a reassuring smile. Rico kept his expression neutral.

Bernstow leaned his bulk back in his chair. The wheels squeaked, as they had every time he moved. He nudged Zee's phone, sitting on the table between them, email displayed. "'I know you saw me,'" he repeated from the message. "You got anything to add, Miss Morani?"

Zee confined her exasperation to a single word. "No."

He pushed the cell toward Sgt. Jones. "Take care of this."

Rico shot Zee a questioning look, opened his mouth, then closed it.

Jones slid sideways from her seat, dodging a drawer in a filing cabinet that didn't quite close. She folded her laptop, collected the phone, and left.

"I remember you, you know," Bernstow addressed Zee. "The Sarpati street gang a couple of months ago." He cracked his battered knuckles, forcing them the way a fighter does, one hand dominating the other. "You got some rotten luck."

Silently, Zee agreed, rotten luck in the person of this detective.

He scraped his chair back, inducing another raw-edged shiver down Zee's spine, and heaved to his feet. Zee made herself sit tall when he leaned across the table. His sandy hair and craggy face filled her field of vision. "Stay here. You need to sign your statements. A sketch artist'll be in."

When he headed for the door, Rico slung his leather jacket over his shoulder and followed.

Zee sagged in her chair as her emotional state executed another ricochet. Under the detective's questioning, she'd zig-zagged from confidence to confusion to anxiety to relief, depending on how well she thought she'd answered. Bernstow's stoic expression never wavered, until that 'rotten luck' comment. His smirk withered the last of her composure, and she wished she could ooze into the cracks in the worn faux-leather seat.

"That wasn't too bad," Fontina said.

Zee's brows shot toward the ceiling. "You think? He *would* bring up the Sarpati. Does he imagine I don't remember?" Reflexively, she rubbed the scar on her arm.

"He knows you do. He's just making a point."

"Which is what? That I'm a dead person magnet?" Two people died in that fiasco, the boy and an innocent bystander just picking up groceries, both her fault.

Fontina stretched to touch Zee's hand. "It's classic domination behavior. And he's still probably irritated at what he perceives as your interference last time."

Zee raked her fingers through her thicket of curls, as if she could dislodge the scene of the shooting from her mind. Careful to minimize friction, she eased her chair back and pressed her forehead against the clammy metal tabletop.

Fontina's wheels squawked.

Zee's head flew up. "For crying out loud, can't they spare a little oil?"

The mild-faced, balding man who stood in the doorway grimaced. "I hate that, too." He approached the table and held out his hand. "David Markham. Sorry about the annoyance."

Zee wrapped her grief into a tight package and stored it in the hollow place beneath her heart. "Not your fault," she murmured.

"I know," Markham said, "but still . . ."

Zee's shakiness faded with his firm grip. She conjured a smile. "Maybe I can use my column to crowdsource a boost in your budget."

Finger to his lips, he darted glances right and left. "Let's not mention budgets, especially where the lieutenant can hear us."

"Oh?"

"Sketching involves a lot of electronics these days." Markham twitched his head toward the open doorway. "Some people weren't happy with my portion of last year's allocation."

"Bernstow can't be a Luddite."

Markham shook his head. "Not that bad. He just always wants more cops on the streets. Thinks more eyes means less crime."

The ghosts of that horrifying night breathed hot on Zee's neck. "He might be right. If the eyes are trained." She met Markham's bespectacled gaze. "I barely saw the man. I don't know how much help I'm going to be."

He gestured toward the door. "You'll be surprised. Sometimes I think we can work miracles."

If he could produce a description from what she remembered, Zee would count herself a believer.

ZEE CINCHED THE BELT ON HER RAINCOAT and followed Fontina and Rico onto the small concrete plaza outside the police station. To one side of the squat gray building loomed the multi-storied, leaden hulk of the county jail. On the other, fourteen long broad steps ascended to the black granite face of the courthouse. Together, the soulless triad formed the stronghold of Valerian law enforcement. Zee shuddered.

Abandon hope, all ye who enter here.

"Three hours in there," Zee said. "Felt like three days."

Despite the earlier rain, the air hung heavy with humidity. More storms were on the way, as the buffeting wind testified. Rico zipped his jacket. "You need to go home and sleep."

"I can't sleep." Zee clawed disorderly locks of hair from her face.

"Why don't we go to that place over there?" said Fontina. "Might be good to decompress a bit." She tugged her woven shawl more tightly around her shoulders. "I personally would appreciate something hot."

"Me, too," Zee said.

A chilly gust rippled across the narrow strip of faded awning. "Shorty's?" Rico said. "Not much good there."

Zee peered at the weathered lettering. "Does that sign say Chop Shop?"

"Cops say it used to be a butcher shop. Name's Shorty's idea of a joke. More like a warning. Breakfast all day, if you can stomach it."

"I'll risk coffee," said Zee.

He shrugged. "Let's go. Weather's coming."

They fought their way across the street and pushed through the shop doorway amid a swirl of crusty brown leaves and the first stinging drops of rain. Zee shivered with relief when the door banged shut, then nearly choked. In the dim light, a miasma of burnt coffee, cold bacon grease, and sugar assaulted her nostrils. Within two breaths, her eyeballs ached. She raised her hand to block the wattage from a dirt-caked, overhead schoolhouse lamp, noticed it was suspended from a wobbling ceiling fan, and sidestepped.

It definitely ranked as a hole-in-the-wall, but the little place was warm and dry.

Three uniformed cops sat at one of the tiny tables, drinking from thick white ceramic mugs. One bit into a doughnut, which fell apart in his fingers, scattering crumbs amid the litter of crumpled paper napkins. The others laughed. "Warned you," said one.

Zee and Fontina sent Rico to the counter to order drinks while they dodged curled edges of worn linoleum tile to claim the least grungy-looking booth. Once safe on the cracked vinyl cushion, Zee's gaze shifted to Rico's tall frame, lingered on the glistening wet strands of his thick black hair. He cut it short, in soft bristles that smelled good after—

She squashed the memory in her fists. They were having coffee, as friends do. Her lapse earlier had done no harm. *Take the victory.*

She twisted to face the window. They'd reached shelter barely in time. Pellets of water pummeled the multi-paned glass. Overhead, the shop's awning whipped and snapped. Pale sidewalks turned the color of melting chocolate, a pleasant sight but for the pile of abandoned black trash bags moldering on the corner across the street. The flimsy skins flinched under the battering. Zee hoped they would hold.

At the clicking of Rico's approaching boots, she turned back to the booth. He pushed two mugs across the table, then slid into the bench opposite her. "I got you cider. You'll thank me."

Bowing her head, Zee let cinnamon-spiced steam wash over her cheeks. She sipped and sighed as warmth blossomed through her chest. "I didn't realize how cold I was."

"Shock and weather," Rico said. "And your unreasonable fear of the police."

"It's not fear. It's animosity." *And maybe some fear.*

This was an old argument between them, though. She had a more pressing question. "Do you think I'm in danger?"

"Detective Bernstow didn't seem too worried," Fontina said.

Rico snorted. "Easy for Bernstow; he sees this stuff all the time. But," he hurried on, "you don't need to be alarmed. The guy sounded more scared than threatening."

"I think so too," said Fontina.

"Reminds me." Rico dug into his jacket pocket. "Here, your phone."

"I thought Bernstow—"

"He didn't need your phone, just your IP address."

Lightning crackled as Zee's fingers grazed his palm. She forced them not to linger. "I appreciate this. You saved me a ton of trouble."

He shrugged. "Bernstow can be a jerk."

She felt blood rush to her cheeks. He did it to challenge Bernstow, not necessarily to come to her rescue. It was thoughtful, but he would have done it for any colleague.

Anger flared. Bernstow had taken advantage of her. If her feelings hadn't been zinging around like pinballs, maybe she would have realized his confiscation wasn't required. She hid her face in a cloud of steam from her mug and wondered how long it would be before her emotions would stop betraying her.

Time to change the subject.

"What's really bothering me," she said, "is having to describe the guy. I told Markham I didn't notice much, but he kept tweaking features, the angle of the eyebrows, thickness of the hair, shape of the mouth. Thing is, everyone says eyewitnesses are notoriously unreliable. What if my mistakes upend some poor soul's life?"

"Maybe," Fontina said, "the *art* of the sketch artist is to tease out those details your vision picked up, but your conscious mind didn't register."

Rico's brows twitched. Zee could have sworn he stifled an eye roll. "The important thing," he said, "is that the police know how to do their job."

Hardness edged his voice and yet beneath that flint, something soft whispered. She'd bet he was thinking about the gang episode . . . or everything that came after.

He'd rescued her, taken her to the hospital, insisted she stay at his place for a few days. A big old house, high on a hill east of the city. His shaded front porch became her refuge. Resting on a padded swing, she followed the progress of the sun: the copper spire of St. Stephen's catching the morning light, the glass roof of the library atrium glowing at midday, the shadows shifting on the *Tribune's* stone angels.

There on his porch might have been where she first felt the foundation slipping under her feet. Sensed the first flickering of urgency to find safer ground.

She wrenched her thoughts from the memory and turned to her companions. "I need to understand this. According to my research, McNeary's drug definitely caused some people a lot of trouble. But, for someone to *kill* him . . ."

"Catch me up," said Fontina.

"About ten years ago, McNeary made what seemed to be an important breakthrough in the treatment of ALS, Lou Gehrig's Disease. After that, as often happens, a big pharmaceutical firm bought the company that employed him."

"Excelco," said Rico.

Zee nodded. "The early trial phases produced positive results. Excelco wanted to cut phase three short and bring the drug to market. McNeary objected, but the company pushed forward. And then the FDA withheld approval."

"Essentially siding with McNeary," added Rico.

"Right," said Zee. "After that, McNeary and Excelco parted ways. The doctor formed his own company, finished the testing, and got approval. The drug went to market in 2012 as Neurish."

"I've heard of it," Fontina murmured. Her voice was hoarse. She lifted her teabag with her spoon and wrapped the string around the tiny sack, squeezing until amber drops fell into her cup. She tugged the thread tighter and tighter, until it snapped in her trembling fingers.

"Fontina?" Zee said.

Her friend waved away Zee's concern, but she did not meet her eyes. "Please, go on."

Zee raised her brows but took up the story. "Neurish worked at first like the proverbial miracle. Then side effects began to appear. Serious infections, cancers."

Beside her, Fontina pulled a thin silver chain from beneath her form-fitting top. Eyes closed, her slender fingers clutched the disc-shaped pendant like a talisman.

"Is everything all right?" Zee asked her.

Fontina swallowed. "Tell you later, okay?"

Uneasy, Zee returned to the narrative. "The easing of ALS symptoms didn't hold. The relapses were catastrophic. Some patients and families claimed the drug actually accelerated the disease."

"Excuse me." Fontina slid from the booth.

Zee moved to follow, but her friend held up her palm. "I just need a minute to myself."

Brows knit, Zee stared at her friend's retreating back.

"She all right?" asked Rico.

"I don't know. Something touched a nerve," Zee said. "Usually she has better control."

"Give her a minute."

Zee swirled her cider. Fontina was strong. The reason for her troubled behavior must be grave.

Rico's fingers brushed her hand.

She jerked her head up.

He withdrew.

Her heart wished he hadn't. Her head told her it was better this way.

"When she's ready," he said. "Meanwhile, don't speculate."

"I can't help but worry." She toyed with her mug. "That pendant on her necklace is an old coin. Her Uncle Ramiz gave it to her before he died." That was not exactly true. Before he died, he gave her his favorite soft brown beret. He told her where to find the coin afterward.

"Significant?" Rico asked.

"They were very close." Zee debated how much to tell him. Pragmatic Rico would probably scoff at any claims of connection to the world beyond this one, but he had warmed to Fontina, and she cared about him. "Uncle Ramiz passed on some years ago, but she . . . talks to him sometimes."

She waited for criticism. Instead, his blue eyes softened. "Could be what she's doing now."

"You're probably right." Tears threatened at his tenderness. She gulped cider, unsure if she could speak more around the lump in her throat.

The cops at the small table scraped back their chairs. Zee tracked them.

"You need a diversion." Rico tasted his coffee and winced, scrubbed at his lips. "You wanted a motive. How about a dying man's revenge?"

Zee forced herself to surrender her concern for Fontina. "Is that what Bernstow thinks? The guy I saw looked gaunt. Big, but his clothes hung off him. And his skin was ashy." She aborted a glance toward the restroom, looked out the window instead. "Ironic, though. If it *was* him, he killed the one person who represented hope. McNeary was close to starting trials with a new drug."

"Would have been a good story." Rico eyed the liquid in his mug as if it had been conjured by Macbeth's witches. He set it to one side. "I looked into him after you left this morning. Did you know he insisted his investors come only from friends and family?"

Zee shook her head. "Guess he didn't want to depend on strangers again."

"Trouble is, you lose a lot of money, things can get ugly."

Zee sucked in her breath. "Bad enough when strangers hate you. Worse when it's people you know and love. I wonder that he even wanted to keep trying. He must've been heartbroken."

Any word but that one. The moment it left her tongue, she wished she could call it back.

Rico rubbed a hand across his shadowy stubble. "Maybe it's all he knew to do." His blue eyes locked on Zee's. "To make up for what went wrong." He held her gaze a moment longer, then slid sideways in the booth. "Gonna try the cider."

He headed for the counter, back straight, shoulders set, stride confident. And yet she'd seen the yearning.

Regret, Fontina told her once, was wishing you had a better past. Zee couldn't deny the truth of that, or the futility. Words once spoken can't be unsaid. Some hurts can't heal. Some hearts are too sabotaged . . .

She stared out the window. The storm had spent its fury. The garbage bags across the street had survived. A burly man in a sodden sweatshirt walked past the pile, stopped, and delivered a furious kick. The plastic skin did not oblige his wrath but merely buckled under the force of the blow. He glanced up and met Zee's eyes. His own narrowed, and he changed course, gobbling the distance between them in angry strides.

CHAPTER 5

Z EE STARED OUT THE CHOP SHOP'S rain-streaked window. She struggled to place the man barreling across the street, jabbing a finger like a dagger in her direction. His sweatshirt looked familiar, gray with a neon yellow panel across the front. Her brow creased as he bounced on the balls of his feet, then darted between two cars. A horn blared. He didn't break his stride.

She swiveled in the booth, scanning the eatery for other possible targets of his ire. No one else there. "Damn," she hissed. "I don't need another confrontation today."

"What is it?" Rico called from the counter.

"Some angry guy just kicked the trash bags. And now it looks like he's heading toward me."

Rico's boot heels clicked across the floor.

Zee's brain rabbited, snatching at details as the man altered his trajectory toward the diner's door. Reddish-brown hair, dark-framed square eyeglasses, patch of beard. She'd seen the guy's face somewhere, although it hadn't been twisted with rage at the time. He'd been laughing.

Laughing.

She spotted the rolled-up newspaper in one fist, and the pieces snapped together. "I know him."

The battered door banged open with a teeth-jarring screech and a furious clanging from the bell above it. A greasy, paper-hatted head popped up in the narrow kitchen window, and the counter clerk ducked behind the sad-sack doughnut display.

Too bad those cops had left. For a moment, Zee wished for Fontina's calm presence, but her friend had retreated to the restroom earlier, obviously struggling to control her emotions. Zee didn't know what triggered such an unusual breakdown. She forced her worry aside.

One problem at a time.

Sodden shoes squeaked on the worn linoleum tile as the man stormed toward the booth. Rico muscled a shoulder in his path. "What's your business, mister?"

Zee held up her palm, relieved that her hand didn't tremble. "I got this, Rico."

His eyes darted to her. She dipped her head once. He let the man pass but shadowed his steps.

"You," the dripping man spat at Zee. "Guess you're proud of yourself." He slammed the newspaper on the table, and stabbed a thick finger at today's *Z Beats*, with its headline *Trash-Talking Trashes Trash Talks*. "I'm on unpaid leave because of you."

"Not my doing." Her heart hammered in her throat, but her voice held steady. He pulled up, surprise written on his features. She pressed her advantage. "You bad-mouthed trash collectors just when they were about to sign the contract. Calling them idiots in public isn't my idea of a great negotiating tactic." She leaned toward him. "How is it you don't know that cellphone cameras are everywhere?"

The man colored but recovered. He planted both meaty hands on the table and angled forward. Rico stepped closer, fists clenched. His leather jacket rustled. Though equal in height to the angry man, Rico outmatched him physically, his muscled torso a clear challenge to the disgraced negotiator's flabby paunch.

Behind his rain-smeared glasses, the man's eyes shifted toward Rico, then back to Zee.

She held his stare. "Are you finished?"

He backed off a bit. Water dribbled from his hair and the strag-gle of beard on his fleshy chin. "You made me a laughingstock."

Over his shoulder, Fontina emerged from the restroom, her demeanor calm, relaxed. She paused, her eyes telegraphing a question. Zee twitched her head in the negative and kept her eyes pinned to her adversary.

His angry glare burned. Zee's fire flared. "I take a dim view of arrogance, especially when it results in the city continuing to fester under a couple hundred tons of garbage. The damage was done when you shot off your mouth, not when I recorded it."

He glowered at her in silence. Behind him, the counter clerk pulled out her phone.

Zee lowered her voice. "If I were you, I'd leave before someone records something else."

He whipped his head around.

Rico tensed.

The clerk lifted her chin and raised her phone. Zee shot her a grateful smile.

Spinning back, the big man snarled at Zee. "Glad I could pro-vide employment for *you*." He scowled at Rico, stomped toward the door, and yanked it open. "Bloodsucking journalists."

The bell jangled into silence. Zee deflated against the cracked vinyl booth, exhaling a low, slow *wooosh* between her lips.

Rico chuckled. "Sure you want to get into more high-profile journalism?"

"Right at this moment, my insides are trying very hard to talk me out of it."

"Don't let them. Good job there."

Zee's pulse, slowing from the encounter, revved again. Romantic debacle notwithstanding, Rico supported her goal. This friendship thing was going to work.

"Appreciate it." Her smile faded. "That guy's the perfect example of why I want it. He thought I was a lightweight. Figured he could bully me. It would be refreshing to get some respect for a change."

"News flash. No reporter gets much respect. Goes with the territory." His grin erased the sting from his words.

"Now I'm discouraged," she teased.

He cocked his head, a question in his eyes. "You weren't afraid of him. What's your problem with the police?"

Zee squashed a grimace. Hadn't she just told him this? "It's not fear." *Not totally.* "I grew up listening to stories about race riots and war protests. Watching the videos endlessly replayed. Viet Nam was my parents' war, but all those emotions blew up again with Desert Storm." She swirled her cider, seeing the past in its depths. "And I can't ever forget Kent State." Where Fontina's cousin was shot.

"That was National Guard," he said.

"Doesn't matter." She shook her head. "It's all law enforcement. Blind, unfeeling bureaucratic machinery. And enforcers are cogs in the machine." She lowered her voice. The employees here might be friends of cops. "That guy was small potatoes, no threat. I didn't mean for him to lose pay, but I was in the right."

"Right is might." Fontina slipped into the bench. Her skin glistened from fresh washing, and the anguished lines in her face had smoothed. Whatever the reason for her earlier sadness, she had recovered.

"You okay? I worried when you left so quickly." Zee's chin dipped. "I should have gone with you."

Fontina's fingers slid to the old coin on her necklace. "It's fine. What about you? That guy was firing thunderbolts."

"She deflected them well," said Rico.

Fontina had engineered a skillful deflection, too, but Zee would honor her friend's desire to avoid a painful topic. "I actually enjoyed putting him in his place. But I do feel a little rattled. Lot of adrenaline." She glanced out the window, buying time to tamp her feelings. The negotiator's aggression had left an angry wake. And her heart squeezed at neglecting her dearest friend in distress. Both good reasons for the skip in her pulse, but it was Rico's compliment that sent it racing.

Fontina's voice interrupted her reflection. "What else did I miss?"

"We were discussing motives," said Rico. "I suggested a dying man who wanted revenge."

Grateful for the opening, Zee let herself rejoin the conversation. "Someone who took the drug and relapsed," she said. "The man I saw looked sick enough to fit the description."

"Anyone who cared about him could have motive," said Fontina.

Others were never far from her friend's mind and heart. Guilt pricked Zee again.

"Who else?" said Rico. "Think broader."

"People who lost money," Zee said.

"Families and friends of those people," Rico added.

"Competitors, worried he might be close to another break-through?" said Zee.

Rico ran a hand through his hair. "Competitors wouldn't kill him, especially not like that."

Not *like that*.

Zee's fragile façade of logical analysis crumbled at the remembered image of McNeary's butchered body. She picked up her cider, but now the crimson liquid reminded her of blood and death. Throat constricted, she set it aside. "I can't wrap my mind around it."

"Despair could push someone over the edge." Fontina's face crumpled.

Zee caught the liquid brown eyes. "What's wrong?"

"It's . . ." Tears glinted in Fontina's lashes. "My niece Teresa has ALS."

Zee's heart fell to the hems of her pants. An only child, she hadn't known the close-knit warmth of a big family. Not until she met Fontina. Shortly after, Fontina's father—Papa Alesandro—adopted her as his honorary ninth child. Suddenly, her world included faces always ready to smile, arms always ready to hug, mischievous game-players, quiet secret-sharers, and big,

wonderful, noisy birthday celebrations and parties. Zee remembered Teresa, a large-boned shy girl, who had grown into an
impressively proportioned woman, with a round face framed by
masses of brunette waves and a voice that always sounded like
bells. "The opera singer?" she said.

Fontina nodded.

"I'm sorry."

"She's in an early stage," said Fontina. "She has most motor control, but the future is inevitable."

Zee slipped her arm around Fontina's shoulders. She refused to
voice platitudes. Amyotrophic lateral sclerosis: slow neurological
deterioration, stealing movement, digestion, breathing, a progressively relentless imprisonment until the release of death. "Are you
able to help her, with herbs and things?"

Fontina touched the coin again. "Tomas doesn't think his little
sister knows anything."

Rico glanced at Zee.

"Fontina's oldest brother," Zee said. "They're fourteen years
apart, and he's . . . not so open-minded."

"It's hard." Fontina gazed into her tea. "Teresa's only forty-two."

"That's rough," said Rico.

"The diagnosis devastated her," said Fontina. "But I can't imagine how she'd feel if she thought she'd been cured, given her life
back, and then had it snatched away again."

"Your point strengthens the revenge motive," he said.

Zee knew that, for Fontina's sake, he was trying to divert the
conversation toward less emotional ground. Torn between supporting his effort and comforting Fontina, she remained silent.

Rico reached across the table and covered Zee's hand with his.
He caught her eyes. "The police will find who did this."

He'd misread her distress, but she didn't care. The warmth from
his palm drew her like a comfortable fire. She curled her attention
around it. "I'm sure you're right. I hope it's not the guy who ran
into me. I believe him when he says he didn't do it."

"Not your problem. You really *should* get some rest."

Zee slid her hand free and covered a yawn. "Maybe I'll be able to sleep now."

"I'll take you home." Fontina dug her keys from her purse.

Zee followed her to the door, then glanced toward their booth. Rico sat sideways at the edge of the bench, head lowered. He cradled his hand, the one that had held hers. Eyes down, he stroked it with his thumb.

She wrapped her hand around her knuckles, the ones he'd covered with his palm. Then, eyes smarting, she shoved her hands into her pockets and stepped outside into the cold wind.

THAT EVENING, HALF A BOTTLE OF CHARDONNAY eased Zee into a stupefied slumber, but the bloodied corpse would not leave her alone. She woke with a cry, throat parched, and rolled to face the bedside clock.

Two-thirty.

With a groan, she swung her feet to the floor and padded the few steps from her bedroom to the island separating her galley kitchen from the great room.

Moonlight streamed through the balcony doors and painted large pale rectangles on the hardwood floor. McNeary's savaged body had haunted her sleep, but on the canvas of lunar luminosity, Rico's face intruded. In the Chop Shop, the light in his blue eyes had danced as he augmented Zee's research with his own, played off her ideas, and listened to her build on his in return.

Like old times.

Zee slammed the empty water glass on the counter. Harder than she intended. Candy's ears shot up. She ran into a patch of silver light, turned toward Zee, and waited, wary.

Familiar coals smoldered behind Zee's heart. After Jeff's motel tryst destroyed their relationship, she'd sworn off men and thrown all her energy into building her career. It was a satisfying life. She dated every once in a while, but never let anything develop; was never tempted. Love was too much work, a complication she didn't need.

Then or now.

Back in bed, she stared at the ceiling, assaulted by every sound: the rattle of the refrigerator, the rumble of a passing truck, even the faint hiss of the distant highway. With a thump, Candy bounded onto the mattress, a tiny, crimson-striped catnip pillow in her mouth.

A memory surfaced. She and Rico, naked and breathless on a late afternoon. Candy leapt onto the tangled covers, lacy red-and-white striped panties between her teeth.

Rico propped himself on an elbow. "Look. It's Candy-pants." He pinched Zee's bottom. "Not a bad nickname for you."

"No, you don't!" She countered with a playful slap.

He rolled atop her, pinned her wrists, and taunted, sing-songing the name as his mouth closed on hers. After that, they forgot the cat.

When they broke up, Zee considered discarding the nickname but rejected the idea. Her faithful feline should not suffer for human foibles.

At four-thirty she gave up trying to sleep.

She'd focused on the riveting details of McNeary's personal story when she prepared for the interview. Not only would they make a good column, but she also planned to pitch them as the hook for an in-depth piece on the human experience of drug development. Rico's information about the investors kindled her curiosity on another angle. How much did it cost to get a drug to market?

While the coffeemaker burbled, she started an internet search. The more she read, the more she marveled that any drug found its way into a doctor's hands. Traditionally, researchers began by identifying a vulnerability in a disease, then sought a potential targeting chemical. The search for a possible match could take two or three years. After that, the trials began, growing progressively larger, as researchers tested safety, dosage, efficacy, and side effects.

The process could derail at any time, sending the whole enterprise back to square one.

Zee leaned back in her chair. She couldn't see how they persisted through year after year of drudgery, slogging their way with no promise of success.

Candy jumped onto her desk and extended a paw toward Zee's face.

"Give me a minute to finish," Zee said.

The cat meowed, yawned, and stretched across the keyboard. Her tail swished, and the window on the screen vanished.

"Argh. I should know better. Your Majesty wishes to eat." Impassive yellow orbs blinked. Zee rolled back her chair, surprised to find her office flooded with sun. "As it happens, Candy-pants, I'm hungry, too."

She toasted a sesame bagel, poured nuggets into Candy's dish, and returned to her computer, resuming her exploration to the delicate staccato of tiny teeth pulverizing Salmon Surprise.

Drug trials, she learned, could eat up six or seven years. Throw in another year or more for FDA approval, and a decade has passed. By then, the cost of a potential drug could mount to an astronomical half-billion dollars or more.

She chewed on the last chunk of bagel and picked up her mug. No wonder the odds against success were one in five thousand, or worse. And that's if all went well.

Her phone's ring cut through the apartment's silence. She sloshed coffee over the rim and flung her napkin at the spreading brown pool while she answered.

"Bernstow here," the gruff voice barked. "You need to come down to the station to look at a lineup."

The bagel turned into a lump in her stomach. Again with Bernstow? Again in that temple of despair? She kept her voice level. "Give me an hour."

"Thirty minutes."

The cords in her neck tightened. She hadn't let the irate garbage guy push her around. Damned if she'd let Bernstow do it. "An hour, no less."

He grumbled something unintelligible. Then, "Don't be late." The call terminated.

CHAPTER 6

O NCE AGAIN, ZEE FOUND HERSELF CROSSING the plaza in front of the police station. She squinted in the late morning sun, narrowing her eyes at the glare from the concrete expanse. Barren, it struck her, heartless as the surface of the moon. Ahead of her, the station's dark doors loomed like black holes, already sucking the energy she needed to face the lineup.

Of their own accord, her feet detoured to a pitted stone bench. She dropped onto it and dug fingers into her thick curls, trying to scrape free her dread. Rico was right: her attitude—call it fear or animosity—toward the police was irrational. Bernstow was not her enemy. And after she'd completed this task, she could put the murder behind her.

At least until the trial, a pessimistic voice in her head nagged.

If it came to that, a stubbornly optimistic one retorted.

Enough.

With a vigorous zip of her hoodie, she stepped toward the doors.

Quiet pervaded the small lobby, its half dozen faded plastic chairs deserted. A worried-looking, baby-faced officer scrutinized her from the front desk.

"Zee Morani to see Lieutenant Bernstow," she said, pleased at the steadiness in her voice.

Relief spread across his bland features. Bernstow must have been harassing him, as if the hapless uniform could expedite her arrival. Irritation spiked in her chest. She forced it down.

"This way," he said with a flick of his hand.

He opened a steel door onto a buzz of activity: voices, phones, computers, squeaking drawers, squawking chair wheels. In a far corner, Zee picked out Bernstow's sandy hair. "I see him," she said.

"Okay." Her escort turned away. Judging from his smile, he was happy to let her proceed on her own.

She maneuvered her way with care among the bustling bodies. Shift change? Or was there that much crime in Valerian, to account for all this busy-ness? She filed the idea for future research.

"Finally," Bernstow said when she arrived at his cluttered desk. He shepherded her down a narrow hallway to a tiny, overheated observation room.

She forced herself to breathe the stale air as a group of men shuffled single-file into a brightly lit space on the other side of the one-way glass. Five middle-aged males, bodies ranging from lean to cadaverous, dressed in an assortment of disheveled clothing. Someone had clearly attempted to present each member of the lineup in a state consistent with her description of the man she encountered.

"Take a good look at each one," the detective instructed. "Tell me if you recognize any of them."

"Number two." Her stomach lurched.

Bernstow rested a light hand on her shoulder. His gentle voice surprised her. "Take your time. Be sure." He keyed a microphone. "Number one, step forward."

Zee inhaled, struggling against the sour taste in her throat. She shed her hoodie and willed herself to study the man. He stood straight and tall, chin up, thin gray hair framing a smooth brow. Despite his rumpled clothing, he exuded good health.

She shook her head.

"Number two."

He flinched as if startled, then advanced on unsteady feet. Zee's heart pounded at the sight of his rucked-up hair, bright wet eyes, and thin colorless lips above the days-old stubble on his chin and jaw. His shirt and pants looked like he'd slept in them.

She swallowed bile and glanced toward Bernstow.

"Step back," he ordered. "Number Three."

Another lanky figure separated from the row. Black-framed glasses slipped repeatedly down his narrow nose, and he kept pushing them back into place. He ran a bony finger under the ill-fitting collar of his over-large shirt.

"Hold still!" Bernstow barked. The man's face reddened.

Perspiration beaded on Zee's forehead. She blotted it with her hoodie. Whatever this jittery unfortunate soul had done, he hadn't barged into her in the lobby. "No," she croaked.

"Number Four."

He stepped up, somber as a funeral, dark jacket drooping from his slumped shoulders. A moustache, barely detectable on his skeletal, sweating face, smudged his upper lip. Except for the facial hair, he bore the greatest resemblance to her lobby assailant.

"It's not him."

Bernstow glanced sharply at her.

"I'm sure." She massaged her temples and fought a desire to loosen the button on her jeans. Why was there no air in the room?

"Number Five."

The last man in the lineup shuffled forward. His scalp glistened beneath thinning colorless hair, and his clothes hung on his slight frame. With palpable effort, he tried to keep his body still. Though he faced straight ahead, his eyes darted around the room. In his hands, he twisted a bedraggled fedora.

Zee felt Bernstow's scrutiny. "Not him."

"You want the hat on?"

"I didn't see a hat." The room wobbled, but she met the detective's gaze. "It's number two. I'm sure."

As if he could hear her, the man standing in the second spot raised his head and stared at the one-way glass. His face showed the ravages of illness, sagging sallow skin, dried-spittle-flecked trembling lips, cheeks etched by pain. His feverish eyes bored into her.

Her stomach heaved.

Bernstow grabbed the trash can, and for the second time in less than forty-eight hours, Zee lost her breakfast.

TWENTY MINUTES AFTER ZEE COLLAPSED onto her couch, Fontina arrived at her door. While Candy meowed a welcome, Zee dragged herself upright. "Did you get a message through the psychic hotline?" she half-jested.

"No intuition needed. Rico called."

Zee wanted to be irritated. She wasn't a child. She didn't need to be coddled. But she couldn't deny that Fontina's presence comforted her.

Her friend sat down beside her, tucking her long legs beneath a soft cotton skirt. "You look a little white."

The familiar joke teased a laugh from Zee, in spite of herself. Her Romanian forebears had bequeathed her an olive complexion. Fontina's toasted cashew skin had been gifted in part by her African ancestors. "Looking a little white" was how they challenged each other in their perennial suntan competition.

Fontina flashed a grin. "Laughter. That's better."

Warmth crawled up Zee's face. "What did Rico tell you? Just that Bernstow summoned me? Or did he find out that I went to the police station, identified the guy, and then decorated the wastebasket?"

"Puking's becoming your new trademark."

"Great. Karl better not find out." Zee puffed a frustrated breath. "Rico defends him, but I notice there aren't any female writers working crime. And he strongly implied I just wanted to compete with Rico."

Fontina arched her brows. "Because you stopped dating?"

"Who knows how that guy's mind works? Or any guy." Zee rubbed her temples. "Seeing that man again . . . this whole business makes me sick."

The smile left Fontina's face. "It would make anyone sick." She wrapped Zee in her arms. "You're shaking. You need food."

Zee eased from the embrace and pushed damp curls off her cheeks. "I can't eat." The man's eyes, piercing, alight in his pallid face, burned in her mind. "He looked like death. If I hadn't just seen a body . . ."

"At least let's have some tea." Fontina rose.

Zee struggled to her feet. "I'll help. Better for me to do something instead of sitting here fighting visions."

The two of them crossed into her kitchen. Candy, ever alert for the possibility of a treat, followed. Lips curving upward, Fontina pulled a catnip mouse from a bag on the counter and secreted it in her pocket. "Mind if I look for some nibbles?" she asked.

Candy meowed meaningfully.

"Human ones." Fontina grinned at the circling cat.

Zee laughed. "Go ahead. They're not as easy to find."

While water heated, Fontina unearthed a twist-tied bag of crackers, a small wedge of cheddar, and to Zee's surprise, an unopened box of spicy windmill cookies. When the kettle whistled, Zee poured hot water over the teabags in the pot and lingered above the fragrant billowing cloud of steam. Ginger-mint. She inhaled, looked at her friend. "You always know exactly what to do."

"Decades together help." Fontina carried the tray into the living room, then tossed the toy onto the old Oriental rug in front of the couch. "Here you go, Candy-pants."

Feline hunter pounced and began batting it between her paws.

Zee sank onto the cushions, shame creeping up her cheeks. "I appreciate you and Rico looking out for me, even if I sometimes resist."

"Sometimes?" Fontina over-widened her eyes.

"Okay, I might be a little sensitive there." Zee held up a hand to forestall any further dramatic expressions of pseudo-shock. "Moving on. I assume Rico learned about my faux pas from Bernstow. Did he find out anything about the guy I identified?"

"He mentioned his name. James Hawethorne."

"Sounds familiar." Zee chased the brain wiggle, but couldn't catch it. "Did he admit to doing it?"

"Rico didn't say."

Zee stopped in the midst of trying to dig her thumb beneath the tab on the cookie package. The visceral memory swept through her, the impact of the shove and the rough slap of the man's satchel. She sucked in a breath and searched for a new focus.

Fontina saved her. "Stimulating, brainstorming together yesterday," she said.

Too much so. "It haunted me last night." Zee pursed her lips and resumed digging at the tightly sealed box. "It seems like just when I feel we can make this friendship thing work, I get ambushed by a memory."

"You're attempting a delicate balancing act." Fontina lifted the lid of the teapot, looked inside, then replaced the cover. "Needs more time." She smiled. "Like you two. Sunface Buddha, Moonface Buddha."

"What?"

"It's a koan. According to one interpretation, Sunface Buddha lives a thousand years. Moonface Buddha lives a single night. We all drag our history with us, but every day is a chance for a new start."

"Sounds like we're trying to be in two places at once." Zee ripped a strip off the top of the box, tore open the inner wrapper, and yanked a cookie free. "No wonder I feel confused."

Fontina's smile softened. "Confusion can be the beginning of wisdom. Think of it as an invitation to stay open to possibility." Her brown eyes twinkled. "Who knows the paths your relationship with Rico might take?"

Only one option for Zee.

As if to argue, the newly acquired windmill cracked in thirds between her fingers. How bad was it when even food defied her? She jammed a piece into her mouth. "How do you come up with this stuff?" she asked, around a mouthful of crumbs.

"Some would say serendipity," said Fontina. "This morning, a former student gave me a brush painting of the Japanese characters. Such a gift, to receive just the right thing at just the right time."

"You lead a charmed life." Zee tried not to sound churlish.

Fontina laughed and reached for the teapot. "Everyone does, if they pay attention."

A pang sliced Zee's heart. Rico's charms had led her into trouble, forced her into a corner. If she'd paid more attention, she could have acted before she hurt him. Forget Sunface and Moonface, she was Stupidface.

A corner of her mouth tugged upward. Fontina's youngest brother used to call her that. It usually earned a reproof from his father, who treated Zee like an honorary daughter entitled to respect. Though the memory was bittersweet, the tightness in her chest eased. "Point taken. Rico and I—"

From her cellphone arose the revving of a motorcycle from a '60s girl group song: Rico's ringtone.

He jumped in as soon as she answered. "Hey, you sound okay. Good." The clatter in the background told her he was calling from the newspaper. "Got good news."

"A confession?" She hoped so. That would end all this.

"No. Hawethorne swears he's innocent. Says the doctor was dead when he got there."

Zee gulped, pushed the bloody image from her mind. "What then?"

"They found a knife at the scene. It's his."

CHAPTER 7

Z EE BOLTED UPRIGHT ON HER COUCH, eyes widened. She waved her cellphone toward Fontina. "Rico says they found the murder weapon."

"They're not calling it that yet." Rico's warning jumped through the phone.

Zee brought it back to her ear. "Why not?"

"Not proven yet."

"I get it. This is high profile. But it's *his* knife, and it was *at the scene*."

Rico chuckled. "D.A. needs more than that." The newsroom cacophony behind him increased. His tone became brisk. "Thought you'd want to know. Might help you relax."

"So, you think he's the killer," Zee pushed.

In the background, someone yelled his name. "Gotta go," Rico said. He disconnected.

Zee dropped her phone on the cushion. "Hairsplitting."

Fontina checked the tea and poured. "They have to follow their protocols," she said over the aromatic ginger-mint steam. "They don't want to lose on a procedural error."

Zee's mind bifurcated, as if she heard Fontina on two tracks, only one of which had to do with the police investigation. Had she lost a possible future with Rico because of a minor misstep? No.

She'd lost because . . . fate would never let her win.

Her left thumb stroked the luminescent opal she wore on the second finger of her right hand, a thorn wrapped in velvet. The maternal bequest should have comforted her, but it carried the sting of her mother's deathbed confession: *Stefan is not your father.*

Zee's heart squeezed. At thirteen, those words shattered her world and seemed to set the trajectory for her life.

"Where are you, Zee-zee?"

She hid her embryonic tears behind her teacup. "Ancient history."

"Don't beat yourself up," said Fontina. "Time moves differently in the heart."

Zee's gaze drifted to Candy, stretched out in a sunlit rectangle on the floor. She lay on her belly, rubbed her face against the catnip mouse, then grabbed the toy between her front paws. Rolling onto her back, she held it aloft, then tossed it to the side, jumped, and chased after it.

Fontina gestured toward the frolicking cat. "I'm glad Candy-pants lives with you."

"Me, too. She's a good therapist, and she works cheap. Sort of."

"I have a theory about animal therapy," said Fontina. "Animals have the gift of bringing people into the present moment. And when you're here and now, you're not fixating on memories of the past or fears of the future."

As if she heard their conversation, Candy abandoned her toy and trotted to lie at Zee's feet, an orange-and-cream sunburst amid the faded reds and blues of the old rug. Zee obliged the proffered furry head with a caress.

In response, Candy stretched her body tall, placed a paw on Zee's thigh, and extended her nose toward the cookie fragments in Zee's hand. She offered a crumb on her fingertip. Candy's tiny pink tongue flicked toward the treat, tasted it, and came back for more.

Zee looked from Candy to Fontina. "You're right. In this moment, I feel better." She scratched gently behind Candy's ears. "Thanks for the gift."

A synapse fired in her brain. Rico called to see if she was all right. He gave her information he thought would help ease her mind. Like Candy with her therapeutic presence, like Fontina with her essential oils and pithy koans and infallible tea, he offered friendship.

Definitely a win.

In the depths of her heart, she wrapped gentle arms around her earlier discouraged self. The tightness in her chest eased. "This has turned into a heck of a story, hasn't it?"

Fontina lifted her cup. "Let's have tea and you can tell me about your adventure."

The lazy sweep of afternoon sun glided across an oak end table as Zee shared details of the lineup. "So, I've identified him," she concluded. "And the police have his knife, probably with blood on it, and he admits to being there." She mimed wiping her hands, slapping the palms against each other. "It's only a matter of time until this is wrapped up."

"Let's hope so." Fontina glanced toward the wall clock. "I need to get back for a self-defense class. Can I help you clean up?"

"You go." Zee grasped her friend's hand. "Thanks for coming over. I'm fine now. And I need to write, though I'll have to rethink the topic." She quirked her lips. "Usually, no matter what happens to me, I can turn it into fodder for *Z Beats*. Can't see how that will work with this."

Fontina opened her mouth, but Zee held up her hand. "I know. Something will present itself."

"You're learning." Fontina rose.

Behind her, rainbow streaks leapt into existence, sunlight through a crystal vase at Zee's elbow. They painted the paneled base of the kitchen island and reflected off the pendant lamp.

Zee smiled. "Your strange powers are rubbing off on me. I'm going to write about the recent rate hike request from Valerian Gas & Electric. I can't believe they want to raise rates because people are conserving *too* much."

"A sort of prudence penalty." Fontina shook her head.

"Clever word play."

Fontina laughed. "Now *you're* rubbing off on *me*."

"Happy to oblige," said Zee.

After one last hug, Fontina left.

Zee carried the tea tray to the kitchen. She opened the cupboard to stow the cookies and met a silent accusation from the sparsely populated shelves. No wonder Fontina felt the need to feed her. She pulled open the refrigerator. Baleful cold breath rolled from its largely vacant racks.

At her feet, Candy meowed.

"Don't worry. I have plenty of *cat* food." Zee patted the silky stripes, then rummaged in a drawer for paper and pen to make a shopping list. She'd go to the grocery after drafting her column.

But by the time she'd typed the last words, exhaustion had overtaken her. Peanut butter-windmill cookie sandwiches sufficed for dinner. As on the previous night, she fell quickly into oblivion.

ZEE WOKE IN THE DARK, hair matted to the pillow, body wrapped in an overheated cocoon. Shucking the blanket, she rolled to a cooler area of the mattress. Moments later, she shivered and covered herself again.

Drowsiness threw filmy scarves across her wakeful mind, yet she could succumb only so far before some perverse instinct whisked away the tantalizing release.

She should be able to rest. No chattering thoughts milled about in her mind's pleasant numbness.

Limb by limb, muscle by muscle, she relaxed. The taut strings unwound. Then when she closed her eyes, the subtle tightening snuck in again, pernicious, exasperating.

She was guarding against something.

Her mind searched. Not the murder, not Rico, for a change. And yet thinking about him had triggered thoughts of fate, and fate had sent her to the memory of her mother's secret.

She winced as the questions crowded in. Why didn't she tell Zee who her real father was? Her dad knew, Zee was sure. Why else did he distance himself, withdraw his affection? She tried to find out, but he wouldn't say. And his heart attack and stroke a month ago had destroyed any future opportunity.

A stroke: nice when it meant caress. When it meant the death of brain cells choked off from their blood supply, it was a horror.

She grimaced at the memory of his trembling hand, the one that still worked. His painful attempts to speak with lips and tongue that wouldn't obey. And the worst of all, his confused, pleading eyes. She wished she could reach inside his head and tell him everything was all right.

In the darkness of her bedroom, she drew in a long breath. She was doing her best. She didn't have Fontina's psychic ability to connect.

Maybe she should ask her friend for help.

Another in-breath, then another exhalation as Zee relaxed her scalp, blinked to ease the tiny muscles around her eyes, flexed her jaw, pictured tension ebbing from her body.

Sleep stood at the door, but would not enter.

She glanced at her clock. Three-twenty.

Worse than pointless. Knowing the time only aggravated her frustration.

She tossed, punched the pillow, turned, studied the rotating blades on the ceiling fan. Sharp edges slicing through the humid air . . . rhythmic *wumph-onk . . . wumph-onk . . .* dripping into her fading consciousness.

A man. His back to her. Knife in his outstretched hand. Bloody blade. Drops falling. Plopping. Nauseating.

Her pulse hammers. She stays back. Circles. Wants to see his face. He turns away. Fear climbs her spine. He knows she's there.

The man whirls. Ian McNeary. Bloodied. Terrifying.

He closes in. Raises the blade. Slashes.

"No!"

Zee thrashed awake at her own cry.

At the foot of the bed, Candy jumped to her feet, teeth bared, yellow eyes huge. Filaments of fur flared, then settled as she surveyed the room.

Tangled in her covers, Zee shivered in a sheen of sweat, her heart a pounding snare drum in her chest. Outside the window, a bare smear of light lit the eastern sky. She extricated herself, slipped on her robe, and crossed the living room to her corner balcony.

From this vantage point, the western firmament bore the indigo of night. Feeling her way by the reflection of the landscaping lights below, she eased into her deck chair. Candy poked whiskers through the doorway.

"It's safe." Zee patted her lap, and the cat leapt up, kneaded, and settled in a warm ball.

Zee leaned back and gazed with unfocused eyes at the fading stars, at the dying leaves drifting from the trees, at a phalanx of geese abandoning their summer home.

When the sky grew fully light, Candy lifted her head and meowed for breakfast. No matter how her human behaved, in cat-world, life went on.

Zee rolled her shoulders and neck, cringing as the cartilage crackled. In a casual display of species superiority, Candy dropped to the floor, shot a glance over an orange shoulder, then flexed and arched her spine in one sinuous stretch.

"Show-off," Zee grumbled.

As she stepped across the threshold, she caught a blinking alert on her phone. A text from Fontina:

Need to talk. 11:30 Farm Fresh?

Zee smiled at the thought of seeing her friend. Then she frowned. *Need* to talk? What did that mean? She glanced in the mirror over the bookcase and caught the lines of strain in her face. The dream had rattled her. She really must get hold of her imagination. With a shake of her head at her reflection, she texted agreement.

While a poppy seed bagel toasted and Candy devoured nuggets of Tuna Surprise, Zee searched the internet for James Hawethorne. After two dead ends—one namesake was deceased and the other lived in Nova Scotia—she found his website, although at first, she could scarcely believe her eyes.

Thick brown hair, wide generous smile, broad shoulders, dancing hazel eyes. Hawethorne as the 2009 Ohio Unofficial Poet Laureate was a far cry from the ragged husk of a man in the police lineup.

Zee bit into the bagel, clicked on his blog, and nearly choked.

False hope is crueler than a knife,
but
a
knife
is
all
I
have.

He had posted it last week. She scrolled backward. A month ago, he'd written:

A snake with poisoned tongue
encroached on my peaceful flesh.
I slept in deceitful embrace
while you slit my veins
to ease the serpent's work.

The lines drove her to the archives, dread spreading. She selected a year and skimmed until she found the answer she suspected, a 2013 diagnosis of ALS. Hawethorne's fans responded with an outpouring of support. They celebrated his recovery with equally heartwarming fervor and heaped praise on Ian McNeary for his groundbreaking treatment.

Grimly, Zee followed the chronicle. Though other patients relapsed, and McNeary was forced to pull his drug from the market, Hawethorne seemed well until early 2017. Then his disease roared back. Over the next six months, his posts grew bitter and increasingly violent, culminating in the one dated just days before McNeary's murder.

Zee stared at the screen, the bagel a boulder in her gut. Maybe the knife-wielding man in her dream wasn't McNeary but Hawethorne.

She shuddered and forced herself to see the figure again. The face belonged to McNeary, but this time she noticed that the angle of the knife seemed odd. The blade had slashed downward, but not necessarily at her. He could have been aiming it toward himself.

That made more sense. The doctor felt remorse. He'd raised powerful hope and then shattered it. Maybe he wished he'd left well enough alone, allowed the sick and dying to make what peace they could.

Questions tumbled in her head. Why would McNeary scream *no*? No, the drug should have worked? It didn't make sense to dwell on the past when he had developed a new drug. No, he couldn't die this close to righting such a terrible wrong?

The rooster crow on her phone wrenched her thoughts from the dream. Time to get ready for Fontina's mysterious lunch date.

She rolled her chair back from her desk and wiped moisture from her brow. The litany of horrors marched before her: McNeary's shocking murder, Hawethorne's haunted face, her terrifying dream, and now the doomed poet's blood-curdling posts. Somehow, she'd sidestepped out of her world and into a circle of hell.

Beyond the balcony, sun gilded a cardinal's scarlet plumage. He perched in an oak tree, swaying with the limb, while Candy crouched at the base of the French doors, ears twitching as she eyed the moving red target. The ordinary world.

"You're an incorrigible optimist, Candy-pants," she called through her office doorway. "You never doubt your chance will come." The cat affected not to hear and kept her gaze on her prey.

Eyes on the prize, good advice.

Zee bookmarked Hawethorne's website. When she stepped into the shower, her mind returned to Fontina's message. It jarred her. Why would Fontina *need*—the word sparked a memory: Zee's desire last night to talk with her dad, her half-serious idea to ask Fontina for help.

Was it possible Fontina sensed Zee's troubled thoughts and responded to them? Could she have penetrated the fog of dementia and the damage wrought by the stroke? Did she communicate with Zee's dad?

Zee lathered her curls. Her thoughts arrowed to the one thing she wished she knew: the identity of her real father.

She was sure her mother had told the man Zee knew as dad. Maybe she thought he would share that knowledge with Zee, when Zee was older. Instead, he withdrew from her after her mother's death, opened a chasm between them. Hurt and confused, she couldn't summon the courage to cross.

The longer she waited, the harder it got. But she always thought there'd be time.

The steaming shower peppered her little toe, broken years ago and poorly healed. Like her dad's—and her real father's—abandonment, the injury didn't stop her functioning. It just always felt a little swollen and sometimes ached.

What if Fontina discovered the truth? The fracture might finally heal. And maybe then Zee could let go of her ghosts, including Jeff. And if that happened, she and Rico might—

She shut off the water. An inviting scenario conjured from vapors and mist, insubstantial as the rivulets spiraling across the tiles into her drain. If she went down that path, who knew in what underground labyrinth she might find herself?

CHAPTER 8

O**N THE SUNLIT PATIO OUTSIDE** FARM FRESH, Fontina's coral
tank top shone like a flower in the garden of green-enam-
eled furniture. Zee waved and threaded her way toward their usual
table.

As she drew near, she picked up the tap-tap of Fontina's nails
drumming against the metal tabletop. Zee frowned. Her serene
friend was never fidgety.

Zee slid into the opposite chair, all her own questions displaced.
Reaching across the table, she captured Fontina's twitchy fingers.
"What happened?"

"I had a most disturbing dream last night." Fontina said.

Zee's pulse jumped. "I had one, too. So horrifying I couldn't go
back to sleep."

"Tell me about it."

Typical of her friend to invite her to speak first, but Zee sensed
Fontina wasn't ready to share yet. She tamped her curiosity and
recounted her dream, ending with the blade's downward slash and
the shrieked *no!*

"This is eerie," Fontina said. "It's been a long time since we had
a paired set of dreams." She paused for the server, a tall young man,
angular in his black apron and green, restaurant-issue t-shirt. "I'll
have the number twelve, Seth."

"Sure thing."

"How's your first week on the job?"

"Good." His ruddy face lit. "The people are great here. Thanks for the recommendation."

"I know Seth from self-defense class," said Fontina.

"I was just about to ask." Zee mustered a smile for him. "You won't have to fight off disgruntled customers in this place. Everything is wonderful. Healthy *and* tasty."

Nothing like those sawdust nut loaves from her parents' experiments with vegetarianism would ever sully one of Farm Fresh's colorful ceramic plates.

As she studied the menu, though, her morning bagel clotted in Zee's stomach, a malevolent presence fed by her nightmare, Hawethorne's acid posts, and the tight lines around Fontina's eyes that betrayed her unsettled state. Something light would be wise. "Just a side salad, please."

"You got it." He scribbled on his order pad and departed.

Zee turned to Fontina. "Your dream?"

Fontina played with the gold filigree dangling from her ear. Sun highlighted lines in her usually untroubled face. "I also saw a man with a knife, whose face is hidden. He's staring down and screaming *no!* I try to see what he's looking at, but I can't until the very end of the dream. It's a body, stabbed so many times it's almost unrecognizable."

Zee's eyes widened. "Sounds like we were definitely linked. I didn't set an intention to dream together before I went to sleep. Did you?"

Fontina shook her head.

"It doesn't matter," said Zee. "Our dreams are clear. I looked up Hawethorne this morning. He was McNeary's patient, and now he's dying. He must've killed the doctor for revenge."

Fontina ran her finger down the side of her water glass, leaving tracks in the condensation. "I'm not ready to draw that conclusion. I didn't see either face, so I don't know who they were. Or if the body was McNeary."

"Nothing else makes sense." Zee tried to curb her irritation. "The dreams are telling us to let this go. The police have the right man."

"I'm not so sure." Fontina's voice remained mild.

"We have the evidence, and Hawethorne's blog is as good as a confession." Zee pursed her lips. "And what about *my* dream? I saw McNeary. And the bloody knife."

"That's the really odd thing," said Fontina. "My knife is shining clean. It flashes in the light so much that my eyes hurt."

Zee studied her friend. The dramatic contrast between the dream knives could be the reason for Fontina's indecision. "What do you think that means?"

"Fresh ground pepper?"

Zee jumped at Seth's voice as he set their salads on the table. "None for me," she managed to say, staring at the vision of delicacies he'd placed before Fontina. Artichoke hearts, garbanzo beans, shredded beets, compared to that, Zee's lunch consisted of a heap of multicolored greens that were, despite their varied hues and profusion of shapes, just leaves. Even the cheery globes of cherry tomatoes and the crescent smiles of red onion paled next to Fontina's choice.

Zee swallowed. Never underestimate the seductive allure of good food.

After Seth left, Fontina nudged her wide, shallow bowl toward Zee. "Want some of mine?"

"I'm fine with this." Zee shook her head, hoping she wasn't drooling.

"You sure? I have plenty to share."

Fontina knew her too well. "Maybe one piece of artichoke . . ." Zee capitulated, sliding her bowl across the table. ". . . and a couple of garbanzos . . . and a few of those beets. I'll trade you a cherry tomato and some slivers of red onion."

"Deal."

Zee drizzled vinaigrette house dressing and speared a clump of lettuce, which looked a lot more inviting with its new culinary enhancements. "Where were we?"

"Discussing symbols." Fontina dipped a chunk of artichoke into the small pot of dressing. "But we're off track. Symbols can be confusing."

Zee halted the fork halfway to her lips. "I can't believe, after all the dreams we've worked on together I forgot the first rule: Don't start with symbols."

"It's tempting," said Fontina, "especially when the symbols are dramatic. The more important question is why our dreams are upsetting. Let's focus on the feelings."

Zee slipped a garbanzo bean into her mouth. Firm, creamy. Farm Fresh always cooked them perfectly. She leaned back in the metal chair and replayed her dream. "I felt terror and horror, vulnerability. And confusion at the end. That lines up with my feelings about the murder, especially after identifying Hawethorne yesterday."

"I get most of that." Fontina steepled her fingers. "How does confusion fit in?"

"Possibly my fear of identifying the wrong person. But finding his knife should have resolved that." Zee sipped ice water to cool her retriggered emotions. "What about you?"

"Horror, but mostly just strong curiosity. To see what lay out of sight." Fontina scooped a forkful of shredded beets, then paused it in midair. "Wonder if that *no* at the end wasn't part of the dream, just your scream."

"It could be. I don't see what difference that makes. Either way, I didn't want him to kill me."

"Or subconsciously you don't accept that Hawethorne is guilty." Fontina gestured with her beet-laden fork. "Bottom line, if our dreams were confirming, they'd have more of a sense of resolution. As it is, I'm consumed by curiosity, and you're uncertain what's going on."

Familiar heaviness took up residence once more in Zee's chest. On the other side of the delicate wrought iron patio fence, a gaggle of young men in Centurions team t-shirts jogged past, their youthful faces shiny with sweat. Once, she had been that young and carefree. *Before she turned thirteen. Before her mother died.* She toyed with an artichoke wedge. "It's possible the dream isn't about the murder."

"You have another potential interpretation?"

Zee described her sleepless meandering thoughts about her dad. "And right before I finally fell asleep, I was wishing I could somehow talk to him. He could be the angry man. And we are cut off from each other, even more now."

"And the fear and confusion?" Fontina said.

"I didn't know for sure what the man was doing with the knife. He could have been attacking me. Or committing suicide. Maybe he was hurling down the weapon in frustration." Zee swirled the water in her glass and stared into the vortex. "I don't know what will happen if I find out the truth about my real father."

A breeze ruffled the leaves of the basil plant that decorated their table. Fontina pinched a leaf, releasing peppery sweet fragrance. "How would my dream fit with yours?" she said.

Zee dredged her fork through a tangle of lettuce. "When I got your text, I thought—We have such a connection, you might have sensed my wish and reached him somehow."

Fontina touched the back of Zee's hand where it rested on the table. "I'm sorry. Perhaps tonight you could set an intention for further guidance. I will, too, if you like."

Zee straightened. "I might, though I believe I'd prefer a good night's sleep without any more traumatizing dreams. I bet I got four hours at most last night, and maybe five the night before."

"All the more reason for your dreaming self to create extreme drama," said Fontina. "To cut through your exhaustion so you would remember."

"And we're back to the big question." Zee captured a single strand of beet on her fork. "Why did I get this dream? What was so important?"

"You'll know, if you let yourself."

Traffic rumbled by a few feet from the patio enclosure. In the distance, a semi downshifted with a throaty growl. Zee tried to relax her mind's tight grip on the question.

She knew Fontina couldn't answer it. Her friend's gift operated on the principle of intuitive *nudging*, a practice she'd honed since her ninth birthday.

On that long ago day, she'd also been fidgety. The next morning, she'd pounded on Zee's back door and spilled out her story as soon as Zee joined her on the porch steps. "I saw my Uncle Ramiz last night."

"In a dream?" Zee said. Fontina's uncle had died a year ago.

Her friend's black braids whipped as she shook her head. "He was there for real. I could see him plain as you. He had light all around him like an angel."

Goosebumps popped on Zee's skin.

"He said he knew why I didn't have fun on my birthday." Fontina lowered her voice to a whisper. "I have a gift. If I pay attention when I feel upset, I can pick up clues about what to do to help make things right. I just have to practice."

It sounded exotic. Exciting. "Are you going to do it?"

Fontina nodded, her brown eyes so aglow that Uncle Ramiz might have left a spark of himself in them.

Across the table at Farm Fresh, a similar radiance shone in her friend's eyes. Or it might have been the sun, catching fire in their depths. Though Zee trusted Fontina, she didn't have to slavishly swallow everything she said.

Her mind reminded her: Fontina didn't *say*; she just pointed.

Zee exhaled in surrender. "You're relentless. Dad always claimed the only commitment must be to the truth. Ironic, coming from him. But you don't let me get away with anything."

"That's because I love you, little sister."

The weight in Zee's chest lifted. Her childhood dad, her faithless fiancé, her biological father, all had deserted her. Through every loss, Fontina remained steadfast, constant. Truth be told, though

Zee disputed with her on occasion, she could no more dismiss her than she could carve a piece out of her own heart.

The Centurion athletes jogged past on the other side of the street, retracing their route, returning to their base.

"Okay, let's say I'm not done with this murder yet," Zee said. "A common dream thread is that we want to see but we can't, not at first. I don't find much guidance in my dream, but in yours, there's the brilliant, shining knife. Is something blinding us?"

"That feels right," said Fontina. "I remember now that I wished I could direct the light. I wanted it to help me instead of getting in the way."

"So, we need to re-aim our light, look elsewhere. Because no way am I going to Bernstow with a dream."

"His eyeballs would probably roll right out of his head," laughed Fontina.

Zee chuckled at the image of the gruff lieutenant cursing as he groped for bronze orbs that skittered just beyond his grasp. "I'm going to picture this the next time I have to deal with him."

"My pleasure." Fontina lifted her wrist in a parody of checking a watch, a gesture that always made Zee wonder if her friend actually perceived the time on her bare skin. "This is a good start, but we'd better finish our lunch. I need to get back to the studio."

"Okay, just one more thing," Zee said. "We've talked about what's in the dreams for me. What do you get out of them?"

Fontina rested her fork atop a curve of red onion. "I believe I need to identify what blinds me." Her jaw tightened. "Violence, of course. More broadly, any highly charged disharmony can interfere with my ability to see clearly." She met Zee's eyes. "This dream actually caused me physical pain. That's why I texted you to meet."

Zee gulped at the price her friend paid for her finely honed sensitivity. "I thought that didn't happen anymore."

"It's somewhat rare," Fontina said. "And that was the drama from my dreaming self."

Zee's heart shrank from causing further suffering, but Fontina's brows narrowed, as if she commandeered their energy to focus her thoughts. Zee ventured a question. "Where have you experienced such disharmony recently?"

The sun glinted off Fontina's gold earrings. She drew her fork through the remnants of her salad, as if she could read the patterns in the leaves. Then she raised glimmering eyelashes. "Teresa. The destruction of ALS. I don't want to think my distress would prevent me from seeing clearly, but . . ."

Zee reached a hand toward her friend. "We're all better at recognizing what doesn't personally affect us."

Beneath her coral tank top, Fontina's chest rose and fell as she collected herself. "Dreams give us gifts to help us. The emphasis for me was curiosity. I'm thinking I should try to approach Teresa's situation with curiosity, a desire to learn, rather than with horror and aversion." She offered a shaky smile.

"And I could approach the murder the same way," said Zee.

Fontina squeezed Zee's hand. "Thank you for helping me see this."

"Glad to help, big sister."

Fontina gathered greens with her fork, and Zee took the cue, returning to her lunch. The imbalance had been righted. Fontina would find her way . . . as Zee would find hers.

She attended to her salad, but despite its flavorful additions, her mind chewed on the dilemma of the murder. What would Shelby do? She twitched her lips. Shelby would have solved it by now. A scrap of fabric, an explanation that felt *off*, a break in the pattern, and she'd have everything she needed.

Zee savored the last bit of curly endive, then pushed a tomato around with her fork. "We need to find other suspects. Trouble is, there are plenty of people who suffered from Neurish."

Fontina patted her mouth with her napkin. "There must be ways to narrow the search."

While they'd been eating, the green lacquered tables on the patio had filled. Seth scurried among the proliferation of customers, seating them, taking their orders, delivering drinks.

His shadow fell across the table as he laid their bills on the surface. "I'll take these when you're ready."

"I'll pay you now. Keep the change." Zee dug a ten from her wallet. As she reached for her check, an odd sense of disconnection made her view the action as if watching a movie. Her hand traveled the distance to the slip of paper, gathered it with her payment, and lifted them into Seth's waiting palm. Upon contact, the illusion dissolved.

After Fontina paid, Zee locked eyes with her. "I just got a great idea for my next step."

Fontina raised her brows.

Zee grinned. "Investors. I'm going to follow the money."

CHAPTER 9

ZEE SAT CROSS-LEGGED IN HER OVERSIZED burgundy leather office chair, attempting to balance a folder atop Candy's purring body. Finalizing her column for the five o'clock deadline had eaten up the rest of Wednesday. She'd been rewarded with a quick approval text from her editor.

Love a utility company complaining because customers aren't using enough gas and electricity. —Penn

The name never failed to elicit a grin—Penn (never Penelope) Sharp.

Now Zee eagerly turned her attention to following the money trail, ferreting out McNeary's investors.

"You're not helping, you know," she said to the cat's closed eyes. Candy's tail swished and knocked a sheet of paper to the floor.

Zee laid the folder on the library trestle table that functioned as her desk, scooted her hands beneath the furry belly, and half-lifted, half-rolled Candy toward the armrest. "I'll share the chair, but I need my lap."

Candy responded with a yawn.

Zee returned to reviewing her notes on Ian McNeary's investors. Her heart constricted as she paged through the clippings. For her planned story, she had researched the human cost of the drug failure as the driving force behind the doctor's determination.

Investors had not been on her radar.

She bent to retrieve the fallen paper, and a sidebar caught her eye. *Actress Threatens Doctor over Financial Loss.* "This might be useful."

Candy raised a lazy eyelid and let it drop.

Beneath the headline, Angelica Street's star-quality photo showed a vivacious woman with long-lashed, sparkling eyes, a full-lipped smile, and luxuriant auburn hair. The story painted her in a less flattering light, as "an inebriated B-movie actress caught ranting in a nightclub."

Zee pursed her lips. Another blunder aided and abetted by alcohol. Still, liquor lubricated and truth often spilled out as a result. She read on.

"I'll make that doctor regret it," Street declared. "I know people, nasty people." However, when pressed, she denied any hostile intention, saying, "I'm distressed only because he diminished the legacy meant for my heirs."

Zee steepled her fingers. The story dated to more than a year ago. Street's situation might be different now. She made a note to find out, then tapped her chin with her pen. The mention of heirs raised the question: Did the doctor leave any? On her computer, she jumped to today's obits, but found nothing relevant.

"Rats." She mumbled her disappointment.

Orange-and-cream ears twitched. Zee stroked the silky fur. "Rico said the investors came from people the doctor knew." Candy meowed encouragement.

Zee set the folder in a corner of the table and pulled up McNeary's vita on her computer. Where to start? His post-grad medical school colleagues, intent on their own careers, probably distanced themselves after his ruin. She scrolled for his undergrad information. He'd earned a Bachelor of Science from L'Ocosta State University, Biology with Laboratory Science Specialization.

She crossed her fingers and searched for the L'Ocosta State website. Her screen exploded with photographs: smiling young people in earnest conversations on green lawns under sheltering oaks, youthful, serious-faced women peering at a complex diagram on a computer screen, grinning lacrosse team members in royal blue jerseys. Every depiction declared itself evidence of the school motto: *An Educational Experience Beyond the Usual.*

Zee lifted her brows. Did any school promise an experience that was merely 'usual'? She snorted, pushed aside the thought.

Facing many possibilities, her hope ticked upward. Surely a younger McNeary would show up somewhere with a few friends. Eagerly, she scrolled and clicked, tabbed, linked, and scanned. With each failure to sight him, her uncertainty grew. She'd thought the site might feature its pre-med student who later became famous. Perhaps L'Ocosta had once been proud of its alumnus but decided to erase him after his spectacular failure.

She scanned the optimistic, unlined faces, wondering how many of them had achieved their dreams. Guilt pricked, but she shook it off. So, she hadn't taken the direct route.

Her dad's words echoed in her head: *You must use your gift to serve the greater good. Don't take the easy way.*

The words stung, as they always did. She had taken the easy way with her career, or so she judged. Humor flowed glibly from her pen. It brought her success, sweet, delicious, and narcotic.

She massaged her temples, as if to dislodge the guilt. Her well-honed skills were transferable for her new career direction. *There are no straight lines in nature.*

Zee smiled. Fontina's father had said that during a heated discussion with Zee's dad.

"Thanks, Papa Alesandro," Zee whispered. Her throat tightened. He'd said she got to call him that, as his honorary daughter. Yet, like all the others she'd depended on, he abruptly withdrew after her mother died. One more reason not to let Rico, or anyone, get close.

She swallowed her sadness and turned back to the L'Ocosta site. A variety of activities beckoned prospective students: Greek societies, theatre productions, dance lessons. Nothing useful, although college life looked like a lot more fun than when she got her degree in the early 2000s.

Norman State at that time was a cauldron of clashing values. The Columbine massacre shocked the nation, but that paled in the wake of the 9/11 attacks. And the country seemed headed for a repeat of Viet Nam when President Bush launched two new wars in the Middle East.

As a journalism major, Zee found herself immersed in debates about guns and the meaning of patriotism, fears about the loss of liberties and the slide toward a police state as a result of the Patriot Act and powers granted to the new Department of Homeland Security. Heavy stuff—no wonder the lighter side appealed to her when she chose a career.

She massaged a crick in her neck, wishing she could drape Candy's warm vibrating body over her aching shoulders. Although on second thought, sweat already dampened her back. Capricious Midwest weather: two days ago, chilly and rainy; today, increasing heat. Mother Nature offering a last steamy kiss before turning her face to autumn.

Zee crossed the room and flipped the switch for the ceiling fan. At least she could achieve that one thing. Her search was pointless. McNeary may as well have been a ghost.

Back at her computer, she nudged a grumbling Candy aside with her hip. A menu item titled *Medicine and the Arts* piqued her interest. Her dad, a philosophy major, loved to draw together the threads of various disciplines. Interdisciplinarity, he'd called it.

She rolled the eight syllables on her tongue as photos splayed across her screen. A name ensnared her: George "Pete" Bottmeyer. The future best-selling author of the medical thriller *Chimera* was shaking hands with a large, ebullient man identified as Dr. Jules Mercy. And the third man in the picture, with his arm slung across Bottmeyer's shoulders, was a boyish, bespectacled Ian McNeary.

Score!

Zee raised her brows at the new possibility. Bottmeyer could be an investor.

A thought niggled—something negative about the famous author—recent.

She opened another window, typed in Bottmeyer's name, and groaned at the list, more than a thousand hits. Nothing for it but to plunge in. She scanned, bookmarked, scribbled, Theseus clinging to Ariadne's thread. An hour later, cramps in her neck and shoulders forced her to close the lid to her laptop.

Candy interpreted Zee's stilled fingers as an invitation and crawled back into her lap.

Zee stretched her arms overhead and pinched her shoulder blades, then summarized to herself. Pete Bottmeyer had established himself as a brilliant writer with a promising career. Darkening his prospects, the gossip sites claimed he had an ongoing drinking problem. It was a leap to compare him with drunken Angelica Street, but if he had invested in McNeary, he might have turned against the doctor, too.

She stroked Candy's head, sliding her delicate ear between thumb and forefinger. Bottmeyer had done two costly rehab stints. His bestseller hit over a year ago. He would need to keep writing, especially if he had invested in McNeary.

A sharp pain sliced across the heel of Zee's palm. "Ouch!"

Candy whipped her head free, twisting to pin Zee with narrow yellow eyes.

Zee jerked her hand clear of Candy's poised claws. A thin trickle of blood welled. Payback for her inattention. Unusual for Candy to break the skin, though. Sitting on Zee's lap, her plump furry body vibrated with tension.

"Something wrong, Candy-pants?"

The cat leapt to the floor and paced, meowing. Did Candy sense an approaching storm? If so, it must be a big one.

Zee swiveled her chair and scanned the view to the southwest through her balcony doors. Glaring sun had turned the sky white.

In contrast, a dark bank of cloud boiled along the horizon. "It's all right." She reached down to pat Candy's head, but the cat shied away. "Okay, I'll leave you to your own devices."

She grabbed a tissue and dabbed at her wound. "Enough research. I've earned some wine."

She washed her hand with generous amounts of soap and water. Cat scratch fever was a real thing. Candy was due for a trip to the groomer.

Fortified with a glass of chilled chardonnay, she settled on her couch and let her gaze drift over trees brushed gold by the late afternoon sun. She'd unearthed an actress and an author as possible suspects. Both could be struggling, but that didn't mean either had motive enough to commit murder. Nonetheless, they were her only leads. Perhaps her friends at the paper would be willing to work their sources.

After she finished her calls, Zee foraged for dinner. The refrigerator yielded rye bread and cheddar. A bit dry, but not yet science experiments. Butter, dill pickles. Voila! Grilled cheese.

While Candy attacked a serving of crunchy Seafood Surprise, Zee carried her sandwich to her computer. She needed to submit her next column by five o'clock tomorrow. Exploring L'Ocosta State had sparked her curiosity about school mottos. That might make a good column. Could be fun to check out a few, and fun sounded great right now.

CHAPTER 10

R ISING SUN TINTED ZEE'S IVORY BEDROOM WALLS rose-gold, a hue all the more glorious because it appeared only briefly with the proper confluence of low angle sunlight and diffuse clouds. It brushed a peachy wash on the Japanese color block print hanging across from the foot of her bed, as if trying to lend optimism to the travelers caught in the rain.

She propped pillows beneath her head, unable to resist a few moments of communion.

The picture always spoke to her. She never thought the peasants needed cheering, despite being caught in a downpour. Several ducked their heads under conical hats, three shared a slatted umbrella, one bent low beneath a woven mat flung across his back. On the wide river beyond the wooden bridge, a lone man poled his long, slender raft in the rippling water.

Like her, they were ordinary folk, not emperors or courtesans in brocades and silks, shielded from life in palanquins borne by liveried servants. These rain-soaked figures displayed no pretense. They were getting wet and doing their best to stay dry.

Their common humanity evoked her empathy. She didn't know if that was what Utagawa Hiroshige had in mind when he created it, but she didn't care.

She bought the two-foot-by-three-foot reproduction of *Great*

Bridge, Sudden Shower at Atake after graduation. A year late because of the fiasco with Jeff, but she finished her degree. This morning, as always, it said, "Rain happens. Keep going."

Damp air wafted through her open window. The humidity was up. Rain might happen today.

On the bedside table, her cellphone rang. The caller ID said her editor.

"Hey, Penn. What can I do for you?"

"Love your column on the school mottos." Penn's husky voice always carried an undertone of amusement. "It's lopsided, though. Mostly public schools. Didn't you find many examples among the private universities?" She chuckled. "You're usually an equal opportunity satirist."

Zee did a face-palm. What had she been thinking, not to check such an obvious bias?

Penn continued without waiting for a response. "I've emailed it back to you with my comments. I'll need the revised version by 5 P.M. today."

"You'll have it." Zee clicked off. That's what she got for focusing on McNeary's murder. And the story it represented, she reminded herself. *Z Beats* needed to come first, though.

The phone rang again.

"Morning, Zee." The voice of Jessica, the paper's Lifestyle reporter, chirped in Zee's ear. "Got some info on Pete Bottmeyer. I can nutshell it, email details later if you want."

Revision could wait a couple of minutes. "Sure."

"He's having trouble with his book in progress. A friend of mine in New York says he'll lose his contract and his nice fat advance if he doesn't produce a finished manuscript by the end of the year."

"That's only three months."

"The guy might be buckling down to get it done," said Jessica. "He's been incommunicado since his daughter's wedding last March. Big society do."

Zee nudged Candy aside and reached for her robe at the bottom of the bed. "So, he might be hurting for money."

"Wouldn't be surprised. He spent his last foray in rehab . . ." Keys clicked through the line. "Looks like right after the wedding, at a posh thousand-dollar-a-week joint. There for six weeks."

"That's a serious chunk of change."

"His problem's more than alcohol. Prescription drugs."

"Ouch."

"One more thing," Jessica said. "His wife had a stroke. She's in a nursing home—very expensive, too."

The image of Zee's vacant-eyed dad in his wheelchair intruded. She shunted it aside, along with the twinge in her heart. "What a run of bad luck."

"Why'd you want to know about him? Doing a column?"

Damn. Zee wasn't ready to have her investigation all over the newsroom. "Can't say."

"Not even a hint?"

That was the problem with reporters. Pushy, especially in their bailiwick. "Maybe it will help me put some pieces together. If it gels, I'll share."

Jessica inhaled.

Zee jumped in before her colleague could press her case. "Have to run. Thanks for the info."

She disconnected and tapped the phone against her chin. "Rehab I knew about, Candy-pants, but not the wife's stroke. A year ago. That'd be after everything went to hell for McNeary and his investors."

Candy stretched and meowed.

"I agree," said Zee. "Lots of financial pressures. Could be the failure of McNeary's company was the last straw. Could be a motive." She stroked the orange-and-cream fur. "So, where was Mister Bottmeyer last Tuesday morning?"

If Candy knew, she declined to comment.

In the kitchen, Zee turned on her radio. Hawethorne's arrest dominated the news. After rehashing the lurid details of the crime scene, the reporter, her voice an appropriate mix of sorry-I-have-to-discuss-this distaste and barely restrained excitement, announced that he would be arraigned at 10 A.M.

"I'm going." Zee could scarcely believe the words as they emerged from her mouth, or the certainty that went with them. Voluntarily enter a bastion of the legal establishment? On impulse, she called Fontina.

"Meet you there," her friend said.

Breakfast and column forgotten, Zee rushed through her morning shower, then took stock of her clothes closet. Left to herself, she preferred cotton drawstring pants or comfy jeans and t-shirts, but not today. She scrutinized her professional wardrobe. It tended toward dark shades, slimming and projecting competence. Today, she needed energy, and maybe courage. She pulled out a brick-red blazer. Perfect.

Suitably attired, she drove to the courthouse. She parked in an overpriced lot two long blocks from the forbidding edifice, and propelled by inexplicable urgency, hurried toward her destination. She needed to do this before she could talk herself out of it.

A flash of light pierced her concentration. Sunlight glinting off the silvery coronet that dangled from Fontina's rearview mirror. Zee shook her head at the sight of her friend's red-bronze Spyder parked only a few feet from the courthouse. At only a dollar an hour for a meter, there was never a space along that curb.

Zee didn't begrudge her luck. The tension between her shoulders eased, knowing Fontina would be with her in the courtroom.

She covered the remaining distance in three strides, but at the base of the imposing flight of steps, she stopped short, her eye drawn inexorably to the granite-faced hall of judgment. From atop its pyramidal platform, the building pressed down upon her, as if to emphasize her position as a supplicant before the mighty throne of the law. No wonder they called the actions inside, pleas.

She snorted, not caring who saw or heard. The impolite grunt loosened the institutional grip on her psyche. Chin lifted, she strode upward, and hit the next architectural statement of human unimportance.

The rise from concrete slab to concrete slab was narrow, prolonging the climb, and the steps themselves were too broad for her to tread easily from one to the next. Forced to continually adjust her pace, she huffed in frustration. Finally at the summit, she shoved against the door, which in a final insult, swung open with ease, thrusting her stumbling into a frigid lobby.

She tugged her jacket straight and brushed a clump of curls from her forehead. The stony-eyed guard at the metal detector barely restrained a smirk. She met his gaze, dropped her purse on the conveyer belt, and passed through the arch while his eyes raked her silk blouse and the gray slacks belted at her waist. Rather than wait for the elevator under his scrutiny, she chose the stairs.

Two flights up, she pushed open the door to a windowless room, painted and paneled in scuffed beige wainscotting. The Stars and Stripes and the pennant-shaped Ohio state flag flanked the judicial dais, a plain-fronted desk laminated in blond wood. It could have belonged to any anonymous office worker, but for the gavel . . . and the bald-headed, black-robed figure in the high-backed chair behind it.

Zee resisted the urge to cower at his disapproving glower. She had a right to be here.

As she slid onto the hard bench along the back wall, Fontina squeezed her hand and whispered, "Glad you made it."

To one side of the dais, a door creaked open. A uniformed bailiff led in a prisoner. Dark hair, slicked back. Not Hawethorne. In a monotone, the judge read the charge, aggravated assault, and intoned the ritual question of the plea. Equally expressionless, a man in a brown suit entered the ritual response: not guilty. The judge consulted a pad on his desk and named a trial date. The bailiff escorted the prisoner back through the door.

The entire arraignment lasted less than two minutes. The gears of the legal system shifted forward one notch.

The next offender entered, and the process repeated, then another after that. Only the details of the unfortunate accused differed. Under the parade of misery, the air in the room thickened. Zee labored to breathe. A brick began to settle behind her eyes.

A young man, hair shaved to a shadow atop his head and a swastika snarling over the jumpsuit collar on the back of his neck, swaggered before the judge.

Zee sucked in a breath. She hadn't been born when the '60s protests dominated her parents' lives, but growing up, she absorbed their anger and fear. The chants of demonstrators, the police bullhorns, the roar of the water cannon, the terrified screams, had all been burned into her psyche.

The police were the enemy. Racism and the war were wrong, but . . . She stared at the cocky prisoner with his proud, abhorrent brand. This veneration of violence and hatred, the forces of the law should protect against that. Even as she formed the argument, the contradictions tore at her logic.

An uncomfortable sensation arose, as if her thoughts were transparent. Imagined scrutiny prickled the hair on her scalp. She fought the urge to scan the room, looking for her phantom interrogator. It would be like Rico to question her, to test—

A bang from the gavel shattered her thoughts. The judge gesticulated, lecturing the young man, who shifted from one foot to the other, telegraphing his disinterest. "We boring you?" snapped the judge. The small mallet thwacked again. "Get him out of here."

Finally, the bailiff led Hawethorne in.

Zee stifled a gasp. If possible, he looked worse than in the lineup. He shuffled on unsteady feet, his thin body shrunken inside an ill-fitting, dingy orange jumpsuit. Stringy gray hair plastered his neck, which glistened with droplets. His manacled hands drooped, so skeletal they might have escaped the cuffs if he but wriggled his fingers.

Zee swallowed. He probably wouldn't live long enough to go to trial, much less serve time.

The judge droned. The lawyer responded. The judge named a trial date.

Done.

Wrapping a thick hand around the prisoner's upper arm, the bailiff began to hustle him from the room. Hawethorne grunted and shrugged as if to loosen the grip. His head turned, and his watery gray eyes met Zee's.

"Lady!" He fought as the officer muscled him toward the door. "You gotta help me. *Please.* I—" The door slammed shut.

CHAPTER 11

THE DOOR'S HEAVY CLANG REVERBERATED through the court-room, as did Hawethorne's desperate cry for Zee's help. She stared at the crosshatched window where the deputy had wrangled the prisoner from sight and wished fervently that she also could disappear. Beside her on the bench, Fontina squeezed her hand.

The judge cleared his throat. Couched in pads of fat behind wire-rimmed glasses, his steely eyes swept the sparse crowd in attendance.

Sweat trickled down Zee's neck. She willed her body to be still.

After an eternity, his black-gowned arm gestured to the bailiff. "Call the next case."

Zee whispered, "Let's get out of here."

She and Fontina hustled down the stairs and, under the leer of the deputy at the metal detector, exited the building.

Already speed-walking in the opposite direction, Zee jerked a finger toward the substandard Chop Shop. "Not there."

"Agreed," said Fontina.

Heat and humidity had thickened during her sojourn in court. Zee pushed her legs hard, sucking in the viscous air and thankful that Fontina's long stride would enable her to easily keep pace. She spared a moment to wonder at the urgency that drove her, first to the courthouse, then away from it. She'd investigate it later, when her heart wasn't thumping in her temples.

A pink-striped awning caught her eye. The gilded lettering above the fringe read, La Patisserie. She darted through the tiny door and sank into a glossy black bentwood chair. "Sorry for the breakneck escape." She inhaled a deep draught of air. "I don't know what's gotten into me this morning. I'm like a person possessed."

"That is curious." Fontina extracted a small brown bottle from her purse. "This might help calm you. It's lavender and passionflower, with a smidgen of valerian root. My favorite go-to." She uncapped it, lifted the stopper, and dripped a drop onto her wrist. "Would you like to try it?"

Zee accepted the vial and mimicked the application.

"Gently rub your wrists together," said Fontina.

Zee followed her lead. The flowery fragrance penetrated, loosening the block of tension behind her eyes. "Nice. Passionflower can be overwhelmingly sweet, but this isn't."

"That's the valerian. Its earthiness balances the floral intensity."

Their server arrived, a pert young woman with bouncy blonde curls and a wide smile. *Robbie*, said the curlicue script on her pink name tag.

"Coffee please," said Fontina.

"Same for me." Zee's eyes strayed to the pastry display. She deserved a reward for skipping breakfast. A plump cherry tart beckoned, but on second thought, the blood-red glaze dampened its allure. Zee turned to Robbie. "And a chocolate croissant."

"Anything for you?" Robbie addressed Fontina.

"I think not," she said.

Robbie bobbed her head and flitted away.

Zee leaned back in the chair, her tension draining in the tranquil emptiness of the bakery. Their only companions were pink rosebuds, one arcing from a slender vase in the center of each small round table. Overhead, a central chandelier shimmered with crystal teardrops, through which drifted subtle strains of Debussy's *Rêverie*.

"You found the perfect refuge." Fontina touched her finger to the tiny blossom on their table. "The flowers are even real. Did you know this place was here?"

Zee shook her head. "I have pastry radar."

"There are worse kinds," Fontina laughed.

Equanimity regained, Zee's thoughts returned to the arraignment. "You sense anything in the courtroom?"

"A great deal of fear." Fontina cocked her head. "And not all of it from Hawethorne."

"I know. I had it under control until there at the end." Zee traced her thumb along a faint pale streak in the onyx tabletop. "I'm glad you were there. I'm sure you have a ton of things to do today."

"I was going to observe a new yoga teacher this morning." Fontina's fingers strayed to Uncle Ramiz's coin on its delicate silver chain. "But I couldn't let you enter the demon den alone."

"I did it before I had a chance to think about it." Zee blew out a sigh. "I shouldn't have bothered you. I did that without thinking, too. But business must be looking up, to hire a new teacher. Lots of new students?"

"An encouraging number," said Fontina. "It warms my heart that so many people are interested in holistic living. The classes are going well, and the herbal products are selling. We're stocking more books, too. It's exciting. This is only the eighth year for Integrated Life, and Emilio and I are making a sustainable profit. We may start offering massage and acupressure."

"Sign me up for massage," said Zee, feeling tension melt from her shoulders at the mere thought. The easing halted at her guilt-puckered brow. "You have a lot going on. I need to stop intruding."

Fontina leaned forward and captured Zee's eyes. "I wanted to be with you. And he's scheduled to teach again this afternoon. That's a more challenging class, which might give me a better idea of his skill."

"You always manage to sound as though everything worked out for the best," said Zee.

"That's because it does. Especially if you trust your intuition. Think about it. You decided to go to the arraignment. Didn't you feel stronger, at least for most of the time?"

Zee nodded.

Fontina straightened. "That's twice in two days you've acted on your intuition."

"Twice?"

"Follow the money?"

"That was originally Rico's idea."

"But you ran with it."

"Come to think of it, I did." Zee smiled.

"Insight isn't always a voice in your head." Fontina deepened her tone to a dramatic whisper. "Don't . . . take the train . . . today-ay."

Zee laughed, remembering it had been a mere spark of interest that led her to the L'Ocosta University website photos of McNeary with Pete Bottmeyer and Jules Mercy, new lines of inquiry that might prove profitable. "Okay, I'm convinced."

Robbie delivered their orders. Zee's croissant sat, plump and golden, on a scallop-edged white plate. A streak of chocolate trickled like a dark river across the glistening crust. Taste buds jumping into overdrive, she broke off a corner of the crescent and popped it into her mouth. Fontina would understand if the conversation lagged for a moment.

But instead of melty, buttery richness, the layers of pastry compressed between Zee's teeth like cardboard. Her tongue quested for flavor, but found only the faintest tinge of chocolate. It might as well have been paint. She chewed the resistant mass, glad she'd taken only a small bite, and forced herself to swallow. With a grimace, she reached for her cup.

"Not good?" Fontina said.

"Intuition failed me this time."

"Too bad. Such a nice feeling to this place." Fontina offered a smile. "If it's any consolation, I don't believe the tart would have been any tastier." She sipped her coffee. "Adrenaline might have muddied your sensitivity."

Zee pushed aside her plate and lifted her cup. "Let's hope the coffee is better than the food."

The bitter brew cleansed her palate but left her wishing for water. She scanned the restaurant. Robbie was nowhere. Probably she was flirting with some guy in the back, who should be baking fresh croissants.

Chiding herself for several unfounded assumptions, Zee refocused on the arraignment. "Anyone broadcasting fear besides me and Hawethorne?"

"Someone else in that courtroom was anxious."

"Any idea who?"

Fontina swirled her coffee.

"What?" pressed Zee.

"I thought for a moment, Rico."

"Was he there?" She flashed on the moment when she'd felt someone reading her thoughts.

"I'm not sure, but if so, only for a very brief time."

Zee wished he had stayed. It would have been nice to see what he thought of Hawethorne's outburst, or just to see him. She quashed a splinter of disappointment. "Anything from Hawethorne besides fear?"

"Anger," Fontina said. "Resentment."

"He's in a bad situation. I'd feel that way, too."

Fontina's voice lifted, betraying surprise. "Hawethorne wishes he *had* done it. He *intended* to kill McNeary."

Zee's eyes widened. "So, it's as I thought from the dreams. It also jives with his posts."

"But he didn't go through with it," said Fontina. "I got that very clearly."

Zee wanted to protest, but she couldn't. Most of the time, Fontina's intuition worked more subtly, which made this unflinching certainty all the more persuasive.

She reached toward the croissant, but stopped her hand halfway. If only it didn't *look* so good. *La Patisserie indeed. More like La Duperie.* She grabbed her coffee. "All right, let's say for the moment we accept his innocence. I did some work chasing down investors, and I have a couple of leads."

"That's great. Tell me about them."

Zee summarized yesterday's research results and Jessica's information, ending with the question she'd posed to Candy. "Where was Bottmeyer at the time of the murder?" She pressed her lips together. "How blithely I'm saying it now, *at the time of the murder.*"

Fontina leaned closer. "The human psyche is wonderfully adaptable. You're not callous. You're doing what is necessary, so you can deal with the situation."

Scarring over a fresh wound—Zee understood that strategy. Her glance strayed to the street outside the shop's tiny window. A street not unlike that one, with a bodega on the corner . . . She pulled her gaze away, stared at the sky to break the hold of the scene. A line of dark clouds chewed their way across the horizon.

"Those clouds look menacing," Fontina said.

"I don't like the look of them, either," said Zee. "Ready to go?"

"Let's."

Zee swallowed another mouthful of bitter coffee and grabbed her purse. Courtesy won out, and she left a dollar tip. The gustatory crime, evidence of which lay on the plate, wasn't Robbie's fault.

When she pushed open the door, a chill gust whipped Zee's face and threatened to push her sideways. She did a quick calculation: wind from the north, a cold front. She wrapped her blazer tightly and quickened her pace.

They turned a corner, and the wind died, sliced by the sharp edge of the building. Cut off from movement, the air hung humid and stagnant. An ache blossomed in her sinuses. A bus rumbled by, leaving a trail of oily fumes that snaked into her eyes. The throbbing in her head expanded.

She pushed on until the Mini's red hood appeared, gleaming at the end of a row. "Here's me," Zee said, no longer envious of Fontina's parking space two long blocks farther.

A muffled buzz arose from inside her purse. Her cell. She caught Fontina's eye. "It's the entertainment reporter. You have a minute to hear this?" It might be useful to have a set of ears that weren't commandeered by painful pulsing.

Fontina looked as though she read Zee's distress. "Let's sit in your car where it's quiet."

Zee spoke into the phone. "Victor, could you hold on a moment please? Let me get in my car. Then I'm putting you on speaker to let my friend here listen."

When they were settled, she laid the phone on the dashboard. "You have something?"

"Of course. *C'est moi.*" Without further preamble, his well-modulated voice launched into his report. "Angelica Street is a poor, faded bloom, not to put too fine a point on it. Her career never reached glittering heights, though to hear her publicist, only the paucity of proper parts kept her from being Lauren Bacall reincarnated."

Zee ignored Fontina's bemused smile. "How's she doing financially?"

"I'm getting to that, sweetheart," crooned Victor. "Dear Angelica is in quite a precarious pecuniary position. She's about to kiss good-bye to at least one of her houses, several of her cars, and definitely that ostentatious yacht."

Zee wrinkled her brow. "You don't have to take such pleasure in her misfortune."

Hurt laced his reply. "I take no pleasure in the fall of gods, but I reserve the right to a certain satisfaction in seeing a pretender's puffery deflated."

She pictured him, elegant fingers tapping his monogrammed silver pen, sculpted lips pouting. "I apologize, Victor."

"Tut-tut. No worries, my dear. The vagaries and vicissitudes of the theatre world are not for the generally honest, straightforward, salt-of-the-earth populace."

Zee's irritation melted. It was fun to listen to Victor, if nothing else for his vocabulary.

"One point of particular interest," he continued. "On her dreadful blog, Angelica waxed quite eloquent about the altruism and brilliance of your Doctor McNeary. I daresay she veered into the fringes of hagiography while extolling his world-shattering breakthrough in improving the lot of suffering humanity.

"However . . ." He hesitated for his usual dramatic effect, and Zee knew that his next comment would thoroughly undercut everything he had just said. "It is my judgment that an unmistakable whiff of desperation infected all her laudatory language. I'd say three-quarters of her admiration for him sprang from the hope that he would rescue her from the financial dungeon into which she condemned herself by her own foolish desire to transcend reality with appearance."

Zee felt out of breath just listening. "Word was she threatened McNeary."

"Ah, the drunken rant." He chuckled.

"Any substance to it?"

"Our dear Angelica cultivated an aura of intrigue by insinuating that she consorted with unsavory types. More the fool she, if there is veracity in any of her fantasies. The rumors she borrowed money from nasty vermin such as Louis Paselly, for example."

Zee leaned toward the phone, brows raised. "Did she?"

His silk jacket rustled, a shrug. "Unknown, my dear. That's the point of mystique, and possibly the pitfall." His amused chuckle drifted through the line. "There you have it, the entirety I have thus far uncovered. I hope it has been helpful to your—what is it you're working on?"

Time to nip his interest in the bud. "Just chasing some ideas."

"I do hope you will share."

"If and when I can. Thanks for your help."

He accepted the dismissal with grace. "Ta, 'tis nothing."

Fontina's brown eyes crinkled as Zee disconnected. "One of a kind, isn't he?" She sobered. "The actress could have a motive, but the act doesn't fit her character, if you'll pardon the attempt to be clever."

"Victor brings that out in people," said Zee. "I think you're right about Angelica Street, but desperation can push people past their normal boundaries. Street, Paselly, and McNeary, those are some strange bedfellows."

"There's also Bottmeyer," said Fontina.

The infusion of energy from Victor trickled away as Zee faced the prospect of finding the elusive author. Even if she managed to locate him, there was no guarantee he'd invested. He might have dropped out of Ian McNeary's life since those long-ago college years.

"Maybe you'll have better luck with him," Fontina added.

Zee tried to match Fontina's optimism. "Maybe." She plucked the parking stub from her dashboard and waved it. "Speaking of luck, how did you manage to snag that primo parking space?"

Fontina laughed. "Luck had nothing to do with it."

"Don't tell me there's a goddess of parking spaces." Zee rolled her eyes.

"Oh, but there is." Fontina grinned. "We call her Asphalta."

CHAPTER 12

ZEE WAVED GOOD-BYE TO FONTINA and started the Mini, a grin on her face at the idea of a Goddess Asphalta. As if to challenge her, the parking lot stub fluttered where she'd dropped it on the dashboard. She grimaced. Ten bucks for two hours. Maybe she would call on the goddess next time she wanted a cheap, convenient spot to put her car.

Her mind turned to the problem of Pete Bottmeyer. She could use some otherworldly help there, too. Given that Bottmeyer had been out of sight for nearly half a year, finding him wasn't going to be easy. She had to do it, though, to chase down the story, if there was one. The reclusive author was her best lead.

If he even was a lead. She couldn't assume he'd invested in McNeary, based on a decades-old chummy college photo.

She shelved her doubts. Penn needed her revisions.

She headed homeward through the southern part of Valerian, a section of the city transforming under gentrification's velvet-gloved, steel-boned fingers. A placard on a chain link fence announced the forthcoming installation of a community garden. Flaking paint on the boarded-up building behind it read *Roman Villa Apts.* These were hardly villas, but home to someone. As usual, her heart fought with her head. Urban renewal was desirable, healthy even, but so was affordable housing.

The derelict apartments bordered a bedraggled dry cleaner, its yellowing shades separated by slivers of dirt-encrusted brick from the gleaming windows of Integrated Life. Zee's lips creased in a smile. Fontina never lost her youthful idealism, just directed it toward supporting herself in harmony with her vision and her gift.

"See, Dad, it can be done," she whispered.

Her heart pinched. She hadn't been to see him since before the murder. Her throat tightened as she counted back. The last visit had been three days before she broke it off with Rico. Almost four weeks.

What a failure of her duty. For three years, she'd spent time with her dad every week, ever since his failing cognition had forced his move into assisted living. Then came the stroke a month ago.

The radical destruction of his brain wasn't his fault. Just as it wasn't his fault that she came to the end of her strength, trying to handle everything. Trying to bear up under the shock and grief and anger and regret that weighed in her chest and crowded her mind like huge, immobile boulders.

And not his fault that, stretched too taut, she snapped, stung Rico, and pushed him away.

She blew out a breath. At least she could remedy one mistake.

A turn at the next light set her on the familiar route to Leehammer Pavilion. She was grateful it had an acute care wing. Unstable as her dad was now, the smaller the disruption in his surroundings, the better for him.

In the half-full lot, she parked the Mini beneath the shade of a sprawling maple tree, resplendent in gold and fiery orange. As the engine ticked and cooled, anxiety tightened her stomach. She should have stopped and bought—what? A magazine? He might not be able to read anymore, but he could at least look at the pretty pictures. She swallowed the bitter taste in her throat. A man of his intelligence . . .

A balloon then.

One of those silvery, shiny, false-colored, desperate expressions of cheerfulness? She'd rather gouge her eyes out.

He liked chocolate. She slammed the door on that thought. Definitely no food. She never again wanted to see him struggle to eat.

Her empty hands screamed thoughtlessness. She reached toward the *Start* button on the Mini's dashboard, but a leftover bit of the morning's fierce determination aborted the move.

She was only procrastinating.

Despite the gulf between them, she loved her dad. *Enough thinking.* She shoved the car door open and propelled herself across the lot.

Beneath the generous portico, double doors eased apart with a pneumatic hiss and a blast of frigid air. She shivered.

"Good morning. May I help you?" A young woman smiled behind the reception desk.

"I'd like to see Stefan Morani." Zee bit her tongue to refrain from asking whether he was in cold storage.

The receptionist checked her wristwatch. "Before lunch. He's probably in the solarium. It's right down the hallway." Her ringed fingers gestured to Zee's left.

Zee sucked the chill air into her lungs, embracing the sharp ache as penance for her dereliction of duty. Her discomfort with this version of her dad, her unwillingness to let go of previous images of him, were shameful reasons to avoid visiting.

She printed Stefan's name, signed hers in the register, filled out a sticky visitor badge, and smoothed it next to her lapel.

The hallway was papered in tasteful pinpricks of plum and navy on a cream background. A sturdy railing ran its length, assistance for walkers and protection from erratic wheelchairs. The thin aroma of boiled meat drifted in the air.

At the wide doorway to the solarium, she steeled herself and scanned the scattered residents. She found him, sitting alone at a small square table. A few feet away, a low wall surrounded a floor-to-ceiling circular birdcage. Her dad's head was tipped back, as if he studied the flitting feathers of red, blue, and yellow, or listened to the sprinkling of trills, chirps, and tweets.

The wheelchair dwarfed him, another insult for a once-hearty man. The image of Hawethorne flashed in her mind. Gray-skinned and skeletal inside his too-big clothing, he appeared hardly strong enough to stab a healthy Ian McNeary with much force.

Zee shook the thought from her head and crossed the maroon and gray checkerboard tile.

Her dad remained fixed on the birdcage as she pulled a chair next to him. His hair, thick and white as hoarfrost, curled back from the mottled skin of his high forehead. She lost herself, staring at his head, imagining all the knowledge inside that skull, locked in that brain. So small a space to contain such vastness . . . and the key was lost.

So much was lost when a brain was destroyed. Both past and future.

McNeary's murder intruded on her thoughts. His promise had been ripped from him, as had the potential of those who took the failed drug. Zee's own experience told of her shock and horror, as she witnessed her dad's destruction. This had occurred by the caprice of nature, not human folly. Surely, the devastation would be compounded for anyone who viewed McNeary's failure as preventable or worse, brought about by his reckless ambition.

Angelica Street's drunken threat echoed in Zee's ears. *I'll make that doctor regret it.* Bottmeyer might have felt the same way.

As a blue-and-white nuthatch hopped head-first down the thick artificial tree trunk in the cage, she stacked the three motives side by side. An actress whose pretentious lifestyle probably took a hit. A struggling author whose dream of debt relief might have been demolished. A poet whose recovered health was destroyed.

All pointed to revenge, but Hawethorne clearly had the strongest reason to kill. And his posts revealed the level of emotion mirrored in the doctor's wounds.

In retrospect, her doubts about Hawethorne seemed naïve. Without even the foresight of a small bird, she'd dived head-first into the unfamiliar territory of murder. Her 'evidence' consisted of a couple of dreams and a gut feeling. She could hear Bernstow's scoff.

Or maybe it was her dad, clearing his throat.

"Dad?"

He didn't move.

She put her lips closer to his ear. "Dad?"

His faded brown eyes looked toward her, but didn't focus.

"It's Zee." She touched his scrawny arm.

His mouth moved, but no words came out.

"Your daughter." Zee kept her voice low, hoping to forestall distress. She repeated her name.

He worked his jaw, and a garbled sound emerged. His face contorted into an irritated mask.

Zee's breath caught.

Cheeks darkening, he glared at her.

She relaxed her jaw, lowered her hunched shoulders, kept her face open, unthreatening.

He stared, opened his mouth.

Fee-bee, fee-bee, fee-bee erupted from the birdcage.

His eyes swept toward the sound. Two black-capped chickadees chased each other from perch to perch. As if washed by their musical notes, her dad's features slackened. The pinched lines smoothed into bland vacuity.

She exhaled her relief. "You always liked birds," she said. "Remember the feeder we had?"

He glanced toward her. Was that a gleam of recognition? If so, it was quickly gone.

She fought down disappointment. At least he felt no disgrace at failing to remember.

Disgrace, another motive.

Damn. The murder would not leave her alone.

Of its own accord, the thought completed itself. More than one person had killed in a twisted effort to reclaim the loss of self-respect.

The lump in her throat surprised her. The white-haired old man happily engrossed in the fluttering birds never meant to hurt her. Though she couldn't understand his aloofness after her mother died, it did not arise from deliberate intent to harm.

Her mother's confession had cleaved the bedrock of their lives. Over time, the break had widened into a chasm, and when she left for college, it was as if a whole section just sheared off. She and her dad lived on the edges of the opposite cliffs. Perhaps he had no more idea than she how to cross the rickety bridge that might have reconciled them.

Blinking back tears, she whispered in his ear. "I love you, Dad." No reaction.

Sadness squeezed upward from her stomach, constricting her throat, stinging into her eyes, threatening to spill in sobs and tears.

Flapping a good-bye in the direction of the attendant, she fled, bolting down the tastefully decorated hallway, across the thickly carpeted reception area, through the gleaming double doors, whooshing open, out into the pale, sticky early-afternoon sun. She yanked open the Mini's door, hurled herself into the driver's seat, jabbed the *Start* button, and headed for the freeway—for wind in her hair and air in her lungs, for trees and grasses to fill her eyes, for the great cleansing wand of nature.

Too late, she accelerated up the ramp. She braked at the edge of a massive traffic jam. *Stuck.*

CHAPTER 13

STUCK ON THE FREEWAY, STRINGS OF TAILLIGHTS stretched like pulsing nerves in front of Zee. She banged her fist against the steering wheel and snarled. So much for her quick escape from Leehammer Pavilion and the specter of her dad. So much for wind in her hair, or any type of fresh air. The sticky heat rolled in waves through the trapped, motionless Mini. Muttering a curse, she raised the windows and cranked the air conditioning.

She drew abreast of a man holding a ragged piece of cardboard. *Columbus* was scrawled across it. His gaunt frame, stringy hair, and disheveled clothing reminded her of Hawethorne, and suddenly, like a chatty, unwanted hitchhiker, the murder rode in the passenger seat.

It peppered her, replaying Hawethorne's anguished courthouse plea for help and Fontina's astonishing declaration at La Patisserie: Hawethorne didn't kill McNeary, even though he wanted, and intended, to.

Zee quirked her lips. Under her friend's relentless probing yesterday at Farm Fresh, she'd been forced to admit to her own doubts. Damn Fontina—why did she always have to be right?

Zee laughed out loud. She asked that question about Rico, too. Curious that she accepted Fontina's behavior much more easily than Rico's.

The dichotomy intrigued her. She eased out the clutch, rolled a few feet, and braked.

She'd known Fontina almost all her life, Rico a lot less. That was a big factor. She tried listing their traits. Fontina was kind, as was Rico. Fontina was generous. Rico was, too. Supportive? He'd been nothing but, and yet, it was as if she stubbed her toe on that idea.

A considerable distance ahead, a tractor-trailer pulled halfway off the road. She grimaced. From such a high perch, the trucker could see much farther than she. If there was an accident, she'd be here until dinnertime. On cue, her stomach grumbled.

Hunger, which had disappeared during her stressful visit, roared back, a rudely awakened sleeping beast. In between inching the Mini forward, she dug in her glovebox, praying she hadn't eaten the last of her emergency cheese sandwich crackers.

"Hallelujah." Her fingers closed around the crinkling plastic. She pulled free her deliverance and groaned. Half the packet was in crumbs.

Nonetheless, it was food. She extracted one mostly whole cracker and popped it into her mouth. Desiccated fragments, yes. Cheese-like filling, yes. Ecstasy for her starved stomach, emphatically yes.

She gulped water, choked down another crumbling square, and crept along.

A billboard to her right seduced her eyes with an enormous, glistening hamburger, crowned with thick slices of cheese, dewy lettuce and tomatoes, and a bun so fresh Zee could feel her teeth sinking into it. *Big Ol' Burger—two miles ahead.*

She licked her lips and tried to dampen her enthusiasm. Probably it would be a cousin of that cardboard croissant. However, enough ketchup could render anything edible, even cheese-cracker dust. She resolved to add condiment packets to her glove box rations and swallowed more taste bud fervor at the thought. Quickly, she averted her gaze, lest she attempt to eat the cellophane cracker wrapper.

Her left foot cramped as she endured another series of clutch-out, roll, clutch-in. As she reached down to rub her calf, a silver Mercedes sped by in the emergency lane. A masculine driver, wraparound sunglasses beneath a shock of hair, chiseled chin thrust forward, driving gloves on the leather-covered steering wheel.

A smile split her face as the Mercedes braked behind the semi. The trucker probably hadn't seen an accident, more likely an opportunity to provide a lesson in humility for Mister *I-Don't-Need-to-Respect-the-Rules*.

Respect. The word dropped into her disarrayed musings like a key. Fontina valued Zee's thoughts, her ideas, her feelings, even when she disagreed with them. Rico appreciated them, too, but he pushed, challenged. His yang to Fontina's yin.

Was that really the only difference? She'd hit upon a part of the truth, but like the mountain whose peak created an island, a great deal more lay below the surface.

A space opened in front of her. She accelerated to thirty. The burst of speed swept clear her mind. She needed to *do* something to get out of this stuck place.

The next exit would put her only a few blocks from McNeary's lab. She could talk to some of the people who saw him every day, like the attendant at the coffee bar. Her pulse quickened, even as her skin prickled.

Ghoulish as the thought seemed, she'd found herself on the front lines of a great story. Sure, not the feature she'd planned, but possibly even better. She swallowed the lump in her throat. No self-respecting reporter would fail to pursue it.

Fired by fresh purpose, she willed the Mini the final half-mile to the exit, abandoned the freeway quagmire, and sped through Valerian's pot-holed southern section to her new destination.

She pulled into the lot across the street, the memory of her last visit beading sweat across her forehead. As she drove past the leaking dumpster, she swore she could see the stench deforming the air above the barely closed top.

Eyes smarting, she angled into the shade of a scraggly tree in a far corner. Too bad she didn't have one of those nylon car shrouds. That penetrating stink might eat the paint right off the bright red Mini.

Heat swamped her as soon as she stepped out, tempting her to leave her blazer on the passenger seat. She resisted. In her experience, the weather inside commercial buildings was always the same: cold. She hurried across the crumbling blacktop, perspiration trickling between her shoulder blades, and pushed open the door.

The Cup o' Joe to Go coffee bar was deserted. A young man wiped one of its three tables. "Be right with you, miss." He gave the faux marble surface a final swipe, stuffed the cloth into the black apron tied around his narrow waist, and loped behind the counter. "What can I get you?"

She sucked in a breath that had nothing to do with the shock of chilly air in the building and everything to do with the friendly, open gaze that looked out at her from lushly lashed, liquid dark eyes. Her gaze dipped to his dark, closely trimmed beard and mustache, skimmed his finely detailed lips, and lingered on his skin, smooth as copper-colored silk. Too late, she hoped her mouth hadn't gaped. What was this Adonis doing in sleepy, backwater Valerian?

He smiled. One front tooth turned slightly inward, disturbing the otherwise perfect line. The discrepancy weakened Zee's entrancement enough to allow her to answer.

"Medium chai iced tea." The jar of biscotti on the counter caught her eye, cranberry-macadamia nut. "And one—no, two—of those." Nuts had protein. And fruit was good.

"Yes, miss." He busied himself with her order.

"Pretty quiet right now." She resisted the urge to lift the lid from the cookie jar and help herself.

"Slow yes, but it will get busy in an hour or so." He flashed another disarming, canted-tooth smile. "People need their pick-me-ups to get through the afternoon."

And when they're starving.

Focus. She needed to get this man to talk. "I'm sorry about last Tuesday."

"Oh, you mean the doctor's . . ." His smooth face crumpled.

She cringed at his pain. "Did you know him?" She searched for a name tag. "Akhil."

He shook his head. "He did not stop for coffee, but Janece, his assistant, would get two cups when she came in." His deep brown eyes softened. "She was always pleasant."

"Perhaps you'll still see her?" Zee infused optimism into her voice.

"She came in a few minutes ago with a police officer. She did not stop." He shrugged slender shoulders. "Would you like whipped cream?"

"Pile it on." Milk was healthy. Her hungry eyes devoured his every move, as he slipped a plastic dome over the cup, topped her chai, and eased a paper-capped straw through the round opening.

"Five dollars and fifty cents."

Through the fog of craving, an idea came to Zee. "What's Janece's favorite drink?"

A smile spread across Akhil's features. "She usually ordered black coffee, but on special occasions she would splurge for a caramel cappuccino."

"Give me one of those," Zee said. "Large."

Akhil grinned as he set to work.

Zee tried again for a sympathetic opening. "It must have been awful, that day."

He froze, pain stiffening his features. "Are you one of those . . . paparazzi? From the newsstand gossip papers?"

Zee's face stung as though he'd slapped her. "No, I'm not," she hurried to say. "I write a column for the *Tribune* and other papers, but no tabloids."

"So, you wish to write about this tragedy?" A flash of anger lit his eyes, and there was steel in his mild voice. "The doctor was a good man. Dedicated."

Zee needed to bridge his mistrust. "I came here that day to interview Doctor McNeary about his new drug. I was inspired by his courage and determination."

Akhil's expression cleared. "I regret misjudging you. And I am glad to be wrong." He capped the drink and slid it across the counter. "Nine dollars, please."

Zee dug a ten and a five from her wallet and pushed the bills toward him. "Keep the change." She considered how to direct the conversation. "Doctor McNeary's death is a great loss. I hope the police catch his killer."

Akhil nodded, and she took a chance—*strike while the iron is hot.* "Did anyone ask directions to the doctor's office that morning?"

"Not from me. But I am very busy early."

Her question hadn't upset him. Maybe he wanted to talk. "You see anything unusual?"

He placed the ten in the register and removed a single. "Thank you," he said, folding the tip into his pocket. "There was a disturbance in the lobby, people scattering, making way for a man who was stumbling. I thought he was ill. He staggered through the doors. A few moments later, a lady came in who had just bought a latte. Very frustrated. She said a drunkard had run into her and caused her to drop the drink on the sidewalk."

Though the shop was empty, he bent toward Zee and lowered his voice. "I gave her another one free. She offered to pay, but I would not take her money. It is a little thing, but such small acts can make a big difference. I made her sun come out again."

Zee smiled at him. "You're a good person, Akhil. I think you're a lot like Doctor McNeary." She thought a moment. "That was a skillful way to take care of an upset customer." Then as if it just occurred to her. "Was anyone upset with the doctor, do you know?"

He knit his perfect crescent brows. "Janece did not gossip, but she seemed disturbed recently."

Zee tugged the cap from her straw to hide her piqued interest. "That's troubling. Do you know why?"

His eyes darted past her. "What may I get you, sir?"

Squelching her disappointment, Zee sketched a small wave. "Best wishes with Janece."

She secured the cups in a cardboard tray and nestled the biscotti between them. As she neared the elevators, a shiver washed over her, as though she'd passed through a ghost. Remnants of the wraith rode with her to the fourth floor. She willed them away, focusing on the crisp cookies with their tantalizing creamy chunks of macadamia and crimson cranberry bits.

Food is grounding, Fontina told her once. She said as her intuition grew stronger, she would sometimes feel untethered, not-quite-here, after an intense experience. Eating, she discovered, was a reliable way to anchor herself back into her body.

Zee thought her stomach might exit her body and directly ingest a biscotti if she didn't feed it soon. She'd been foolish to start on her upward journey without unwrapping a cookie, though now that she thought about it, she couldn't see eating in that haunted elevator or in that dingy, dimly lit hallway. No matter how much she wanted to wolf down sustenance.

Soon, she promised her gut. There was a distinct tone of skepticism in its answering rumble.

At the end of the hallway, she rapped on the half-open door.

"Come in," called a female voice.

"Stay right there!" shouted a second one.

Zee stilled her body in the doorway.

McNeary's assistant looked up from the desk. Towering beside her, a uniformed policewoman glared at Zee. "This is a crime scene. Back away from the door."

"I just wanted to bring this to Janece." Zee held out the cappuccino. "From Akhil downstairs."

Janece's brows lifted, but she covered her surprise. "Thank you. That's very kind."

The officer kept one eye on Zee. "You get what you wanted?" she barked at McNeary's assistant. Without waiting for a reply, she jerked her head toward the door. "Let's go."

Janece's hand closed around a paperback on the desk blotter.

"Leave it," snapped the cop.

"I don't see why I can't take it with me." Janece lifted the book toward a large leather bag. "It can't have anything to do with . . . the crime."

The uniform hooked her thumbs on her utility belt. "My orders are your pills and the case study logbook. That's all."

"But—"

"Read something else for a few days."

"This is unreasonable. No one—"

"You want a trip downtown?" The policewoman yanked the book from Janece's grasp and tossed it on the blotter.

Zee clamped her mouth shut. It wouldn't do to make things worse.

Inhaling a slow breath, Janece straightened her shoulders and stepped from behind the desk.

Zee held out the coffee as Janece crossed the threshold, the officer a glowering blue warden behind her. "Akhil said this is your favorite."

Warmth flickered in Janece's brown eyes.

Behind them, her law-and-order escort made a show of locking McNeary's door. She shadowed Zee and Janece to the elevator and punched the down arrow.

Zee pitched her voice low toward Janece's ear. "Is there a place we can talk?"

"Lunchroom on three," she murmured.

The bell dinged and the officer got in. She folded her arms across her chest and tapped her foot. "You two coming?"

Zee locked eyes with her. "Think we'll take the stairs."

CHAPTER 14

ZEE SHOOK HER HEAD AS THE ELEVATOR doors closed, shutting in the über-cop and her petty authority. Alone in the hallway with Janece, she was tempted to return to McNeary's office and retrieve the forbidden novel, but that would only bring trouble for the doctor's assistant. Zee could handle that, but Janece might be better off letting it go. The small woman's hands quivered as she gripped Zee's cappuccino offering.

Resentful of the cop's attitude, Zee followed Janece down the stairs. Though the passage was poorly lit, the atmosphere seemed to brighten the farther she got from McNeary's office. When Janece pushed open the third-floor entrance, light flooded the hallway through wide double doors to the lunchroom.

The bright space hosted the expected institutional-grade tables and seating, but Zee raised her brows at the well-upholstered couch and padded club chairs.

"The law firm people gussied this up after they bought the building." Janece twisted her lips. "Hand-me-downs from their most recent renovation. They couldn't be expected to sit their thousand-dollar-bottoms on plebian plastic." Her hand flew to her mouth. "Oh, I hope I haven't offended you. I don't usually blurt out my thoughts like that. I'm just not myself."

Zee brushed away Janece's concern. "Don't worry. It seems to me the only winners in lawsuits are the lawyers. I even heard one firm boast that they wouldn't charge the client more than the settlement received. How generous!"

"Thank you." Janece exhaled and stuck out a plump hand. "Janece Renford."

"Zee Morani."

"I recognized you from the television feature." Janece sank onto the couch and held up the cappuccino. "Thank you for bringing me this."

"Thank *you* for being quick on the uptake." Zee offered a biscotti. "Want one?"

"Oh, I shouldn't." Janece fluttered her hand. "Diabetes. This is bad enough." She sipped. "Oh, but it's good."

Zee settled in a club chair, stirred whipped cream into her iced chai, and indulged in a long drink. Smooth, sweet, and robust with just the right amounts of cardamom, cinnamon, nutmeg, and ginger. A hint of pepper lingered as the chilled liquid slid down her throat. She barely suppressed an audible sigh of contentment.

"Akhil makes a good chai," she said.

Janece's face softened. "He's sweet."

"He seems a little sweet on you," said Zee.

Janece dipped her head, but her cheeks colored. She busied herself digging a tissue from her pants pocket, removing her tortoiseshell glasses, and dabbing at her eyes.

Zee mulled how to proceed while unwrapping a cookie. Akhil had remarked that Janece seemed upset recently, but Zee didn't want to betray a confidence. She waited until Janece replaced her glasses, then caught her eyes. "Akhil held Doctor McNeary in high regard. I'm sorry I didn't get to meet him. I'm wondering if there's still a way to tell his story."

"I'd love that." Janece sighed into her cappuccino. "It breaks my heart that the only thing people will remember about him is his failure." She raised her eyes. "I'd help if I could, but I don't see how."

Zee leaned forward. "Maybe you can. I hoped to better understand the challenges he faced. Like," she guessed, "had he been receiving threats?"

"No more than usual."

"Oh?"

Janece pulled her already snug sweater more tightly across her body. "I suppose I'd gotten used to it. People were angry when Neurish failed." She shuddered, her short brunette ringlets rippling. "The hate mail. You wouldn't believe it. But the vitriol usually stopped there. No one ever came here . . ." She bent her head.

Zee sipped chai to ease the lump in her throat. At least Janece had not seen the doctor's savaged body. She gave the assistant time to regain control before speaking again. "He wanted to tell me about the new drug."

Janece's face lit, and Zee glimpsed beauty beneath the lines of strain. "He was very excited. He had high hopes." Behind tortoiseshell glasses, her eyes met Zee's. "He drove himself too hard, though. I should tell you I argued with him about giving you an interview."

That's why the researcher set up their meeting so early. "Was he ill?" Zee had not uncovered any problems with McNeary's health.

Janece shook her head. "But some other doctor kept pestering him. For some reason, he believed he should be in charge of the project. I offered to block his calls, but Ian—Doctor McNeary didn't want to do that."

Zee kept her face neutral at that slip of the tongue and focused instead on the troublemaking colleague. Possibly he was the reason McNeary agreed to the rare interview in the first place. "Can you give me that doctor's name?" she said.

Janece chewed her lower lip. "Marks . . . no. Merit?" She shook her head. "I'm afraid my memory is just mush right now."

"That's all right." Zee set the empty biscotti wrapper on the tray, found a card in her purse, and pushed it across the polished table between them. "If you remember, call me." She waited while Janece tucked the card into her pocket. "Did Doctor McNeary have any other appointments that day?"

"Just his chief lab assistant. John Flann. They usually met over at the Medical Center, but lately he's been coming to the lab here."

"The lab adjoins his office, right? Do you have to go through the office to get into the lab?"

Janece nodded. "There's an exit door to the hallway, but no entry. Doctor McNeary insisted on security."

Zee recalled the door without a handle in the fourth-floor hallway. One way in, but two ways out. Lucky for her. She suppressed a shudder.

Janece worried the tissue in her hands. "I suppose I'll be asked to help hand off the project to whoever takes it on." Her voice hitched. "I don't know how I'll face going in there." Tears trickled down her cheeks.

"Would the lab assistant help? Or Doctor McNeary's family?" It seemed likely they'd want to ensure the work continued.

"His father's all he has," said Janece. "He lives in New York. Arrived today to, to claim . . ." She sniffled.

He might know of investors. Zee kept her voice solicitous, disguising her interest. "Do you know how to contact him?"

Janece dove into her copious handbag as if glad to be given a task. "I have his number on my cell. Where is the dumb thing?" She began to pile the excavated contents on the table. "Poor man's very distraught. The police won't give him any information. Ah!" She pulled the phone free, scrolled, and read the number. Her face softened. "Maybe you could talk to him for me? Share whatever you might know?"

And ask him a few questions. "I'll give him a call." Zee repeated his number. "I can't imagine how it would feel to be kept totally in the dark."

"Mercy." Janece's eyes lit.

"Yes, you'd think they could tell him *something*," Zee said.

"No," Janece said. "Jules Mercy, that's the other doctor's name. I knew it started with an *M*."

Jules Mercy, the other man in the college photo with McNeary and Bottmeyer.

Janice's face clouded. "I wonder what will happen to Ian's work now. And to me." She cried harder.

"Why don't you go home?" Zee made her voice gentle. "I'm surprised the police let you in today."

Janece inhaled a ragged breath. "I'm in a diabetes study. I have to take the pills at lunch and keep a log. I had enough at home to last a few days, but I needed the supply I keep here." She raised wet eyes. "Doctor McNeary got me in. He was a kind man."

"I'm learning that about him."

Hands shaking, Janece refilled her bag. "You've been very kind, Miss Morani. If I can help you . . . if you decide to write . . ."

"Of course."

Zee accompanied Janece to the elevator. After the doors closed, she munched on the second biscotti. Light, crumbly, delicately flavored with anise, sweet-tart with cranberry, and rich with macadamia chunks.

Worlds away from La Patisserie. Maybe it boded well for finding more rewards here. Perhaps even a witness. She tossed the wrapper and her empty cup into the trash bin and, brushing crumbs from her blouse, started down the hall.

Her first destination was a door decorated with a giant, smiling tooth. Hours emblazoned along the molar's side showed that Ferguson Family Dentistry had been closed three days ago. Zee went in, anyway. Over the squeals of two children playing in a corner, the polite receptionist confirmed the information. *No help there.*

She walked the length of the corridor to the law offices of Heberle, Hatchett & Crick. When she pushed open the heavy oak door, a smartly attired woman was on the phone, inquiring in a faintly aristocratic British accent how she might direct someone's call.

Zee's eye took in the lobby: honey-colored leather sofa and two armchairs, gleaming softly in light that filtered from antique parchment shades atop brass floor lamps. On the golden teak coffee table, an enormous vase barely containing an explosion of red, orange, and yellow chrysanthemums. On one matching side table, a volume of Shakespeare.

The arrangement gave the impression of someone's living room . . . a very wealthy someone. Zee would like to get on the law firm's hand-me-down list.

"How may I help you?"

The patrician tones scolded Zee's attention back to the matter at hand. "Lovely office." She offered a card, which the receptionist accepted and studied. "I'm wondering if someone was here around seven on Tuesday morning."

"The office opens at nine."

Not exactly an answer.

During Zee's ill-fated ride on the morning of the murder, several people had gotten off the elevator on this floor. "Don't associates come in early?"

The woman's expression did not change. "I would have no way of knowing that."

Nice evasion. The lawyers had trained her well.

"Was there something else?" Her manicured hand reached for a folder on the desk.

Zee accepted she would get nowhere with this gatekeeper. She thanked her, and stealing another envious glance at the furnishings, crossed to the heavy door. An idea caused her to turn back. "I understand the law firm bought this building," she said. "Will there be space for lease?"

The woman picked up Zee's card. "I can have our agency contact you."

Zee approached the desk. "Perhaps you could just give me their information."

The phone emitted a discreet brrrr. The gatekeeper answered, glanced at Zee, and asked the caller to hold. She handed Zee an embossed card, then turned her attention to the call. Zee nodded her thanks.

In the hallway, she tapped the agency's card against her fingertips. Based on the elegance of the office, it was a good bet the rents were going up as soon as current leases expired. That could be another reason McNeary wanted to make his work public. Perhaps it would garner financial support and allow him to keep control of his project.

She suffered a pang of guilt for her covetousness as she took the stairs down a flight. She needed to remember the cost that others might pay, or had paid, for the law firm's opulence.

The second-floor hallway was dominated by a series of large frameless portraits: dark-lashed, brooding men; sultry, pouty-lipped women—all close-up, larger than life. Their sepia eyes followed Zee as she made her way toward a frosted-glass door.

Etched in the glass was a stylized outline of a woman, the perfect image of poise. One impossibly long leg, slightly forward, positioned her at a three-quarter angle, the better to accentuate her subtle curves, sleek shoulders, long slender neck, and hair in such volume it surely would have toppled an ordinary female of the species.

Zee opened the door, and a svelte woman in a black silk sheath glided toward her.

"Welcome to the Sandhurst Beauty, Talent, and Modeling School. I'm Barbara Sandhurst, proprietor." Her delicately tinted lips turned upward in what Zee supposed was a smile, but it did not mask the subtle shifting of her eyes. In preparation for the courtroom, Zee had worn dove gray slacks with a matching blouse, topped with her brick red blazer. One of her better-fitting professional outfits, but under Barbara's scrutiny, it might have been a cardboard and paper suit.

The agency owner lifted an elegant hand toward an arrangement of large velvet mushrooms perched on low metal corkscrews. "Please have a seat."

Zee glanced toward the precariously balanced upholstered mounds. Perhaps it was a test. If you could sit on one of those and not fall off, you could be a model. "No, thanks. I won't take much of your time. My name is Zee Morani."

"Oh yes, I saw you on the television." Barbara's perfect features shaped themselves to project conspiratorial camaraderie. "You've made a wise choice. Upon reaching a certain level of celebrity, many people find their image can benefit from a bit of burnishing."

Zee didn't know whether to be flattered or insulted. She tried for a pleasant smile. *Catch more flies with honey.* "That's quite astute. Seeing myself on television was revealing. Perhaps we could discuss your services at another time."

If Barbara felt disappointed, her malachite orbs did not betray her. "How may I help you today?"

Zee explained her connection with McNeary. "I wonder whether anyone saw him that morning," she finished.

Barbara's lips pursed faintly.

"I'd just like to learn all I can about him," Zee added, infusing her voice with harmless, friendly curiosity.

Barbara gave a fractional nod and stepped toward a waist-high glass counter. Zee followed, blinking at the glittering array of tear-drop-shaped crystalline bottles, golden-hinged discs with jeweled clasps, and ebony-handled brushes with bristles that looked soft as sable.

"Veronique," Barbara called, somehow projecting her voice without raising it. "Could you come out front please."

A dark-haired woman appeared in a doorway behind the counter. The planes of her face gleamed pristine as Christmas snow, so featureless that her dark eyes and red lips seemed to float on the surface of her skin.

"Veronique is here at six," said Barbara, by way of introduction.

"Our protégés often must have hair and makeup early in the day." Veronique flashed Zee a dazzling smile.

Barbara gestured with slender fingers toward Zee. "Miss Morani is interested in the doctor upstairs." She spoke of him as though he hadn't been the victim of a horrendous crime.

Zee kept her expression neutral. "Did you see the doctor on . . . that day?"

"No, but I did see a strange man." Veronique flicked her lashes toward Barbara. "I expected Clarissa for her appointment, and I looked down the hall when I heard the elevator bell. But a man stepped out."

"You didn't recognize him?" Zee said. "He wasn't maybe his lab assistant?"

"He was no one I have seen." Veronique shivered delicately. "I thought perhaps he was homeless, or ill. He was very thin. Or perhaps it seemed that way because of his hat. It was quite large and made his head look out of proportion to his body." The barest blush tinted her alabaster cheeks. "I did not wish for him to see me. I ducked behind the counter display."

"I would have done the same thing," Zee said.

Veronique rewarded her with another diamond-bright smile.

"Did you see anyone else?"

She shook her head, a single, apologetic gesture. Economy of movement must be part of the curriculum here.

"Did your client mention anything when she arrived?"

Another elegant negative.

Zee shifted to Barbara. "Did any of your other employees say anything?"

"I heard nothing."

"Would you mind if I spoke to them?"

Barbara's green eyes narrowed the tiniest bit, a practiced movement no doubt to maintain her facial barricade against wrinkles. As if any crease would have the effrontery. "Do you plan to write about . . . the incident?"

She'd made an acknowledgment, at least. Not of murder, more on the level of a forgotten item on the grocery list. "I don't know yet what I'll do. I liked the doctor."

"We had nothing to do with it."

Barbara's smile seemed forced. Maybe she *couldn't* move her muscles any more than that. "Of course not," Zee said. "I—"

"And it would not be the kind of publicity we'd prefer, you understand."

Zee closed her mouth. She would learn nothing more in this place. Handing Barbara a card, she thanked the two women and turned toward the door.

"Please take a brochure." Barbara touched Zee's shoulder and pressed a glossy trifold into her hand. "Let me show you what we can do."

Zee slipped the folder into her pocket. "I will," she said. *Just not this lifetime.*

The Department of Motor Vehicles office on the ground floor was thick with disgruntlement. Zee decided not to take a number.

She flashed Akhil a smile and a wave as she crossed the lobby. Too bad he couldn't have seen the light in Janece's eyes at the mention of his name. Perhaps those two would find their way together. She grinned faintly at the thought of matchmaking; not her forte.

Outside, the heat of the day struck her, brutal and wetly stifling. Her curls, their unruliness magnified by the humidity, tangled over her cheeks in the hot breeze. As she skirted the stinking dumpster, she resisted the urge to fling in Barbara's slick advertisement. Too far, anyway, it would only add to the ugly mess.

She wrinkled her nose at Sandhurst's pretentiousness. Give her Janece any day. She might be less polished, but she was loyal, caring, and spunky.

And she'd provided a lead. Energized by the thought, Zee slid behind the wheel, found her cell, and punched in the number for McNeary's father.

CHAPTER 15

PERCHED ON A SILK UPHOLSTERED CHAIR in the St. Deirdre lounge, Zee waited for McNeary's father. Finally, she had an opportunity to catch her breath. She'd been going at breakneck speed since this morning, when that excitedly regretful radio reporter announced Hawethorne's arraignment—she glanced at her watch—six hours ago.

Her gut grumbled a reminder she'd skipped breakfast, and the abomination at La Patisserie was worse than no food at all. The cheese-dust crackers hardly counted, and even the biscotti from the Cup o' Joe had no staying power. Promising more substantial sustenance soon, she sipped a spectacular café mocha from a wafer-thin porcelain cup. Worth every penny of its eight-dollar price, it slid velvety across her tongue, the espresso a sharp-edged, dangerous paramour only partly tamed by creamy milk and the lingering kiss of dark bitter chocolate.

She smiled. Her mouth was happy, though her stomach didn't seem much mollified.

To watch the entrance to the lounge, she sat facing away from St. Deirdre's famous back wall mural, a colonnaded walkway crowned by a luscious grape arbor. Romans used these frescoes to add the illusion of space to their cramped rooms. It performed the same function in the intimacy of the lounge, but with one departure from the typical scene. A statue of St. Deirdre, an emerald-robed Irish beauty with creamy skin and cascades of fiery red hair, graced the verdant garden beyond the columns.

Her lustful father, the story goes, murdered Deirdre's husband, and in fine tragic tradition, she killed herself. Zee was fairly sure suicide was frowned upon by Christianity, but someone must have devised a work-around for that little detail.

She indulged in another sip. To her relief, the coffee settled her stomach. The last thing she needed was to call attention to her gastric distress. In the hushed atmosphere, two business-suited men clinked their glasses at the polished bar. A young woman, the only other occupant, hunched beneath a blue-swirled pendant lamp in a corner booth, nails clicking against her laptop keys.

The staccato taps pricked Zee, Penn's impatient fingers tapping. Zee had used the time before her appointment with Fenton McNeary to uncover several private schools' mottos. She needed only to incorporate them into the revision of her column. She should be doing that now.

She raised her cup. Over its rim, a tall figure appeared, wealth quietly evident in his finely tailored charcoal suit, immaculate shirt, and expertly knotted pewter tie. His thick, iron-gray hair shone in the dim light as he slipped into the chair opposite her. Zee sucked a silent breath. The same steel-blue eyes had stared from Ian McNeary's lifeless face.

A waiter in a pinstripe waistcoat approached. McNeary's father waved him away and extended his hand toward her. "Miss Morani." Not a question. He'd done his homework.

Grateful for a reason to tear her gaze from the haunting apparition, she shook his hand. Soft skin, nails expertly trimmed. "I hope I can help, Mister McNeary."

"Fenton." He pinched the razor crease on his trouser and crossed his legs, then laced his fingers in his lap. A slight lift of his chest betrayed a controlled inhalation. "Janece said you found my son. I'd be grateful for any information you can share." He clipped the words, as if each one threatened to crack the dam holding back his grief.

Zee bit back a surge of sorrow for him and began with the encounter in the lobby. Fenton's tanned face tightened when she recounted entering his son's office. Try as she might, she couldn't keep the horror from her voice. "I'm sorry."

He held up his palm. It trembled, though his speech remained steady. "I needed to know. I regret you had to see it." He lowered his hand to his lap and ran his thumb over the signet ring on his little finger. "Do you know anything about the investigation?"

Zee's chest constricted. *Damn law enforcement paranoia.* If anyone had a right to know, he did. Bernstow had charged her not to talk about the murder. She shoved that concern aside and told Fenton about the arrest and the discovery of the knife at the scene.

Anger fought with grief in his flattened lips. "Why wouldn't they tell *me*?"

"I don't know. To protect their case?" If so, she'd just exposed it.

He pulled a monogrammed handkerchief from his pocket and pressed the folded snowy square briefly to his eyes. "But if they know . . ."

Zee leaned toward him. She hated that she could sense his vulnerability and yet scheme to use it. To bring him closure, she told herself—and because he was an invaluable source that belonged solely to her. Swallowing her self-disgust, she plunged. "Maybe, like me, they aren't sure."

He raised his head, eyes narrowed.

Now or never. "I don't believe he did it."

His face hardened. "Why not?"

She flinched from the anguish roiling beneath his response. His entire being must be screaming for an end to his agony. Instead of offering relief, she scraped his raw wound. Her heart recoiled from causing added pain, but he might be able to help her get to the truth. His son—and Hawethorne if he *was* innocent—deserved justice.

Damning her quarrelsome internal voices, she met his gaze.

At the very least, having provoked his question, she owed him an answer. "Hawethorne's motive might be powerful, but having seen him, I don't think he's physically strong enough for such a brutal attack."

He winced. She cursed her failure to soften the vicious image.

"You think the police haven't considered this?" he said.

"I'm not saying that. But I have a personal stake here." The words left her lips with surprising conviction. The question of Hawethorne's innocence had staked a claim on her conscience. "I'd like to see it through."

His jaw remained set.

Her bruised heart protested pushing further, but she overrode it. "Fenton, my instincts tell me something's wrong. I need to follow up before the trail goes cold." She cast her final hook. "I'll keep you informed."

His eyes sliced through her defenses, sharp as an incision. She tried not to fidget, but she felt floodlit, exposed, ashamed for selfishly exacerbating his suffering. Yet determination stiffened her spine.

He broke their connection, pocketed the handkerchief with deliberate care. "Janece trusts you."

She held her breath.

His posture relaxed a fraction. "All right. How can I help?"

The knot in Zee's chest loosened. "Do you know anyone who invested?"

"I did. Ian had a good heart and a fine mind." His brow furrowed. "I believe Angelica Street did, too." He leaned forward. "A news report said she threatened him, but I considered that melodrama."

Well said. Zee filed his response.

"Also, Louis Paselly. I warned against him."

Zee's breath quickened. "Why?"

"He had a sleazy reputation. Nothing pinned on him but enough slime to make me wary."

She forced down her uneasiness. "Anyone else?"

"Ian was close-mouthed after that. He thought fear clouded my judgment. I thought guilt clouded his."

"Guilt over Neurish?"

"Over his mother. She died of complications caused by ALS."

Zee had found no reference to this in her research. Such a personal loss went far to explain the doctor's relentless quest. "I'm sorry."

A deep weariness rolled out on his sigh, carrying with it the ashy taste of a burden, lonely and long carried. "I tried," he said, "but Ian couldn't see she loved every moment she lived. Such spirit, the joy she squeezed out of life. Ian saw only the disease. I suppose doctors are trained that way."

Heat rose in Zee's cheeks. She'd reacted the same way to Fontina's news about her niece. She shrank from the memory. There'd be time later for a more sympathetic conversation with her friend. "May I run a couple of names by you? Possible investors?"

"Go ahead."

"Doctor Jules Mercy?"

He shook his head.

"Pete Bottmeyer?"

Tension washed from his face. His ramrod back softened. "They were best friends in college. Like brothers, though they drifted apart in later years. Still, I wouldn't be surprised if he invested."

The steel-blue eyes shone with unshed tears. Zee attended to her café mocha to give him time to recover.

Three deep chimes drifted through the lounge doorway as the clock in the lobby struck the hour. Fenton glanced toward his wrist, where an ebony watch face glimmered. "I must go, make arrangements." He clasped Zee's hand. "Thank you for talking with me. And for your principles. I want justice for Ian. He was a good son, trying to do good in the world."

Zee offered her card. "Call me anytime."

He extracted a silver case from his pocket, placed her card inside, and handed her a discreetly embossed slate rectangle. "Stay in touch."

"I will."

With disciplined purpose, he rose and strode toward the doorway. No one seeing his confident figure would suspect the tragic weight he bore.

Her own heart heavy, Zee turned from the sight and drank the rest of her coffee. She had gained new leads, but they did not cheer her.

Her stomach emitted a loud growl, an alien disruption in the subdued, elegant atmosphere. Behind the bar, the waistcoated waiter lifted a brow.

A menu lay on her table, a marbled sheet of paper slipped like a piece of art into a black leather frame. The presentation alone told her the prices would be gallery-worthy.

She could go get a burger, but somehow that felt like betrayal. McNeary's father had just bared his soul. She couldn't dishonor him by tearing into a bag of potato chips.

What the hell. She beckoned the waiter, then inspected her choices. The stylish script provided nothing so gauche as a price to guide her. All right, she'd let her taste buds decide. "I'll have the brie croissant," she told his attentive face.

"Another café mocha?"

"A glass of chardonnay." Might as well go whole hog.

The waiter inclined his head and glided away.

Having decided to eat, she was instantly ravenous. To distract herself, she pulled her phone from her bag and tapped Louis Paselly in her browser. Fenton's comment marked the second time his name had come up in a discussion—and in a negative light. She blamed the twisting in her gut on hunger and hit Search.

Louis and his sister Beatrice inherited their wealth after a plane accident killed their parents. A plethora of pictures revealed that the son enjoyed the high life of the equine set. In the daughter's rare photo appearances, she wore apprehensive expressions. Maybe she worried Louis was running through the inheritance.

Zee enlarged an image of him. His narrow skull pushed his feral features forward, turning an already long nose snout-like and crowding his teeth above his pointed chin. He looked like a weasel, with none of its cute, redeeming qualities. A shiver snaked up her back and curled into her temples.

"Your chardonnay." The waiter set the glass of golden liquid atop a square, leatherlike coaster.

Just the thing to get the taste of Paselly out of her mouth. She laid the phone aside and touched the wine to her lips.

The initial citrus tang tingled, then mingled with toasted oak and a pleasant mineral flintiness. She closed her eyes and sipped again, savoring the sensual ballet. She would have to upgrade her stock.

A soft clink on the table announced the arrival of her croissant. She lifted her glass in acknowledgment to the waiter.

Research could wait. Wine this good deserved her full attention, as did the repast before her. Perfectly positioned in the center of a square white dish, the flakey croissant rested like a buttery waxing moon, its arms enfolding generous wedges of soft brie. Small crystalline dishes of butter and apricot preserves sparkled at opposite ends of the pastry crescent, each accompanied by a tiny silver serving knife.

Almost too pretty to eat. Almost. She refused to calculate what this lunch might do to her expanding waistline and gave herself to enjoyment.

The first bite ensured her the promise of gustatory delight would be fulfilled. Smooth creamy cheese with the barest nuance of tang married perfectly with succulent slivers of glazed, sweet-tart fruit, the whole layered on a bed of lightly buttered, tender pastry. She suppressed an audible exhalation.

In the next bite, she included a bit of the cheese rind. Slightly chewy, it released a subtle earthiness, a perfect accent for the epicurean pairing of cheese and fruit. The textures and flavors lingered on her palate until she was ready for the faultless cleansing of the crisp chardonnay. Sacramental nectar from the gods.

Zee's taste buds absolved her for La Patisserie's travesty.

When the memory of the last crumb had melted, she tried and failed to summon the energy to leave. The men at the bar were gone, though the woman in the corner continued to click away on her keyboard.

In Zee's languorous state, the woman's tapping seemed louder, steadier. Zee sharpened her attention. Not a computer. Rain.

A thunderous rumble penetrated the sanctuary of the lounge, heaven's blessing on her wish to linger. She leaned back in the chair. After her long day, a nap would feel idyllic.

Her eyes snapped open. *Not here.* The pattering rain through the thick walls dissuaded her from leaving, however. She picked up her phone. She'd use the time to learn about Jules Mercy.

He was easy to find, and as she read, the remnants of tension from the predator-like Paselly dissolved. Mercy appeared to be a polar opposite: kind, thoughtful, and generous, a well-regarded clinician and researcher. His articles were published in top-ranked medical journals. He was devoted to service to the community. His website told her he was giving a free public lecture tonight.

Quiet descended in the lounge. The storm must have spent itself. She contemplated the glass chandelier in the lobby, letting her thoughts drift among the jewel-toned swirls and curls.

Mercy seemed to possess personal and professional integrity down to the bone. Such unblemished character almost defied belief.

On the other hand, McNeary's heroic sense of ethics had led him to sever a lucrative partnership. The two doctors could simply be birds of a feather.

Or they could be fighting cocks, if Janece's version of Mercy was accurate.

Four chimes from the clock interrupted Zee's musing. She signaled the waiter, who approached bearing the bottle. She shook her head with regret. "Just the check please."

"It's been paid." He presented the wine, new, unopened.

Zee scanned the label. Kongsgaard Chardonnay. Her eyes

widened.

"With Mister McNeary's compliments," said the waiter.

She blushed. He really *was* grateful for her information. Or he'd seen her clumsy attempts at manipulation and forgiven her. Accepting the bottle, she vowed not to fail him.

Two new leads beckoned. Paselly seemed a nasty piece of work. She'd avoid him if possible. Mercy, on the other hand, seemed harmless enough . . . and she could meet him tonight.

CHAPTER 16

CRADLING THE EXPENSIVE BOTTLE OF WINE, Zee crossed the spotless lobby of the Hotel St. Deirdre. A young woman in a crisp black-and-white uniform sprang to hold it open. "Enjoy your evening," she said. Professional and competent, yet personable, warm.

Zee found herself smiling an acknowledgment. She could get used to pampered living.

Fenton's tortured eyes flashed through her mind, crumbling her fantasy. Luxury, however great, did not protect against life's suffering.

Yet, Ian McNeary's father had known profound joy in the midst of loss. When he spoke of his deceased wife, his voice softened and grief lifted his weighted brows. Whether or not she got a good story out of it, Zee would ensure the killer was brought to justice, for Fenton's peace of mind and her own.

Beneath the watchful eye of the valet, she nestled Fenton's gift in the Mini's trunk.

The storm had banished the stifling heat, but below the cool surface, humidity and warmth worked invisible fingers steadily upward. Already, steam curled from sunlit pavement. Zee would bet money on more rain. She hoped to get to Mercy's lecture before it started falling.

Humming, she pointed the Mini west toward home and Penn's deadline. The jazzy zing of progress thrummed in her veins. New details to sort, new avenues to—

Her phone erupted with a motorcycle's throaty growl. Rico. She pushed the answer button on the steering wheel.

"Hey." His voice was light, casual. "I saw you at the courthouse."

Elation surged. She *knew* he'd been there. Then why had he left if he'd seen her? Confusion swallowed her triumph.

"I heard Hawethorne," he continued.

"Who didn't?" she snapped. And immediately regretted it. He wasn't to blame for her frayed sense of well-being. She relaxed her tone. "Fontina and I left before that judge showed any more interest in me."

"You need to deal with your irrational fear of judges."

Zee's aggravation rose. "I'll decide what fears I face and when I face them." She caught herself. This was not the time to relive their breakup. She forced conciliation into her voice. "And it's not fear. It's . . . intense dislike."

"They got a job to do." Pushing.

Her good mood evaporated. "Yeah, their job is to grind soft, vulnerable humans between the unfeeling gears of the legal bureaucracy."

"It's not a perfect system, but it's the one we have."

Zee stomped the brake as the taillights in front of her flared. "Is this why you called?"

An audible intake of breath, then softly, "I called because I know you."

And now they came to the real reason. "Rico—"

"Don't get involved."

"Too late. I've done some digging—"

"Zee, it's *murder*."

Her knuckles whitened on the steering wheel. "I can't ignore him." She strained to keep her voice calm, reasonable. "Could you?"

"That's different." He hurried on before she could object.

"Besides, you're already carrying a lot with your dad. You don't need to add more."

The load she carried. That's what she'd tried to explain when she broke it off with him. After that disquieting desire to cool their relationship, the first inklings of which she felt on his front porch, she'd been relieved when he told her Karl was sending him to Chicago to follow up on the gang story.

She grabbed the chance to escape.

In her familiar safe zone, she thought she was healing well until her dad, already fading with dementia, had a heart attack. The stroke that followed launched his downward spiral. He had rallied, but he was forever changed.

Her life splintered. Swallowed by doctors, tests, procedures, consultations, she'd missed Rico's calls. She didn't call back. Running— to appointments, said her mind; from him, said her heart.

The traffic signal changed to red. She slumped in her seat, awash in memories of the hospital cafeteria where they'd had their last talk. The overcooked coffee, the food too long in the warmers, the pervasive undercurrent of antiseptic—the pain she'd caused.

She'd been at her nadir when Rico found her there. He pulled out a chair, squinting in the fluorescent light. Raindrops glistened on his leather jacket.

"You're back," she'd murmured. Then wished she'd been more welcoming. She blamed it on soul-crushing fatigue.

Worry glimmered in his dark eyes. "Just got in. Finally wrapped up Chicago. Came right here. I wanted to see how you are."

She shrugged, a mighty effort. "As good as can be expected."

He fidgeted. Rico never fidgeted. "How's your dad?"

"Same. It's been a helluva—" She looked around for a calendar on the gray-green institutional walls. "What day is it? I don't know anymore."

"Zee, I—" His eyes seemed to study her for clues.

The throb of machinery ground at Zee's ears. She snapped at him, more harshly than she intended. "What is it, Rico?"

"I missed you."

An alarm went off in her foggy brain. She couldn't figure out why. "I've been overwhelmed with Dad and . . . everything."

His gaze shifted to her arm. "No more sling?"

"I couldn't do anything with my arm like that."

"Are you still on the meds?" He shifted again in his chair.

The alarm grew louder. If he had something to say, he usually just said it. Then again, maybe he had. *He missed her.* She swallowed a trickle of fear. She wasn't thinking straight, but she wanted him gone.

"I'm okay on OTC stuff." She was aware that her untamed hair and rumpled clothing belied that statement. She tried to smile. "You look a bit ragged. You've done your friend duty. Why don't you go home?"

"Zee." Rico reached and turned her face to his. Warmth from his palm rippled through her. "You're more to me than just a friend." His voice was husky. "Every day, I fall—"

She whipped her hand up, breaking contact. "Don't say it. Please."

He trapped her fingers in his, twining them. "Why not?"

The warning bells were ringing loud now, a full-blown, five-alarm clanging. She searched desperately for the right thing to say. Depleted, she found nothing.

"I don't want to play games," he said. "Not with you." He loosened his grip, stroked his fingers along her forearm, igniting her skin. "I love you."

Hot tears built behind her eyes. "I tried love once."

He brushed his thumb across her damp cheek. "I did, too. Her name was Julia. She disappeared with a team of doctors in Eritrea. I didn't think I'd ever find someone again. But here you are."

Droplets shimmered in his thick black hair, in the dark stubble along the line of his jaw, on the outline of his velvet upper lip. She pulled herself from his magnetic gaze and tried to infuse strength into her voice. "Look, I hate that my past still messes with my life, but this isn't the time."

In one liquid motion, he was out of his chair and wrapping her in his arms. She melted into his embrace, lost herself in his heartbeat. "I know you're afraid," he whispered, "but I'll be right there with you."

Her comfort fled. She didn't want him right there. She wanted him to stay in the box with the other guys she'd dated. She wanted her orderly life, the life before Rico, to resume.

She wriggled her hands onto his chest, struggling to create space between them. "Please. I can't do this now."

He loosened his arms, regret in his eyes. "I'm sorry. I should have realized." He smoothed an unruly curl from her brow. "You're under a lot of stress. We can talk about this tomorrow."

She sank into the chair and looked up at him. "I don't know when I'll be ready to talk." And he should know the truth of it. She might never be ready. She hesitated. That moment, exhausted, in pain, and scared, was definitely not the best time to make life-changing decisions. To say things that couldn't be unsaid.

Desperate, she flung toward him the only safety net she could find. "I don't want to lose you as a friend, Rico. Please."

The pain in his face scoured the depths of her soul. Worn from his trip, he'd come to see her, to offer his help, to declare his love. And she'd crushed him.

The sigh seemed to come from the deepest well of his being. "If that's really what you want." The chair screeched as he slid it back.

A horn blared behind her. She jerked.

"You there? Zee, can you hear me?"

How long had he been trying to get her attention? "Yeah. Sorry. Traffic." She eased the Mini forward.

For a moment, she wished she could agree to stop investigating, but she'd committed to Fenton. And she was on the trail of the story of her career. Rico should understand that. Her annoyance ebbed. She loosened her grip on the Mini's wheel. "I appreciate that you worry about me, but I'm not going to do anything dangerous."

Rico's frustrated huff echoed through the phone. "At least tell me what you learned."

A reasonable request from a friend. Fontina had asked the same. Zee marshalled her thoughts. "Okay. Maybe some of it will be helpful for the police." She summarized her findings on Street and Bottmeyer, but decided against mentioning Paselly.

"Interesting," he said when she'd finished. "Cops won't bother with it. They have their guy."

"I know." Zee pursed her lips.

He added, conciliatory. "I'll say this, Hawethorne doesn't ring like a killer."

She raised her brows at his concession. "So, we have to pursue it, especially if the police aren't."

"*We* don't have to—"

She swore she could hear him bite his lip. "Tell you what, I'm following up on a lead tonight. Want to come with me?"

He was wary. "What is it?"

"A lecture on DNA splicing. The presenter apparently wanted in on McNeary's project."

He yawned theatrically. "Pass."

"See? A bunch of researchers and students and a few interested members of the public. All very sedate and civilized. The worst danger will be if I fall asleep and snore."

He laughed. Genuine relief. "Have fun." Then added, "Please, be careful."

CHAPTER 17

The Medical Institute lecture hall buzzed as Zee found a seat at the front of the second tier. Attendees in lab coats occupied half the lower-tier seats, a sea of white across which sailed an occasional tweed jacket. Students in scrubs collected in the uppermost ranks of the auditorium, their gray-green uniforms blending into the darkness near the ceiling. In between, moored a handful of 'civilians' like Zee.

Penn had approved the revised version of *Z Beats*. Conscience clear, well, feeling only a little guilty for making such an error to begin with, Zee settled in to make the acquaintance of Dr. Jules Mercy.

At precisely seven p.m., he strode to the lectern. His L'Ocosta State photo had not deceived. Though older and heavier, he radiated enormous energy, filling the stage with his presence.

"I'm here tonight," Mercy's baritone boomed, "to speak in praise of frustration."

Chuckles rippled through the audience. Mercy grinned. Big. Toothy.

"Gene-splicing research is painstaking," he said. "It can feel like cold molasses moves faster, but researchers endure it because," he shrugged, "that's how things work. Or at least they did until MIT graduate student Feng Zhang got frustrated and created something better, the CRISPR system."

He clicked to his first slide. "CRISPR stands for Clustered Regularly Interspaced Short Palindromic Repeats. In plain English, snippets of DNA that recur at intervals."

The next slide showed a strand of the familiar spiral as a long string of various combinations of the letters A, T, C, and G. Mercy pointed to sequences highlighted in blue. "These are CRISPRs. Researchers had been aware of them of course, but Zhang's breakthrough changed their work dramatically."

He illustrated with an animated slide. As a cartoon-like calendar peeled off the days, one lab mouse slowly materialized on the left, while on the right, a fanciful proliferation of eight others popped into existence. "Zhang's method," said Mercy, "cut the time to produce a genetically modified mouse by more than 87 percent, from six months to three weeks. In this case," his smile widened, "*impatience* was the mother of invention."

Zee joined in the laughter.

After the crowd quieted, he continued, lacing his lecture with dramatic gestures and pacing between the far edges of the stage, his suit jacket flapping with the energy of his stride. At times, he peered into the audience, as if by force of will he could compel their comprehension.

To Zee's delight, he proved himself adept at explaining complex ideas in simple terms, slipping in definitions and liberally employing drawings and charts. And with impeccable timing, he leavened the density of the topic with well-placed humor.

She glanced around to see if others were as affected as she. Every face behind her was riveted to the stage. In the front rows, each head craned forward—almost. In an otherwise empty row behind the lab coats, three men were engaged in inaudible communication. Gestures flew, restrained yet stiff and tense. One man ticked off points on his fingers. Two heads shook, nodded. The point-maker glanced toward the stage.

Nonplussed, Zee followed his gaze. Mercy stood before a photograph of a boyish looking man.

"Zhang and the Broad Institute have made their discoveries freely available," said Mercy. "They've trained thousands to use the tools." He flicked his hand toward a quote on the screen. "In Zhang's own words: 'If someone had protected the HTML language for making Web pages, then we wouldn't have the World Wide Web.'"

The doctor's resonant voice softened. "Such an ethical stand is rare, my friends. And marvelous."

Mercy's somber tone carried a hint of sadness. Maybe he heard in Zhang, as she did, echoes of McNeary. Zee chided herself for her earlier doubts about Mercy's integrity.

Excitement quickened her pulse. Fontina continually pushed her to trust her intuition, but not every nudge had to be about the murder. Here was article-worthy material. In her mind's eye, Penn gave her a thumbs-up.

MERCY'S POST-LECTURE RECEPTION WAS HELD in a large, carpeted room with floor-to-ceiling windows framed in heavy red drapes. White-cloth-covered tables offered finger food, but judging from the traffic, the bar provided the main attraction. Zee stepped aside to avoid a stampeding herd of white coats.

"Never get between an academic and alcohol," said a voice behind her.

She swiveled and met a smile from a gray-haired man in a lab coat. "That was true in my own college days," she said. "Some things never change."

"Unlike what we heard tonight." The man scrutinized her. "You look familiar." He proffered a thickly veined hand. "Doctor Ferdinand Wilson." He gestured to the white plastic name badge near his lapel. "Call me Ferd."

Zee shook his hand and introduced herself.

His eyes lit. "Ah yes. Saw you on television. Good feature. You here to do a story?"

"Yes." She just decided, but he didn't need to know that. "Doctor Mercy has a way of clarifying complex topics."

"It's definitely one of his talents." He lifted a hand toward a small round table, which held a tray of crusty bread ovals spread with cream cheese and topped with slivered salmon. "Hors d'oeuvres?"

Zee had loosened her belt once today already. One small piece wouldn't hurt, though. She selected a slice, then attempted to steer the conversation. "How did Doctor Mercy get into gene research?"

Ferd's lips flattened. Then he seemed to remember himself and eased their tension. "An unusual road. He'd be the better one to tell you about it." He scanned the crowd. "He should be here soon. You'll know when he comes in."

"Doctor Wilson." A slender woman in a well-cut turquoise pantsuit laid a hand at his elbow. "A word?" She guided him toward a potted ficus in the opposite direction of the bar. Zee had enough time to note her name badge was gold, not enough time to read it.

She ate the crostini. Salty. Dry. Her gaze strayed to Ferd and the sleekly dressed woman. Zee smothered a grimace. She'd never get a figure like that, eating stale bread, or cheese-dust crackers, or extravagantly delicious croissants.

Her thirst sent her to the bar queue. As it snaked forward, she speculated on what Ferd meant by *an unusual road*. According to Janece, Mercy insisted he should be directing the project. Did his unorthodox past connect to this claim?

Zee swallowed a dryness that had nothing to do with physical dehydration. Every light cast a shadow. What hid in Mercy's?

The bar line shuffled forward, and she caught McNeary's name. Off to her right huddled the three men she'd noticed earlier. She perked her ears.

"Ian was a hard worker," said a balding man whose lab coat hung loosely on his skinny frame.

"Took too many risks," said the other lab coat, a dark-complexioned man with thick hair and a narrow beard.

"Can't fault his ethics, though. In my most honest moments, I wonder if I'd have the courage." This from a man in a rumpled gray suit, whose thinning hair covered a sweaty pate.

Zee tried to ignore a hard crostini crumb stuck between her teeth. Her thoughts wandered to the chilled bottles of water sitting along the bar top.

"Think that fellow in custody did it?"

She snapped her attention back.

Gray-Suit cleared his throat. "He seems unstable enough, but I don't want to think so. Where would we be if we had to worry about distraught research subjects coming to take revenge?"

"Then who killed him?"

The queue advanced. Zee cursed silently as the researchers passed beyond her sight. She edged toward the side of the line, straining to stay within earshot.

"You know what I think—"

"Yeah, O'Deneigh, you're stuck on the investors—"

"Just one. I warned Ian. If he wasn't so stubborn."

Paselly's weasel face leapt into her mind. She shuddered.

"Wonder who recommended that guy."

"Wish *I* hadn't recommended anybody. Sorry I got involved."

Zee squelched the urge to turn to see which of the three spoke.

"Jules plans to reimburse them."

Her eyebrows rose. This was news.

"You believe that? He wasn't as generous to that grad student he trampled all over last year."

"Yeah, that was—"

"Hey, lady."

Zee jerked her head toward the young man in line behind her.

He gestured to the gap in front of her. "You going to the bar or not?"

"Sorry," she squeaked from her dry throat. "Changed my mind."

She stepped aside, and spotting a sprawling potted dieffenbachia, hurried down the line and cut through. Hidden among its broad leaves, she pretended to search her purse while she homed in on the trio's voices.

"—probably not an investor. They have tools to manage risk."

"Smart ones."

She dared a peek in time to see Gray-Suit mop his brow with a rumpled handkerchief. "Unfortunately," he said, "several were unusual investors, and they may have made naïve mistakes."

"That's my point." Dark-and-Bearded punctuated his assertion with a raised index finger. "I told him not to get involved with that guy. Jules better hope he doesn't come after him."

Sweat blossomed on Zee's forehead. Her earlier dismissal of danger, expressed blithely to Rico, seemed less certain. If Mercy was involved with Paselly—

"So, he *is* taking over the project," said Baldy. "Guess he'll finally get the credit he thinks he deserves."

Somebody jostled Zee, pushing her against the huge leafy stalks. "Oh, excuse me," a woman's voice said. "Are you all right?"

Zee didn't want to tear her eyes from the threesome, but anything else would call attention to her eavesdropping. "I'm fine," she said, turning.

Hazel eyes met hers, eyes that belonged to the woman in the turquoise pantsuit.

Zee ducked her head toward her purse and pulled out lip balm. "Just looking for this and not paying attention to where I was. Sorry if I got in your way."

"No, it was my fault." Her steady gaze said there was truth to that, but no apology.

Forcing a smile, Zee uncapped the tube.

"Chancellor." A man approached. "Could I have a moment?"

With a final assessing sweep of her eyes, the woman moved off.

Zee exhaled. So, that woman was the Chancellor of Valerian University, ranked higher even than the dean of the Medical Institute. No wonder her glance could shrivel an underling.

Grateful she didn't fall into that category, Zee angled her head toward the dieffenbachia foliage while pretending to apply balm.

"—sketchy, is all I mean," said Gray-Suit. A handkerchief corner drooped from his pants pocket. "I never believed Ian stole his idea."

Zee's eyes widened. So, that was the reason for Mercy's badgering.

"My opinion," Gray-Suit went on, "he should be glad the police have a suspect, or they'd be looking at him."

Zee rocked back on her heels, fighting the sensation that she stood on the lip of a chasm. There were dangerous depths in the relationship between McNeary and Mercy. At the same time, her vow to Fenton impelled her to step toward the hazards.

For a moment, she considered simply passing the information to Bernstow. *Passing the buck*, her conscience reproached. Besides, she had a story to write.

She stared through the leaves at Gray-Suit. What did he know that made him suspect Mercy?

She needed to talk to him. If she could make her parched mouth work. She swallowed fish breath and circled to bypass the plant. "Excuse me, gentlemen. I heard you mention Ian McNeary. I'm—"

"We know who you are," interrupted Dark-and-Bearded. He glanced at his colleagues. "A reporter." He wrapped the words in barbed wire. "We have nothing to say to you."

Zee infused her voice with friendly, non-threatening interest. "Doctor McNeary agreed to give me his first interview in years. He was on the verge of a great breakthrough and felt it was time to let the world know his story."

The men exchanged glances. Gray-Suit dropped his eyes. He stuffed his handkerchief the rest of the way into his pocket.

"This isn't the place," said Baldy.

She proffered a card. "We can talk whenever and wherever you want."

No one moved. They could have been a tableau, but the tension among them crackled in the air. Finally, Gray-Suit extended his hand.

Zee dropped the card into his palm. "Call me when you're ready." She let her gaze rest on them, memorizing their name tags. "I'm sorry he didn't get to fulfill his dream." They stared back, noncommittal. They must learn those patient masks in medical school.

Gray-Suit pocketed the card. "Nice to meet you." He turned toward his companions. "I need a drink."

Zee accepted their dismissal. She could reach them if she wanted.

"We shouldn't be talking about this," Dark-and-Bearded muttered as they walked away. "Who knows who he has listening?"

Zee scanned reflexively. No one seemed to be paying attention to the trio, or to her. Best to keep it that way.

She skirted the edges of the crowd, considering what she'd learned. Mercy was taking over McNeary's project. Investors might recoup their loss. So, none of them would have a motive to kill McNeary.

If Mercy intended to reimburse them. Which he might not.

If they knew about his intent. Which they might not.

If they would wait. Which they might not.

She passed behind the turquoise pantsuit. That interaction had been awkward. Did the chancellor suspect Zee was snooping? It hardly seemed credible that a poised, polished executive would stumble into someone.

She had also interrupted Zee's conversation with Ferd, and rather rudely.

Dark-and-Bearded had said *he* might be listening. It wasn't the chancellor he feared. Did he refer to Mercy? What had happened to that unfortunate grad student?

Her meandering brought Zee to the doorway and its inviting tide of cool air. She stepped through into the main lobby of the institute.

Relief washed over her. Despite its size, the other room could not handle the press of bodies, the excited chattering, the sheer energy that Mercy had ignited in the audience. Someone should have opened those elegantly draped windows.

Glad to be out of the stuffy atmosphere, she strolled across the polished tile, indulging in deep, lung-clearing breaths. In her freshened mind, the overheard conversation began to lose its sinister cast. Internecine rivalry was a staple of university life, and the chancellor's behavior could be explained as merely engaging in political gatekeeping. Of course, she'd want to control information, minimize the connection to McNeary's death, possibly protect Mercy in his new role, and certainly safeguard those all-important, scandal-averse funding sources.

Zee shook her head. Bottom line, Mercy as a killer was hard to reconcile with the evidence of her own eyes. She'd stick to her plan to interview him for her column. He might even be part of the bigger story she planned on drug development. Not everything had to revolve around the murder.

A large oil portrait of the Medical Institute's first dean snagged her attention, a white-haired, suitably somber-faced gentleman in nineteenth-century formal dress.

She detoured to examine it. The manicured left hand of Doctor Noah Hedding lay casually on an open book. His right rested atop a silver-headed walking stick. In the dimly lit background, a caduceus stood in a tall bookcase. A stuffed duck wearing a bowler hat kept it company.

Zee grinned. Everyone should have a little mystery.

Next to the framed picture, an ornate board displayed a list of the building's occupants. On an impulse, she checked for Mercy's office. Number 309. If he hadn't yet arrived at the reception, maybe she could catch him there and set up an appointment.

She hurried to the elevator. On the third floor, its brass Art Deco panels opened at the center of a long corridor full of closed doors. She oriented herself to the numbers and turned right. Mercy's office would be toward the far end.

As she approached 309, an unmistakable baritone filtered into the hall.

"Of course, I'm upset," Mercy barked. "We've worked for months to get here. A delay is *not* possible."

Zee flinched. This was not the same affable lecturer who had entertained an auditorium of admirers.

Behind the door, quiet settled. Mercy's tone calmed. "The people we're dealing with are skittish. You know that. We—"

More silence. Then abruptly, "Don't worry about him. We have to handle this delicately."

Zee wished he'd drop a clue about the topic. She had no reason to assume it was McNeary's project.

Mercy's footsteps thumped against the carpet, then stopped. "Look, I have to get to a reception. Go have a drink. To quote Lady Macbeth, 'Screw your courage to the sticking place.'"

Cold sweat popped on Zee's brow.

His laugh erupted, jarring and harsh. "Good. That's the spirit."

Zee had come within a foot of his nameplate. It no longer seemed a good time to arrange for an interview. And she didn't want to be caught lurking outside his door.

A drawer slammed inside his office. Zee sprinted toward the EXIT sign glowing red at the end of the hall. Behind her, a doorknob squeaked.

She flattened herself into the shallow niche surrounding the stairway door and prayed he would not look her way; also that he wasn't one of those fitness nuts who always took the stairs. She pressed her back against the wall, sucked in her stomach, and entreated the gods for invisibility.

At the same time, she almost laughed at her alarm. Five minutes ago, he was a good guy. Okay, with a few tendrils of darkness curling around his halo, which she had decided to ignore.

With slow deliberation, she drew in a quiet breath.

The vinyl flooring creaked to the rhythm of long strides. Zee strained to decipher the direction.

The squeaks retreated.

The elevator bell dinged, the doors hissed open, then glided shut. The motor rumbled, hummed, and faded into silence.

Satisfied she was safe, Zee poked her head beyond her refuge.

And nearly fainted.

Backlit by illumination from a window to the parking lot, a

figure stood far down the hall. By its side, something long and narrow dangled from one hand.

A key clicked in a lock. An office door opened. An interior light shone. The yellow cone spilling into the hallway fell on a cleaning cart.

Zee expelled her breath, shoved open the stairway door, and fled.

CHAPTER 18

CHEERY CHIMES CASCADED INTO ZEE'S EAR. She opened one eye to a bedroom full of gray light.

"What the . . . ?"

Her phone alarm continued to play, relentlessly upbeat music that spoke of butterflies flitting through green meadows. She rolled, fumbled on her bedside table, and swiped to silence the sanguine torment.

Flopping back on the bed, she stared at the screen: seven o'clock. Way too early to get up on a Saturday. Her mind offered a sleep-dazed recollection: Fontina's 8 A.M. hatha yoga class.

Forget it. She snuggled into the pillows.

Her conscience poked her. Replayed images of yesterday's breathless spluttering as she hurried from the courthouse, of her lungs gasping for air after the mad dash down the Medical Institute stairs. The previous day's diet paraded before her, with scarcely a fruit or vegetable in sight.

Sleep disappeared. The nagging memories prodded her from the bed and through a small bowl of instant oatmeal—envelope dusty in the back of the cupboard but contents edible. Stilling any qualms about what kind of preservatives might enact that miracle, she trudged out the door, grumbling but determined.

Under a heavy gray sky, a gust of wind whipped open her

raincoat. She yanked it closed and hurried toward the Mini, dodging a rolling foam cup and several scampering scraps of cardboard.

Infernal garbage strike.

A blustery breeze lifted a sheet of paper plastered against her windshield. The corner snagged on her wiper, and a jagged strip peeled. Spatters of rain stuck the fragment to the glass. The larger piece sailed across the lot and pasted itself against a car tire, loosening moments later to join the other attempted escapees in a row of bushes.

Stifling a flash of irritation, Zee snatched the scrap. She frowned at her building's overflowing trash bin. No way would she get near that filthy mess, much less touch it, which she'd have to do if she wanted the paper to stay put. She couldn't bring herself to just drop it on the ground, either, where it would add to the debris that already aggravated her.

Grimacing, she stuffed the litter in her pocket. How easily she seemed to slip into annoyance these days. Fontina said yoga calmed a person. If it worked, Zee resolved she'd make it a regular practice.

Twenty minutes later, she relaxed in the spare simplicity of the studio, with its softly gleaming hardwood floor and pale daylight filtering through muslin shades. Delicate flute music floated beneath Fontina's voice as she guided the group into the first asana, the concave and convex flexing of the Cat. Zee pictured herself as Candy and smiled.

At Fontina's instruction, she sat on her heels and bent forward to rest her head on the floor in the Child pose.

This yoga stuff really *was* relaxing, and not nearly as hard as she thought.

"Now move into the Cobra," instructed Fontina. "Slow and smooth. Legs extended behind you. Hands flat on the floor. Lift your chin and curl your spine upward like a snake, but keep your hips squarely on the floor."

Zee's back muscles stretched and pulled. Sweat bloomed on her forehead as she held the position for the eternity that Fontina claimed was only thirty seconds.

From there, the class shifted into the Plank, a rigid position balancing the body on toes and forearms; then into Downward-Facing Dog, an opposite flex to the Cobra; and from there, to the Standing Forward Bend, what ordinary people called touching your toes.

Arms dangling, Zee glanced at the man next to her. His face brushed his knees. She stared at hers from a foot away.

"Now that we are loosened up, let's flow through four Sun Salutations," said Fontina.

Loosened up? Zee's joints creaked and seized like machinery left outside to rust.

She grit her teeth and followed Fontina's instructions through the twelve bending, arching, lunging, and holding positions that comprised each salutation. By the time she placed her palms together in the last *namaste*, every pore in her body churned out salty rivulets.

"Lie on your back."

At Fontina's words, Zee dropped gratefully to her mat. Surely, everyone in the studio could hear her sucking noisy draughts of air. She must have lost her mind, deciding to take this class.

"For this next part, we will work from the floor," Fontina said.

Zee stifled a groan.

"Move first to the Shoulder Stand and then into the Plow. As always, go slowly and only as far as is comfortable for you."

Zee managed to lift halfway into the Shoulder Stand, but when she tried the Plow, which required her to lie on her back, lift her hips, and extend her legs to touch her toes to the floor behind her, she capitulated. She was in over her head in more ways than one. Collapsing on her mat, she let her screaming muscles rest, and tried to catch her breath.

This couldn't go on much longer.

It did. For twenty additional excruciating minutes.

Zee persisted, forming caricatures of the positions everyone else seemed to effortlessly achieve. The Lunge, the Warrior, the Archer, the Mountain. She accepted she carried a bit of excess weight for her five-foot-six, but in this roomful of elongated, sinuous bodies, she felt short, squat, and lumpy. And she moved like she was dragging sandbags. By the time Fontina began to guide the class through relaxation in the Corpse pose, Zee thought she might do her body a favor if she actually died.

Every muscle and tendon ached. Her hamstrings burned like fiery cords. Perspiration stung her eyes. Following Fontina's soft voice, Zee slowed her breath and visualized the tension washing from her limbs. Despite the flicker in her brain at the name of the asana, quiet pervaded her mind. No cacophony of voices clamored with ideas and questions. No adrenaline-fueled disaster scenarios played their scripts. She exhaled with an audible sigh.

When she opened her eyes, Fontina came to kneel beside her. Her friend's lemon-yellow tank top was barely moist. She offered a white sweat towel. "I'm glad to see you here this morning."

Zee pushed herself to a sitting position. "I'm sure it did me a world of good." She mopped her face and pulled her sticky t-shirt from her back. "Although if I don't get into a hot shower soon, I won't be able to move for a week."

"Guessing you don't want to stay for my self-defense class." Fontina chuckled.

Zee waved a limp-noodle arm. "If I had any strength left, I'd punch you for that."

Fontina twisted her lithe body sideways in a mock avoidance maneuver. "Didn't touch me," she teased. She patted Zee's knee. "You did well. Go home and get your shower. You'll feel better."

"I trust I will," said Zee. "I'll slather on some of that herb for soreness."

"Arnica."

"That's the one."

Zee wriggled her protesting arms into her raincoat and hobbled to the door. As she crossed the street, she spied a folded square of paper trapped beneath her windshield wiper.

Asphalta, that better not be a ticket.

Annoyance frayed the calm she'd enjoyed mere moments before. She pulled the document free and unfolded it. It was not a ticket. Her body chilled.

The lined sheet had a ragged edge, as if torn from a spiral-bound notebook. It bore a note written in blocky letters. THE POLICE ARE WRONG. IT'S ABOUT THE MONEY.

Zee whipped her head around. No one was on the street, yet she felt eyes upon her.

A gust nearly snatched the note from her fingers, and she stuffed it into her pocket. Her hand froze as she encountered the earlier wadded-up litter. Two pieces of paper stuck to her windshield in one morning? Windy though the weather was, and rife with trash, this strained coincidence.

She pulled out the crumpled strip she'd found outside her apartment building and smoothed it. THE POLICE AR . . . She swayed as though she'd been kicked in the chest.

Again, she could have sworn she was being watched.

This time when scanning the street, she noticed an elderly woman, sitting beneath a bus stop shelter halfway down the block. Ignoring complaints from her muscles, Zee hurried toward her.

The woman's sharp gray eyes assessed her as Zee lowered herself to the hard plastic bench.

"Just came from yoga. I need to do it more often." Zee smiled to offset her sweaty, disheveled appearance. She pulled the folded paper from her pocket. "Sorry to bother you. Someone left this note on my car—the red-and-white Mini Cooper. I wonder if you saw who did it."

The woman's pale parchment face relaxed a fraction. "I saw a lady about fifteen minutes ago."

Zee resisted the urge to launch into interrogation. She kept her voice light. "She must be playing a joke." Inventing information, Zee shaped her voice into a conspiratorial tone. "Was she tall with long red hair?"

The elderly woman hesitated. "I don't want to get in your business, you understand."

"Of course not," said Zee. "But my friend is famous for this stuff."

The woman glanced at the small fluffy-haired mongrel who lay at her feet. A large white bandage covered a shaven area on its side. "Louisa here had surgery a week ago, and we have to take breaks on our walks." She reached a gnarled hand to scratch the dog behind her ears. "This bench is a good place to rest out of the wind. It's natural to watch."

"Of course." Zee clenched her teeth behind her smile. "The lady?"

The old woman's posture eased. "She was trim, in good shape like you."

Zee tried to ignore the flush of pleasure. Maybe she was too hard on herself. She did feel slimmer after that workout. Then again, her raincoat hid most of her sins.

"Wearing skin-tight pants," the old woman continued, "and a stretchy blue shirt."

Zee's elation faded. If she wore an outfit like that, her new friend's admiration might wane a bit. She'd best get back to business. "Did you see her face?"

"No. She had a straw hat with a floppy brim and rather large sunglasses." She chuckled drily. "The wind darn near blew that hat away. She had to run to catch it."

"Do you remember her hair color?" Zee cringed. She shouldn't grill the poor woman.

Her companion seemed unfazed. "Beautiful shiny blonde." She touched her own gray strands. "Like mine used to be. How my Franz loved to see it loose in the wind." Her eyes misted.

Zee fought the impulse to hurry her, yet every heartbeat ticked off another lost second. Louisa stirred, sniffed at Zee's ankle, and began to wash it with a small pink tongue.

"She likes you."

Candy's going to love that. Zee patted Louisa's head. "Anything else you recall?"

"Tallish, I'd say. Although those Minis are little cars. Cute. We had one, before Franz passed." She smiled at the dog, whose liquid brown eyes gazed upward while her tail wiggled. "You're getting much better, Louisa. Soon we'll be able to walk to the park, and you can play while I sit by the lake."

Zee bit back an irritated huff and remembered to keep up the pretense. "That wouldn't be my friend Ann. Did you happen to notice her car?"

The elderly woman pursed thin lips. "Let me think. I'm afraid I didn't pay much attention at first. The U-turn caught my eye, but I didn't think much about it. People do that all the time."

Zee hid her frustration and nodded encouragement.

The woman pointed over Zee's shoulder. "I wouldn't have thought anything of it, but she came back a few minutes later, parked behind you again, and put the paper under your wiper. I said to Louisa, 'That's odd.'"

The dog shifted her brown eyes to Zee, as if confirming the account.

"I didn't get a good look at her car until she left," the woman continued. "She drove straight down the street past me." She shrugged apologetically. "Just an ordinary car, I'm afraid. Not too big. Not one of those SUVs."

Not a lot of help. "Do you recall the color?"

"Beige, tan, something along those lines. She drove very fast. I remember thinking she should slow down. Her tires even squealed when she turned the corner."

Zee resisted an irrational desire to run to the Mini and pursue the mystery vehicle. Instead, she climbed to her feet, stifling a grunt at the effort to move her leaden limbs. "Thanks very much. I hope you enjoy the rest of your walk." She'd begun to turn away when the plaintive voice stopped her.

"Was I any help?"

She owed the woman some reward. "I have an idea," she lied. "Thanks to your sharp eyes."

A sad smile spread across the wrinkled face. "An old woman is invisible. No one sees us."

Zee swallowed a lump in her throat. She might be the only person this lonely lady talked with all day. She fished out a card. "If you think of anything else, please call me."

The gray eyes brightened. "I'd love to help you solve your mystery." She looked at the card. "Zee. An unusual name. I'm plain old Mary, by the way."

"Nice to meet you." Zee scratched behind Louisa's ear. "You, too. Best wishes for a speedy recovery."

She hustled to her car as quickly as her testy muscles would allow. Adrenaline urged her to act, but behind the wheel, she paused. The furtive note-writer had come from around the corner behind her and gone on down the street when she left. Zee pulled the two notes from her pocket and studied them. The earlier one had been written on plain unlined notepaper. It had no ragged edge. If the writer saw the wind rip the original note from Zee's windshield, she'd know it had to be replaced.

Zee's skin crawled at the thought of someone stalking her. She closed her eyes and pictured the scene in the apartment parking lot. She walked toward her car, saw the paper on her windshield rip, the larger portion fly across the blacktop and lodge against the tire. She forced herself to concentrate on the vehicle. Bland color, possibly dulled by the gray morning, definitely not a truck or SUV, though—a car.

Little to work with, and yet Zee could not escape the conviction that the car belonged to the note-writer. Who had watched her. Fresh sweat prickled along her spine.

She played out the scenario. If the writer had seen the original note escape, she might follow Zee, and after discovering her destination, go in search of paper for another note.

Zee forgot her fatigue. She whipped the Mini into a U-turn and set off in the same pursuit.

CHAPTER 19

ZEE WHEELED THE MINI AWAY from Integrated Life, her thoughts scrambling ahead as if on their own, they could search out the source of the spiral notepaper and from there, the woman who used it to leave the note on Zee's car.

In her rearview mirror, elderly Mary still sat with her dog at the bus shelter. Zee's face softened. The sweet old woman wanted to be helpful, and truth be told, she observed quite a few details about the mysterious lady. The hopeful part of Zee's brain asserted they might somehow lead to her identity. The rational part dumped on her optimism, insisting it was a long shot. Yet Zee could see no other option than to try to track her moves and hope for a bit of luck.

Her muscles, complaining under her sweaty t-shirt, disagreed. They'd been promised a hot shower after the yoga class. If she had any integrity, instead of chasing the furtive note-writer, she'd go home and give them their due.

Soon, she promised.

Halfway down the block, she spied a string of small businesses: dry cleaner, bakery, camera shop, drugstore, sports bar. The drugstore seemed the most likely option.

Frigid air conditioning blasted from an overhead vent, frosting her scalp as she hustled through the door. Shivering, she joined the checkout line.

Balding and overweight, the lone clerk looked to be in his mid-fifties, tired, and bored. His lethargic movements never varied, as though each one exacted an enormous mental and physical toll. She hoped she could rouse his interest enough to help her.

When her turn came, she beamed at him. "Hi. I'm hoping you can help me. I'm looking for a woman who might have come in earlier today."

Not a muscle moved on his pale pudding face. Zee pressed on. "Nice looking. Blonde hair, wearing tight pants and a stretchy blue shirt, possibly a big floppy straw hat and sunglasses."

The clerk's dull eyes regarded her through thick smudged lenses. "Lady, I don't know anything about anything," he mumbled. "You wanna buy something?"

His blank countenance sucked at Zee's energy. She tried again. "She was a good-looking lady. You would have noticed, I'm sure."

He stared at her, unblinking. "Not paid to notice. You gonna buy something?"

Zee clenched her jaw. "No. Thanks anyway."

Outside, the hot wind burned her skin, but she welcomed it after the drugstore deepfreeze. On the other side of the camera store, someone exited the bakery. Zee lifted her nose. A sugar-glazed, fresh-from-the-oven aroma curled beckoning fingers.

"I deserve a treat," she declared to the plastic bag skittering across the blacktop. She pushed open the door, and the fragrance of roasted coffee and sweet baked goods wafted a mouth-watering welcome.

A single barista tended the small shop. Miranda, according to her name tag, embodied the energetic opposite of the nearly coma-tose clerk in the drugstore. Light dazzled from a gem in her eyebrow. A hot pink patch leapt from her black hair, which appeared hacked in three or four jutting angles that jostled like mismatched panes whenever she moved.

"Coffee and one of those please." Zee pointed to a cherry cheese Danish. While she waited, she concentrated on not drooling.

Yoga certainly revved a person's appetite.

Her body had stiffened during her arctic sojourn at the drug-store. She accepted her order from Miranda and sank onto the near-est seat, a wooden chair at a small round table. Her thighs rebelled at the lack of padding, but their message faded, eclipsed when she bit into the Danish. Buttery pastry and sweet-tart cherry burst in her mouth, with exactly the right amount of sugary zing from the icing. Zee closed her eyes and lost herself in taste bud nirvana.

Maybe she'd go to yoga class more often.

A motorcycle rumbled from her phone. Rico. He could leave a voicemail.

She returned to savoring her pastry. The coffee, rich and mel-low with a tinge of bittersweet aftertaste, provided the perfect acidic complement.

Lilting notes announced a voicemail message. It could wait. She muted the annoying reminder.

When she'd licked the last rich cherry-suffused flake from her lips, Zee picked up her phone, tapped the icon, and keyed in her password.

Urgency edged Rico's voice. "If you're digging into the Paselly clan, you need to stop right now. They're . . ." His words faded and became indistinct.

Zee strained to hear.

". . . damn . . . I just charged . . ." His voice died.

Zee listened to the silence. She replayed his message, increasing the volume to try to catch any additional details. It merely exacer-bated the assault on her ear.

The buttery Danish aftertaste congealed on her tongue. Here was yet another warning about feral-faced Paselly. She swallowed coffee to warm the chill in her chest.

If there was a link, surely the police knew.

And were doing nothing about it.

She pulled up her contacts, intent on calling his office phone. Her finger paused. He would have used it if he were there. She punched in Fontina's number instead. When the call transferred to voicemail, she spilled out the news about the note, the writer, and the conversation with Mary.

As she ended her message, she became aware of Miranda standing a few feet away.

"Excuse me." The barista stepped closer. "The woman you were talking about looks like a lady who came in earlier today."

"Oh?" Hope lifted Zee's voice.

"She wasn't wearing the hat and sunglasses. But the outfit sounds right, and especially the hair."

"When was she here?"

"About eight-thirty." Miranda fixed blue-green eyes on Zee. "And if she's the one you're looking for, she's Shandra Somerworth."

"Of Somerworth Farms?" Zee furrowed her brows. The Somerworth family reigned at the top of Valerian society. Originally cattle ranchers, they'd branched into real estate, and more recently into thoroughbred racing. What would a member of that exalted family be doing in this humble shop? "Are you sure?"

The barista blushed. "I like the uh, society pages. She's in there a lot. And last month, *Fashion Extravaganza* did a feature on a charity horse show sponsored by the Valerian Ladies Circle. Lots of photos of the latest designs." She shrugged and the edge of a tattoo peeked from her neckline. "Guess a punk like me shouldn't be interested in all that, but I am."

Zee smiled. "Be interested in anything you want. Don't let anybody pigeonhole you."

Miranda grinned back, perfect teeth gleaming against her merlot lips.

In the next moment, doubt prodded Zee. "Has she been here before?"

Miranda shook her head. Pink flashed among her ebony tresses. "First time I've seen her. She came in this morning and ordered a skim milk latte." She wrinkled her nose. "I hate skim milk. It tastes like chalk, and it's so . . . pretentious."

Zee liked the barista more by the moment. "Did she have a notebook?"

"Yep, and I think she just bought it. While she was waiting for her order, she kept trying to peel off the price sticker."

Zee felt new irritation at Mr. Dead Eyes in the drugstore, but she pushed it aside. "Did she write in it?"

"Don't know," Miranda said. "I got busy with customers." Her tongue toyed with the glinting stud in her lower lip. "Does this help?"

"Yes, it does." Zee stood and slung her purse over her shoulder, which responded as though she'd hoisted a bowling ball.

Miranda indicated Zee's cup. "Want a refill to go?"

Thoughtful. "Thank you, Miranda, that would be nice."

Armed with fresh coffee, Zee headed to the Mini. The mystery had only deepened. She could think of no reason why Shandra Somerworth would stick a note on her car. Rain spit in Zee's face and she scowled. If Shandra knew something, she should go to the police, not play games with Zee.

She pulled the door open and got in, but didn't start the engine. Instead, she drummed her fingers on the steering wheel, unfolded the note, and scrutinized the printed message. She weighed the paper in her hand, willing it to speak its secrets.

IT'S ABOUT THE MONEY.

Money would be something familiar to a wealthy socialite.

Adrenaline surged, the scent of the hunt in her writer's nose. She should, she *would* take the note to Bernstow, but not yet.

A quick search on the internet provided an address. Mind made up, Zee started toward home to shower and change. Sweet elderly Mary hadn't minded her redolent post-yoga presence at the bus shelter, but those who breathed the rarified air of McKinley Heights would surely wrinkle their upper-crust noses. One did not enter their domain stinky and sweaty, much less with pastry crumbs clinging to one's sodden workout clothes.

CHAPTER 20

FRESHLY SHOWERED AND SUITABLY ATTIRED in fawn trousers with a matching silk tunic, Zee drove north toward the wealthy enclave beyond Valerian's outskirts. She considered how to approach Shandra Somerworth with the note she left on Zee's car. *May* have left, Zee's pesky mind objected. Miranda had been certain of Shandra's identity, Zee's stubborn mind retorted, and Shandra's behavior in the bakery certainly fit.

It's about the money, the careful printing said. What did Shandra know?

Zee itched to go on the attack—shove the note in Shandra's face, catch the sneaky woman off guard. That might boomerang, though. Society people expected respect. Entitled egotists.

Friendly curiosity seemed most advisable, laced with a healthy dose of entitlement herself.

The GPS led Zee unerringly to the Somerworth home. *Manor*, Zee revised, when she reached the end of the quarter-mile curving driveway. Wings of tan brick stretched left and right of the central edifice, where a slanting three-story facade of gleaming glass thrust itself at visitors like a pugilist's jaw.

She pulled to the side of the front porch and parked at the edge of a fifty-foot square of herringbone-patterned brick. Under an overhang of heavy gray clouds, in stifling humidity that presaged hard rain, she crossed toward the expressionless glass-sheeted face the Somerworths presented to supplicants.

No pseudo-Roman kitsch here. The nymph pouring water into the fountain was carved from white Italian marble, and the bowl into which the clear water splashed was glazed in shades of blue, from pale cornflower and green-tinged cerulean to deep, rich cobalt—the color of Rico's eyes, except when anger darkened them to midnight. Zee lifted the bronze horsehead knocker, wondering how Rico would react to this impulsive decision.

A middle-aged woman in a black, high-necked dress and starched white apron opened one side of the pair of massive carved doors. Her iron-gray hair matched an implacable expression and a similarly unyielding tone. "Yes?"

Zee pasted on a smile. "I'm here to see Shandra."

The guardian's plucked eyebrows rose a fraction. "Is she expecting you?"

Zee kept her face relaxed. "I'm here at her invitation." Leaving a note on her windshield was an invitation in her book.

"I see." The maid's face said she clearly did not. "I will check whether she is available."

She started to close the door. Zee fixed her smile in place. "That's fine. I can use the time to take photos." As if to call her bluff, a single drop of rain left a half-dollar-sized splat near her feet. Zee hoped she wouldn't regret leaving her ten-year-old raincoat in the car. She'd imagined she'd make a better impression on the status-conscious Somerworths without it.

The heavy wooden door halted. "Are you a . . . *journalist*?" Iron-Maid invested the word with the type of horror one might reserve for lepers.

"I'm sure that's why she contacted me." Zee offered a card.

The stone-faced woman ignored it, but she widened the doorway another foot. Zee stepped into a grand foyer, tiled in travertine and featuring an assortment of generously fronded greenery and pristine alabaster statuary. Twin polished mahogany staircases curved to a landing twelve feet above, over which presided an enormous, half-moon stained-glass reclining odalisque.

"Wait here." The maid turned on her heel, halted, and swiveled. She held out her hand. Zee dropped her card into it just as Shandra appeared in a doorway.

"What is it, Margaret?" Shandra looked at Zee. "What are you doing here?"

Margaret spun back. "Just as I thought—"

"I'm Zee Morani." She circumvented the fuming servant and held out her hand. "We haven't yet met in person, but you invited me to see you."

Shandra's enormous blue eyes widened. "I don't recall."

Zee withdrew her untouched hand. "I'm sorry you don't remember. You left the note this morning." Margaret positioned herself at Zee's side. At her employer's command, the maid's energy screamed, her pincer grasp would forcefully escort this interloper to the exit.

Shandra kept her gaze pinned to Zee. "Margaret, you may leave."

The maid inclined her head a fraction, during which she shot a poisonous sideways glance at Zee, and stepped back.

Zee followed Shandra through a doorway flanked by potted palms. In contrast to the chill formality of the foyer, this room exuded intimacy, with deeply padded seating, softly gleaming tables, and richly textured cream-and-pink drapes framing a pair of arched windows. The ivory marble mantelpiece showcased a half-dozen photos framed in brushed silver.

Without waiting for an invitation, Zee seated herself in a rose leather armchair, then hastily repositioned her body as the buttery soft cushion threatened to swallow her.

Shandra composed herself on a matching loveseat. She wore a sleeveless silk jumpsuit the color of sea foam. A braided gold chain lay below the notch of her collarbone.

Zee hid her disappointment. She supposed it would have been too much luck to catch the socialite wearing this morning's outfit. If it actually was her.

Zee squashed the niggling doubt.

Shandra crossed her legs, picked up an old-fashioned glass, and sipped the amber liquid. "Understand I am seeing you only because you piqued my interest. I know nothing about a note."

Zee locked eyes on her adversary. "I'm here about the murder of Doctor Ian McNeary."

Shandra held Zee's gaze a moment, then shrugged tanned shoulders. "What about it?"

"You know something." Zee fought to keep the irritation from her voice. "And for whatever reason, you won't take it to the police." She moderated her tone. "I don't mind that you contacted me, but I need more information to help me follow up."

"You are mistaken." Shandra studied the ice in her beverage. "I read that the poor man was stabbed rather horribly. The police have arrested . . . someone. That's all I know."

Zee caught the hesitation. She leaned forward and spoke slowly. "The police are wrong. It's about the money."

No flicker of recognition marred Shandra's untroubled face. "Is that so?"

Either she was one hell of an actress or she didn't write the note. Zee sharpened her voice. "Someone left that message under my windshield."

"How dramatic." Shandra lifted plucked eyebrows a millimeter and sipped her drink.

Zee pulled the note from her bag and snapped it open. She extended her arm and let the paper dangle. "Two witnesses identified you."

Cool fingers flicked sideways, dismissing her. "Really? I don't see how that is possible." Shandra leaned over and made a show of examining the note without touching it. "This is clearly not my handwriting."

Zee ignored her protest. "Both witnesses described you."

Shandra set her glass next to a hardback book on the rosewood side table. Pete Bottmeyer's last best-seller. A perfectly cut curtain

of shiny blonde hair brushed her shoulders. "You no longer interest me. I'll have Margaret escort you."

Not yet, you arrogant—Zee sharpened her voice. "Why are you
lying?"

"I'm not lying. I couldn't have—"

"You couldn't have what?"

Shandra's cheeks colored.

A crack in that carefully crafted façade.

Zee switched to a softer tone. "Come on, Shandra. You wrote
the note. You put it on my car. Now why? What do you know?"

The socialite plucked the note from Zee's fingers and bent her
face as if to study it, but she could not quite contain the tension
that tautened her smooth features.

"Shandra? Oh, there you are." A large head poked through the
door. Zee caught a glimpse of dark wavy hair receding from a glistening forehead. "I'm off to meet Dad at the club. Don't forget dinner—oh, I didn't know you were entertaining."

A scrawny scarecrow of a man stepped into the room. His head
seemed overlarge for his matchstick neck. His once crisply-ironed
shirt had wilted across his narrow chest, and his trousers had lost
most of their sharp crease. "Henry Somerworth." He extended a
hand so bony that his enormous wristwatch slipped to his knuckles.

"Zee Morani." She stood and stifled her revulsion at his damp
handshake and the realization that he bit his nails.

He squinted behind square gold-framed glasses. "The newspaper columnist?" He frowned at Shandra.

"Just a social visit," Shandra said. She did not rise from the loveseat. "No need to work up a sweat."

Henry's face darkened.

Close-up, Zee could see he oiled his hair. The man looked wet all
over. She glanced at Shandra. No mistaking the gibe in her cool gaze.

"Go on, dear. Enjoy your lunch," said Shandra. "Dinner at seven-
thirty with the Leehammers. I'm fully aware."

Henry curved thin moist lips upward. "Have a nice day, darling."

He settled a fedora on his greasy hair, exaggerating Zee's earlier impression that his head was too large for his body. He turned, paused. "By the way, Samson called. Looks like someone bailed out James Hawethorne. I thought you'd like to know." He did not wait for a response.

Zee stared at the composed woman on the loveseat. A faint smile played on Shandra's meticulously painted pink lips. Tiny lines of tension around her eyes eased. She enjoyed sniping at Henry, but the news about Hawethorne also pleased her, Zee would bet on it.

Shandra's laugh interrupted her thoughts. "Henry always gets nervous when he has to meet with his father. He shouldn't. Henry's every bit as smart, perhaps I should say devious, as Edward. He just needs to learn how to assert himself."

That was a problem Shandra obviously didn't have.

Zee nodded automatically while searching for a way to refocus the discussion. Damn Henry's timing. However, he had provided another opening. She returned to the armchair and infused her voice with friendly curiosity tinged with disappointment. "Shandra, clearly you knew that Hawethorne had been arrested. I saw it in your face. Why the big charade?"

Shandra's expression gave nothing away, her control locked in place once more. "I'm simply glad that they're going to release Jim. He could never kill anyone."

"How can you be sure?"

Shandra leaned back in the loveseat. "Papa introduced me to him at a writers' conference. He's a wonderful, talented man, and completely incapable of murder."

Zee's eyes darted to the book jacket photo, then to the mantel display. Her brain made the connection. This woman was the daughter of Pete Bottmeyer, the struggling novelist last seen at his child's society wedding, potentially one of McNeary's unlucky investors.

"You'd be surprised who's capable of murder," Zee said.

Another of those ephemeral smiles flitted across Shandra's face.

"I didn't say he was incapable of deep feelings. Have you read any of his poetry?"

Zee recalled the venomous posts in Hawethorne's blog and chose not to answer. "The note says it was all about the money. Why would . . . someone . . . say that?"

Shandra gave her a withering look. "Isn't it obvious? The doctor's superiority complex ruined many people. Of course, it's about the money. *Everything* always is."

"So, you think one of McNeary's investors killed him? Paselly?"

No reaction to the name.

Zee took a chance. "Or your father, for that matter?"

"You leave Papa out of this," snapped Shandra. "He's suffered enough. I won't let you make it worse."

Zee held her hands up in a gesture of placation. "I'm not making accusations. I'm simply trying to learn what you think."

"What I think doesn't matter." Shandra scowled. "But I won't have you or anyone thinking he was involved." Her voice rose. "Papa is an honorable man who's had enough struggles in his life. You leave him alone."

The socialite's vehemence knocked Zee off balance, but it compelled her to persist. "Did the police question your father?"

Shandra produced a noise that in a less well-mannered person would have been considered a snort. "The police are fools. You saw how quickly they arrested Jim. Poor man." She shook her head. Her tresses swung as one glossy blonde drape and fell back, every hair in place.

Zee wished she had hair like that.

Shandra's voice climbed to a screech. "I don't want to even *imagine* what Jim went through all this time in jail." She fixed Zee with an ice-blue stare. "I do *not* intend to have Papa endure *anything* like that."

"I'm sure—" Zee choked off her reply. Swift, sinuous, and menacing as a tiger, Shandra rose from the loveseat and advanced on her. Zee scrambled to her feet. She barely had time to snatch her purse before Shandra sank sharp nails into her elbow.

"We're finished." She propelled Zee through the travertine foyer. "Look elsewhere." The massive wooden door slammed shut.

Zee trudged across the herringbone parking area, stunned by the strange turn of the interview and thankful the rain had ceased. She climbed behind the wheel and drove slowly down the long, curving driveway, her thoughts trying to sort themselves. On the street, she pulled to the shoulder, nestled the car beneath a canopy of wind-swept trees, and shut off the engine. Leaning against the headrest, she closed her eyes.

Shandra had attacked like a wounded predator. She knew more than she'd shared. Snarling pounce aside, there was that flickering smile at Hawethorne's release, the not-quite-quick-enough recovery when she'd seen the note, the too-smooth way she'd dismissed the murder as being "of course" about the money.

Despite all that, Zee had failed to unearth any useful information.

Tires squealed behind her. Zee snapped upright as a car roared out of the Somerworths' driveway. A faded gold Mustang. Zee glimpsed the sheaf of blonde hair and jabbed the Mini's *Start* button.

CHAPTER 21

FROM HER VANTAGE ON THE SIDE OF THE ROAD, Zee kept eyes on the gold Mustang as it fishtailed from Shandra's driveway and sped away. She drummed her fingers on the Mini's wheel until the Mustang rounded the corner, then pulled from the shoulder in pursuit. As they threaded through the sparse traffic of McKinley Heights, she hung back, hoping Shandra wouldn't notice a red-and-white Mini Cooper among the silver Mercedes and black Cadillacs. When Shandra rolled onto the freeway, Zee exhaled in relief.

Once on the open road, the gold car roared ahead as if propelled by afterburners. Zee downshifted the Mini, said a silent prayer that the gods of law enforcement would take a nap, and gave her sporty car its head.

Shandra wove through the traffic, seeming unfazed by the angry horns from swerving cars. Zee stuck to the middle lane, grateful to blend into the commotion in the Mustang's wake.

After fifteen minutes, Shandra lurched for an exit. Zee's luck held; an ancient, rust-pocked pickup fell in line behind the gold car. Zee maneuvered to shelter in its boxy profile.

The ramp decanted them onto a two-lane country road. Both Mustang and truck turned left. Zee followed. The road led the trio through a small town, barely two blocks of weathered storefronts. When the truck peeled off at a gas station, Zee ducked in as well.

Without a barrier to protect her, she had no choice but to allow Shandra to get out of sight.

She used the opportunity to mute her phone. She disliked being out of touch, but better to miss a call than suffer another inopportune disruption. If only Henry hadn't popped his sweaty head into Shandra's sitting room, Zee might have learned something useful.

She tamped her disappointment and pulled back onto the road. The gray ribbon snaked between rolling bucolic fields dotted with giant cylinders of yellow hay. The Mini's nimble handling shone on winding country roads, and Zee grinned as she goosed the accelerator.

In minutes she spied the barred taillights of the Mustang. She let Shandra's car crest a gentle rise and sink out of view. When Zee topped the rise, a flatbed truck, its stacks of straw bales tilting precariously, trundled toward her along an intersecting lane. She slowed to allow the overloaded lorry to lumber between her and the gold car. With such a dearth of traffic, as long as the vista remained open, she would be able to see if Shandra made a turn.

In her rearview mirror, the humongous grill of a jacked-up truck appeared and quickly closed the distance. The dirt-encrusted chrome bore a jagged depression along the right side that made it look like a prize fighter who'd lost a tooth. The black beast backed off, then drew near again. Zee waved a hand out her window. "Come around," she said, though she knew the driver couldn't hear. The truck fell back.

Ahead, the flatbed crawled, spitting bits of straw behind it. Zee forced herself to keep a distance, scanning the countryside every time she crested one of the undulating hills. She saw no roads, no houses, no path to deviate from the unrolling asphalt strip. Also no gold car.

Zee consoled her anxious mind. Shandra had not escaped. Even if she took the Mustang cross-country, a foolish move for certain, Zee would have seen her. She glanced in her rearview mirror. At least the monster truck was no longer tailgating her.

She lost the protection of her hay-laden guardian just before the fields yielded to forested land. Miami Woods, a vast tract of mostly unspoiled nature centered around a small body of water marked on maps as Bath Lake, but which locals called, predictably, Bathtub.

The road twisted and the thickening woods obscured her view. Zee tapped the accelerator, increasing her speed in cautious increments. A driveway appeared on the left. She slowed and passed a deserted lodge.

Once more she picked up the pace. The road threaded through the trees, then climbed a sweeping incline. No Mustang. At the top Zee steered through a curve and, as she entered the long downward slope, she caught sight of Shandra's car far ahead. Its brake lights glowed and angled into a right turn.

Zee glued her eyes where the Mustang had disappeared, hardly daring to blink. In her peripheral vision, she noted an abandoned campground on her right. Halfway down the hill, she glimpsed a cabin on her left, half hidden by trees and approached by a narrow gravel driveway.

Shandra's car sat in another such turnoff. Zee rolled past the battered mailbox on its leaning post: number 364, except the 4 swung upside down, hanging by one nail. She steered the Mini to the side of the road and shut off her engine.

Woods and underbrush, agitated by the wind, crowded the passenger side. Zee fought against the gale and managed to exit, but once outside, a gust tore the handle from her grasp. The door slammed, loud as a thunderclap, but far more alien.

Zee held her breath.

No one came to investigate.

Satisfied, she started to sprint toward the gravel opening, then stifled a grunt at her protesting legs. Why did people think exercise was good?

She moved as quickly as she could to the side of the driveway and sought shelter behind a large bush. Bare branches slapped against her silk tunic. Too late, she remembered the raincoat, abandoned in the back seat for her entrance into Somerworth Manor.

Thickets of curls whipped her cheeks. She pushed them aside and dared a look around the edge of the shrub. Not fifty feet away stood a small cabin, its front porch partially obscured by Shandra's car.

Zee adjusted her position and peered through a rattling lattice of mostly denuded twigs. Shandra's voice filtered through the clacking and rustling, but Zee couldn't resolve it into words. Whatever she was saying carried high emotion, judging by the way she paced the wooden floorboards and periodically flung her arms and hands in the air.

The porch's other occupant, a scrawny-armed, barrel-chested man, seemed focused on weathering the onslaught by shrinking into the shelter of an ancient Adirondack chair. After Shandra's third pass, he got to his feet, raked his tangle of stringy gray hair, and nodded. Shandra responded by wrapping him in a hug so fierce, Zee feared his bent back might break.

Had to be Papa.

Zee chortled. She'd discovered the reclusive Pete Bottmeyer. And when Shandra left, she was going to talk to him.

A flash of lightning cut short her triumph. Thunder ricocheted overhead. Thrashed by the chilly wind, her sheltering shrub turned against her, its branches snatching her clothing, her hair, her skin.

Time to retreat.

She hurried to her car, through bushes and trees that swayed like an army of drunks. The first drops of rain spattered her windshield as she started the engine.

Urgency pushed her to escape. She'd risk less chance of discovery if she drove the way she was already headed. The problem was there was no place to hide before the road ahead dipped from sight.

She eased the Mini forward until she could see what lay beyond the drop. Shimmering wet, the asphalt descended sharply and curved into the trees. Once over the rise, she'd have no chance to observe Shandra's departure.

Her best bet was to retrace her path, but that meant passing the cabin. Hoping Shandra lingered with her father, Zee pulled a quiet U-turn. She resisted the impulse to floor the accelerator. Dangerous on a slick surface and besides, a speeding car calls attention to itself.

Picturing the Mini as invisible in the fine gray curtain of rain, she drove quietly past the driveway, where the gold Mustang still sat, and steered her car up the long slope. Near the crest, she spied the campground. A burst of wind nudged the car sideways toward the entrance.

Great idea, Mother Nature.

The gravel driveway dipped several hundred feet to a parking area. Zee turned around in the muddy space and drove back until she had a clear view of the road. She snugged her car against an overgrown nest of shrubs. Trying to ignore the sawing of branches against her passenger door, she settled in to wait.

Shandra would not stay long at her father's cabin. The socialite's hurried departure after the conversation with Zee screamed spur-of-the-moment, and she had that dinner date.

With the Leehammers, for whose generosity Leehammer Pavilion had been named. Zee's thoughts strayed to her dad as lightning snaked across the angry purple sky. In the past, he'd never been afraid of storms. She hoped someone would comfort him if needed.

With no further preamble, the storm broke in a torrent of rain, battering the Mini's roof like fists. Zee could see no more than a foot in any direction. Her chest tightened. She'd parked near the top of the sloping driveway, but at the rate the rain was falling, it wouldn't take much to create a tide that washed her to the bottom and mired her in the mud.

She was alone. No one even knew where to find her.

Then as if the allotment had been reached, the cataract stopped. A new anxiety squeezed Zee's stomach. This weather pattern meant trouble. She should go home.

Overhead, clouds roiled, mirroring her mental state. Chasing leads was exhausting. Usually she chose a topic for her column, did her research, set up interviews as needed, and drafted the result— all very organized.

This was miles from anything resembling structure. Since she found McNeary's body four days ago, her ordered world had been subsumed in escalating madness.

Yesterday, she'd dashed to the courtroom for Hawethorne's arraignment; interviewed Akhil, Janece, Veronique, and Fenton; and gotten scared out of her wits outside Mercy's office. Today, she'd found a cryptic note on her car, tracked down the likely author, and been thrown out of the manor for her trouble. Now she sat in what most certainly was a lull between violent thunderstorms, debating her next move.

The gold Mustang sped past in a rooster comb of road spray and skidded around the curve.

Zee's pulse jumped. Investigating a murder was chaotic, true, but it was also exhilarating. A columnist might go home. A reporter would not.

CHAPTER 22

FROM HER SHIELDED PARKING SPOT on the campground driveway, Zee watched Shandra's taillights drop over the hill and out of sight. Impatience prodded her hand toward the Mini's *Start* button. She should grab this chance to interrogate 'Papa' Bottmeyer about his connection with Ian McNeary.

Lightning flickered on the horizon, staying her reach. The storm had abated to a fitful drizzle, but she was not fooled. A churning sea of charcoal clouds hung low overhead, and a restless wind scraped branches against her car. This was tornado weather. Late in the season, but nature didn't care a fig for the human calendar.

She started the engine, vowing not to stay long.

Carefully steering on the slick road, she made her way back to the cabin. A banged-up beige sedan, invisible to her earlier, hunched at the edge of the parking area. Beyond the empty porch, yellow light shone through a thinly curtained window.

Heeding some cautionary impulse, Zee backed in, bumping along muddy ruts in the gravel driveway and coming to rest at the edge of a murky pool. She sighed, resigned to sacrificing another pair of shoes, and picked her way through the squelching mess, mounted the creaking porch steps, and rapped.

The planked slab of wood banged open. "What do you want now?" Bottmeyer's rheumy eyes widened. "Who are you?" He swayed and whiskey rode almost visibly on his breath.

"My name is Zee Morani, Mister Bottmeyer. I'd like to talk to you about Doctor Ian McNeary. May I come in?"

Bottmeyer squinted. "Ian? Someone killed him, damn shame. We were close once." His hand gripped the door handle, but Zee suspected he used it to steady himself rather than prepare to slam the door. "I don't know anything else."

"You were one of his investors," she said. A guess.

"More's the pity."

Wind blew rain in needles against the back of Zee's neck. Bottmeyer blinked as drops struck his face.

"Could I come in, Mister Bottmeyer? I'd like to ask you a few questions."

He shrugged. "What the hell. I'm not getting anything done anyway. And call me Pete, or I'll think you're from the IRS."

He laughed at his joke and turned his back, leaving her to follow and close the door while he made his way on wobbling legs to a sagging couch. A bright pink-and-cream crocheted afghan lay over the back, a decorating attempt that succeeded only in drawing attention to the original upholstery, a faded plaid of sickly brown, yellow, and green.

Bottmeyer fell heavily onto the cushions. The impact released a puff of dust and musty odor. Zee stifled a cough.

"Hand me my drink." He stretched a thin arm toward the listing, battered coffee table. Despite his broad chest, he seemed shrunken, as though he lived inside a husk of his former self.

Zee picked up the glass of amber liquid, surprised at its weight.

Bottmeyer shaped colorless lips into a crooked smile. "A relic from my former life." He drained it in one long draught and held it up to the dim lamplight. "Used to have lots of these."

Without warning, he hurled the glass against the far wall. Zee cringed. The squat tumbler bounced off the pine paneling and spun to a stop on the stained wooden floor. Its intact form sat among the shards of previous projectiles.

"God damn son of a bitch," Bottmeyer snarled. "Even when I want to, I can't break it."

Zee ducked her head to hide her raised brows. The evidence of his previous success lay at the foot of the wall.

"Probably a moral there." He flicked his wrist. "The universe is willful. A thing decides for itself when it wants to be destroyed."

"Interesting way to put it," said Zee.

"Yeah, I'm full of that crap." He ran big square hands through his greasy hair. "You said you had questions. I get one first. Why are you interested in Ian?"

Zee edged onto the drooping lip of the armchair, grateful to have wriggled into her raincoat before leaving the car. At least she had a barrier to protect her trousers from whatever lurked in the discolored cushion. "I discovered his body."

The old man's mouth fell open.

Zee hurried on. "I was supposed to meet him that morning. And now I find myself entangled in his murder." She detailed her encounter with Hawethorne, his email message, and his court-house plea for help. "I believe James Hawethorne is innocent," she ended, "but if he didn't kill Ian McNeary, who did?"

Bottmeyer bared his teeth in a smirk. "You think I did."

"Did you?"

He hacked and cleared his throat. "You've been reading too many books."

"You lost a lot of money."

"Money." He spat dryly. "Ian was a good friend, a fraternity brother. We used to hunt together. We lost touch the way people do when life takes them in different directions. But then he called, and the years between us disappeared. Might have been better if they hadn't."

He dropped his voice almost to a whisper. "What a fool. A blind, stupid fool."

Was he still talking about McNeary? "I don't understand."

"I wouldn't have killed him over the damned money. If any-thing, it'd be the other." He leaned forward and pointed to a group photograph on the mantel above the empty fireplace. It showed a happier, clearly more prosperous man and a smiling woman, standing on either side of a grinning young lady in cap and gown.

"That's my wife and I at our daughter's college graduation. You can't see it in the picture, but Shandra's got her arm wrapped around my waist, hugging me so tight I can barely breathe." He blinked wet eyes. "She's a daughter any man would die for. Smart, funny, beautiful, completely devoted." He belched loudly but didn't seem to notice.

Zee struggled not to recoil at the pungent stench.

"Shandra was always my baby. You know, her first word was *Papa*."

Zee cast about for something that would pull him from his reverie. "Did Doctor McNeary harm Shandra?"

Bottmeyer jolted upright. "The damned s-o-b just about wrecked my whole family. The other beautiful lady is my wife, Helena. On one of her good days. She fought depression all her life. But that mess. It destroyed her."

He lifted his hand, seemed surprised that it was empty, and let it fall heavily into his lap. "Drugs didn't help. She just got worse. And then a scan showed brain cancer."

"I'm sorry, Mist—Pete."

Like a pricked balloon he deflated. "They did the surgery. Now half the time she doesn't recognize me, and the other half, she's in so much pain, I wish . . ." He coughed and his voice cracked. "I know she's never coming home."

He looked around the single large room. Zee followed his gaze through the sad, bedraggled place. A threadbare rug demarcated the living room area. Next to the front door, two spindly chairs leaned into a chipped and scarred dining table. Across from them against the opposite wall sat a half-size refrigerator, two-burner stove, and rust-stained porcelain sink.

"Home," Bottmeyer muttered. "She'd never recognize this miserable place as home." He sighed heavily. "Get that glass for me."

Zee stood and crossed the room, questioning why she did as he asked. Except that it was such a small request, and he was pathetic, this broken man with a broken life because of Ian McNeary. Her neck hair prickled. He'd revealed a powerful motive for murder.

On the mantel above the vacant hole of the fireplace, she noticed a second photograph of Shandra. Sans graduation regalia, the exuberant young woman smiled from a brushed silver frame decorated with jeweled hearts. A skinny, shiny-faced young man draped his arm over her shoulders. Henry Somerworth.

Zee carried the picture across the room. "A happier time," she said.

Bottmeyer took the photo in one hand and stroked Shandra's image with his thumb.

Zee blushed at the intimacy of the gesture.

He laid the picture on the sagging couch, picked up the tumbler, and dumped in a generous splash from the bottle on the table. *Old Elijah*. Single barrel. Aged ten years. The novelist still had some money.

"Damn near thought he'd be another casualty of this whole mess."

"What do you mean?"

Bottmeyer pulled a plastic vial from his pants pocket and shook free a couple of pills. He swallowed them with his drink.

Alarms rang in Zee's head. The guy clearly hadn't kicked his alcohol addiction. It appeared he'd failed to rein in his drug use, as well. She sat on the edge of her chair. "What mess, Pete?"

His eyes roamed past her, unfocused. "It was insane. Everybody's emotions high. So much going on." He drained his glass. "It blew over."

Meaning lurked somewhere in there. "Not immediately," Zee pursued.

He seemed not to hear her. "I should tell that story. I can't seem to write anything original. It's like my mind is dried up." He raised a pained face. "Head's like a desert. It's all sand and rock and jagged, sharp, prickly things. Nothing that bears fruit."

Zee struggled to corral his melancholy. "I'm a writer, too, Pete. We all have those tough spells, but you're very good. You'll come out of this, I'm sure."

He snorted wetly and wiped his mouth on a wrinkled denim sleeve. "You sound like Shandra."

"Shandra loves you and wants you to succeed. Isn't that why she came here today, to encourage you?" She held her breath at her mistake.

"I don't know why she came here," he snapped. "No, that's not true." His shoulders slumped. "It's always for the same reason, to *see how I'm doing*." He swept his arm wide and nearly lost his balance. "See those boxes? She keeps bringing me stuff. Towels, a tablecloth, new curtains, furniture covers. Decorative pillows, for chrissake."

That explained the lime green pillow on Zee's chair.

Bottmeyer scrubbed his hands across his face. "Don't listen to me. I'm in a bad place right now. I need to be alone."

Sympathy bunched in Zee's throat, but anger surged, too. This alcoholic drug addict was voluntarily destroying his brain cells. Unlike her dad, who'd probably give anything to have his back.

"Mister Bottmeyer," she blurted, "*did* you kill Ian McNeary?"

He stared toward the empty fireplace. "Damned if I know."

Zee tried to read his face but failed. "What do you mean?"

He hefted the tumbler in his hand and reared back his arm. At Zee's grimace, he laughed, a loud, belly-shaking sound that devolved into a wracking cough. He lowered the glass to the table. "Got no more of these. Better keep it. Wouldn't want old Ian to have the last laugh."

Had he failed to hear her? Was he ignoring her? Had he completely disconnected from reality? She tried a different tack. "Mister—Pete, where were you Tuesday morning?"

He swept his eyes around the shabby cabin. "Here. Home."

"Alone?"

A crooked grin pulled at his sallow cheeks. "No, I was entertaining

the queen." He pushed to his feet, towering over her. His face darkened and the smile vanished. "Who are you again?"

Zee wriggled out of the chair.

Fierceness twisted Bottmeyer's features like a sponge, squeezing out any remnants of the blabbering, blubbering drunk.

"Thank you for seeing me." She backed toward the door. "I'll
go now."

He lunged, flailing, and made a grab for her. "Just a minute.
Who—"

She sidestepped and, much as she wanted to flee, caught his
arm to break his fall. "You should sit down." She pulled out one of
the spindly dining chairs and maneuvered him into it.

His eyes darted left and right, searching. *We used to hunt
together.* Did he have a weapon? She wouldn't stick around to find
out.

Releasing him, she ran to the door. As she yanked it open, the
chair clattered to the floor.

She splashed through a chilly rain, wishing she could stand in
it and let it wash her clean. Bottmeyer's misery clung to her like
greasy film, overlaid with fury. Footsteps pounded onto the creaking porch behind her.

She jumped into the driver's seat and punched the starter, eyes
darting to the rearview mirror. On the rickety porch, Bottmeyer
wielded something that, through the Mini's rain-streaked back
window, looked like a shotgun.

Zee slammed the car in gear and peeled out onto the road, leaving a spray of stones in her wake, and praying he didn't decide to
get behind the wheel.

CHAPTER 23

WHEELS SKIDDING ON THE RAIN-SLICK ROAD, Zee sped from Bottmeyer's pathetic cabin. She goosed the accelerator, spurred by the image of the drunken man swaying on that rickety porch, brandishing a long, slender, dark object. Was it a shotgun? Would he really have fired at her?

Maybe she should rethink her desire for a career change. Even her most caustic comments in *Z Beats* had never jeopardized her life.

Distracted by the thought, she plowed into standing water left by the storm and nearly lost control. She forced her foot to ease from the gas.

As she started into the long upward sweep of glistening blacktop, she kept eyes on the rearview mirror. Bottmeyer's car did not appear.

Her mind returned to the strange encounter with Shandra's father. At first, she'd discounted him as a viable suspect. His dissipated state argued against the ability to execute a plan. His transformation, though—that revealed a frightening depth of passion and will, as well as alarming irrationality. She no longer doubted that, if provoked, he could kill.

Questions popped like the fat raindrops spattering her windows. Was Shandra shielding her father's guilt? She was certainly protective enough. Then why write the note? Maybe Shandra didn't know her father killed the doctor. In that case, visiting him was simply the action of a dutiful, devoted daughter. Then why the rush to see him?

She wished she'd heard their conversation on the porch. Why was it important for Shandra to continually, as he put it, *see how I'm doing*?

As she crested the hill, the resurgent storm decided to unleash its fury. Rain burst across the Mini's hood and sheeted down the windshield faster than the wipers could clear it.

Her stomach clenched. She was in the worst possible situation, at the head of a long slope on a part of the road where the contours of the land funneled the rushing downpour directly across her path. In moments, the banked curve became a broad watercourse. Foot barely on the gas, Zee crept through the rippling flood. Her tires slipped, then caught. Then slipped again and didn't catch.

"Slow and steady." White-knuckled, she whispered the mantra that was her best chance of getting out of this in one piece.

Trees reached for her. She nudged the steering wheel away from their dark clutches. The car failed to respond. Like a blindfolded seeker, her front left tire found the sloping edge of the road. The hood began to dip.

The tire grabbed.

In front of her, the pavement rose, exposing the boundary of the flood and beyond it, blessed, pebbled asphalt. Hands shaking, handling the wheel with the delicacy reserved for brain surgery, she guided the car to safety.

On solid ground again, she allowed herself a breath.

The rain continued to pour. The world disappeared beyond the tunnel created by the Mini's headlights. She rounded a bend and confronted a newly created pond in the dip of a rolling hill. Shoulders hunched and jaw clenched, she feathered the brakes and rolled into it.

Fontina's instruction from yoga class echoed in her ear: *When you notice tension, see if you can release it, even a little. Try forming a smile.*

At the time, Zee had been stretching in a sideways bend, every tendon taut as a bridge cable. She'd nearly laughed aloud at Fontina's suggestion and then realized that even that tiny bit of relaxation enabled her to hold the position with fractionally more ease.

Worth a try in this situation. She forced her lips into an upward curve as she forded the mini-lake. Tension trickled from her neck and shoulders. She gained the other side.

She was going to make it through this brutal beating.

A soft brush across her arms made the hair stand on end. She had barely registered the sensation when a bolt of lightning exploded in a fireball, electrifying a water-choked ditch.

She jumped in her seat, and the Mini skidded. Another fork of lightning struck among the hay rolls in the field. Her heart clawed its way into her throat.

Ahead, lights glimmered. The town gas station. Relief as big as any stormy wave broke over her as she aimed the Mini's lights toward the haven.

She sloshed her way toward a cluster of refugee vehicles, pulled into a spot behind a Jeep, and shut off the engine. Grateful to be sheltered in protective metal and glass, she flexed the stiffness from her fingers. Almost without thought, the stretch morphed into a cathartic all-over body shake, wriggling and wiggling from sweat-drenched curls to muddily-shod toes.

The storm continued its furious onslaught, but safe now, she could enjoy the spectacular display. Late-summer afternoon thunderstorms were Nature's specialty in the Midwest. Thousands of heavy drops hurling themselves to earth like kamikaze divers. Lightning cracking its way through unseen channels, unstoppable.

She flinched as another streak seared her retinas.

Death to anyone in its path. Visible death, that's what she saw. Though if it struck her, she'd never see it coming.

Zee shuddered. *Enough nature.* She opened the glove compartment, grabbed a notebook, and flipped to a clean page. She'd use this time to organize her chaotic thoughts. In the center of the sheet, she printed *Shandra Somerworth*.

She drew a circle around Shandra's name and began to create a web diagram to map the connections among her pieces of information. A notepaper version of a police murder board, she realized with a shiver.

She jotted: *the note, Hawethorne, denial,* and *relief,* then drew lines to connect them. The note and Hawethorne belonged together, and all four items tied to Shandra. She wrote *Henry,* linked him to Shandra, and penned *tension* along the connecting line.

Tapping her pen against her chin, she lifted her eyes to the scene outside. Another rain-swamped vehicle pulled into the gas station. It passed the two empty pumps and several parking places.

Back on the page, she started a smaller web with a bubble marked *Pete,* connecting his name to Shandra's. She scribbled: *guilty, Shandra warning, drunk, fierce!* She lined in the connections.

She paused, then wrote *misjudging Shandra?* She left it floating free, not knowing how to link it.

No more ideas came. She flipped the page, wrote *Jules Mercy,* then added *Lady Macbeth, weasel-faced Louis Paselly.*

Her head ached in the dim interior of the Mini. The rain had abated, but the afternoon had darkened to green-tinged twilight. A distant wail rose, faded, rose again. *A weather alarm.*

She pulled out her cellphone to check the radar. Four voicemails and two alerts. A severe thunderstorm warning, read one. *No kidding.* The other sounded a tornado watch. Not a warning, no twister sightings—yet. Caution born of experience urged her to abandon the Mini for the safety of the gas station until the danger passed.

She reached for the door just as hail began to fall. In mere moments, icy projectiles enveloped her car in a rattling onslaught. She let go of the handle and decided to check the voicemails.

The first three were from Rico. Zee tapped *play,* jammed the phone against her ear, and covered the other ear with her hand. The noise outside diminished to a rumbling kettledrum.

"Call me."

That's it? She advanced to the next message.

"Call me right now."

She huffed a breath. *Next one'd better have more.* She tapped the icon.

"Dammit, Zee, where the hell are you? Call me. Please."

Zee stared at her voicemail icon as the hail pummeled her car. He was worried. Fear quivered in her chest.

The final message was from Fontina. On the surface, her friend's voice exuded her usual calm, but distress vibrated beneath the words. "Zee-zee, please call me right away. And please be careful."

Fontina's request alarmed Zee even more than Rico's. Zee punched in her number as the cacophony around her increased. Those hailstones must be the size of quarters. Wind gusts rocked the car.

Her friend answered on the first ring. "Where in creation are you? It sounds like you're inside a drum set."

Zee tried to keep her voice light. "It's hail. I'm waiting it out at a gas station."

"Zee-zee, listen, you're in danger. I'll explain when you get home. For now, leave as soon as you can, and don't stop anywhere for any reason."

Midway through Fontina's tumbling words, the hail gave way to heavy rain. Zee grimaced, resigned to more white-knuckled driving. "Okay."

She glanced in her rearview mirror and groaned. A dark hulk barred her escape.

Irritation flashed, then melted into trembling fear. She hunched in her seat, acutely aware of all her windows, transparent holes in her protective shell. "I can't leave now. I'm blocked in," she said to Fontina. She squinted toward the building. *Lights. People.* "I'm going into the store."

Before Fontina could object, Zee dropped the phone into her purse. She slung the strap over her head and across her body, grabbed the door handle, and pushed.

In seconds, she was drenched. Cold and half-blinded, she fought through water that ran like a river across the tops of her feet. When she gained the shelter of the building overhang, she caught her breath, turned, and clicked the lock button on her key fob.

Her breath snagged in her throat. Parked behind her, its huge, dented grill snarling at her bumper, was a black monster truck. It couldn't be. Whipped by fear, she scrambled into the store.

Her skin prickled in instant goosebumps. Ice scabbed her scalp, and she was sure frost clumped her eyelashes. Resisting a desperate urge to shake herself like a dog, she clenched her chattering teeth and scanned the area. "Need some coffee," she mumbled through stiff lips.

The middle-aged, bespectacled clerk raised her brows as if to say, "Obviously." She jerked her head toward the back of the store.

Zee swallowed a retort and set off, zigzagging among the aisles of snack foods. Her soaked shoes squeaked, and her drenched trouser legs slapped against her ankles. Unprotected during her dash across the parking lot, her sopping hair drizzled frigid rivulets down the back of her neck.

The odor of old, burnt java guided her to the coffee station. An assault on her nostrils, but at least the brew was hot. She wrinkled her nose and grabbed a foam cup.

The urn was dispensing brownish-black sludge when the bell over the door clanged. Zee jumped. She wished the last image during her note-taking hadn't been Paselly.

Get a grip. Just another sodden soul seeking refuge.

She kept her eyes on the rising liquid in the cup, while her ears told her what she feared. Footsteps approached, heavy, sloshing on the wet floor.

A large figure stopped next to her. A dripping sweatshirt-clad arm stretched forward and hard-knuckled fingers closed around a foam cup. Zee moved to step aside, but his other hand fell on her shoulder.

"No need to move, little lady. I got all the space I need."

His guttural voice froze the cry in her throat.

He squeezed. "I'm just making friendly conversation. You don't want to look foolish now."

A twinge crept across her back.

"Nasty weather out there," he said. "Be sure to keep your lights on. For safety."

Zee craned her neck to look up at him, but he'd pulled the black hood tightly around his face. Reflective sunglasses hid his eyes. Rain had transformed his dark mustache into twin dripping rat tails.

"Coffee don't look so good. I changed my mind." He loosened his grip. "You oughtta change yours." He gave her shoulder a pat, a little harder than was friendly. Then he walked away.

Coffee ran over the lip of Zee's cup and jolted her brain into a semblance of functioning. A voice in her head chattered non-stop, but she couldn't understand the words. She poured some of the vile beverage into the drain grate, while her mind churned, trying to find order. The voice continued. With a start, she realized that it came not from her head, but from her purse.

She fished out her cellphone and put it to her ear. Fontina was chanting.

"Fontina, I'm here," Zee said. The sound on the other end stopped.

"Thank creation! What happened?"

Zee told her. She kept her voice low, her eyes continually scanning the store.

Fontina exhaled with a whoosh. "Oh Zee-zee, be careful. Come straight home. Okay?"

Shaken, Zee acquiesced.

She didn't want the coffee, but she bought it anyway. The middle-aged clerk arranged her face in a look of careful disinterest, but Zee suspected she was memorizing her appearance and planning to save the security tape.

The rain had slowed to a steady drizzle. Except for pothole lakes, most of the deluge drained into streams along the edges of the lot. Many of the vehicles had left, including the monster truck. Zee's stomach eased, then clenched. He could be waiting elsewhere. Watching her, or watching *for* her.

She whirled. She didn't want to see the truck, never wanted to see the hateful thing again, but it felt safer to know its location.

Nothing tweaked recognition.

Reflexively, she sipped the caffeine-sludge. As awful as she had feared, but the sharp taste cut through the thrall of the thug's intimidation. She would not behave like a frightened schoolgirl.

She dumped the cup into the trash and strode toward her car. As she neared the Mini, her shoes crunched on the larger pieces of glistening gravel. She stopped, her attention caught by the reflecting shards of light in front of the Mini's bumper. Bending closer, she saw them more clearly, the shattered remnants of one of her headlights.

CHAPTER 24

DREGS OF THE LATE AFTERNOON THUNDERSTORM draped the gas station in heavy mist. In the mostly abandoned lot, Zee stared at the remains of her Mini's shattered headlight, anger boiling in her gut.

The ghost of the thug's heavy hand landed on her shoulder, so real she jerked her head to check. No one there, of course. His 'friendly' advice—keep her lights on for safety—stoked her rage, and she clamped her jaws to keep from screaming.

Ignoring the chilly drizzle and her saturated feet, she whipped out her phone and snapped photos of the destruction. Seething, she circled the Mini but found no other damage except a few dimples on her roof and hood from the hail.

Despite the murky gray that blended discrete objects into indistinct blurs, she scanned for cameras. She could pick out nothing. And she wasn't going back inside to ask the suspicious clerk. The deluge might have rendered their lenses useless, anyway. Let the police follow up on that.

Even as the thought occurred, she cringed at another intersection with law enforcement. Who'd probably never find the culprit, anyway.

She swiped droplets from her face with a sodden sleeve, got into the car, and rotated the light switch. Her right headlamp glowed, a lone beam that emphasized the void on the driver's side. She cranked the heater, as much to warm the ice from her veins as to chase moisture from inside the Mini, and sat back to calm her breathing.

She should call the police right now, and at least report the vandalism. Her stomach twisted at the idea of waiting in this god-forsaken place for the arrival of a cop car. Adrenaline ebbing, she plucked her phone from the passenger seat.

A black SUV with heavily tinted windows pulled into the station. It passed the first pump and glided into place at one directly across from her. Huge headlights flooded the interior of the Mini. Fontina's warning echoed in Zee's ears.

Her mouth went dry. She dropped the phone on the seat and jammed the car into gear. She could call the police later, when she was safe.

Her foot stayed. She'd be leaving a crime scene.

Better than creating another one.

She remembered at the last moment to avoid the broken glass. Tires spitting gravel, she gained the road and sped away. The nagging voice followed her. It wasn't too late to turn around.

"I might not be terribly brave," Zee said to the disappearing roadway behind her, "but I'm also not entirely stupid." Shelby's version of the difference between discretion and valor.

The brightening horizon beckoned like the gates of heaven. As she flew up the highway on-ramp, sun penetrated a gap in the clouds. Shafts of light streamed like blessings, then broadened to spill benevolence on long stretches of roadway.

Steam rose in plumes from the asphalt, spectral despoilers, reminders. Despite the comfort of sunlight, she checked her mirrors every few seconds, her gut contracting whenever she caught sight of any dark-windowed vehicle.

Between adrenaline spikes, she lectured herself. Message delivered. She doubted there'd be further contact, but her pulse still thumped by the time she steered the car into its parking space at *Legate I.*

She groaned.

Rico's Road King leaned on its kickstand, sleek, black, and studded with globular remnants of the storm. Beside it reclined Fontina's red-bronze Spyder, silvery coronet hanging from the rearview mirror.

On top of everything else, Zee didn't have the energy to deal with people, even well-meaning ones she loved.

In soaked pumps, she trudged the stairs to the third floor. With every step, her saturated hair leaked cold droplets down her neck. Beneath her sodden raincoat, her tunic and trousers stuck to her skin.

She was clammy all over. All she wanted was to shed her clothes, steam herself in a hot shower, and curl on the couch with Candy and a glass of wine. She'd thank her friends and tell them to go home, promise to catch up later.

In the hallway, she squared her shoulders, then opened her door into a maelstrom.

"You do *not* know who you're messing with." Rico boiled up from the living room chair like a thundercloud.

"Whom," Zee corrected, her voice icy. "And nice to see you too."

"Sorry, Zee-zee." Fontina rose from the couch, still in her lemon-and-gray yoga wear. "He was camped outside your door when I got here."

Zee concentrated on slow breaths, in through her nose and out through her mouth.

"Don't start that yoga-breathing shit on me," Rico snapped. "Why don't you answer your damn phone?" He prowled the living room, a compact, leather-clad storm.

Zee glared at him. She wasn't at his beck and call, but she was too tired to take up the argument. "I'm sorry I didn't get your message." She steadied her voice. "I'm here now. I'm safe. Can you calm down?"

Rico whirled. He opened his mouth, then closed it. He clenched his hands into fists and shoved them into his jean pockets.

An effort at self-control—good. His mood wasn't her responsibility. Beneath his taut black t-shirt, his muscled chest rose and fell. He locked eyes with her. A light flickered in their depths.

Fear.

The world shifted, and she glimpsed the day from his perspective. He knew something about the Pasellys. Something that alarmed *him*, the tough crime reporter. Who said he loved her, even if she couldn't say it back.

Chastened, she stripped off her sopping coat and, buying time to adjust to this new perception, hung the dripping garment on a bar chair near the kitchen counter. She ventured one step toward Rico. "I'm all right. Really I am. We can talk about this later."

He shook his head. "With you, later never comes."

"That's not fair." Zee's voice broke.

Maybe it was fair. She hadn't told him about her past. Maybe she should lay it all out, show him clearly why she was broken. She could easily recite the story, had told it to herself ad nauseum. The problem was, although the explanation soothed her mind, it didn't heal her soul.

And why drag it out for him? He was supposed to be just another guy.

She felt his eyes upon her and risked a glance, knowing what she'd see. The hurt. He'd risked his undefended heart, and she'd sliced through it. She hadn't meant to, didn't realize, couldn't be skillful enough . . .

She'd been right to do it, of course, rational, logical, prudent. She wasn't ready for love. Not until she faced the razor wire waiting in the recesses of her darkest place. Not until she answered the question: why?

Why had her mother strayed? Why had her dad pulled away? Why had her real father abandoned her? And why did Jeff cheat?

She wanted to take it a step at a time. He wanted to take her hand and jump.

Foolish, reckless, beautiful man.

He couldn't know they'd hit a darkness more terrifying to her than a thousand Pasellys.

Candy poked her head around the bedroom doorway. Her plaintive meow spurred Zee to action. She swept her gaze from Rico to Fontina, who had resumed her seat on the couch. "I don't care if you go or stay," Zee said, "but I wish you'd trust me."

She crossed the living room, scooped the cat into her arms, and shut the bedroom door. In her bathroom, she slid to the floor and let the tears come, loosing emotion she'd held at bay since the nightmarish incident at the gas station.

Snuggled against her collarbone, Candy purred. Tension leached from Zee's limbs, flowing out along the river of soft vibrations. Her heart rate slowed.

Kitchen sounds trickled through the walls, the clunk of a cupboard door, water drumming into the hollow of the kettle. The music of Fontina's voice mingled with Rico's bass.

Zee's heart warmed. Despite what she said, she was glad they stayed. She wanted to share her burden.

Releasing Candy, she hauled herself to her feet. Her skin itched. She peeled off her sticky clothing, cranked the shower to hot, and soaked in the spray until the ice in her bones melted. Deliciously warm, she toweled herself dry and slipped into the bedroom to dress.

When she returned to the living room, Rico had settled on the couch, but whereas Fontina relaxed against an arm, he perched on the edge of the cushion.

"Tea?" Fontina offered Zee a cup.

She accepted and sank into the armchair. Candy curled into her lap.

Rico spoke first. "Sorry I yelled at you. The Pasellys—"

Zee held up her hand. "I know. And I don't blame you, after what happened today."

He started up from the couch, but she waved him back.

"What happened?" asked Fontina.

Zee inhaled the sweet fragrance of chamomile and lavender. It seemed to float up into her brain like a benevolent mist, soothing her agitated synapses. Loathe to disrupt the spreading sense of ease, she opted for the easier path. "You first," she said to Rico. "What did you want to tell me?"

He twisted a water bottle in his hands. "Louis Paselly is trouble. McNeary's failure slammed the family business. Louis invested a chunk, latest in a string of bad bets. Big sister got mad and cut him off."

Zee's eyes widened. Rico had continued to investigate, despite his assertion that the police had their man. Like her, he wasn't satisfied.

"Good. You're getting it." Coiled energy propelled Rico to his feet. He skirted the coffee table, paced toward the balcony, and turned, pinning Zee's eyes. "He always bought his way out of trouble. Now the spigot's off. He'll find another way to solve his problems." He closed the distance and punctuated his words with his water bottle. "If *he* killed McNeary, *you* are his problem."

Zee's breath caught in her throat. "Oh my god."

"What?" Rico and Fontina demanded as one.

Candy stirred and lifted her head. Zee stroked the soft fur, letting the silky texture soothe her until she regained control of her voice. She swallowed the lump in her throat and described the encounter at the gas station.

Rico's face darkened, his eyes chips of cobalt fire. "I told you. Leave this to the police."

Zee lifted her chin. "I'm not giving up just because some creep threatened me." She held Rico's stare until he broke contact.

He backed a step, then another. "You are so stubborn."

"Persistent. Anyway, I was invited to this party." Zee regretted the words the moment they left her mouth. He had conceded. The standoff had ended. Now she'd opened the door again.

Rico spun, brows pinched like dark spears.

Zee pointed to the couch. "Sit down. Please. And I'll tell you."

He grumbled an unintelligible complaint and settled beside Fontina. She laid a hand on his shoulder, which he did not shrug off. Her pacific touch: Zee resolved to learn that magic.

She allowed herself a slow breath. Candy purred in her lap, a tuning fork that spread through Zee's solar plexus. Her jumbled emotions sorted. Her thoughts cohered.

"I found a note on my car," she began. Matter-of-factly, she reported the conversations with Mary, Miranda, Shandra, and Bottmeyer.

When she finished, Rico ran a hand through the bristles of his soft black hair. "You're being played. I don't like it."

"I don't like it, either," said Zee. "But I tugged this string, and I'm going to follow it."

He rose and began pacing again, boots thunking against the floor. Typical when he was thinking. Sifting, weighing, looking for patterns as if his footsteps forged a path, clearing the useless data, saving the useful.

Zee hoped he would see the next step. Something niggled at her consciousness. She tried to focus on it, but like a faint star, it winked off when she strained to see it.

"Why would Shandra hide the fact that she knew Hawethorne?" said Fontina.

Zee nearly spilled her tea. It was as if Fontina reached into her mind and snagged that elusive pinpoint of light. "I wondered that, too."

"Something going on between them?" said Rico. He stopped pacing to sit on the arm of the couch.

Zee thought of Henry, nervous and sweating, and of Shandra's taunting. Hawethorne, though, was practically a cadaver, hardly someone with enough energy for a fling. "Unlikely," she said. "Though I believe her marriage isn't particularly fulfilling. And she admires Hawethorne's poetry. And passion."

"There," said Rico, as though that settled the matter.

"I wouldn't rule out Bottmeyer," said Zee. "Although for a while, I doubted he had the energy to do it."

"Bottmeyer has motive enough to hate McNeary," said Fontina.
"Forget Bottmeyer." Rico got to his feet again. "In fact, forget
all this. Paselly's involved. You're out of your league." He crossed
to Zee and stuck out his hand. "Give me the note. I'll take it to the
police. You need to stay out of this."

Frustration drove Zee to her feet, heedless of the startled Candy,
who leapt for safer territory. "I can't stay out of it. I'm a reporter
like you. And I feel an oblig—"

The electronic bird trilled from her phone. She snatched it from
her purse.

"*Now* you respond," he growled.

Zee ignored him. James Hawethorne had sent an email. A
phone number and three words:

Please call me.

CHAPTER 25

Hawethorne's email rooted Zee to her living room floor. Fontina and Rico stared at her.

Zee read the email again. She knew she would call Hawethorne as he asked, even though doing that would twine the murder's cold tentacles more firmly around her ankles.

Fontina rose from the couch. "What is it?" Rico's eyes held the same question.

Zee forced lightness into her voice. "An unexpected development for a story I'm working on."

Not exactly a lie.

Rico narrowed his eyes. His rapid breathing told her he was unconvinced. "Another not-so-subtle message from Paselly?"

"No." She laid the phone on the table and faced him. "And don't worry, you'll be the first person to know if any of his thugs contacts me again."

The furrows in his brow eased a fraction. "Call the police first, then me."

"Deal." She aimed a smile at both her friends. "Thank you for coming over, but now I need to get some work done. And I'm sure you have things to do."

Rico stretched his hand toward her. "The note."

"I'll take care of it." Zee broadened her smile. "Can't let Bernstow think I'm afraid of him."

"Got a point there." He held her gaze.

The concern smoldering in those blue depths nearly pulled Hawethorne's message from her. She sucked her lower lip, trapping her tongue. She could certainly make a simple phone call.

"I'll leave you to it," he said. One final glance didn't quite hide his tension. "Stay safe."

On her way out, Fontina wrapped Zee in a lime-scented hug. "Be careful."

When they'd gone, Zee grabbed her phone, stepped into her office, and sat at her desk. Her professional surroundings would keep her mind focused. This was, after all, a business call.

Hawethorne answered, his hoarse voice cutting in before the first ring ended. "Thank you for calling me back."

"Are you all right, Mister Hawethorne? What's going on?"

"I, I want to tell you something." He coughed and cleared his throat. "Something I didn't tell the police. Can we meet somewhere and talk?"

"If you know something, go to the police." Zee squelched the hypocritical stab from her conscience.

"I can't," he said. "I . . . it's too dangerous. I'm leaving and getting far away. But I can't go before I tell somebody." His voice cracked. "I trust you."

Ice gripped Zee's spine. Paselly had to be involved. Yet she couldn't refuse Hawethorne's request. "Where do you want to meet and when?"

"Ten o'clock tonight." The words came quickly. He'd thought about this. "The rest stop at exit 42."

"I'll be there."

Barely had he disconnected when she realized she shouldn't drive the Mini with only one headlight. It was illegal, not to mention dangerous. As if to affirm that recognition, rain pattered against her office window.

Maybe she could borrow Fontina's car.

"Thank you for calling," her friend's voicemail answered. "Please leave your number, and I will call you back. Be well."

Zee left a short message.

That task accomplished, she turned her attention to filing a police report. As she attached her photos to the online form, anger surged afresh. There was no way to connect the thug to his implement of destruction.

Caustic frustration burned in her chest. She hated feeling helpless. In her column, she tackled bureaucratic stupidity, mocking it to hold offenders to account. That tactic wouldn't work for this personal invasion of her space.

A temple bell tolled from her phone.

"First things first," said Fontina. "Of course, you can borrow my car. Do you need to leave your car at the repair shop?"

"I do," said Zee, "but not tonight." She related her conversation with Hawethorne.

"I feel uneasy about this," said Fontina. "If you hadn't just told us about that guy at the gas station, I'd make a joke about Hawethorne going all 'cloak and dagger.' But now it's . . . let me go with you."

Relief washed through Zee, but Fontina didn't need to be involved in this. "That's not necessary, though I appreciate the offer. I should be safe."

"You shouldn't go alone." Fontina's voice grew stern. "Remember, he wanted to kill McNeary, even if he didn't go through with it. And he sounds desperate."

"Which is why I'll be safe." Zee raised her voice against the rain drilling at her window. "He wants to tell me something, and it's not so he can then turn around and kill me."

Fontina drew in a breath. "The danger might not be from him."

The ice between Zee's shoulder blades returned. "How did I not realize that?" She could almost feel Fontina relax.

"That's why you have me. I'll pick you up at nine-thirty."

A FEW MINUTES BEFORE TEN, THEY PULLED into the rest stop, a lonely outpost set back from the highway and screened by a stand of trees. It was clear why Hawethorne had chosen this spot. A handful of vehicles dotted the parking area. Several lights were out, creating pools of darkness. Zee parked in one of those.

Fontina laid a hand on Zee's arm. "Take it slow. Give me time to find a place where I can observe and step in if I'm needed."

Zee squeezed her friend's hand. "Got it."

Light wind tugged at Zee's raincoat as she walked toward the vending area. A shape moved in the shadows. She tensed.

"It's me." Hawethorne spoke in a hoarse whisper. "Stay out of the light please." He motioned toward a shaded bench a few yards away. Zee fell in step behind him.

His shambling gait reminded her of Bottmeyer, wobbling in his cabin, but without the miasma of liquor. A cautious hand extended, she closed the gap to catch him if he lost his balance.

When they reached the bench, he collapsed in the center. Zee sat beside him on the damp wood and studied his slumped figure. His shabby jacket hung loosely as he leaned forward, forearms on his knees, head bowed, breathing heavily.

The back of Zee's neck prickled, but it was only Fontina, slipping among a cluster of softly dripping trees.

Hawethorne's breath sawed. Zee faced him. "I was surprised to get your email, Mister Hawethorne."

He raised a colorless face, made ghostlier by eyes that peered from great dark caves. Goosebumps pimpled Zee's arms. He seemed already dead.

"Call me James." He sucked in a raspy breath. "This isn't easy. But I don't have much time . . . and I have to help you." He squeezed his eyes shut and swallowed hard. "I wanted to kill him. I'm ashamed of that."

Fontina had been right, as usual.

Hawethorne pulled off his ball cap and scrubbed his hands through stringy hair. "Facing death, people say your priorities get clear." He laughed, a harsh rattle. "Not true. Mine disappeared down a black hole."

Pity constricted Zee's throat, but his self-recrimination wouldn't advance her investigation. "James," she said, "what do you want to tell me?"

He turned a despairing gaze on her. "I agreed to threaten him. Scare him so he'd get this guy his money."

Those tentacles Zee had felt in her living room crawled upward. "Who—"

He interrupted, the confession, once begun, pouring from his lips. "He was dead already. I didn't even have the satisfaction. And then, oh god, I was horrified to see it and relieved that I didn't do it and then horrified all over again because I knew I wanted to." He collapsed, coughing.

The contract had to be with Paselly, which is why Hawethorne wouldn't go to the police. Knowing she had to ask, she swallowed to ease the strangling in her throat. "Who hired you?"

His colorless lips stretched into a ghastly rictus. "He didn't give his name." He crushed the ballcap between his hands. "But his voice, squealy, snarly, like a trapped rodent."

Zee jolted backward, as if the last word could strike like a poisonous fang. She twisted on the bench, eyes darting.

Hawethorne jerked his emaciated frame upright. "What's wrong?"

Zee steadied herself and willed the tension from her voice. "I've heard of someone who fits that description. Not good things."

"All of them true, no doubt." He raked his fingers across his scalp, then pulled away his hand. "I'm sorry. It's rude to claw at my head. I don't like hats, but . . . I feel safer."

She understood his desire to hide, more than he knew, but she pushed. Sympathy could not override her need for information. "How did you come to this arrangement? Why didn't you tell the police?"

"He found *me*." Hawethorne shifted knobby shoulders beneath his jacket. "He offered money. And medicine is expensive. I was scared to tell the police."

Zee recalled the massive expenses involved in drug development. But driving a man to despair, costs like that didn't show up in a ledger.

Silent tears leaked from the dark recesses of his eyes. "What devil possessed me?" He brushed at his gray cheeks. "I hope I wouldn't have gone through with it."

His tortured frame bowed as if all the strength had left it. Whatever danger existed for her did not come from this broken man. He'd made a bad decision, contemplated doing a terrible thing, but he'd also been exploited in his vulnerability. Her coiled caution loosened. "None of us can be sure what we would do in an extremity."

"You're kind," he said. "But I didn't even call nine-one-one. I heard a noise in the next room, and I ran. Didn't even realize I dropped my knife."

"Someone else was there?" The spring tightened again.

Hawethorne's weary gaze met hers. "We both had a close call, didn't we?"

Zee nodded. An unlikely bond—a major shift from her first impression of him, stumbling into her in the lobby, both of them moments from a scene of death. She smiled at him, and in that moment, she glimpsed the man he had been. His eyes softened, and the light of intelligence glinted in them. His pasty skin even seemed to sag a little less.

He straightened. "Thank you for meeting with me."

In a nearby copse, Fontina moved. Startled, Zee lifted her hand to stop her.

"What is it?" Hawethorne attempted to stand.

"A friend." Zee eased him back onto the bench. "I was uncertain about meeting you here alone." She softened her voice to take the sting out of her admission.

Hawethorne's eyes roamed her face.

"Not police," Zee said. "Why don't I ask her to join us?"

He gave the briefest dip of his head.

Fontina emerged from the shadows. Zee made the introductions, and Fontina settled on the other side of the dying man.

It could have been a trick of the wind, but Zee felt measurably warmer.

Hawethorne's posture relaxed.

"Can you remember anything else about that morning?" Zee said.

He chewed dry lips, then shook his head. "I'm sorry. This disease, or the medicine . . ." He dropped his head into his hands.

Fontina touched his shoulder. "It's all right. You can reach us if something comes back to you."

He unbent. Zee thought he held himself more upright than when they'd met a short time ago.

"Where are you going now?" Fontina said.

"I don't know," he said. "I'll just drive. Find a place to stay. Then go on the next day and the next. Until I run out of days."

"You're out on bail," said Zee. "You can't leave the city."

"Don't you have anyone to stay with?" said Fontina.

Hawethorne shook his head.

An idea struck Zee. "What about Pete Bottmeyer?"

Hawethorne fixed her with a look of such profound sadness that it nearly stole her breath. "You wouldn't ask that if you knew," he said.

"I heard you and Pete were friends." Zee faltered.

"We are." Hawethorne winced as he shifted his bony body. "But Pete doesn't need me around right now. He's got enough problems."

"With his book, I know," said Zee.

Hawethorne pushed back the ballcap and scratched at his head. Filtered moonlight mottled his pained face. "That too, but I meant his daughter."

"Shandra?"

In the dim light, Zee could have been watching a silent movie. His face telegraphed empathy, but colored with wariness. Hawethorne knew a painful truth but was hesitant to speak it.

"Pete doted on her," he said. "He was devastated when Henry broke the engagement."

Broke the engagement? Bottmeyer had glossed over that detail.

Hawethorne exhaled a long, rattling sigh. Guardedness gave way. "I'm not sure it was such a bad thing."

Zee knit her brows. "I heard they had a rough patch."

He barked a laugh that ended in a cough. "That's putting it mildly." He lifted the cap and fanned himself. Moisture glistened through his thinning hair. "Shandra loved that guy. Seems he loved her. His parents, different story."

"They didn't want them to marry?" Zee said.

He scrubbed his hands across his face. "McNeary broke Pete. Financially. Some people put a lot of store in a big bank account."

Shandra lived in rose-leather luxury. "They must have resolved it," said Zee.

Hawethorne stared into the distance as though he'd forgotten them. "What people think they need." Bitterness dripped from his words. At himself? At the Somerworths?

Fontina laid a hand on his thin forearm. "Time to let it go."

Crumpling forward, he buried his head in his hands. He labored to draw air, then expelled it in a wracking cough.

Zee dug in her purse and found her water bottle. She pushed it toward him. "Here, take this."

He groped blindly, as another coughing spasm contorted his body. Zee pressed the bottle into his hand. He drank, cleared his throat, dragged his sleeve across his mouth. "Sorry."

"I don't like the idea of you going off into the sunset by yourself," Zee said.

Hawethorne wiped wet eyes. "I'll be all right. Hearing me out, it's a great burden lifted." He grimaced at Zee and Fontina. "One I just laid on you." He grasped Zee's fingers in his cadaverous hands. "You're young. You have energy. You'll see that justice is done."

"I will." Zee knew she shouldn't promise, but she couldn't bring herself to equivocate. She pressed her card into his palm. "Please call me if you need anything."

He pushed the card into his shirt pocket and eased to his feet. Zee refrained from helping him. Let him have what dignity he could manage. Observing with the air of a man taking his final leave, he turned in a circle, then shambled toward the parked cars.

As he disappeared beyond a pool of light, Zee turned to Fontina. "Now what?"

Fontina fingered Uncle Ramiz's coin. "When in doubt, get tea."

Fifteen minutes later, they huddled under eyeball-stabbing fluorescent light at a table inside a truck stop. The urn had dispensed hot water, and Fontina had produced packets of chamomile from her bag.

"Talk about bombshells," said Zee.

Fontina met her eyes. "I know what you're thinking."

"The connection with Paselly is unavoidable. And given what happened to me today . . ." Hoping to thaw the ice in her gut, Zee dared a sip of her steaming brew. It burned all the way down, but the fiery path melted some of her tension. Seeking to change the subject, she said, "Why did you step forward?"

"Something was missing in Hawethorne's confession. Like his words had woven a piece of cloth, but there was a big threadbare spot."

"He was holding back?"

Fontina shook her head. "Whatever he knew, he was unaware of its importance. He was ready to leave. I had to do something to stop him."

Zee sipped her tea. It no longer seared her throat, or maybe that first swallow numbed a layer of cells. She cast her mind over Fontina's conversation with Hawethorne. "Why'd you ask him where he planned to go?"

"It was the first question that came to mind."

Such a banal answer provoked a pang of disappointment. No intuitive leap, no hoped-for brilliant lead. She swallowed her discontent. "I felt terrible at his reply. Going off to die by himself."

"As did I." Fontina blew on her tea and sipped. "But if I hadn't asked, we would not have learned about the break-up and Henry's parents. And with that, the fabric of the confession felt complete."

Zee fell silent, digesting this. She doubted she would ever grasp the mysterious workings of Fontina's intuition.

Her gaze strayed to the display of doughnuts. Sweet, sugar-glazed, pillowy soft dough, they would melt in her mouth with every bite. Her stomach strained toward the tray in the glass case. 'Fresh,' the sign promised.

The bell over the door jangled Zee from her fantasy. Seriously? Truck-stop doughnuts?

She re-focused on Fontina. "I need to look further into the Somerworths."

"Careful, Zee-zee. They're a powerful family."

"Nothing I like more than mucking around in the basements of the untouchable elite." Zee yawned. "But not tonight."

Fontina checked her watch. "Nearly eleven. Way past my bedtime."

"Mine too. Candy's going to demand an explanation." Zee dredged up a weary laugh. "Or at least a cat treat."

CHAPTER 26

ZEE WOKE IN PRE-DAWN DARKNESS. In the twilight of neither sleep nor wakefulness, her mind churned: *Hawethorne. Bottmeyer. Shandra. Paselly. Broken headlight. Knives, shining clean and dripping red.*

She snorted, turned, punched the pillow. Wished for Rico. His muscled chest, his blue eyes, his strong hands. Hands she'd last seen extended for Shandra's note. The note Zee promised to deliver to the police . . . to Bernstow.

She threw back the covers. Fontina led a morning meditation on Sundays. Maybe that would calm the images careening in her head.

Her cellphone display read sixty-two degrees, good sweatshirt weather.

A news alert caught her eye. *Trash collectors settle dispute.*

She threw a fist into the air. "Hooray and halleluiah."

Candy raised her head and blinked.

Buoyed, Zee dressed in jeans, an indigo t-shirt, and her favorite teal sweatshirt. When she got to the parking lot, Venus winked at her from the sky.

First the promise of clean streets, now the favor of the goddess; all boded well.

Cool air scoured the remnants of sleep from her eyes. She

grinned at the paper cup dancing across the parking lot. "Let's go for a ride," she said to her Mini.

She drew up her mouth in a silent laugh. What giddiness infected her? She never talked to her car. Next thing she knew, she'd be giving it a name, like Fontina did with hers. Although according to Fontina, the automobiles named themselves. *Diana*, her current Spyder, honored the former Princess of Wales.

Zee regarded the Mini's shiny red exterior, white roof, and racing stripes. "You'll require an exciting name."

Her sporty car's broken headlight admonished her. She laid her hand on the hail-pocked hood. "I'm not getting any psychic messages. Guess for now I'll call you Master Po from the old *Kung Fu* series. Although he was totally blind, and you're only halfway."

She tapped her fingers against the metal. "So, half a name. *Po*."

Chuckling at her choice, she wound through nearly deserted streets. When she parked across from the still-dark windows of Integrated Life, the sun had begun to spread red-gold over the horizon.

Just as it had the morning of the murder.

A string of lilting notes signaled a text. She pulled out her cell: Rico. Warmth blossomed in her chest, banishing her previous dark memory. This day would hold no such malevolence.

She clicked open the message. *FYI: Knife not murder weapon. Be careful.* The comfort he'd brought died.

A realization peeked from a tiny corner of her mind. Until this moment, despite everything, she'd been harboring the possibility that Hawethorne might be proved the murderer. That meant the mystery was solved. It meant she was safe.

Rico's message decimated that illusion.

The killer was at large. And, thanks to her poking around, he probably knew her name.

She rolled down the Mini's window. Reining in her fear, she breathed in the quiet of the morning. No danger existed here on this peaceful street.

Her thoughts veered toward last night's meeting with Hawethorne. He'd said someone else was in McNeary's office. Logically, that person had needed to escape in a hurry. He couldn't know that Hawethorne wouldn't call the police.

A stroke of luck for him, they found Hawethorne's knife on the floor. Certain misdirection while the killer tossed the actual murder weapon.

Uneasiness nagged at the edge of her mind, a distant thought approaching. She didn't want to let it in, not this morning. She shook her head to derail the train.

Through her windshield, she focused on the burgeoning day. The first rays of sun caught the cross atop St. Stephen's spire, setting it afire. Across the street, a light bloomed inside Integrated Life. A pale rectangle shimmered on a pile of dark plastic trash bags.

Against her will, the thought-train chugged into her consciousness, hauling an image. Where she might find the murder weapon.

She grit her teeth. Not her job.

A voice in her head argued.

She snuffed it, reached for the door handle, hesitated.

If the trash collectors got there first, the knife could be buried forever.

If she acted . . .

She could crack this whole thing. That would take the fierceness out of Bernstow's hard bronze eyes. A grin crept across her face. She pulled her fingers from the handle and started the car.

"Our first adventure under your new name." She patted the dashboard. If Po questioned the wisdom of their inaugural escapade, he kept quiet.

McNeary's lab lay due north, a short distance as the crow flies. Unfortunately, the Mini needed to take the land route. Opting to avoid the great hulking construction of the Cardo Maxima Viaduct, she headed east, winding past the dilapidated dry cleaners and the chain-linked Roman Villa Apartments. She skirted Farm Fresh, where early shift workers labored behind brightly lit windows, then turned north, and crossed the railroad tracks, an obstacle the viaduct was designed to eliminate in time for Christmas.

On the corner of McNeary's block, a poster-size pile of potatoes dragged her eye from the road. She slowed, her gaze lingering on the golden mound of fried spears, their crisp edges sparkling with hard-edged crystals of salt.

Her stomach rumbled, reminding her she'd eaten only a handful of stale pretzels before leaving home. Potatoes were nutritious. Nothing wrong with French fries for breakfast.

Not now, ambition argued. *No time to waste.*

As she had twice before, she parked across the street from the four-story edifice that housed McNeary's lab. The buildings on the block eyed her like stone-faced guards, each before its deserted inner sanctum. She hoped the street remained empty until she secured her prize.

The image of victory quickened her steps across the parking lot and down the narrow strip of cracked concrete alongside the structure. At the end, she spotted her quarry, a large gray-green dumpster that squatted amid a pile of rubble.

She cast a mournful glance at her jeans and sweatshirt. Especially the teal sweatshirt. It sported the Roman Eagle logo of the Valerian Conquerors, the football team of her high school alma mater.

This was why she didn't work the crime beat.

Her chest tightened. She could call Rico, but he would scoff, then argue vociferously. She squeezed her shoulder blades to ease the tension. He'd change his tune when she recovered the murder weapon.

Having scoped the task, she returned to her car. An excavation in her zippered cargo carrier produced an old blue bandanna and a pair of gardening gloves, a remnant of the days before she realized how easily squirrels could plunder tomatoes on a third-floor balcony.

Once more, Rico intruded upon her thoughts. His idea to keep the gloves and bandanna in the trunk, along with a cache of plastic grocery bags and a few other potentially useful items she would have discarded.

Why was he *always* right?

A tiny voice suggested she linger on that thought.

Nonsense. With brisk movements, she folded the faded square of cotton into a triangle and tied it around her neck, then stuffed a couple of bags in her back pocket.

As she pulled on the gloves, she retraced her steps along the concrete strip and faced her adversary. The scarred metal box, five feet high and dented, bore the weathered remains of spray-painted gang tags and unidentifiable streaks of gray, brown, and muddy red.

Shunting aside speculation on the origin of the stains, she dragged a hunk of cinder block close to the dumpster, stepped up, and flipped back the lid.

It clanged against the back of the bin. Her eyes ricocheted in all directions. The last thing she needed was attention.

The alley remained empty. The metal reverberation faded.

She leaned over the open maw and jerked back, gagging. Stench billowed, drowning her in a miasma of rotting food and decomposing carcasses. She twisted to the side and blew out forcefully, squeezing her lungs until they felt like squashed bags. Head turned away, she sipped air, fighting the sensation of the reek crawling up her arm where she gripped the dumpster.

Maybe she should trust the police . . . just this once.

Her ears picked up the distant clank and whine of machinery. *Trash collectors.*

The yawning cavity beckoned, goading her.

Clenching her jaw, she secured the bandanna over her nose and mouth. Bernstow would thank her. Using the block to give herself a boost, she clambered over the lip and dropped inside.

She landed with a loud squish, staggered, and caught her balance. Breathing relief, she surveyed the dank cavern.

Lumpy shrouds sloped downward from one side, leaving a partly cleared space in which to work. Reason dictated the knife would not be inside a big trash bag, but she lifted one and examined it anyway. Wary, she patted across the surface. Nothing of note, no sharp protrusions. She set it to the side and picked up another.

Methodically, she worked her way through the pile. Beneath the top layer, she uncovered the disintegrating debris of consumption, coffee grounds, chicken bones, and oozing unidentifiable sludge.

No knife. Nothing even resembling a knife.

In the background, the noise of the trash truck waxed and waned as it worked its way through the streets. She bumped a foam carryout box. The lid sprang open, and flies boiled up from the gaping mouth, buzzing at her disturbance of their feast. She swatted at them, wishing she'd thought to cover her hair.

As she nudged aside the pool of slop, a slender object poked into view. Her breath caught. She used two fingers to grasp it and eased it from the goo.

A broken cane. Disgusted, she tossed it aside.

Lips clamped beneath the bandanna, she continued to burrow. Mounded bags rose in unsteady walls around her, shifting and settling with each fruitless addition.

Hopelessness gnawed at her resolve. This search was looking more and more like a bad idea, but she couldn't stop now.

A few inches from the bottom, she used her feet to sift the debris, bending periodically to stare at a potential find. She found nothing. Sludge seeped through the edges of her sneakers. The cloth over her face clogged, and she was forced to pull it away so she could breathe.

She prodded a bulky package. The smell of rotting meat ballooned in her face, rocking her back on her heels. Something crawled high on her cheek. She slapped at it and cringed, horrified at what she had just smeared across her skin.

A revolt threatened at the base of her esophagus.

The trash truck was only a few blocks away. She ought to quit now. Get out while she could. She was filthy, she stank, and she'd learned nothing.

Leaning against one slimy wall, she fought tears. With an effort of will, she called to mind Hawethorne's words. *You'll see that justice is done.* She had promised—like a fool.

As she pushed herself upright, her foot slid in the oily layer on the bottom of the bin and bumped something solid beneath a small lumpy mound.

It was oblong, but plumper than she expected if it hid the weapon. She pressed on it with her sodden shoe. The exterior yielded with a wet rustle and then resisted. Pulse quickening, she grasped the object with a thumb and finger and eased it free.

Her eyes picked out a bedraggled edge in the wrapping. She loosened it, forcing herself to move with care. A section of the outer layer separated with a staccato hiss. One after another, she pulled apart the sticky folds.

A gleam of metal caught her eye.

Her pulse jumped.

She steeled herself not to rush.

Another layer peeled. Her eyes probed like a miner seeking the glint of gold.

There.

Her heart soared. She'd done it. Then her mind assembled the fragmented impressions born of hope. She stared at the revealed object.

A broken, torn collapsible umbrella.

She flung the tattered filthy frame against the far wall. "Damn it to hell!" she cried, just as the open space above her went dark.

CHAPTER 27

SOMETHING LARGE AND HEAVY DROPPED through the dumpster opening and smacked Zee in the face. She screamed and flailed at the shifting mass. A bulky black garbage bag bounced off the front of her filthy shirt.

"What the crap?" A startled face appeared in the space above her. "Lady, what are you doing in there?"

In spite of herself, tears slid down Zee's grimy cheeks.

"Oh, never mind," said the young man. "Give me your hand."

"Thank you." Zee extended her hand, then realized it was smeared with gunk and studded with bits of flotsam. She stripped off her glove. "Sorry."

Wrist and forearm steadied in his strong grip, she grabbed the lip of the bin and clambered out.

Her rescuer released her quickly, stepped back, and scanned his uniform, an orange and brown shirt with the logo of a burger place stitched above the left breast pocket. Then, as if embarrassed by his self-concern, his pale cheeks flushed. Large blue eyes met hers as he pushed black-framed glasses higher on his shiny nose.

Zee collapsed on the cinder block. In the stronger daylight, she could see the mess she'd made of herself. Brownish-black sludge coated her shoes and spattered her jeans halfway to the knees. Unidentifiable rot clung in clumps to the sleeves of her sweatshirt.

She didn't care to think about what was sticking to her face. She combed slimy curls from her forehead. "Thank you again."

"Listen, lady, come across the street and I'll get you something to eat." He gestured toward the Big Ol' Burger on the corner. His face colored more deeply. "Sorry for dropping that on you, but ours is full. Stupid garbage guys."

Zee managed a smile for his sake. "I'm okay."

He slapped his forehead. "Oh, dopey me. You don't want to go into a restaurant like that; I get it. Sorry. Stay here and I'll bring you something."

Zee forced herself to her feet. "Really, I'm fine. I appreciate your help getting out of there." She turned away, then thought better of it. "You know you could help me. Do you have a couple more of those garbage bags? I could use them."

He cocked his head and pushed his glasses up again. "Okay, sure. Be right back."

He darted toward the street, and Zee settled again on her concrete perch. The seat of her jeans squelched, and she tried not to think about what soaked through to her clammy skin. What had she been thinking? Only an idiot would try something like this.

Guilty as charged.

She pulled at the hem of her putrid sweatshirt . . . probably ruined. She tugged it off, turned it inside out, and used the relatively clean interior to wipe her face and rub as much goo from her hair as possible.

Nearby, a car door slammed. Zee unburied her head from its grubby teal shroud and watched a pair of men stride down the alley toward her. As they crossed into the sunlight, she groaned. One wore a police uniform. The other she recognized.

"What have we here?" Detective Bernstow stopped a few feet from her, hands on his hips. The corners of his mouth twitched upward.

Zee mustered as much dignity as she could. "Good morning, Detective." She hid her clenched fists in the balled-up sweatshirt. "Just a citizen trying to help the police."

His amusement vanished.

Zee tried for conciliation. "This dumpster could have gotten emptied. You guys figured you had the murder weapon—"

"Every cop in the city's looking for that knife," Bernstow growled. "We don't need your help."

"Maybe you do," Zee snapped. Markham had pointed out Bernstow's budget frustration. "More eyes on the street."

He advanced a step. "Don't get smart."

The storm on his brow warned her she'd poked a sore spot. She shifted tactics. "Detective Bernstow, I regret that we got off to a bad start. The circumstances made this murder feel personal to me. That led to mistakes." She swallowed. Nasty tasting. She wished desperately for water. "I apologize."

The rigid lines in his face eased a fraction. "You should have listened to me back at the station."

"I know." She met his bronze eyes. "I wanted to. I still do. But I keep getting dragged back into this."

Sandy brows lowered. "Explain."

Zee sucked in a breath. "Hawethorne called me. Told me he was hired to threaten McNeary."

"What? When'd this happen?"

"Last night."

The hard lines reappeared. "And why am I finding this out *now*?"

Zee decided a bit of truth-stretching was in order. "It was midnight. I figured I could call you today."

"You should have called me right then. Better yet, you should have sent Hawethorne to me."

"He said he wouldn't talk to the police, only me. I didn't want to lose the chance." She spread her grimy hands. "At least this way we learned something."

Bernstow closed the remaining distance between them, jabbing his finger toward her, but stopping short of actually touching. "*We* didn't learn anything. There is no *we*. Get it?"

Zee raised her palms in surrender. "Yes, Detective."

He towered over her in silence. She lowered her eyes. He rocked on his feet as if considering his next move. When he spoke again, he had eased his commanding tone. "Did he say who hired him?"

"He didn't know, but he said the guy had a voice like a rodent." Zee's neck itched. She resisted scratching, then figured a hint of contamination could work to her advantage. She scraped her hand below her chin.

The ploy worked. Bernstow backed a step. "I don't suppose you know where Hawethorne is."

Zee shook her head and peeled away a curl that stuck to her cheek. "And while I'm confessing, there's more that could be connected."

He scowled. "Go on."

She detailed the threat and the damage to the Mini. "I filed a vandalism report, but I don't know if you got the information."

He screwed his face as if in thought. "We'll follow through on it." He hesitated. "Thank you."

Zee exhaled. Maybe Bernstow wasn't such a bad guy.

He scanned her, and the twitch returned to his lips. "You're not cut out for police work." Then, as if he caught himself softening, he roughened his voice. "Miss Morani, I'm choosing to believe you're only a klutz who bumbled into this investigation under the misguided notion that you're helping. But if I see you one more time, or I find out you've failed to provide me with pertinent information, I'm going to revise that evaluation. And you won't like the consequences." He lowered his face to fill her vision. "Understood?"

"Yes, sir." His words stung, but Zee kept her expression contrite. "Thank you."

A few feet away, the officer worked his hands into a pair of latex gloves.

Zee abdicated the cinder block. "Here, use this. I'm leaving."

Bernstow's eyes raked her. "Just a minute." He turned to the uniformed man. "Search her."

Zee thought to protest, but dismissed the idea. Best not to fail the first test of cooperation, even if she detected a barely concealed grin on the detective's face. Let him throw his weight around now. It might not land on her later.

"You *were* in there. I have to be sure you didn't take anything out." Bernstow wrinkled his nose. "Other than what's obvious."

She bit back an acerbic reply and submitted to an efficient but thorough pat-down.

The officer stepped back. "She's . . ." He rolled his eyes. "Clean."

Behind him, the young restaurant worker stood, mouth agape. Zee smiled and reached for the garbage bags. "Thank you for these."

Big Ol' Burger-boy gulped and thrust a brown paper bag toward her. "Here, I brought you some French fries." He glanced quickly at Bernstow. His voice cracked. "I found her here."

"Did she give you anything?" Bernstow barked.

The kid quaked and shook his head.

The detective jerked his thumb toward the burger joint. "You work over there?"

"Yes, sir." He nodded like a bobble-head doll.

"Okay." Bernstow dismissed him with a flick of his hand, which he broadened to include Zee. "You too," he said.

Zee let the young man get down the alley and then trudged to her car. She used the garbage bags to cover the driver's seat and seat back, then stared at her shoes. No amount of stomping and scraping would free them of their sticky coating. She pried them off, retrieved another plastic grocery bag from her pocket, and stuffed them inside. She added her grimy, slick socks.

Breathing a prayer that she wouldn't be busted for driving barefoot, she slid behind the wheel and started the engine. Even with the windows down, every movement vented gag-inducing vapors.

"I'm sorry, *Po*. Maybe you wish your *nose* had been broken. I wish mine was."

Her glance fell on the bag of fries. She pulled it open, buried her face in it, and inhaled. At least something in the car smelled good.

Zee lingered under the steaming shower, skin pink from scrubbing, hair squeaky from shampoo. *Nirvana*. As close as she hoped to get. When the water turned tepid, she abandoned her Eden for a fluffy bath towel.

"I'm *never* doing anything like that again, Candy-pants." She scratched behind soft orange ears. "Glad I didn't eat much breakfast, or I would have spoiled yet another trash receptacle. No matter that this one was already filthy."

Candy meowed, turned her slender body toward the kitchen, and flicked her tail.

"Right. You didn't volunteer to go hungry." Zee wrapped the towel around her and padded barefoot to the kitchen. She poured a serving of Tuna Surprise nuggets into a dish and set it on the floor. As Candy attacked the food with as much relish as her feline superiority would allow, Zee examined the contents in her refrigerator. Half a loaf of rye bread, one egg, and a dried heel of cheese. She shut the door with a thunk. "I deserve a treat."

After she pulled on sage-colored cotton pants and a melon-hued t-shirt, she spared a rueful glance at the bag containing her odiferous gym shoes. "Sandals, it is." On her way to the door, she grabbed a can of disinfectant spray.

The Mini smelled surprisingly fresh, but she dosed it for good measure. Any number of nasty microbes probably lurked from her excursion, despite her precautions. She stowed the canister in her trunk cargo carrier, Rico's voice in her ears. Never know when it might come in handy. Then she fired up the engine. She hoped Miranda was working today.

The black-haired barista welcomed her with a smile that bounced light from the stud in her wine-dark lips. "Hi! Nice to see you again."

The rich aroma of coffee coaxed excitement from Zee's taste buds. She returned Miranda's greeting and maneuvered past four people chattering at one of the tables. "Those look delicious." She gestured toward a tray of glazed pastries topped with slivered nuts.

"Almond horns." Miranda leaned forward, and the pink patch in her chopped hair winked into view. "Try one? They're to die for."

"Sounds good to me." Zee grinned, her spirit recharged. Talking to Miranda was like mainlining energy.

"I'll bring one over. Coffee?"

Zee nodded, then chose a table near the window.

The arc of the sun had taken it above the trees, and radiance lit a few tiny puddles remaining from yesterday's storm. Not a cloud marred the blue bowl of the sky.

"Beautiful day." Miranda set a mug of coffee and a small white plate on Zee's table. "Too bad I have to work. I'd be at the Minerva Festival."

"Is it the end of summer already?"

"Equinox today."

Zee sipped the coffee. Robust, rejuvenating . . . familiar. "Is this Dutch?"

"Great stuff, huh?"

Zee savored another velvet swallow.

"You going?" Miranda's question broke through Zee's reverie.

"To the Minerva? I just might."

The bell over the door jingled. "Let me know what you think of the almond horn," Miranda said as she turned toward the newcomer.

Zee bit off a tip. Buttery flakes melted on her tongue, leaving a slightly salty richness that was in turn supplanted by tiny, sweet grains of almond paste. The moist filling perfectly complemented the dry crunch of slivered almonds scattered across the top of the horn and held in place by the merest hint of sugary glaze.

She had not realized she'd closed her eyes.

Did she moan out loud?

None of the foursome at the other table stared at her. Miranda had ducked to retrieve a muffin from the display case. The man at the counter studied his phone.

Zee sipped her coffee, resolved to keep her gustatory enjoyment private, and indulged in another mouthful of delight.

Rico would mock-scold her dietary choice. Only because she complained her clothes no longer fit. He made it clear he thought every inch of her body was delectable.

The Minerva Festival: an afternoon at the park, children splashing in the lake, dogs romping, the entrancing smell of fresh popcorn, ordinary people doing ordinary things. After the morning she'd had, that sounded heavenly.

It would be even better shared with Rico.

She sipped the rich coffee. He hadn't been happy when he left yesterday, but he had given her the space she requested.

Maintaining friendship boundaries required practice. She pulled out her phone and punched his number. No time like the present.

CHAPTER 28

T HE BROAD SWATH OF LAWN IN CROSSWINDS PARK was polka-dotted with picnic blankets and knots and clusters of people enjoying the warm afternoon sun. Zee leaned back on her elbows and rested her gaze on distant Minerva, presiding over the fountain at the center of the artificial lake. The picnic Rico brought lay between them, a baguette of French bread, a wedge of dilled Havarti, a dish of soft butter, and a plate of enormous ripe strawberries.

All her favorites.

She inhaled, pushing to expand her ribs, but her chest felt unyielding as the golden breastplate shielding Minerva's shapely bosom. She was goddess of war, but as the owl perched on her right hand and the snake twining the spear in her left attested, she also ruled the arts and medicine. Zee wished for help from those quarters.

She wanted to accept Rico's food offerings as a thoughtful gesture, even an apology of sorts for the acrimony between them yesterday. After all, she was attempting a similar rapprochement with her invitation to the festival.

Why didn't his effort feel like enough?

Because his accusation scraped a sore spot on the inside of her breastbone.

He was wrong. She was not a coward, not weak, not a liar. And though he'd said none of those things yesterday in her apartment, she'd heard them all in his "later never comes." A judgment that slipped through her defenses like the blade of a stiletto.

The problem was, nothing could hurt like that unless it held a grain—or more—of truth.

Somewhere behind her, fingers began strumming a guitar. Hands joined in, patting bongos. A harmonica warbled. With children splashing at her feet, the compassionate goddess sent song to sweep up Zee's dark thoughts and balm to ease her heartache.

She breathed a prayer of thanks. Enough mucking through the ruins of life for one day. She'd figure it all out some other time.

She stretched her bare toes to graze the tips of Rico's polished leather boots. He reclined on one hip as a noble Roman might, devouring a huge red strawberry. All he needed was a toga.

The image brought a smile to her lips. Seconds later, the vision of draped fabric revealing his muscled arms and chiseled chest compelled her to dampen a quivering too deep for comfort.

Searching for a distraction, she picked up a diagonal slice of crusty bread, buttered it generously, and topped it with a thin slice of Havarti. She extended her hand to Rico. "Would you like?"

He reached for it. "Sunshine, sweet words, good food." He grinned. "Works for me."

The cincture in her chest loosened. Yesterday she had, almost literally, pushed him out the door. To be fair, he had blindsided her. Today, though, it seemed both of them wanted to restore ease to their friendship. Perhaps her plan, though more hope than strategy, was going to work.

She'd passed the first test, his offer of a ride to the park on the Harley. The proximity, the intimacy of wrapping her body around his, feeling the rumble of the powerful engine reverberating through her body. Too much too soon, she feared, at least for her. However, the other option was *Po*, redolent of dumpster. Not acceptable.

The music drifted through his soft dark hair. His cobalt eyes held Zee's as he bit through the brown crust, trailing a sprinkle of tender crumbs onto his black t-shirt.

He left them there. On purpose.

Or maybe it was Minerva teasing.

She resisted the urge to reach across and brush them from the taut muscled expanse.

Lifting his chin, he flashed an insouciant smile, teeth gleaming in contrast to the shadowy stubble along his jawline. "Some foods are not neat."

She met the dare in his gaze and picked up her tumbler of chardonnay. "They're often tasty, though."

He touched his plastic glass to hers. "Good things are worth the mess." The crinkle fell away from his eyes.

Zee averted hers.

Laughter like the tinkle of bells drew her attention to the Fanciful Fabrications yard art booth. A wizened old man reclined in a lawn chair, surrounded by whimsical animals created from old rakes, saws, springs, and other found pieces of metal. Under his kind, watchful gaze, a handful of giggling children circled, brushing their fingers along this year's signature attraction, a six-foot-tall dinosaur with an undulating spine fashioned from a vibrant red bike rack.

Close by, squeals peeled from youngsters playing in the shallow lake. The jets at Minerva's marble feet throttled to a mist, and rainbows winked on and off in the shifting breeze.

Zee swirled her wine, savoring the nuances of vanilla and clove. "This is *so* what I needed."

"After your morning dumpster diving?"

"Hey." She punched his arm, her fist just tapping his hard muscle. "You promised not to mention that again." Her skin tingled from knuckles to elbow.

Down, girl. Boundaries. Space.

He feigned a grimace at her assault. "Couldn't resist."

She took her cue from his banter. "Tsk, tsk. So little self-control. Good thing Burger Boy found me. You'd have taken pictures." She bracketed her cheeks with her hands in mock horror.

"You bet." He chuckled.

"Poor kid. And Bernstow only added to his anxiety." A smile touched her lips. "My guardian angel."

"Who? The kid or the cop?"

"Maybe I have more than one." Her index finger toyed with a lock of hair behind her ear. She jerked her hand away, rubbed the back of her neck instead, horrified at how close she'd come to twirling a curl.

Dial it back, oh goddess of medicine. There is such a thing as an overdose.

"Zee." Rico sat up and faced her. "Let's get serious for a moment."

Okay, enchantment broken. She studied his sober face in the dappled shade.

"This morning. You could have been in big trouble. You know you could be a suspect."

"That's ridiculous."

"It's not." His eyes pinned hers. "Standard procedure: police *always* suspect the person who found the body." Zee opened her mouth to object, but he held up his hand. "You dodged that. Then Bernstow catches you searching the dumpster. He could have hauled you in for obstruction." He ran a hand through his soft bristles. "Be glad you didn't find the knife. You'd be in a cell by now."

The wine churned in Zee's stomach. "I thought . . . the garbage strike was over, but—"

"Think of it his way. You claim you're trying to find the murder weapon. Who would do that? Then you spring Hawethorne's confession on him. He's got to wonder." He leaned closer. "Listen, Zee. Every time Bernstow turns around, you're there. You're *making* yourself the prime suspect."

Zee's eyes widened. "I didn't realize." She wrapped her arms around herself, suppressing vertigo. She hadn't seen any danger. Her ill-considered pledge to Hawethorne rose to haunt her. And yet she wanted, needed to honor it.

"You need to stay out of his way." Rico broke into her thoughts.

She straightened, scanned his grave countenance. "I'll be careful, and cooperative. But I can't do nothing. I made a promise." And she wasn't giving up on this story.

"I know." His finger trailed electricity along her jawline and rested beneath her chin. "I admire your sense of justice."

Her resistance melted in the pull of his magnetic blue gaze.

"If you *come across* any other information, get it to him immediately."

The spot on her chin sizzled. She nodded, not trusting her voice.

He laced his fingers in hers. "Or share it with me. I'll take care of it."

She lost herself in the comfort of his words. It would be a relief to stop slogging along on her own in this dangerous territory.

A small plastic football bounced a few feet away, shattering the hypnotic spell. It careened on a collision course with their picnic until Rico pinned it with a booted foot. He smiled at the boy who toddled over to retrieve it. "Quite an arm you got there."

The child's eyes lit at Rico's compliment.

Zee's heart warmed. He was a good man. He was good with kids, a good friend, too.

She left him talking with the animated boy and pillowed her head on her rolled-up jean jacket. The worn denim smelled of motor oil and Rico's scent, juniper and wild orange. Closing her eyes, she drew in a deep breath. This afternoon had turned out perfectly. They were easy with each other again. She winged a silent prayer of thanks to Minerva.

Laughter and conversation, low and throaty, wrapped her in a world of ordinary innocence, far from blood and death. The savory fragrance of corn on the cob floated by, supplanted by the mouth-watering aroma of fresh-from-the-oven, giant chocolate chip cookies. Perhaps she'd dispatch Rico to buy one.

As she cracked her eyelids, a chorus of shrieks erupted. Down near the edge of the lake, a young girl in a dripping swimsuit ran toward a group of adults. "Mom! Dad! Look!" At arm's length before her, she held something shiny.

Beside Zee, Rico jumped to his feet.

As girl crossed the lawn, a trail of other children followed, filling the air with shouts. Dogs caught the excitement, spreading the word along the canine information highway.

"Stay here," Rico said. He jogged toward the gaggle.

Heart thumping, Zee scrambled to stand. She squinted toward the scene, but could not discern what triggered Rico.

A crowd had gathered by the time the girl reached her destination. Voices rose, sharp-edged. The mass of bodies swallowed Rico.

"Where'd you get that?" A man's words cut through the melee.

Amid the jumble of sounds, heads turned in the direction of the lake. The girl's shrill wail lifted above the crowd. Zee searched the shifting throng for Rico while fear spread barbed tentacles through her midsection.

She stepped tentatively toward the commotion, but stopped at the appearance of a uniformed police officer. Knots of people loosened as she forced her way toward the center. Another officer arrived. Under his urging, the crowd dispersed, thinning to a sparse ring.

From her vantage, Zee angled for a better view and spotted Rico. His entire body telegraphed alarm.

The first officer patted the sniffling girl's shoulder and held out a hand toward an older man. He laid something gleaming in her blue-gloved palm.

Rico whirled and sprinted back to Zee.

"What's going on?" she said.

He snatched the bread and threw it into a canvas bag, his face stormy. "We need to get out of here. They just found the murder weapon."

CHAPTER 29

Across the lawn, the excited crowd shifted and buzzed around the girl, the cops, and the newly discovered knife. Rico knelt on their blanket and tugged Zee's arm. "Help me get this stuff." He shoveled picnic items into a bag.

Zee bent to close the wine bottle. Her mind reeled. "The murder weapon's here? In the park?"

Her eyes strayed over his shoulder. One police officer followed the girl who found the knife as she led him toward the lake. The other officer hurried in a different direction, cradling the dripping knife in her blue-gloved hand.

Rico bundled their blanket. "We need to go before you get sucked into this."

She snapped her head side to side.

"Relax." He circled her waist with his arm, drew her close, and murmured in her ear. "We're just a couple leaving the festival."

His lips brushed her cheek as he spoke. With an effort, she did not lift hers to meet them. "Right," she breathed.

Easing his embrace, he twined their fingers. "Casual. Don't attract attention."

Hand enmeshed in his, she matched his pace across the lawn, trying to quell the uptick in her heart rate. When they reached the Harley, Rico stowed the picnic bag and wadded blanket. "I'll take you home. Then head to the station."

"I'm going, too."

He drilled her with his eyes. "You forget Bernstow already?"

She fought the urge to scream. "It's damn frustrating. This is my story, and I can't follow it up."

"There'll be other stories." He brushed his thumb along her jawline, trailing fire. "Other chances."

An argument chafed in Zee's throat, but she suppressed it. When she got home, she could always take half-blind Po . . . and hope she didn't get a ticket.

Which might be the least of her problems. Rico was right; she was already on the detective's radar. One more link—however incidental—between herself and the murder, and she'd jump from the periphery to the crosshairs.

Arrive with Rico, and she brought down destruction. Arrive without him, and she'd learn nothing. With more vehemence than necessary, she snapped on the helmet and mounted the bike.

As the engine growled to life, she wrapped her arms around his waist. Her body vibrated, synchronizing with his. Her irritation crumbled. None of this catastrophe was his fault.

They thundered out of the parking lot. Snugged against his leather jacket, she gave into the ride. Her curls whipped in the wind. Her heart thudded in her chest. The roar of the Road King swept her mind clean. She lost herself in the sensation of flying, open on all sides to the landscape around her, feet on the pegs, inches from the long gleaming exhaust pipes and the blur of asphalt beneath them.

At a stoplight, she leaned back and caught her breath. Late afternoon sun bathed leafy maples, brick facades, wrought iron light fixtures—even the ubiquitous garbage bags—in honeyed light. She inhaled, drawing in the golden moment. Beneath the face shield, she tasted the scent of his after-shave. Woody, clean, spicy with a tang of citrus, and of course, undertones of motor oil and leather.

When the traffic light changed, she closed her eyes and nestled against his back. The engine revved, and the Harley glided forward.

A rumble erupted on their right. Rico's shoulders tensed beneath her cheek, and the bike slowed.

The braking force pressed her to him, warm, solid, safe. Acceleration eased them apart once more, freedom, exhilaration. The dance of nature's forces. Their dance.

The bike picked up speed, then slowed again. Rico cursed under his breath. Curiosity prompted Zee to abandon her sightless cocoon and peek over his shoulder.

The huge tailgate of a dirty black Chevy pickup dominated the view. Zee's spine branched ice. Surely, this couldn't be the same one that followed her down the country road and trapped her at the gas station, where the thug left his warning in the shards of her headlight. She imposed temperate logic on her frozen fear. These trucks were commonplace, no threat.

Hoisted on oversized tires, the behemoth lumbered down the road. As Rico followed the black monster's sedate pace, he wove the Harley right and left. The Chevy repeatedly skewed in front of him, thwarting any attempt to pass.

Zee wished she had a bullhorn. A few choice words would wake up this clueless driver. Maybe the blockhead was drunk. Or just liked messing with people. Zee squashed the idea of malevolent intent. All the same, she craned her neck to see the license plate. Mud covered it.

Her jaw clenched, mirroring the tightness in Rico's corded neck. She willed herself to relax. Perhaps she could ease his impatience by osmosis.

A clear path opened on the left. Rico's shoulders loosened, and he goosed the gas. Relaxing, she leaned with the bike's slant.

Rubber screeched against her eardrums.

Rico shifted his weight. The Harley's brakes grabbed. Momentum propelled Zee hard against his back. As the bike's tires squealed, the Road King's massive frame inclined, wavered, then tilted farther and farther.

She clamped her knees against the sides of the seat, gripping with all the strength in her legs. A patch of roadway reared, reached for her.

Fire ignited along her arm and shoulder. Her helmet slammed the surface. The world screeched to a halt and dissolved into cacophonous darkness.

She opened her eyes to find she lay sideways, partly beneath the bike. Arms clasped around Rico, her body jangled with a thousand alarms. As she lifted her head, stars swam into her vision. Her gorge rose.

Breathe.

She scanned the sensations engulfing her: throbbing elbow and shoulder where the bike had hurtled into the asphalt, searing sharp-edged needles where she'd been dragged along it. She flexed gingerly: fingers, toes, arms, legs. Everything worked.

A careful inhalation. Ribs hurt but no piercing pain.

Rico lay still.

Fear lanced through Zee's midsection. She tried to speak to him, but managed only a raw croak.

Her head seemed a hand's breadth from the pickup's huge rear tires. The truck's engine rumbled, echoing along its greasy, mud-encrusted undercarriage, gagging her with the stench of burnt rubber and exhaust fumes.

Terror liquified her joints. The front half of the bike was under the truck. If the driver moved . . . She had to get out . . . and help Rico.

She forced down the trembling in her shocked limbs. Jerking, clumsy, fighting for coordination, she scrabbled free of the Harley and crawled up next to Rico's head.

He stirred, coughed, lifted on one elbow. "You all right?" His voice was muzzy through the face shield.

A wave of relief dizzied her. "I think so. You?"

"Good enough." He took in the situation. "You get out of here."

"Not without you." She heaved against the saddlebag and managed to nudge the heavy bike.

"I got this. Go," he said. "Please."

He'd be fine. He knew what he was doing. She didn't move, couldn't bring herself to leave him. She stared, unsure how to help, as he wrestled free of the bike.

"Come on." He grabbed her hand. Together they stumbled to the side of the road.

At the curb, she sank into a sitting position and, mindful of a mounting headache, eased off her helmet. Tiny firebolts pricked her eyes. She waited until the bright points faded, then stared at the scene on the road.

Rico had managed to lay the bike down without hitting the Chevy. The Road King sustained scrapes and dents but otherwise looked free of major damage.

Rico removed his helmet and ran a hand across his matted black hair. "Son of a bitch brake-checked me."

Zee's sluggish mind struggled to decode the statement.

"He *meant* to wreck me." He laid his helmet on the ground and maneuvered to his feet. As if waiting for him, the truck gears clanked and its engine roared. The massive black monster pulled forward at an angle and then backed over the Harley, crippling the front wheel. Just before the beast peeled away, Zee glimpsed a jagged depression in the front grill.

She broke her stunned silence. "What the *hell*?"

Rico staggered backward as though he'd been sledgehammered. He broke into a run after the truck, but a few feet down the road, faltered to a stop and spun toward the mangled carnage of his bike.

Zee scrambled to rise, overriding her stiff limbs and the stab of pain across her shoulder. As she fought another wave of vertigo, Rico reached the felled Harley. He stood at the untimely grave, fists clenched.

On unsteady feet, she ran toward his rigid figure, tripped, and pitched forward. For a sickening moment, she teetered on the edge of balance. Her eyes took in every stony shard of gravel, every jagged fragment of rock. The roadway wavered and shifted, then raced toward her flailing arms. She squeezed her eyes shut and braced for the impact.

It did not come.

Strong arms broke her fall.

Rico pulled her upright and crushed her to his chest, where she buckled against him. She hung, unable to find any strength in her legs. Gradually, her trembling eased. When she straightened, he loosened his embrace but did not release her.

"Zee." He lifted her chin. "I *will* get the guy who did this."

"It's Paselly, I know it. He's trying to scare me off." She met his dark eyes with a fierceness that surprised her. "And *we* will get him." Her gaze caressed his stubbled jawline and lingered in the narrow crevice formed by his parted lips.

He brushed his thumb across her wet cheek. When had she started to cry?

"Don't worry," she said. "I won't fall apart."

"I know." He fingered a tangled curl on her forehead. "You're stronger than I give you credit for."

His breath held traces of strawberries from their picnic. She hungered to taste them, to taste him.

Don't do it.

The distance between them shrank.

Was she moving? Was he?

She willed to hold her boundaries.

Her body refused.

Trembling fingers burrowed into the soft bristles behind his ears. Under the slightest pressure, he yielded.

She opened her mouth to his, gave herself to the rising flames that threatened to devour her. The truth was so obvious, she couldn't remember why she thought she should deny it. His low growl obliterated the last vestige of her resistance. Blood roared in her ears as she melted into him.

The world shrank to the tide of their breathing. She rode the ebb and flow while he tightened his embrace, dug his fingers into her curls, and answered her passion with his.

"Need help?"

They broke apart, their abrupt separation like an electric jolt. She turned toward the source of the interruption.

A middle-aged man climbed out of his car. "You two okay?"

CHAPTER 30

$\mathbf{L}$EANING ON FONTINA'S ARM, ZEE COMPELLED her stiff legs to
negotiate the few steps from the elevator. "I didn't know there
were so many places a body could hurt."

Fontina slipped a key into Zee's lock. "I have a few tricks up my
sleeve that might help with that." One arm around Zee's waist, she
guided her through the door and over to the couch. "Rest here. I'm
going to run you a nice medicinal bath."

Zee wanted nothing more than to collapse, slowly and carefully, in solitude. "You've done enough. I already ruined your dinner with Emilio and his parents."

Fontina shook her massed black waves. "Nonsense. Everyone
understood." She lifted one brow. "Although I am a bit surprised
that Rico didn't insist on taking you to urgent care. He could have
dealt with his bike later."

An electric current swept across Zee's lips at the memory of their
kiss. She shut out the sensation, unprepared to handle Fontina's
intuition. "I could see he was torn. I called you to relieve the pressure." *In more ways than one.* She sank against the cushions, imagining what might be happening if Rico had brought her home.
Stop.

Fontina pulled back. "Did I hurt you?"

"Oh." Had she spoken out loud? "No. I was reliving . . . the crash."

The brown eyes narrowed.

Zee endured the searching gaze until she could stand no more. "Look, I'd just declared that I wouldn't fall apart. I was showing him I could handle my own problem. So, he could be free to handle his."

A smile spread across Fontina's features. "Good for you. The best relationships are built by equal partners."

Rico's ardor had certainly matched Zee's. His surrender, too. What might they have done had they not been interrupted?

Fire scorched in her face. If she didn't get rid of Fontina, she'd spill the whole story. And she wasn't ready to do that. Not until she understood it better herself.

She dredged up enough energy to speak. "I'm okay now. You can go. Really. I'll take care of myself."

Hands on the hips of her figure-hugging scarlet dress, Fontina fixed Zee with a stern gaze. "Zee-zee, I'm not a taxi. I don't just take you for medical care and drop you off at home. You're having a healing bath, and I'll see you safely tucked in bed before I leave." She turned on her heel and disappeared into the bedroom.

Too depleted to protest, Zee turned sideways and reclined on the couch. If she moved with care, she could minimize reminders of the assault on her body. When the bike began to go over, she'd reacted as Rico taught her, bringing her knees up tightly inside the roll bars. Her rigid musculature protected her, but at the price of widespread pervasive soreness.

Her shoulder and elbow stung, despite the numbing ointment applied by the nurse. The unforgiving pavement had lacerated her skin and embedded threads, gravel bits, and other debris in an angry seeping rash.

She grimaced at the plastic bag Fontina had left near the coffee table. Her shredded jean jacket, another wardrobe casualty of this investigation.

Candy trotted toward her. Sounds of running water floated out, along with Fontina's lilting hum. Zee extended an arm. "She's creating healing vibes, Candy-pants."

The cat yawned, stretched, and crawled up beside her. Zee stroked the soft orange-and-cream fur and reveled in the comfort created by this small ball of warmth and the animal intuition that guided Candy to choose a safe resting spot. As if accepting her due, Candy arranged her face in her best inscrutable expression and blinked.

Zee closed her eyes. Her body burned with the memory of his, pressed against her. His arms, his legs, his chest, his hands, his lips. She sucked in a breath and shook her head to loosen the power of the image. *Big mistake.* Cymbals clashed inside her skull.

Part of her wanted to dissect the experience, unravel its meaning for their relationship, but her synapses were busy firing pain signals. Analysis would have to wait.

Unwelcome, a warning arose. As she well knew, good decisions were not made in the heat of a crisis. She and Rico might have fallen prey to shock, given into the raw physical need for comfort.

The clanging in her head subsided to a throbbing ache. Each pulse rippled through her body. She would be smart not to read too much into that moment with him. Right now, he was probably questioning his rash behavior. She must leave him a graceful way to retreat.

Oh, who was she kidding? He wasn't the one with doubts.

"Bath's ready, Zee-zee." Fontina dropped a lifeline into Zee's whirling thoughts.

An hour and a half later, Zee lay in bed, the day's events banished behind a scrim of tea laced with an herbal supplement and a dash of brandy. Despite her exhaustion and Fontina's ministrations, sleep refused to lower its velvet curtain. Her mind wandered. Tension snuck into her heavy limbs, hijacking their peace.

Maybe a little more brandy.

She levered her distressed physique from the bed and shuffled to the kitchen. Accompanied by a small glass of brandy, she positioned herself on the couch, feet propped on a pillow on the coffee table, and channel-surfed.

Candy crept up beside her. Feline, and then human, fell asleep.

Zee woke with a cough. Beyond the flickering television, darkness cloaked her balcony. She swallowed to moisten her dry mouth and stretched her stiff neck with exaggerated care. Surprisingly little pain. Bless Fontina.

On the screen, a hard-nosed detective was grilling a young suspect. Under garish light, he paced the interrogation room, badgering and taunting the youth. Zee snorted. Police didn't act like that anymore, did they? She hit the power button, yawned with caution, and pushed herself to her feet. Time to get her battered body to bed.

As she settled her head onto the pillow, the detective's actions reverberated at the edges of her awareness. The scene had sparked an idea in her, a different way to look at the murder. Though she reached for the memory, she couldn't grasp it.

She should call Rico. He might see what she could not. Halfway to the phone, weariness overtook her hand. She sank against the pillows, heavy eyes shuttered.

Maybe tomorrow.

CHAPTER 31

A MID-MORNING TIDE OF SUNLIGHT ROLLED ACROSS the folds of Zee's cotton bedspread. Overnight, her limbs had stiffened. Fiery cables stretched from her shoulder to her elbow.

Outrage flared as yesterday's scene came back to her: the roar of the truck, the mangled bike, Rico's still body. She sucked a quick breath at the sharpness of the memory. The moment before he moved. It was as if she'd been shot in the chest with a nail gun.

A furry head wriggled beneath her hand. Zee stroked it, breathing carefully while her heart stitched up the wound. The effort exhausted her. "How about I stay in bed all day, Candy-pants?"

The cat apparently thought little of the idea. She leapt onto Zee's midsection, provoking a needle-sharp spasm, which she amplified by pacing to and fro.

Zee's efforts to soothe her met with increasingly indignant yowls. "Slave-driver." Capitulating, Zee shifted her legs over the edge of the bed and dumped the cat to the floor.

Her head drummed its objection to movement, and she groaned.

Candy shot her a look, as if to say it served her right, then turned, tail high as a crown, and stalked toward the kitchen.

Zee shambled after her. "Food's coming, you tyrant."

With a grunt, she reached for the Tuna Surprise, then stopped with bag in hand, stymied by the dish on the floor. Bending was out of the question. Her head, heavy as a bowling ball, might fall off. Also impossible were squatting, kneeling, or sitting, not with muscles already on fire. Perhaps she could just let an avalanche of nuggets fall from the bag. *Some* of them would hit the target.

Candy twined herself around Zee's ankles and locked eyes with her.

"New plan." Zee set a cereal bowl on the counter and made a show of scooping a portion of food into it. "Just for today." She slid it toward Candy. "We will *not* make a habit of this."

Monumental task completed, she swallowed pain medicine and made for the couch.

Zee cracked her eyes. Sun filled the living room with benevolent light, casting rainbows from the crystal vase on the end table, and transforming her favorite decorative pillows into glimmering jade and garnet. Even her mother's antique floor lamp, a usually somber rod of wrought iron, lost its stern face as golden light burnished its pebbled surface.

She raised herself on one elbow. Her head throbbed, but it didn't threaten to topple from her neck. The pain from her other injuries had also lessened, though she felt stiff and sore, and her skin burned where the asphalt had done its damage.

Candy, indicating she had forgiven Zee's earlier behavioral infraction, meowed and leapt up beside her. Zee ruffled the soft fur. "I'm hungry, Candy-pants. That's a good sign."

After a few shaky steps, she found her balance and crossed to the bedroom bath. A careful splash of cold water refreshed her face; a toothbrush erased the brandy film from her mouth. She shrugged at her wild curls in the mirror. A shower was the only way to tame them. That wasn't an option with the bandages on her arm. And her ablutions had sharpened the need for nutrition.

She dropped her last bagel in the toaster and leaned on the counter, surveying the apartment's spacious living area. The generous illumination that cheered her also highlighted the accumulated dust and clutter, including the garbage bag that held her clothing from the dumpster excursion. It looked innocent, sitting there. Only Candy, who sniffed and backed away as if physically struck, divined its secret.

A memory tickled the edge of her consciousness. She held her breath, hoping to coax it from the shadows. The detective paced, sneered at the young suspect, needled him.

With a clank, the toaster sprang the bagel, shattering her focus. Zee started to shake her head in annoyance and thought better of it. Instead, she lifted her hands in front of her, palms out, as if to stop her spinning thoughts.

Maybe she should take a break from murder today.

Usually, vigorous activity could silence her squirrel-in-a-cage mind, but that was out of the question. Still, the idea of cleaning appealed to her. Reasserting control of her life. Progress would be slow, but who cared?

She ate her buttered bagel standing, eager to begin. Though her legs protested, she lugged a basket of clothes to the shared basement facilities. She dropped her rank dumpster-diving outfit, including the soiled shoes, in the washer.

Back upstairs, she rested a few minutes to catch her breath, then put on a blues-rock CD and got to work, albeit at half-speed. When she carried a pile of mail to her desk, her blank computer monitor precipitated a twinge of anxiety.

Her next column was due on Wednesday, two days away.

She chewed her lip. Her back argued for sitting. Her mind countered. She knew where thinking would lead her. "Later," she promised the impassive screen.

Instead, she tackled the dusting. As she wiped and rubbed, her muscles loosened and her steps lightened. A snatch of boogie notes escaped her lips. She must ask Fontina what she infused in that bath.

Her sneakers proved reclaimable, another delightful discovery. When she set them to dry on the balcony, her stomach grumbled.

Too late she realized her limited energy might have been better spent getting groceries.

Elves had not stocked the refrigerator since yesterday, though she did unearth a bottle of ketchup and a container of what might have been rice in a previous incarnation. The freezer offered a better choice, pistachio ice cream.

Nuts and milk were healthy. She'd shop later.

She lifted out the carton, dismayed at its light weight. It might not offer as much nourishment as she hoped. As she began to close the door, a frost-coated, oblong object caught her eye. She pulled it free.

A microwavable burrito.

Restraining the urge to throw her arms up in victory, she performed a small bow for this manna and tore off the wrapper. She purposely declined to check the 'use-by' date. Best not to look too closely at a gift from the refrigerator god.

As she ate her tortilla-wrapped beef, beans, and cheese, only a bit leathery with age, she took stock of her physical state: no fearful knot in her stomach, no watchful tightness in her shoulders, no frustrated tension in her brow. Only clean, honest achiness from hard work. Okay, and from yesterday's assault, but that was fading. Despite the overall soreness, she felt refreshed.

She glanced toward her office, the next target of her ministrations. The monitor's blank countenance reprimanded her professional negligence. Another unrelenting boss, did it take lessons from Candy?

The thought brought a smile and a solution. She would buy off her conscience with one quick phone call. Set up an interview tomorrow with Mercy to learn about CRISPR.

She hoped he would be in a cooperative mood. He'd threatened someone in the phone conversation she'd overheard. A frisson of unease rippled through her stomach at the memory. On the other hand, that might have been the burrito.

"I'm being ridiculous," she said aloud.

From her perch atop the couch, Candy executed a slow blink. Zee ruffled her fur. "Glad you agree."

A trip through a telephone labyrinth finally landed her in Jules Mercy's office. "He's out this week," a bored male voice informed her.

There went a great plan. "Can I make an appointment for next week?"

"Um." The voice hesitated. "I'm not sure what his schedule is."

Zee's patience frayed. "Can you check?"

"Well, here's the thing. He's in South America with some doctors who are treating poor people in villages. And the lady who usually takes care of this stuff is at lunch right now."

God, Mercy really was a saint—or he was Jekyll and Hyde. "Okay, never mind." Her brain tickled. That trip could be a cover story. "What's the name of that group?"

"Um, I don't know. Think it's in a foreign language or something."

Zee repressed the urge to gnash her teeth. It would only make her jaw hurt. "All right. I'll call later."

Relief sprouted in the young man's voice. "That'd be great."

For a moment, she considered asking him to transfer her to O'Deneigh. He or one of his companions had said if the police hadn't arrested Hawethorne, they would be looking at Mercy.

However, working the phone system might be beyond the young man's capacity. And the clarity of simple cleaning beckoned her to return. There was always tomorrow.

After a third CD, Zee opted for big band swing. She'd just piled her dried clothing on the bed to sort and fold when a motorcycle roared from her phone.

She answered with a spring in her voice.

"You sound good," Rico said.

"I'm definitely better than I expected." She inspected her still-stained sweatshirt with a pang of regret.

"I . . . after yesterday . . ." He seemed to choose his words with care. "I'm glad."

Glad she was recovering? Glad they kissed? Glad they stopped? "Is that swing?" He broke into her thoughts. "You must be cleaning."

How well he knew her. *Though not well enough.* "The place needed it. How are you?"

"Okay. Listen, I got news." His voice became brisk. "The knife the kid found? Turns out it's special-order. Commissioned for Pete Bottmeyer."

Zee gulped air.

"Hey, you all right?"

Zee nodded and then felt foolish. "Just a sad end for such a talented man." She recalled the writer's dingy cabin, his drunken rage, her shock when he hurled the liquor glass.

"Gotta go." Rico's voice pulled her from the memory. "They're bringing him in. Get that note to the police and you're done."

The note again. Zee cringed. "Will do."

She searched for something to say, so her false promise wouldn't be the last thing he heard. "How's the bike?" she blurted and immediately regretted bringing up the painful subject.

"Bad." He clipped the words. "But Eddie'll fix it."

Zee felt the ghost of Rico's embrace, his lips on hers. If only she knew his feelings. She cast about for a neutral, but open-ended, response. "Helluva day."

"I'm handling it."

He probably referred to his Road King, but he could have meant her, them, that moment. She suppressed disappointment. After all, distance was safer. "Good." Her response left the lump in her throat, but she could think of nothing else to say, short of directly asking him.

"Gotta move." *All business.* "I'll keep you posted."

She returned to sorting and folding the laundry, but peace had fled. She and Fontina had suspected Bottmeyer. They'd been proven right. Yet her restless mind continued to sift what she knew.

Zee cocked her head to look sideways. "Come on, Shelby, help me see through this mess." She sank to the edge of the bed, as the memory of last night's scene on the television replayed.

Her breath quickened. The detective's behavior—that's what snagged in a crevice of her addled brain the night before. She dug her fingers into the crack. Her thoughts shifted to Shandra and her husband. There was something highly suspect in that relationship. The way Shandra needled Henry, a smug cat toying with a mouse. Why did he submit to her taunts?

A switch flipped, as if her mind had patiently waited for her to lift her gaze from the shadows. The truth blazed like a neon sign.

Henry did it.

Henry murdered McNeary.

CHAPTER 32

H ENRY SOMERWORTH KILLED IAN McNEARY. Zee should have
seen it sooner.

Her body buzzed like a live wire. She needed to call Bernstow.
He was going after Bottmeyer, but the detective didn't know what
she knew.

She tossed the half-folded t-shirt on the bed and hurried to
the living room for her phone. From her perch on the arm of the
couch, Candy perked her ears.

"You feel it, too, don't you?" Zee said. "I've solved the case."

Elegant whiskers twitched.

Zee paused her finger over the number pad. "You're right,
Candy-pants. This kind of news should be delivered in person."
She allowed herself a chuckle. "I can't wait to see the look on
Bernstow's face."

Although . . . Rico should share her triumph. She started to
scroll to his number, but stopped. He would be at the station
already, waiting for the police to bring in Bottmeyer. She grinned,
imagining his pride. Who knew that cooperating with the police
would be this rewarding? Only a week ago, they'd been the enemy.

All the weariness from the day's cleaning vanished. She changed
into fresh jeans and a sweatshirt, dumped Tuna Delight nuggets
into the cat dish, and snagged her keys from the demilune table

by the door. "Don't wait up, Candy. After this, I'm going out to celebrate."

As she headed down the stairs, her mind churned, assembling a logical presentation even Bernstow couldn't dismiss. She could easily demolish the first hurdle. True, the murder weapon belonged to Bottmeyer. That didn't mean he used it.

Her major weapon was Shandra's taunting mockery of Henry. She must impress upon Bernstow that Henry tolerated such treatment because his wife knew he was a killer.

And when the detective demanded more than that, Zee would relay Veronique's description of the man in the hallway. A scrawny man with an over-large head, emphasized by his hat—undeniably Henry.

She pushed through the door and drew a deep draught of crisp air. Her mind felt as clear as the evening sky. All the pieces connected, like stars in a constellation.

Except . . .

A tiny doubt wriggled in her brain. What was Henry's motive?

Bottmeyer had a clear one, financial ruin. According to Hawethorne, that devastation caused Henry to call off the wedding.

Car door half-open, Zee froze. Broken engagement—she knew that pain. She held her breath, braced for the piercing stab of Jeff's betrayal.

It did not come.

A deep ache pulsed in her chest, but the razor sting was absent. For the first time in memory, thinking of Jeff didn't feel like a knife in her heart.

She sank into the driver's seat. Carefully, she exhaled. She wanted to trust this unexpected relief, but if she looked too closely, the mirage of grace might dissolve.

If it didn't dissolve, though. If it was true . . .

She tasted Rico's strawberry kiss.

Gently, she laid the precious gift aside. After she fulfilled this evening's obligation, she could return to cherish it and ponder what it might mean for her and Rico. For now, it had illumined more clearly Henry's motive.

She pushed the Mini's *Start* button. She'd had years to learn to live with the anguish of shattered idyllic dreams. Henry had felt its keen edge only recently. He had rescued his marriage, but who knew what damage had been done? If it continued to despoil his life, he might have wanted to kill the man responsible. Rage could lurk beneath Henry's cowed exterior; enough to fuel murder.

If. Might. Could. Suddenly she heard her argument with Bernstow's ears. Hesitation chipped at her confidence. Unless she had something stronger to present, he would send her on her way.

Shelby would tell her to back up a step or three.

What did she know for sure? McNeary ruined Bottmeyer's life. By her own witness, Bottmeyer was capable of violence. And Bottmeyer's knife killed McNeary.

She was way out on a limb here, a limb that might not even be attached to a tree.

Her spirits crumbled. On cue, a chorus of aches erupted in her body. Her shoulder and elbow burned. Her brain sank like a heavy weight inside her skull, pushing down on her brows and pressing against her eyelids.

One small light glimmered. She hadn't made a fool of herself in front of Bernstow and Rico. She'd merely come damn close.

She killed the engine. She'd done enough for one day.

THE NEXT MORNING, ZEE SCROUNGED the cupboard for breakfast. "No matter what else I do today, I'm going shopping," she declared to Candy. Skeptical eyes blinked.

In the bedroom, her muted phone buzzed. Zee hurried as much as her re-stiffened limbs would allow, but by the time she reached the bedside table, the caller had gone. She gave the person time to leave a message, then tapped the icon.

To her surprise, she had two voicemails. The first came from Fontina, late yesterday evening. "Hi, Zee. I hope you're feeling a bit better by now. I remembered something I haven't told you. I'm in a training session all morning tomorrow. Can we meet about noon? Text me."

Maybe this was the clue she needed. Zee carried the phone to the kitchen, intending to text her agreement.

The second voicemail began. Hawethorne's ragged voice issued from the speaker. "Please listen. The police are wrong."

She closed her eyes and pinched the bridge of her nose.

"Henry Somerworth couldn't kill a flea. Bona fide . . . Caspar Milquetoast."

Zee frowned. Hawethorne had to be confused. The police had gone to question Bottmeyer.

Several phlegmy breaths rasped in her ear. "Will you look into it?"

What was there to look into? Last she heard, Henry wasn't under suspicion, even though he should be.

"Consider it . . . the request of a dying man."

The message ended.

Zee punched the call-back icon. If Hawethorne wasn't delusional, she was about to be vindicated. The distant phone sounded in her ear. One ring, two, three . . . seven. The echoing emptiness at the other end offered no answer and no option to leave a message.

She fought the urge to throw the phone across the room. Instead, she glared at the cat, who responded to her ferocity with a placid stare. "Candy-pants," she said, "would you be really disgusted with me if I had wine for breakfast?"

Candy gave her a look that said she didn't care, as long as food appeared in her dish first.

Zee obliged her with Salmon Surprise, thought better of the chardonnay in her refrigerator, and pulled out the pistachio ice cream instead. She paced, wolfing spoonfuls straight from the carton. All yesterday's arguments replayed themselves.

She caught her galloping thoughts. She'd nearly torpedoed her credibility last evening. Before she acted today, she'd get hard facts.

Her mind turned hopefully to Fontina. Now would be a great time for an intuitive breakthrough.

The blank monitor in her office reminded her a column due date loomed. She had a couple of hours before meeting Fontina, time to earn her pay, at least write a draft.

She dumped the empty ice cream carton in the trash and forced herself to sit in her desk chair. Her fingers dawdled on the keyboard.

She wanted to write about the Minerva, but all she could see was the girl, the knife, the police, and Rico's worried face. And the crumbs across his chest. And the wreckage of the bike . . . and herself in his arms.

The sunny morning disappeared behind descending clouds, and still she had not enough words on the screen. Her phone emitted a rooster crow. Time to go. Relieved to end her fruitless work session, Zee shut off her computer.

She drove to Farm Fresh under a dripping sky. In the gloom, *Po*'s single eye reproached her negligence. "I'll take you to Al's today," she promised.

Fontina was a sunny splash of gold-orange, easily visible in the restaurant's brightly lit window. Zee hurried inside, glad to escape the humidity coalescing on her face and seeping through her collar, to say nothing of the explosion it was unleashing in her insubordinate curls.

Those curls Rico had tangled in his fingers while his lips demanded hers. A tingle spread deliciously through her chest and lingered as she shed her raincoat and pulled out the chair. She gestured toward the dripping landscape. "That was like walking through a cloud."

Fontina laughed. "As opposed to walking *on* a cloud."

"Wha—" Zee's hand flew to her mouth. "You know!"

"I suspected when I picked you up after the wreck. Something in the air. And then just now."

Zee blew out a breath. "Look, what happened, I mean we, I don't . . ."

"Relax." Fontina held up her hand. "Things will be as they will be." Her amused expression softened. "You look better."

Relieved at the change of subject, Zee grinned. "I'm surprised at how good I feel." A magical kiss did that. She gestured toward the tall glass. "What are you drinking?"

"Carrot-kale juice."

Zee stifled a grimace. Fontina's physique didn't come from eating ice cream for breakfast. Zee nodded to the hovering waiter. "Same for me." Almost at once, she regretted her decision. The dark flecks that floated like flotsam in Fontina's drink bore an unsettling resemblance to the bits of material in the dumpster bin goo. She pulled her eyes from them. "What did you want to tell me?"

"I have an update on Doctor Mercy. Seth mentioned it to his professor, and she brought it up for discussion in class."

"Seth? Oh, your love-struck server, student of business law."

Fontina's eyes crinkled. "The professor did a bit of research. She told the class that McNeary had made Mercy a partner, but he stipulated that they would share any profits with the original investors. Mercy agreed."

"Wow, that's . . ." Zee groped for an appropriate word. "Ethical."

"And sad that we should be surprised." Fontina stirred her greenish-brownish concoction with the straw.

Zee hid a gulp. No way she could drink that. She wrenched her mind from the image. "It's irrelevant now. You know the knife was Bottmeyer's, right?"

"I didn't." Fontina lifted her brows.

The server arrived with Zee's drink. She sniffed it while pulling paper off the straw. "Even more pointless for Bottmeyer to kill McNeary. If he'd only waited."

"Hm-m."

Zee stuck her straw into the mixture in the glass. "Rico said the police pulled him in. I guess he'll be arrested today if he wasn't last night."

"Hm-m."

Zee lifted her straw partway, grimaced at the thick green coating, and set the drink aside. "Okay, my friend." She fixed her eyes on Fontina. "Out with it. What's bothering you?"

"Bottmeyer doesn't feel right. I'm going to ask the pendulum." Fontina unhooked her bracelet, a string of carnelian beads with a heavy brass teardrop at one end that slipped through a braided metal loop on the other. She held the strand by the loop, steadied it, then released.

The beads jiggled, catching the gray light through the window. Beneath Fontina's motionless hand, the bracelet began to circle counterclockwise. Long after it should have settled, it continued. She caught the teardrop in her hand. "Bottmeyer's not guilty."

This wasn't the lead Zee hoped for. "I don't know where to go from here. Mercy's living up to his billing. Despite the lack of information from the kid who answered the phone, the trip he referred to was legit. I learned from Mercy's website he's out with *Médecins Sans Frontières*."

"Doctors Without Borders. They do good work."

"Agreed." Zee's stomach twitched. Couldn't be from the juice; she hadn't tasted it yet. With a jolt, she recalled Rico's story about Julia, disappeared in Eritrea while on a medical mission. Who knew what happened in a foreign country, far from the watchful eyes of home?

Mercy's harsh phone conversation wormed its way into her thoughts. The criticism from his colleagues echoed, and Ferd's enigmatic comment. She caught Fontina's eyes. "I'm unsettled about him. I know he's not the killer, but I'm starting to wonder whether interviewing him, having anything to do with him, is a good idea."

Fontina sipped. "We don't know what pressures he may have felt that evening. One colleague murdered; another perhaps getting cold feet about traveling. Maybe he thought the foreign mission would be ruined."

Frustratingly reasonable, it did little to soothe Zee. "I thought my intuition was getting me a great story." She stirred her reckless order. "Now I'm full of doubts. I'm not sure what to do next."

Fontina gestured toward Zee's glass. "Aren't you going to try it?" Like that would help her see clearly?

Fontina smiled encouragement.

Zee lifted her straw and touched the end to her tongue. Carrot dominated, its sweetness rounded and deepened by the earthy kale. "Hey. This is pretty good."

"Drink some then." Fontina grinned. "You're going to need it."

Zee followed Fontina's amused gaze. Through the window, she caught sight of Rico, leather jacket glistening in the fine mist of rain as he muscled shut the door to his battered van, fallback transportation while the bike was in the shop.

The bell over the entry jingled. He flicked a gloved hand in greeting and made for their table. "I rattled by your place, Zee."

Zee's heart skittered in her chest.

"Didn't see your car. Guessed you might be here." He reversed a chair and straddled it, resting his forearms on the curved back.

Entrancing droplets clung to his dark eyelashes. A hope, tiny and wild, tried to scrabble through Zee's ribcage. She slammed the door with a sharp, and she hoped silent, exhalation.

Rico's gaze lingered.

"Good guess," Zee managed to say.

He shifted in the chair and cleared his throat. "The police arrested Henry Somerworth."

"What?" Zee and Fontina spoke at once.

"Cops went to the daughter's house. Said they needed to talk to her father. She went ballistic. Demanded to know why. They tried to calm her, told her it was about his knife. She went white. Said it belonged to Henry."

Zee gripped the table. Dammit, she *should* have gone to Bernstow. *Defeat snatched from the jaws of victory.* "Henry say anything?"

"Clammed up. Told his wife to call their lawyer."

"I'm surprised," Zee said. "And yet yesterday, I suspected Henry. I couldn't figure out why, though."

"Always one of the three *L*'s," said Rico. "Loot, lust, or love."

That word on his lips—below the table, Zee pinched herself. No time to get distracted now. "Not love, not the way Shandra treated him. Unless he was trying to win her back." She stirred her carrot-kale juice. "Not lust either, if it implies overpowering desire, or powerful emotion of any kind. Hawethorne called him a Milquetoast."

"When did he say that?" Rico frowned.

Zee cursed her betraying blush. "I got a voicemail from him this morning." She summarized the message.

Rico's voice sharpened. "You called Bernstow, right?"

"I didn't know what to make of it."

"*You* don't need to make *anything* of it." Rico pinned her with eyes like blue lightning.

"All right. I'll tell him, but I don't see—"

"They're still gonna want to talk to Hawethorne. And I can't believe we're having this conversation. Again."

Zee reached across the table and grasped his hand. "I'm a slow learner sometimes." His damp fingers were cool, but heat sizzled up her forearm.

His eyes softened. "Slow's not bad. As long as you get there."

The wild hope in Zee's ribcage started scrambling again. She released his hand, cut the current.

Rico glanced at Zee's drink. "What the heck is that? Grass and mud?"

Grateful for the distraction, Zee drew a slow swallow through the straw. "Yum. Want a taste?"

He wrinkled his nose. "Dumpster cuisine?"

Bantering, that's how they'd started on Sunday. Did he want to go down that road? Not trusting her own desires, she pulled the glass out of range. "I'm not telling. You'll never know what you missed."

Rico chuckled and reached. "Okay, gimme. I'm an adventurous guy."

"Oh no. You've already blown your promise not to mention my other adventure. If you don't like this, I'll never hear the end of it."

Smiling, he leaned back, stretching his legs. It struck Zee how much the pose mimicked his bike-riding stance. The jittering in her chest extended downward, and she sucked a long draught of juice, cooling the fire.

"So, this time the police have the right man?" Fontina said.

"And we can all sleep safe in our beds," said Zee, and then cursed herself silently.

Rico's eyebrows twitched a fraction upward. A smile ghosted across his lips as he untangled his long frame from the chair. "Gotta go. Just wanted to update you." He met her eyes, searching. "And see for myself how you're doing."

Voltage streaked all the way down to her toes. "I'm good," she managed.

He glanced at her glass. "Might want to get checked for loose screws."

"My screws are tight," Zee retorted, then did a face-palm.

Rico laughed, low in his throat, and headed for the exit.

Toying with her straw, Zee tracked his departure. "Wow," she said, as the door banged closed.

"I'd have to agree," said Fontina.

Zee swiveled to face her friend's broad grin. "I meant the pendulum got it right."

"Of course, you did," Fontina jested, refastening her bracelet. "I wonder how Hawethorne knew Henry'd been arrested."

"Good question. I called him back, but it just rang." Zee pulled out her cell and punched the icon. She got the same result as earlier.

"It appears we have a conundrum," Fontina said.

Zee pocketed the phone. "I wish I didn't believe Hawethorne."

"But you do." Fontina said it like a tenet of faith.

"I believe *me*."

"Are you going to tell Lieutenant Bernstow?"

Zee gulped the liquid in her glass. "Rico told me to stay off his radar . . ." She met Fontina's eyes. "I need information. And I have an idea where to get it." She flashed a crooked smile. "Think I could borrow your car?"

CHAPTER 33

A L's GARAGE WAS THE OPPOSITE OF THE SHINY showroom-type of facility, but Zee wouldn't trust her car to anyone else. *Po* sat on the pockmarked concrete floor in the single usable bay. Al's massive tow truck filled the other one.

He surveyed the damage to her headlight. "Have ta get one of those in. Straighten out the housing. Shouldn't be a problem. These," he brushed a calloused palm over the dimples from the hail, "I can pop 'em out. Car should be done tomorrow. Come on in and I'll write ya a ticket."

Zee followed him through the adjoining door into his customer 'lounge,' a pair of 1950s bench-style car seats, faded, cracked, and seriously devoid of stuffing. "Hi, Frieda." She held out her hand to the pony-sized Doberman.

Frieda licked a customer's hand if she got good vibes and snarled if she didn't. Fortunately, Zee had never been the object of a snarl. After receiving the canine seal of approval, Zee scratched the dog's massive head. "You're a good judge of character."

Al scribbled on a grease-stained pad of paper. "Ya need a ride?" He winked. "Or is that biker comin'?"

Heat rose in Zee's cheeks. Hard to keep a secret on a Harley. A flash of red-bronze outside Al's smudged front window saved her from a tongue-tied response. "There's my ride now. Thanks." She patted Frieda's head, failing to avoid a second swipe of her enormous tongue.

When she dropped Fontina at Integrated Life, her friend hovered at *Diana*'s door. "Keep me informed, okay?"

"As if I could avoid that." Zee laughed, but she was grateful—mostly—for the uncanny connection to her sister of the heart.

She jumped on the freeway, heading north. As she shifted the Spyder smoothly through the gears, resentment against Hawethorne muscled to the fore. Playing the *dying-man* card. That was low.

A flash of insight yesterday had revealed Henry's guilt. News of his arrest today proved her intuition right. That should have been the end of her involvement. She'd fulfilled her pledge to see that justice was done. Fine, except for the unnerving conviction that a sick man facing death would hardly lie.

She passed the central section of Valerian. In the distance, the rooftop garden of the Hotel St. Deirdre spilled lush greenery against the drooping clouds. She pushed aside her irritation at Hawethorne. He wasn't the only one she'd made a promise to. For Fenton's sake, she'd learn what she could.

And for Janece. McNeary's story deserved to be told, his legacy to be more than his heartbreaking failure. That's how she would pitch the story of his murder to Karl, as soon as she was sure she had the whole story.

She powered down the off ramp before the freeway veered east to cross a tributary of the Great Miami and skirt Miami Woods. Her eyes sought the stone angels of the *Tribune*, standing watch on their lofty tower, reminding reporters of their high calling, the diligent pursuit of truth. Stopped at a traffic signal, she gazed across the rooflines at their steadfast figures.

Where was the line between justified perseverance and bullheaded stubbornness? The scar on her arm throbbed. Getting shot should have clarified that for her.

She'd been new to the *Tribune*, the paper having picked up *Z Beats* when it bought out the smaller weekly *Star*. Seeing a chance to prove herself a serious journalist, she'd proposed to chronicle an after-school program for inner-city, middle-school kids, one of those keep-them-off-the-streets enterprises.

The story was developing just as she'd hoped. Over several weeks, she focused on two teens, Banner and Jazmeen, documenting the effects of positive role models, wholesome activities, and challenges that involved more than how to get away with the five-finger discount.

Rico tried to warn her.

She bristled, refused to listen. She wasn't that easy to fool. Only later did she realize how much she wanted those kids to be saved, how much she'd let hope blind her.

Then came that night.

Banner, swaggering down the street. Zee, concealed behind a rusting van, sad to see him but relieved Jazmeen wasn't with him. And then there she was, skipping toward him. Zee hissed, gunfire erupted, Zee rushed out, and a forty-three-year-old father of three, stopping on his way home to get groceries—oranges—emerged from the corner store.

A flash of lightning jolted Zee from the memory. Thunder cracked overhead, sending tremors through the silvery coronet that dangled from *Diana's* rearview mirror. The traffic light changed.

Zee shifted the car into gear. Her past mistake wasn't the problem, nor was her aggravation at Hawethorne. She didn't need dreams or pendulums or even Shelby to know that something was off about this whole case. If she didn't find it, it wouldn't be for lack of trying. Even if she had to use unorthodox methods.

She steadied the tiny, jiggling crown and headed through the glistening streets. Twenty minutes later, she sprinted through the drizzling remnants of the storm to the massive double doors of Somerworth mansion.

Margaret's reception was as starched as her uniform. Frowning, she allowed Zee to enter, then disappeared, soft shoes silent on the travertine tile.

Zee waited in the cavernous foyer under the heavy-lidded eyes of the reclining odalisque. A faint strain of salsa music drifted on the air, and she amused herself with speculation. She pictured the sultry stained-glass beauty, freed from her brittle prison, undulating with sensuous power, her ebony body pulsing to the hypnotic Latin beat.

A chill on Zee's neck announced Margaret's return. Without a word, her stiff-backed figure showed Zee into Shandra's sitting room. Moments later, Shandra entered, patting her forehead with a towel and carrying a bottle of water. She seated herself on the rose leather loveseat and gestured Zee to the chair.

"Sorry you had to wait." She uncapped the water, swallowed once, and fixed her large blue eyes on Zee. "I find that exercise helps keep me sane."

A flash of envy caught Zee by surprise. Shandra looked glamorous. Her face glowed with a dewy sheen. And she must own expensive, moisture-wicking workout clothes, because the sky-blue tank top revealed no unsightly half-moons under her arms or splotches on her chest.

Zee forced her mind to the purpose of her visit. "I'm glad you have an effective method for dealing with the stress."

Shandra twisted her lightly lipsticked mouth upward. "I'm not sure how well it works." She set the water bottle on the rosewood side table. Her fingers meandered to the cover of Bottmeyer's last bestseller and curled around the spine as if cradling a talisman. One thumb caressed his author photograph, a slow, intimate gesture that triggered an uneasy stirring in Zee's memory. Before she could pursue the fleeting impression, Shandra released her grasp and stood. "Would you like a drink?"

The hospitable offer sent Zee's eyebrows soaring. She yanked them down, grateful the socialite had already turned her back.

Shandra glided toward the glass-topped bar, sleek as a panther. Zee scowled. Liquor was loaded with calories. Why wasn't she fat, dammit?

Shandra dropped three cubes into a cut crystal glass and poured enough amber liquid to lift the ice. She turned her head to look at Zee. "This is a fine bourbon, very smooth."

"No, thank you." Zee bit back any further comment. She might have had chardonnay instead of ice cream for breakfast, had her husband just been arrested for murder.

Shandra's eyes narrowed, as if trying to discern condemnation in the refusal. Then she shrugged, picked up her drink, and returned to the loveseat. "Why are you here?"

Zee blinked. She hadn't rehearsed what to say. What was it Fontina did? Oh yeah. She inhaled a deep breath and said the first thing that came to mind. "Do you think your husband is guilty?"

Shandra choked in mid-swallow and coughed. She stared at Zee for a long moment. "I don't know." Her voice cracked. Wetness shone in the corners of her eyes. "We sleep in separate rooms. When I came down for breakfast, Margaret said Henry had already gone to the office." She drained her glass in one long gulp.

Opportunity.

Zee pressed. "He didn't come in to say good-bye?"

A flush tinted Shandra's face. The tears brimmed, and she turned her head as a drop rolled down one smooth cheek.

Zee shifted her gaze to a photo on the mantel, a twin of the graduation picture in Bottmeyer's cabin. No companion picture with Henry, though. They'd married six months ago. That was a short honeymoon.

Unbidden, the odalisque danced before Zee's eyes. Did Henry have a paramour? She squelched a grin at the thought of scrawny, sweaty Somerworth with the voluptuous slave.

"We were so happy before." Shandra's voice pulled Zee's attention back. Moisture beaded the socialite's lashes. "I loved him more than I thought possible. How could he think money meant that much to me?"

Even as Zee struggled to accept the implication, Hawethorne's words echoed. *Some people put a lot of store in a big bank account.*

"What do you mean?" Zee said.

Shandra lowered her head. Her hair shimmered like a wind-blown curtain across her face. "He was a silent investor with Doctor McNeary. He didn't want the family to know. Not even me. That hurt."

Zee recalled Henry's browbeaten face and Shandra's description of her husband as smart and devious, just needing to learn to assert himself. "He wanted to show them a success," she guessed.

Shandra nodded, closed her eyes, and massaged the space between her carefully sculpted brows.

Motive. Henry's defense was looking thin.

Zee studied the bowed figure. Trust was the cornerstone of relationship. It seemed the newlywed Somerworths built their dreams on a foundation of sand.

She pursed her lips, trying to sort her thoughts. Such a difference between this picture of heartache and the icy cruelty of only a few days ago. Which one was true?

Maybe both were. Zee flashed on the two faces Mercy had shown. She reached for something to say. "What will you do now?"

The blonde hair flared as Shandra snapped her head up and dashed the tears from her eyes. "One thing is certain. I'll not throw myself on the mercy of my in-laws." Her tone could have re-frozen the ice-melt in her glass.

She might have patched things up with Henry, but not with his parents.

"It's ironic." Shandra laughed bitterly. "If I hadn't written that note, maybe Henry wouldn't be in jail."

Zee blinked, clinging to the tail of Shandra's whipsawing train of thought.

"Why *did* you write it?"

Shandra lifted her glass and seemed surprised to find only shards of cubes. "As I told you, I just wanted Jim released. How could I know where it would lead?"

"But you'd be living with a murderer."

The tanned shoulders shrugged.

The casual gesture stunned Zee. It must be the shock. Shandra couldn't mean she would overlook what he did. However, until it all fell apart when the police came, that's exactly what Shandra had been doing. Perhaps she hadn't been sure of Henry's guilt.

Zee tried for clarity. "I know Henry seems so mild-mannered that it's hard to believe he could do such a thing."

Shandra crossed to the bar, dropped one cube of ice in her glass, and filled it near the brim. She drank half the contents, then faced Zee.

"Appearances can be deceiving. Henry was a risk-taker, despite his mild manner." She laughed, a harsh expulsion from her throat that seemed to cut through the soft luxury surrounding her. "After all, he married me."

With careful steps, she maneuvered across the room and lowered herself onto the loveseat. A bit of bourbon sloshed onto her hand, and she licked the wet patch. "Can't waste good *Old Elijah*." She looked to Zee as if for confirmation.

Zee nodded, aware of another tickle in her brain. She focused, but the illusive idea, as if spooked by the clinking of ice, slipped beyond her grasp. Frustrated, she switched to analysis.

Shandra's information solidified the case against her husband. And though Zee couldn't reconcile Henry's demeanor with McNeary's bloodied body, people always warned about the 'quiet ones.'

Shandra's wistful voice broke into her thoughts. "*I* was a leap of faith for him. I loved him for that. I really thought we had a chance." Her tears ran unchecked.

Feeling like a voyeur, Zee turned her attention to the room around her. Bottmeyer's volumes filled two rows in the low bookcase. A fan of magazines on another rosewood table displayed covers featuring his picture. A parade of photos along one wall tracked his success, as he accepted awards, shook hands, and hobnobbed with celebrities, including a bubbling Angelica Street.

Shandra appeared in every picture, beaming by his side. A chill crept over Zee.

"Papa was relieved that we managed to save the marriage." Shandra jolted Zee from her uneasy contemplation. "He just wanted me to be taken care of." She dropped her head backward, resting it on the rose cushions. The liquid in her unattended glass sloshed close to the edge. "That plan didn't work so well, but that's all right. I'll move back in with him."

"I thought he sequestered himself to finish his book."

"I'll help him." Shandra straightened and lifted the bourbon like a toast. "We've always been a team."

A soft knock interrupted them. Margaret stepped just over the threshold. "Ma'am, Mister Fredrikson is here."

"My attorney," Shandra explained to Zee. She addressed the maid. "I'll see him in a moment." Margaret ducked her head in a miniscule bob and left.

Zee stood. "I'll go now. You have a lot to do." She offered a smile. "I'm sure the lawyer will mount a good defense."

"I'm certain you're right, whoever it is. Fredrikson is handling the divorce."

Shandra must have seen her shock. She stretched her lips in a thin line. "He broke my heart. Papa's too. He's going to pay for it."

Margaret ushered Zee through the foyer, accompanied by a cloud of frigid displeasure. When the carved front door thudded behind her, Zee resisted the urge to shake like a dog to throw it off.

She reviewed the conversation as she made her way across the wide expanse of herringbone-patterned brick. In retrospect, she wondered why Shandra divulged so much—another departure from her frosty aloofness in their previous encounter. Of course, the socialite's world had crumbled around her.

Suspicion and sympathy warred in Zee's brain. She doubted Shandra had been exercising. The water bottle was fresh. Her form-fitting clothes were not even damp. And she had an appointment with her lawyer. Who exercises before that? Lying about such a trivial matter did not bode well for her veracity elsewhere.

When she reached Fontina's car, she turned back for another look at the huge house. To the left and right, the wide wings of tan brick rose fortress-like, their lightless windows impenetrable. The three-story central glass façade could have been the gate to a moat, mirroring choppy water instead of turbulent clouds.

As she stared, a ray of sun pierced the gray expanse. It should have been beautiful, uplifting, a sign that the storm had passed. Instead, its diamond brilliance stabbed her eyes and forced her to turn away.

She left McKinley Heights with a sense of relief. Money often earned its soiled reputation as a breeder of corruption, but the hunger for it, like all addictions, usually masked a deeper need. Unfair of her to tar all wealthy people with the Somerworth brush, yet the sour taste in her mouth betrayed her guilt.

She slowed, waited for a sleek Porsche to pass, then shifted *Diana's* gears to accelerate onto the freeway. If only she could redirect her thoughts as easily.

Something didn't fit right in the relationship between Shandra and her father. Zee's skin crawled at the memory of Shandra stroking Bottmeyer's picture, of all the mementoes of him that crowded the sitting room. Add candles and it could be a shrine.

Secrets inside secrets inside secrets. Her head ached with the burden of duplicity and the struggle to know who to believe.

The ghost of Frieda loped through her mind. How did the big dog know who to trust? Did liars smell bad? Maybe Al should hire out the Doberman. Sloppy swipe or sinister snarl, her character test could be a nice source of ancillary revenue.

The idea tugged Zee's lips into a smile. She pictured Frieda assessing Shandra, or taking the measure of her father.

The image pulled her musing up short. Bottmeyer probably didn't know about Henry's investment. She'd also bet he wasn't aware of the state of Shandra's soon-to-be-dissolved marriage.

Zee pursed her lips. Father and daughter hid things from each other, but she sensed the deception went deeper in this unnerving symbiotic relationship. The chance to delve further with Shandra had passed, but maybe Zee could find a key among what Bottmeyer held buried.

On impulse, she ducked down the next exit, pulled over, and tapped his address into *Diana's* GPS.

CHAPTER 34

THE SUN BROKE THROUGH AS ZEE backed the Spyder onto the rough gravel driveway in front of Bottmeyer's cabin. The parking area was vacant. No light leaked from behind the thin curtains. Leaves cluttered the porch and congregated undisturbed near the chair legs.

Zee locked *Diana* and crossed the driveway. Despite the indications that no one was home, her skin crawled with the sense of being watched. The soaked wooden steps creaked beneath her feet, an alien intrusion in the soft drip-drip of leaves shedding the remnants of the storm.

She knocked on the warped door. No response.

She rapped again. "Mister Bottmeyer?"

Greeted only with silence, she peered through a gap in the drab drapes. On the dining table beneath the sill, his laptop faced a vacant spindly chair. The tiny kitchen, the ratty couch, even the bathroom across the dim interior, were empty.

Before she could talk herself out of it, she pushed against the door. It scraped open.

"Mister Bottmeyer?" She stepped into the eerie silence, the hair on her neck quivering. Her foot brushed against a wastebasket. She clenched her jaw. There was not going to be a body here. Still, good to know where to find a trusty friend if she needed it.

She forced herself to tiptoe farther beyond the door, scan the floor, and check the corners. No corpse appeared, only the dismal evidence of Bottmeyer's descent into despair. Disappointment settled on her shoulders. No crime scene, but also no answers for her questions.

As she turned to go, the crack of a branch outside startled her. She jumped, caught her foot on the chair leg, and fell against the dining table. Her hand landed on the laptop keyboard, and the screen lit.

Frozen in the bright glare, she waited.

No one crossed the threshold. Outside, only the whisper of leaves broke the silence. Adrenaline drained from her limbs, and her heart crawled back into its accustomed place.

She shifted her attention to the monitor. A message inquired: *Restore previous session?*

What had she done? Did she close a browser? Should she hit *enter, go back, escape*?

She chewed her lip.

Surely, Bottmeyer didn't leave his computer this way. She moved the mouse away from the text box and clicked on the screen. The message disappeared.

A sketchy outline stared at her: *CRSPR tests. Surprising results. Trouble.*

Perhaps this was research for his next novel.

Five tabs appeared across the top of the screen. McNeary's name popped out. Her fingers hovered over the keyboard. Already, she'd committed an unforgivable invasion, but since she was already across the bridge . . .

A gust of wind drummed a shower of drops on the tin porch roof. She jerked her hand away. He could return at any minute, and she'd have no explanation for her presence.

The unlocked door had blown open and she'd gone in to investigate. Just being a good person.

Even *she* wouldn't believe that line.

Then she'd best move quickly.

She slipped into the chair, clicked McNeary's tab, and scanned the list of search engine hits. They offered the expected chronicle. The familiar pang touched her heart.

She opened an article that hinted at new research. It mentioned Jules Mercy.

Back to the list. James Hawethorne's name appeared, but he and Bottmeyer were friends, nothing nefarious there.

Zee leaned back in the rickety chair. The searches told her nothing new, and time was ticking. Her eye strayed to the bottom tray, where a document icon stared at her. She clicked it open.

Her blood turned to ice. A question ran across the top of a page of notes: *How long does it take to die?* Beneath it, he listed various causes: overdose, gunshot, strangulation, stabbing.

The letters swayed. She gripped the table to steady herself. He was a writer, working on a novel. She of all people should know how misleading research notes can be.

Her scalp prickled a warning. She needed to get out of there. Clicking 'X's in rapid succession, she erased her trail. Fear rumbled below her belt like an agitated swamp that, at any moment, could disgorge a monster.

"Damn!" She stared at the monitor. She'd closed his outline. Maybe he wouldn't notice.

Ears straining for any tiny sound, she replaced the spindly chair against the table and glanced around the room. Nothing revealed her unauthorized visit. Satisfied, she tugged the cabin door closed and darted to *Diana*. Heart pounding, she pulled the car out of the driveway.

As she rounded the first curve in the road, a dilapidated sedan approached. Bottmeyer clutched its steering wheel, eyes straight ahead. Zee averted her face as he passed. At least she wasn't driving her red-with-white-racing-stripes Mini.

ZEE TOSSED FONTINA'S KEY ON THE DEMILUNE TABLE by the door. "I need some wine," she declared to Candy, who misinterpreted the comment, meowed, and trotted toward the kitchen.

"Yes, Your Highness. Wine for me, dinner for you. Will Tuna Delight suffice?" The slender body twined around her ankles, manacling her steps. "Despite the fact that you're hobbling me, I'll take that as a *yes*."

Feline nourishment provided, Zee poured a glass of chardonnay, wandered to the balcony, and sank into her deck chair. She fought a wave of revulsion. She'd always played by the rules, yet here she was. Listening to a private conversation outside Mercy's door hadn't seemed too bad, but entering someone's home without permission, and snooping through his computer, that crossed a line for sure. And had she learned anything from these transgressions? Precious little.

Her integrity was as soiled as Bottmeyer's disgusting couch. Was this the price for chasing the story?

She sipped the wine. Buttery, oaky, slightly citrus. Good, but not nearly the caliber of Fenton's gift. A fresh onslaught of shame swept over her. Was it possible to investigate a despicable crime and keep one's honor? Spend enough time with sick people, it seemed, and one was bound to fall ill. And yet, she had promised.

She lifted her glass, an offering to nature for healing.

The storm had hung a curtain of mist in the trees shading the lawn between *Legate I* and *III*. Damp foliage glistened, yellow, red-limned maple, nut-brown oak, fiery scarlet sweetgum. A breeze rippled the leaves, launching some, ballerina-like, on their final voyage.

Autumn, the season of dying. Death should be like this. Coming in its own time, graceful, even exuberant.

On the table beside her, a motorcycle rumbled.

"Hey, Zee." Upbeat, a spring in Rico's voice. "You up for dinner? I feel like celebrating."

Her heart leapt toward the invitation. "Absolutely." She caught her eager agreement and added, "Where do you want to meet?" She would drive there herself. Better not to presume too much.

"How about the Loose Goose?"

"I know where that is." The same strip mall as the bakery where Shandra had written the note. *Damn.* She still hadn't told him. Zee squelched a pang of guilt. "Meet you there in half an hour."

She spent the next fifteen minutes getting into and out of clothes. Silk blouse? Too sexy. Cotton tee? Too indifferent. Tank top? Might work. Knit slacks? Maybe. Sandals? Fine. With heels? Without? Spangles? Plain?

Candy meowed from her perch on the bed pillow.

"You're right," said Zee. She donned the blue jeans and deep red pullover she'd worn when she'd seen him earlier at Farm Fresh. It wasn't like this was a date.

She tugged a brush through her curls, swiped on a bit of eye shadow and lipstick, and grabbed *Diana*'s key.

When she pulled into the strip mall lot, her palms broke out in a sweat. Rico's tall, muscular frame leaned casually against the Road King. She parked next to him, smoothed damp hands across her denim-clad legs, and stepped from Fontina's car. "You got your bike back."

Rico raised his hand in a fist pump. "Eddie knows I need my ride."

"Biker's version of phantom limb syndrome." She smiled at his obvious pleasure. More than once he'd referred to the Harley as an extension of himself.

A curvy hostess in a tight black tee and low-slung black pants led them to a booth, presented twenty-four-inch laminated menus, and assured them their server would arrive soon. When she left, Zee glanced around at the packed tables. Her stomach growled. *Soon* could be a while.

She scanned the list of beers, wines, and spirits that covered one side of the plasticized sheet. On the other, she had worked halfway through the creatively titled super-burgers, when a string of chirping syllables interrupted her.

"Hi-my-name-is-Mandy-I'll-be-your-server-tonight-can-I-get-you-something-from-the-bar?"

While Mandy's considerable cleavage heaved inside her snug black t-shirt, Zee flipped the menu. "I'll have a glass of house cabernet," she said.

Mandy turned her wide brown orbs to Rico. She leaned forward, further defying the thin fabric across her bosom. "What would you like?"

"What do you recommend?" he asked, blue eyes all innocence.

Zee resisted kicking him under the table. Since when did he not know what he wanted?

"The Lagunitas IPA is very popular," Mandy said.

"I'll have that."

As Mandy hustled toward the bar, Zee cocked a brow.

Rico shrugged and grinned. "Seems like a day to experiment. And I don't see mud-and-grass juice on the menu."

Zee dropped her eyes. Silly to be annoyed at his response to Mandy's flirting. He was giving Zee space—which she swore she wanted. Besides, she shouldn't be in a rush to test her newly healing heart. She swallowed the lump in her throat.

Mandy returned, bouncing and breathless, to serve drinks and offer appetizers and entrees.

With effort, Zee brightened her voice. "Share a plate of loaded potato skins?"

"Sounds good." Rico pointed to the menu. "I'll have the Blue Goose Burger."

"Excellent choice," enthused Mandy. "And for you?" She turned to Zee.

"I'm fine with just the appetizer."

Mandy tried to hide a pout, spun her tightly wrapped buttocks, and left.

A thought scampered across Zee's awareness, pinching her brows, but it disappeared before she could catch it. She puffed a frustrated sigh, then caught Rico's narrowed eyes.

"She triggered something," Zee said, "but it's not important."

He touched warm fingers to hers, obliterating any further

inclination to pursue the elusive idea. "No chasing ghosts tonight."

She raised her wine in agreement. *No chasing possibilities of any kind.*

Amid the happy chatter in the Loose Goose, they made small talk as they shared the potato skins. Rico bantered, yet Zee thought she sensed tension in his repartee. Or maybe she imagined it.

His Blue Goose Burger arrived, juicy, spilling over with melted cheese and golden onions, dominating the small platter. As he hefted it for a bite, she reached across the table and plucked a straggling caramelized onion.

She lifted her chin, daring him to object. His eyes crinkled, and she popped the morsel into her mouth. "Couldn't resist." Tender, the perfect combination of savory-sweet. She licked her lips and lowered her eyes, conscious of the hot flush in her cheeks. "Those are good."

"Glad you're enjoying my food." His chuckle robbed the words of any sting.

She snuck a glance over the rim of her glass. The light above the table accentuated his chiseled jaw and sparked animation in his eyes. She stilled the impulse to visibly shake off her attraction.

If she couldn't stand the heat, she should get out of the kitchen. *Or go down in flames.*

Persistence prevailed. As dinner progressed, she found herself laughing more easily. Feeling giddy. Noticing and savoring the admiring glances from other tables.

Had she ordered a second glass of wine? Deliciously, she didn't care.

Rico's laughter seemed easier, too. She loved that he was sensitive to her moods.

He'd devoured most of his burger when the twinkle in his eyes faded. He reached across the table and covered her hand with his. Prickles spread through her arm and into her chest. Was she chilled, or was he hot?

"I know I said no ghosts tonight, but Zee, you need to stay clear of the McNeary situation."

"It's over, isn't it?" They arrested Henry. Why was he warning her?

"Yes and no," Rico said. "There are some loose ends."

Zee's stomach flipped. "You mean Paselly."

"I mean let it go now."

"I never wanted to be part of it." She grimaced. "Murder is not exciting. It's depressingly banal."

"Criminals are not the sharpest knives . . ." He squeezed her hand and let it go.

Zee ignored his faux pas. "The whole business is sad. Did you know—" She clamped her lips.

"Did I know *what*?"

Moisture dampened Zee's neck. *Just tell him.* She needed to break the habit of holding back. "Henry invested in McNeary's company." She hoped he wouldn't ask how she knew.

"That's motive," he said. "We know he had means. Only a matter of time 'til we find opportunity."

The evening's joyful ease drained in a bead of sweat down Zee's spine. "Can we stop talking about this?"

He laid a scorching hand on her forearm. "Sure."

Zee straightened, breaking contact. "I'm off-balance." She compelled herself to laugh. "Too much wine. May I eat a bite or two of your burger? Food would help."

"Eat the rest." He pushed his plate across the table. "Just like old times."

A sharp pang pushed Zee to the edge of a precipice. She grabbed the burger for safety and bit into the remnants of the sandwich. An aromatic explosion of blue cheese stung her sinuses. "Agh! That's powerful." She coughed and swallowed with difficulty, then drained half her glass of water. "You could have warned me." Her eyes smarted, but at least she was anchored firmly in the present.

Rico seemed to sense her narrow escape. He sipped his beer. "Think that new quarterback will give the Conquerors a chance this year?"

The image of her dumpster-ruined sweatshirt flashed in her mind. Zee dismissed it. "I'm cautiously optimistic."

"Schultz has promise."

The conversation staggered to safer ground, light talk that skirted the chasm of that which remained unsaid. The police would learn soon enough that Shandra couldn't alibi Henry. Zee had no responsibility to tell them, or enlighten Rico.

By the time she finished eating, a precarious sense of balance had returned. "I should head home." She wiped burger juice from her fingers.

Rico's smile seemed strained. Did he want more from their not-date? Did he sense she withheld information? As he walked her to Fontina's Spyder, she wrestled with a bigger dilemma. She wanted to risk a kiss, to feel her lips against his skin.

Her fearful mind fought to stay on familiar ground. Her cursed heart, daring to hope, resisted.

Maybe a feathery brush against his cheek.

She reached for the door handle, but paused at his touch on her arm. Her pulse quickened. Straightening, she locked his deep blue eyes. She should act now.

He acted faster.

Pulling her close, he swept his lips below her ear. "Stay safe."

His scent drowned her in spice and wild orange. "You, too," she murmured.

Then he freed her, stared hard for a moment, and strode to his bike.

Zee fumbled with *Diana's* door and fell into the driver's seat, jostling the shiny coronet. It arced, catching flashes of the Road King's chrome. She halted the silver crown's wild swing.

"Am I a fool?" she asked it.

The charm did not reply, but Fontina's voice whispered: *The Tarot Fool is one who believes in herself, no matter what others think.*

"That," Zee murmured, "is the heart of the matter."

CHAPTER 35

I N THE PARKING LOT AT THE LOOSE GOOSE, Zee fingered *Diana's* coronet. Silly to think the talisman would bring good fortune. Yet she rubbed it anyway, for luck . . . and grounding. Clarity. If only it could divine the meaning of Rico's whispered near-kiss.

The yearning for intimacy throbbed in the hollow in her heart. Tugging against it, the fear of loss shackled her tongue.

All that she hadn't told him crowded in: She didn't have the note. Shandra couldn't alibi Henry. Hawethorne confessed to being hired. She knew why she didn't mention the last item, but it lodged one more secret below her breastbone.

Her temples pounded. She wished she could unscrew the top of her head and dump all the turmoil, fear, and doubt swirling in her brain.

The silvery crown ceased its swing. Zee released a deep exhale. The universe declined to provide answers tonight. She shifted the Spyder into gear, pulled out of the lot, and turned left. In her rear-view mirror, Rico followed, but turned right. She watched his taillight shrink and disappear.

She swung around the corner and stared down half a block at twin strings of scarlet lights.

Just what she didn't need.

Suppressing a groan, she pulled a quick U-turn. Maybe she'd

fare better in the other direction. She passed the restaurant and turned left at the first opportunity. The gambit rewarded her with lighter traffic. She blew out a breath. Dodged that mess.

Zig-zagging through side streets, frustrated but adapting her route at each cluster of taillights, she crept toward home. Must have been a serious accident to cause such a snarl.

At the thought, a twitch pinched her gut. She brushed it aside, but it wouldn't stay away. Stopped at a light, she drummed her fingers on the console, then yanked her hand into her lap.

There was no reason for her nerves to fire like this.

She crooked her neck left and right, loosened the kinks, rolled her shoulders.

The light turned green. She jumped and stalled the engine. Aggravated, she restarted the car, as behind her, a horn blared. Teeth clenched, she laid rubber.

"Sorry, *Diana*. I—"

The apology caught in her throat. Her face split into a grin. Fontina said the life force always wanted to move. Very well, Zee would take the freeway home. No matter that it was the longer route. She'd roll down the windows and let the fresh night air scrub the malaise from her system.

Her heart lifted, and she prodded the gas pedal, smiling at the Spyder's sultry purr. Smile wide, she turned the next corner—into another traffic jam. Forced to leash her kindred spirit, she frowned at the blinking blue-and-white lights skittering across vehicle roofs.

No escape this time. She joined the crawling string of cars.

Dread tightened her jaw. She deliberately relaxed it. This had nothing to do with her. Yet her anxiety ratcheted the nearer she approached the strident strobes.

The smashed remains of a wreck crept into view.

Gulping air, she whispered a prayer.

She was forced to creep past, unwilling to look, but unable to avert her eyes. The driver slumped sideways, his head canted against the window. In the distance, a siren wailed on a futile run.

It had to be an accident.

Except it wasn't. She knew it in her sickened bones.

The sightless skull-eyes gaping through the glass had once looked upon the world as James Hawethorne.

An officer stepped into her line of vision and swept his arm forward. "Move along."

Numbly, she obeyed. Not knowing how, she found herself several blocks away before she came to her senses and pulled to the curb. She shut off the engine and waited for the world to stop spinning.

SUNLIGHT FILTERED BENEATH ZEE'S EYELIDS. She lay motionless in her bed, taking stock: body relaxed, pulse normal, breath easy. Mind calm.

Somehow, she'd driven home, then sat up half the night on her balcony, her mind stunned into stasis. Every once in a while, a thought floated past. Call Rico. Get a glass of wine. Call Fontina. Change out of her sweat-drenched clothes. She didn't move from her chair. She couldn't remember getting into bed.

In the light of day, she steered her thoughts to the scene on the road. It was horrific, yes, but an accident, nothing more . . . and yet.

Firmly, she pushed aside any other speculation.

Nestled in the hollow between her shoulder and neck, a furry head stirred. Zee scratched behind the velvet ears. "You're a good therapist, Candy-pants. Add this visit to my bill."

Candy meowed an invoice for Chicken Surprise.

"On its way." Zee smiled with parched lips. "Please allow ten business days for delivery."

The cat yawned, stretched, and leapt off the bed. Another meow floated up as she trotted toward the kitchen. The feline calendar obviously ran differently than the human one.

As the accident images faded, the evening at the restaurant resurfaced. Zee latched onto it, relieved to focus on something other than Hawethorne's vacant eyes. She'd enjoyed herself, maybe too much.

Still, nothing had happened.

Well, almost nothing.

She threw back the blanket, padded to the kitchen, and filled the cat dish. As the nuggets fell, they reminded her of flipping calendar days, the way old-time movies showed the passage of time.

For twenty-eight days, she managed to stay on her side of a tenuous boundary. Until that kiss. Leaning against each other at the graveside of the Road King's carnage, falling into each other, stepping into the abyss.

Though she'd scrambled to safety, the border had been breached. Last night, she'd crossed again. Their dinner, her ease, the phantom brush of his lips. Her visa had been stamped. She had officially entered the country of bewilderment. And the carefully ordered land that had been her home was gone.

Her cell rang. Her breath seized, even as she registered that it was not his ringtone.

"Miss Morani? This is Janece. Can we meet?"

Zee grimaced at the voice of McNeary's assistant. Why couldn't this damned case die? Still, she owed Janece the courtesy of listening. "Yes, certainly. What's this about?"

"Akhil and I, we're seeing each other. We try not to talk about the murder." She sucked in a breath and exhaled the words in a rush. "But when they arrested Mister Somerworth, Akhil told me something that happened at the coffee shop. It's probably not important, but I thought you could help us decide."

Zee waited a beat. Janece had come to her for help, but why delay the inevitable? "If you know something, you should go to the police."

"Akhil won't, that is, he doesn't trust them."

Zee's gut twitched in solidarity. "All right. But I can't guarantee that you won't have to speak to the police anyway."

"We'll accept your judgment."

"Where should we meet?"

"We thought the little garden by the library?"

"I know the place. Ten o'clock?"

"Perfect. Thanks."

Zee glanced at Candy. "The downside of encouraging people to call me, is that sometimes they actually do."

CHAPTER 36

ZEE THREADED HER WAY THROUGH the annual juried pho-
tography exhibition in the library's spacious atrium. Despite
her curiosity about the information Janece and Akhil had to
share, the images snagged her attention. She couldn't pass up the
opportunity to appreciate one of her favorite parts of Valerian, its
architecture.

The Emperor's statue sheathed in the rose-gold of morning gar-
nered an Honorable Mention, as did the Cardo Max viaduct, its
girders and beams a steel spiderweb glistening with rain. She skirted
an astonishing photo that captured one of the *Tribune* building's
angels just as a bolt of lightning cut the sky. She wondered why that
didn't merit the grand prize until she came upon the winner.

The photographer had captured the setting sun as it cast fire on
the Forum pavilion in the town square. With scalpel-like precision,
the low angle incised the elaborate acanthas leaves crowning each
of the nine Corinthian columns, and cast deep dramatic shadows
on the Capitoline Triad of Jupiter, Juno, and Minerva aloft on the
triangular pediment. What gave the picture its power, though, was
the lone actor on the stage below.

Hoisting the skull of Yorick, a pensive Hamlet seemed offer
his own evanescent life in homage to the gods. He would make
that sacrifice in the next act, his final effort to avenge his father's

murder. A synapse twitched in Zee's brain, but disappeared before she could grab it.

She must be getting old. In the past, her brain had never teased her like this. A spike of fear drove itself into her skull. Dementia. It wasn't necessarily hereditary. She'd researched it. The odds were higher if a parent had it, but lifestyle could mitigate the risk. Or exacerbate it. Zee glanced at the snug snap on her jeans and resolved again to get to the grocery store.

Smothering her anxiety, she turned her steps toward her destination, the Peace Garden, a mid-town oasis of multi-colored foliage bounded on three sides by a serpentine brick wall.

Janece and Akhil sat with their backs to her on wire mesh chairs, her brunette ringlets resting on his slender shoulder. As Zee pushed open the door, Janece reached up and stroked Akhil's smooth dark cheek. He captured her plump hand in his large fine-boned fingers and brought her knuckles to his lips.

Struck by the tender gesture, Zee slowed her steps to circle into their line of sight.

Akhil stood at once, tugging at his immaculate jacket. "Thank you for seeing us, Miss Morani." He waited until Zee sat before positioning himself on his chair, body still and composed, but no longer at ease.

"I'm glad to help if I can," Zee said.

Akhil's coffee-colored eyes held hers. "I do not like speaking of another man's troubles, but in this situation, I have an obligation. Perhaps it need go no further."

Zee laced her fingers in her lap and mirrored his posture. "Please, tell me what happened."

"A few days before the doctor's death, young Mister Somerworth came into the coffee shop, arguing on his phone and in an agitated state. He ordered a black coffee and then sat at a table. I could not help but hear."

The shop with its three tiny tables sprang into Zee's mind.

"His words were not always coherent," Akhil continued. "It

appeared he had planned to start a company, but he had lost his money. He kept pleading with the other person not to back out. His begging seemed to make no difference, because he became very angry. I felt sorry for him, but I also feared he might lose control of himself."

"Did he behave violently?"

"He struck the table with great force. And jumped to his feet. I was glad there was no one else in the shop. He was a small man, but anger made his presence very big."

"I see," Zee said.

"Then he began to blame 'her father,'" said Akhil. "He said her father told him to take a chance, that he understood the desire to escape a dominating family." Akhil swallowed. "There was silence. He seemed to be listening. Then he shook his head and said if he couldn't make this deal, his life was ruined. He might as well kill himself."

A shudder crawled across Zee's back. "What happened then?"

"He seemed to become aware of me. He stared—such cold eyes made me shiver—and then he left." The tightness drained from Akhil's body. He unscrewed the cap from a water bottle, drank, and smiled at Janece, revealing his endearing crooked front tooth.

Zee steepled her fingers. His temper provided more ammunition against Henry. If he was determined to kill himself, he might have decided to take the cause of his despair along with him. She looked into the expectant faces. "This is significant information."

"But since the police already arrested Mister Somerworth . . .?" Emotions warred on Janece's round face. Worry for Akhil? Loyalty to McNeary? Duty versus distaste?

Zee recalled the dictatorial policewoman in McNeary's office, her insensitivity to Janece's shock, the petty exercise of authority in her officious denial of the assistant's harmless request for her novel. Whatever Akhil's feelings, Janece had no love of law enforcement.

Zee shook her head, and squelching an internal accusation of hypocrisy, leaned toward the couple. "I'm sorry, but you have to tell the police. Every piece of information has potential. It's their job to decide what's important."

Janece's face fell.

Akhil squared his shoulders. "We will go right now."

"Will you come with us?" The words rushed from Janece.

Zee wondered how to tell them her presence might do more harm than good.

"That is not necessary." Akhil wrapped Janece's hand in his. "Do not be afraid."

They departed hand in hand, while Zee leaned against the back of the chair, digesting this new data. Henry Somerworth's passions ran much more deeply than she had first believed. This final loss could have spurred him to action.

Breeze ruffled her hair. Her glance fell on the winding gravel walkway. A cluster of yellowed leaves huddled at the edge of a curve as if gathering their courage, then skittered in a herd across the path. The universe affirming her theory? Zee laughed. Fontina might say so.

Her cell rumbled Rico's ringtone.

Not now. A lost traveler in the country of bewilderment, she didn't know how to answer.

It sounded again.

She shivered at the ghost of his breath on her cheek. She should stay silent. At least until she gathered her bearings.

The third time drove her finger to the answer icon before another thought could intervene.

"Hi, Zee. Just came from the police station. Interested in an update?" Again his voice was upbeat, friendly, untroubled.

"Sure." She would just consult her wanderer's dictionary of non-verbal translation. "There's a new bakery a few doors down from the Loose Goose."

"So, you found Schreinhardt's?" He chuckled. "Opened eleven days ago. You're slipping."

"What, was there an office pool?"

"Your love of sweet treats is legendary." Another throaty laugh. "Heard they have good pastries."

Too good.

Half an hour later, Zee pushed open the bakery door, noting the name in script on the window. Another observational failure.

"Hi." Miranda waved a greeting. "We got cherry Danish again today."

Zee blinked.

Miranda colored and dipped her head. The neon pink patch flickered among the angles of her jet-black locks. "I have a really good memory. Almost photographic."

"Fantastic. Wish I had that." Zee glanced around at the empty tables.

"Looking for someone?"

"Black hair, leather jacket, insanely hot." *Oh crap.* Her cheeks warmed.

Miranda's grin reached the silver circlet in her eyebrow. "I'll be sure to let you know."

Hiding her face, Zee studied the baked goods behind the display glass. "I'll have one of those." She pointed to a nut-studded confection. Nuts were nutritious, and she'd skipped breakfast, another bad habit she needed to break.

"Ooh, almond pretzels. My fave," said Miranda. "Don't let the shape fool you. They're nothing like regular pretzels." She reached for a ceramic plate.

Zee spied the society section of the *Tribune* on the rear counter, and inspiration struck. "What do you think about Henry Somerworth's arrest?"

The barista paused in mid-stretch and sucked her lip stud. "Honestly, I'm surprised. Didn't think he had it in him." Her brows flicked upward. "But you know what they say. The nice man next door turns out to be a serial killer with a basement full of body parts."

Zee grinned. "You just hope you didn't eat his barbecue."

"Ugh!" Miranda laughed. "Good reason to stick with pastry."

Zee refrained from mentioning *Sweeney Todd*. She rubbed a knuckle across her chin, contemplating how to steer the conversation toward her goal. "Maybe Henry had a dark secret. I know he had a temper."

Miranda propped her elbow on the counter. "Don't know it was much of a secret, but his marriage was in trouble." She arched her brows to her hairline, lifted her chin, and looked down her nose in a perfect parody of snootiness. "His parents considered Shandra beneath his class, but her father had money, so they overlooked Henry's"—she affected an accent—"vulgar choice.'"

"The dilemmas of the upper crust." Zee smirked.

"When her father lost all his money, the Somerworths tried to get Henry to break off the engagement." Miranda wrinkled her face. "Seemed like Henry was going to cave, but then he defied them. Caught *me* off guard. Based on everything I read, I thought he was a big wuss. He even looked wimpy in his photos."

Zee pursed her mouth. Another nail in Henry's coffin, and some light on Shandra's icy attitude. She gestured toward the *Tribune*. "Any other news on that in today's paper?"

"Not about them," said Miranda. "The big story today is that Angelica Street tried to commit suicide."

The floor at Schreinhardt's wobbled beneath Zee's feet.

"Not a lot of details, looks like the actress overdosed," Miranda said.

Black spots danced in Zee's vision. She blinked furiously. There was no reason to automatically suspect the hand of Paselly, but the discomfiting thought pranced like an imp in the back of her brain.

The bell over the door jangled, and Miranda darted a look over Zee's shoulder. Her eyes widened, then she winked her approval. "I'll bring your pretzel. Black coffee?"

"Yes, please."

Rico joined Zee at the counter. "Same for me."

Zee released a quiet exhale. His presence, real and solid, pulled her from speculative scenarios about the demise of Angelica Street. Her fingers stretched toward his soft leather sleeve. Just a touch, to anchor her. She slowed and curled her hand back.

"Got it," said Miranda.

"But not," Rico jutted his chin to the display case, "any of those, scrumptious though they look."

Zee resolved, again, to start exercising.

She and Rico settled at a small table. When Miranda brought their orders, Zee pushed aside any food-oriented guilt and bit into the almond pretzel. Crisp parchment-thin wafers and sugar chips showered the plate.

"M-m-mm." She licked crumbs from her lips.

Rico chuckled and sipped his coffee. "Hey, this is good."

"It's your favorite."

Pleased that she'd surprised him, she indulged in another bite of pretzel, cupping her palm to catch the flakes. Buttery layers crunched between her teeth, releasing interleaved sweet almond filling, the whole delicacy finishing with a caress of frosting on her tongue.

Zee opened her eyes. When had she closed them? Rico leaned back in his chair, studying her with a bemused smile.

"Would you like a bite?" she said.

"Wouldn't dream of it." His grin widened.

Heat crept up her neck. To cover, she grabbed her coffee. "So, the update?"

"A couple of things. One, Somerworth doesn't have an alibi. Says he can't remember anything from the time he went to bed 'til he woke up around nine next morning."

"Is that unusual?" Zee eyed the pretzel but restrained herself.

"Said he hadn't slept well in months. Always woke up at night. Usually got up before dawn. Claims to be mystified at having slept nine hours straight."

"Maybe that's because he *didn't* sleep nine hours." Zee tried breaking off a piece of the pretzel instead of biting it. The result was another pastry-sugar shower. Ignoring Rico's amusement, she popped the piece into her mouth and licked her fingers. "I'm sure the police asked, but did Margaret verify that?"

"Her day off. And how do you know Margaret?"

Maybe she hadn't mentioned the Iron-Maid when she told Rico and Fontina about her meeting with Shandra, the day of thug and the broken headlight. Rather than defend herself, she decided to ignore the question. She slipped out her tongue to snag a crumb clinging to the corner of her lip. "Maybe he passed out."

Rico's jaw tightened. He shifted his gaze from Zee, and the tense lines relaxed. "Says he doesn't drink."

Zee snorted. "Guess his wife makes up for that."

"What do you mean?"

Oh hell, might as well come clean. "I went to see Shandra yesterday."

"Why?"

Zee tried for exasperation. "I thought she might need cheering up. You know, her husband in jail for murder and everything."

"Yeah, right." Rico's brows lifted over the rim of his coffee cup. "New role for you, church-lady."

Zee lowered her eyes and dusted shavings from her hands. "Rico, I don't want to argue."

"Me neither." He reached, and enclosed her fingers.

Electricity spread up her arm, but she did not pry her hand free.

"So, what happened?" he asked.

Zee tore her attention from the voltage prickling her chest. "Shandra was halfway drunk. In ten minutes, she downed two glasses of"—her free fingers formed an air quote—"'a very fine bourbon.'"

He grinned. "Sucks to be rich."

"It loosened her tongue, though. Henry lost more than money when McNeary failed."

Rico leaned forward, tightening his grasp on her hand. The current spiked.

"What I learned this morning corroborates it." Zee focused on keeping her voice steady as she recounted Akhil's story. The strategy worked. Her inner turbulence subsided. Having crossed the border into the foreign land, she pitched her tent with surprising ease.

"They need to go to the police."

His voice startled her from her musing. "I told them that, too."

"Good." He squeezed her fingers and released them.

Zee recaptured his hand. "And the second thing?"

He cocked his head.

"You said two updates."

"Oh, right. Somerworth told the cops the knife was a wedding gift. He couldn't remember when he'd seen it last."

"He can't remember a lot of things."

"This one's not so surprising, given he's not a hunter."

Zee pinched her brows.

"His father and his brother hunt," Rico said. "Henry said it was too violent."

"And yet he stabs a guy multiple times?" Zee dropped his hand, leaned back, and blew out a breath. "Do you believe him?"

"Not my job." He stretched across the table and lifted her chin. "Or yours."

She met his eyes. *A mistake.* Their blue depths swallowed her, submerging her in their dark swells. She fought them, clutching her coffee cup like a life preserver. With a flash of insight, she understood Shandra better. You love who you love, good for you or not.

Rico drew back.

His soft gaze told her he sensed her turmoil. She eased the grip on her cup, raised it, and sipped, hiding behind the china wall until equilibrium returned. When she peered around the barrier, Rico appeared engrossed in his own coffee.

She waited until he set it on the table, then strove to pick up the conversation as though she had been musing about Somerworth instead of trying not to drown. "You know, Shandra's not a likeable person, but I feel sorry for her. She loved Henry. But at the same time, there's steel in her. Her divorce lawyer arrived just before I left."

"Hell hath no fury . . ."

She nodded.

"Cutting her losses," he said.

So matter-of-fact, his voice. Like he was cutting his losses, too.

Zee yanked her attention from the painful constriction in her chest. "She's planning to move back in with her father." She studied the dark depths in her cup. "Rico, there's something, I don't know . . . unnatural about that relationship."

He squeezed her forearm. "Don't see more than there is, Zee."

A stone tied itself around her heart and sank it to her stomach. "You're right." She rubbed the goose bumps from her arms, glanced at her watch, and pushed to her feet. "I should go home and finish my column. I have a deadline today."

Rico stood and clasped her shoulders with both hands. "The police will figure it out. Prisons are full of quiet killers." A shadow crossed his face. "And parents and kids? Messed up since time began."

He flashed a smile, bent toward her, and brushed her cheek with his lips. Before Zee could react, he pulled back. "Take care of yourself."

Then he was through the door.

Zee sank into the chair. She toyed with the unfinished almond pretzel, tracing patterns with her finger through the litter of pastry shavings and frosting chips.

Once she would have licked the plate clean. Maybe if she did, she could clear the clutter from her mind. She broke the pretzel remnant in half, creating another downpour of fragments. Her eyes searched the scattered shapes. Not even Fontina could divine these dregs. There weren't enough crumbs in the world to show her the way forward with Rico.

McNeary posed a different quandary. She hadn't actually told Rico she would stop. He knew her well enough to understand that. It could explain his parting words.

Her cell sounded, an old-fashioned car horn.

"Al here, Zee. Your Mini's ready."

She pushed the plate aside. The familiar. The safe. The sane. At least for the moment, one space of solid ground where she could set her foot.

CHAPTER 37

ZEE SANK DEEPER INTO HER COUCH, glad that Fontina had time for a quick visit after they met at Al's to pick up *Po*. Glad also that Fontina hadn't been available until four o'clock. Zee had spent the intervening hours cobbling together a column on the photo exhibition. Not a gem, but it would do. She'd grimaced as she hit *Send* to submit it. This murder took up too much brain space. It was an obsession that had to end.

She cradled her wine glass. On the other side of the coffee table, Fontina sipped tea, her amber face veiled in steam. Candy sat on the floor between them, meticulously cleaning a front paw. Zee wished she could clarify her thoughts as easily.

"I can't make sense of Henry," Zee said. "Why did he use that knife?"

Fontina tipped her cup toward Zee. "The whole case turns on that choice, doesn't it?"

Zee recalled McNeary's savaged body. "For a while, I thought the attack happened in a blind rage. I figured the killer acted on the spur of the moment. Hawethorne could've just grabbed a kitchen knife, but Henry's particular weapon wouldn't be handy like that."

"It seems unlikely," Fontina said. "I'm bothered by the disparity between the ferocity of the attack and your impression of Henry, which I trust despite Akhil's description of his violent behavior."

"That's a problem for me, too." Zee swirled the wine, as if she might read the answer in the chardonnay shimmering golden in the late afternoon sun. "I'm missing something."

Fontina paused, cup halfway to her lips. "Perhaps he considered the knife a symbol. An icon of destruction to destroy the man who destroyed his new life with his new wife."

"Would Henry think that symbolically?" Zee shook her head. "That's more like James Hawethorne." Her gorge rose. She forced her mind from the horrific scene of the wreck.

"Henry thought his life was ruined, though."

Zee met her friend's gaze. "Shandra loved him. They could have worked it out."

Fontina's mouth curved upward a tiny bit.

"I saw that," Zee snapped. "We're not talking about me and Rico." A gulp of wine stung the back of her throat, and she struggled to contain a cough.

Abandoning her paw, Candy leapt to the couch and curled in Zee's lap. Her purring warmth soothed the cold stone in Zee's stomach.

"No, we're not." Fontina smiled as she poured more tea, releasing traces of orange and mint on the breeze through the balcony door. She set the pot on the table and straightened. "But now that you mention it . . ."

Zee exhaled. "Maybe we can find our way. Find what, I hope, he still wants." There, she'd admitted it—to Fontina, not to him. Fear quivered in her gut.

"And I saw that." Fontina leaned toward Zee, her deep brown eyes full of compassion. "You just took a really big step, Zee-zee."

Forget the tent. She was building a house in unexplored territory. "Okay," Zee said, "but enough for now."

"Then," Fontina sat back, "return to the facts, Shelby."

Zee took a slow sip. "Maybe Henry doubted Shandra's love. After all, he nearly broke off their engagement."

"Why do you think he changed his mind?"

"He decided she—they—were worth fighting for?" Zee fidgeted on the couch cushions. Dammit, she felt like she was giving herself a pep talk. She refocused. "If he wanted to save the marriage, why did he wreck everything?"

"I can think of one reason," said Fontina. "He'd given up."

Zee's breath quickened. "Maybe he thought he could command some respect, though. Is it possible he used that knife to guarantee he'd *get credit* for decisive action?"

Fontina's slender fingers toyed with the bloodstone drop in her earring. "A desperate, irrational move."

Shame for her stupidity flared in Zee's chest. Desperate to cling to what they valued, people did foolish things, like push away people who loved them, for the illusive safety of hiding from life.

She flashed on Pete Bottmeyer's complaint about Shandra. Always coming over *to see how he was doing.* His tone left no doubt he wished she'd leave him alone. Would he regret that attitude later?

"Drachma for your thoughts?"

Zee's reverie splintered. "Shandra's father. He's another victim of this mess. He saw Henry as a savior. Shandra said he was happy the marriage had gone through, because she would have someone to take care of her."

A neighbor's four-foot wind chime tolled deep tones. A death knell for so many hopes.

"Shandra?" Fontina arched her brows. "She doesn't strike me as a person who needs anyone to take care of her."

"You didn't see her break down when she talked to me after Henry's arrest." Even as she countered Fontina's argument, Zee's synapses twitched. Shandra had cried, but she'd also made a speedy appointment with a divorce lawyer.

"People often act differently in extremity," said Fontina, "but they usually revert to character sooner or later."

Zee grimaced. "She's as irrational as her father. She writes a note to get her friend out of jail, then shrugs when I suggest that she'd be living with a murderer if Henry got away with it."

"But by then, as you pointed out, she knew she wouldn't be living with him. And unless she signed a prenup, she'll likely come out of this in good financial shape. So, her father's hopes are actually fulfilled."

The hair on Zee's neck prickled. A half-formed thought, jagged and dangerous, lurked at the edge of her awareness.

Fontina glanced at her watch. "I have to go. Emilio and I are having dinner before the movie."

Zee lifted Candy from her lap. "Thanks for lending me *Diana*."

"*Po*," Fontina smiled at the Mini's new moniker, "looks as good as new."

"I like the name. Even if he's no longer blind."

Fontina winked. "Master Po always saw very well." She tossed a shawl around her shoulders and paused. "I wonder, Zee-zee, what kind of relationship Shandra and Henry would have had if this hadn't happened. Given Shandra's almost fanatical devotion, would Pete Bottmeyer have become an unwelcome third presence?"

The elusive idea snuck in from the shadows, poked a barbed finger into Zee's spine, and triggered a memory of Shandra's sitting room. "He may have been well on his way to that already," Zee said.

At the doorway, they hugged. Fontina stepped back and locked eyes with Zee. "I know you're chewing on this. Please be careful."

Zee dredged up a smile. "Don't worry." She closed the door behind Fontina and sagged against it. If only she could take her own advice. Dissatisfaction pestered her as she fed Candy, contemplated the barren refrigerator, and made ancient microwave popcorn for dinner.

She dumped the misshapen kernels into a bowl and carried it to the balcony with a cup of tea and a legal pad. Time to think her way through this, to lay her nagging unease to rest, once and for all. The *Tribune*'s reporters, all enamored with their computers, would laugh at her, but when she wanted to sort her thoughts, nothing worked better than writing by hand.

At the top of the page she wrote: *Means, Motive, Opportunity*, and along the left, she listed everyone involved: Paselly, Mercy, Hawethorne, Street, Bottmeyer, Henry, Shandra, even Janece, Akhil, and Veronique from the Sandhurst School. Then she crossed out the first four. Her pen paused over Paselly, but he'd had his chance and failed. And the last three didn't meet the criteria. That left Henry, Shandra, and Pete.

Zee stared at the names until they danced before her eyes. No matter how she conjugated that unholy trinity, she could discern no clear path to the truth.

She leaned back in her chair. Dusk transformed the landscape into a pointillist painting in which dots of surface color continually dissolved, revealing the gray beneath. Her shoulders sagged. The seeping darkness seemed an infection, draining the vitality of light and hue until all that remained were shadows.

She rubbed her temples. The gloom contained the rot she sought, the fetid bed from which the violence had erupted. She had to find a way to see beneath the enchanting colors in this case.

Landscape lights winked on, resurrecting pots of mums and hydrangea from the field of ash. The orchestrated focus of illumination destroyed her concentration—so much for divining the dark.

Unexpected, Rico's advice sounded in her ears: *Don't see more than there is.* And on the heels of his warning came a thought: What she saw depended on where she shone the light.

Zee started in the chair. She grabbed the pen and scribbled to keep up with her unspooling thoughts. When she stopped, she gaped at the page.

It made sense.

Trembling, she reread what she'd written. Line by line, her pen traced the inked path of logic. Sweat peppered her forehead. The map on the page revealed a calculating, pitiless murderer, and one unforeseen consequence that placed another innocent person in peril.

Unless she intervened.

She bolted to her feet. A startled Candy skittered a few feet away, spun, and hissed. Zee barely registered the cat's annoyance.

Or was Candy warning her? Zee stopped in her tracks. The scenario answered all her questions, but it rested on speculation. No proof, nothing she could take to Bernstow.

She sank onto her seat. An orange-and-cream head ventured near enough for her to stretch out and touch. "You don't need to be cautious, Candy-pants." Zee drew her fingertips along the silky fur. "But I will be. I won't try this without backup."

Mollified, Candy crawled into Zee's lap and allowed Zee to stroke her velvet ears with one hand while with the other, she tapped Rico's number. She'd need to convince him to go with her, but stay in the car. Her chances of success would be better if she confronted her quarry alone.

After six rings, the call went to voicemail. Zee disconnected without speaking. If he wouldn't agree to follow her lead, he might be a liability. She couldn't risk an interruption.

Someone should know where she went, though. She called Fontina, aware she would be shunted to voicemail, and left a message.

Her knees quaked as she pocketed the phone. Candy meowed and wriggled upward to nuzzle her neck. Zee buried her cheek in the soft fur, feeling her heart knock against the cat's ribs.

Maybe she should wait.

A chorus of voices rose in her mind:

Fontina: *Trust your intuition.*

Rico: *You're stronger than I give you credit for.*

Hawethorne: *You'll see that justice is done.*

A pang stabbed her chest. Fiery and fierce, it disintegrated the icy tentacles of fear. She would not let another blameless man die.

She got to her feet. "I see no alternative, Candy-pants." She hugged the cat and released her. "Wish me luck."

CHAPTER 38

U RGENCY PUSHED LIKE A FIST against Zee's ribcage, but she forced herself to drive cautiously on the dampening road. Drizzle misted her windshield. Oncoming headlights blossomed into chrysanthemums before *Po's* wipers obliterated them.

While her tires ate the distance, strategies circled like fighters sizing each other up. A blunt declaration might trigger an admission—although it hadn't worked well before—and with an unstable person, finesse might be wiser, and safer.

The rain picked up. She increased her wiper frequency but kept the speedometer steady. Would her quarry be drunk? That could advance Zee's purpose or spark further danger. Her thoughts darted from one scenario to another but made little progress, only wore themselves out like the rubber blades on her windshield in their fruitless quest for clarity.

A downpour pummeled the roof of the car as she exited the highway. She flipped on her high beams. Perhaps she should try a compassionate approach. Sympathy creates a powerful bond. She might be able to exploit that. It would be like walking a tightrope. One false step . . .

The curve was upon her before she knew it. The tires skittered as she let off the gas. *Po* corrected. Zee sucked a gulp of air.

Enough of spinning scenarios. She needed to focus.

The rough surface twisted and climbed as she remembered. Visibility shortened. Trees and underbrush pressed in on all sides until she felt as if she were driving in a tunnel. She crept, scanning left and right whenever she dared to take her eyes off the bright cone that illuminated her path.

As her physical vision narrowed, distractions stripped themselves from her mind. A plan emerged. Fraught with uncertainty, but feasible.

Shelby would do it. "Half of detecting," she liked to say, "was being a good actor."

People might fall for that on television.

Zee tightened her jaw. She wasn't Shelby, a fictional detective. She was a real-life reporter, with a passion for truth and a conscience that demanded she keep her promises.

Were it not for the light in the cabin, she would have missed the dilapidated structure. She backed, killed the headlights, and pulled into the gravel driveway. A few tense moments passed while she waited for her vision to adjust. No one twitched the threadbare curtains or cracked open the door. The beat-up sedan sat alone, stoic under the water streaming off its roof and hood.

With a prayer that her faith in herself would prove true, she opened the Mini's door.

Rain exploded in her ears. Thousands of tiny drops drummed on thousands of leaves and the tin roof of the drooping porch. She shouldn't have worried about the engine announcing her arrival. The storm swallowed her footsteps as she hurried up the driveway.

A furtive glance through the thin curtain told her that Bottmeyer was alone. His back to the door, he slumped on the worn couch, a three-quarters empty whiskey bottle on the floor at his feet.

She squared her shoulders, knocked, and pushed the door open. "Hey!" He jerked and spun toward the entryway.

Zee stepped quickly inside. She pitched her voice low, non-threatening she hoped. "Mister Bottmeyer, I'm here as a friend."

She locked her eyes with his and stayed out of his reach as she circled to face him. He tracked her but made no move to stand.

Sparing a sideways glance at the sagging armchair, she pulled a spindly, hard-backed seat from the dining table and lowered herself into it. "I understand how very stressful life has been, and I think I can help you."

"Help me how?" He stared at her, his gaze unfocused. "What are you talking about?"

Stifling a gag at his reeking breath, Zee leaned toward him. "I know everything."

"Everything about what?"

"McNeary's murder."

He squinted at her, then picked up the bottle. *Old Elijah*. His hand shook as he poured half the remaining amber liquid into his glass, but when he spoke, his tone had hardened. "What is it you think you know?"

She infused her voice with sympathy. "I know you love your daughter, Mister Bottmeyer. It must have hurt to see her happiness nearly destroyed. You were under a lot of stress, with your wife's stroke and the pressure to finish the book to save your career. It seems clear that you just snapped and struck at the man who caused it all."

She held her breath.

Bottmeyer stared at her, then set the glass on the scarred coffee table. He leaned forward, hands braced against his bony knees, rheumy eyes now chips of flint. "You better take me through it step-by-step."

Zee swallowed. "All right. Here's how I see it. Shandra is betrothed to a wealthy man, who will ensure that she's well taken care of. Your father's duty is done. Everything's fine until McNeary's enterprise fails." She watched his face as the memories played across it. "It must have burned to see the Somerworths' naked hypocrisy."

He barked a laugh. "Bunch of rats."

Zee nodded. "But Shandra rescues the situation. You're relieved when she saves the engagement. It stung I bet, to see your daughter grovel and beg, work to prove her worth. Did she have to convince Henry himself?"

Bottmeyer dug a filthy handkerchief from his pocket and blew his nose and wiped his eyes. "I don't know how she did it. I don't want to think about it, but yeah, it stung like a bitch."

"I can't imagine."

"No, you can't." His face purpled. "He didn't deserve her, but she loved him. I had to choke it down and smile." He gulped a slug of bourbon.

Zee realized she'd been gripping the sides of her wooden seat. She relaxed her hands in her lap. First step accomplished. She must convince him now. "So, the marriage takes place. Maybe at first you were able to put aside your doubts, but as time went on, you could no longer deny Shandra's misery. That's when you set your plan in motion."

"My plan?" Bottmeyer ran a hand through his stringy hair.

Zee laced her voice with equal parts admiration and accusation. "You're a writer, Mister Bottmeyer. You concocted an ingenious way to exact your revenge."

Bottmeyer sloshed some whiskey as he refilled his glass, then sat back on the ratty couch as if to enjoy a show. "You figure I killed Ian as an ingenious plan for revenge? Okay, I'll bite."

So far, so good; Zee had counted on his curiosity and his ego. She began ticking off on her fingers. "Revenge number one: McNeary is dead, the man who drove you to bankruptcy, ruined your wife's health, and destroyed your ability to write. You even said you should tell Shandra and Henry's story, since you couldn't seem to write anything original."

Bottmeyer's thin lips formed a bemused smile. "Go on. This is fascinating."

At least he was listening. She continued. "Revenge number two: Henry is accused of murder, the man who rejected your beloved

Shandra, whom you yourself described as a daughter any man would die for."

His eyes misted, but anger flared in their depths.

"Revenge number three," Zee plowed on. "The Somerworths are embarrassed by a nasty scandal, a society family's worst nightmare."

His mouth twisted in an ugly sneer. "Delightful thought."

Zee waited, but he said nothing further. She tapped her fourth finger. "And revenge number four: Shandra comes out of the whole thing with a chunk of the rich folks' money." She sat back, hoping she exuded confidence.

Bottmeyer rubbed a heavy-veined hand over his unshaven chin. "I have to admit, it's a darn good plot."

It wasn't the only one at work here, but she couldn't read him to know whether her plan was succeeding.

He swallowed half his drink and squinted at her. "What led you to me? Other than conjecture, you got any evidence?"

She inhaled. Time to play her trump card.

"It came down to the knife. I just couldn't figure out why Henry Somerworth would commit a murder with a weapon easily traced to him. Then I found out you gave it to him as a wedding gift. That was particularly sly. If Shandra didn't divulge Henry's ownership, you would simply tell the police when they came for you."

Bottmeyer's mask cracked. His jaw worked. He glanced at her, then quickly looked away, but not before she saw the pain in his eyes. She held her breath, watching him fracture. He did not speak.

The silence lengthened. Sickened by what she felt forced to do but spurred by McNeary's brutal murder, she searched for another weapon to break him. An idea occurred. Weak, might even backfire, but it was all she had. She leaned into his line of sight. "Need more?"

He lifted his tortured eyes to her.

"Shandra will undoubtedly share her good fortune with you when she returns to live here. As you counted on." She gestured to the pitiful room. "Your daughter never really left you. It's obvious in the ways she tried to brighten this place. She even provides your favorite bourbon. And now she's coming back. Just the way you planned."

As if she'd dropped a weighted net on him, his body sagged. His face crumpled. His sallow skin grayed.

Zee started from her chair. "What is it?"

He held up his hand. "It's all right, Miss . . ."

"Morani," Zee supplied. She remained perched on the edge of her seat, eyes trained on him.

"It's a brilliant plot, and I wish I'd thought of it. For a book. But you're wrong." He dropped his head into his hands. "I can't believe . . ."

Zee didn't dare move. She could feel him teetering on the edge.

Bottmeyer's thin body heaved. His hand trembled as he picked up his glass.

She tensed, searching his face for any sign of violent intent.

He drained the whiskey and met Zee's eyes. "I'm not your killer, but—God help me—I might know who is." He sucked in a ragged breath. "It wasn't my idea, the knife. Shandra badgered me and pestered me until I agreed to give it to him."

Tears ran down his sunken cheeks. His body seemed to collapse in on itself, as though some piece of interior scaffolding had given way. He fixed her with a bleak stare. "You knew, all along, didn't you? You just needed me to see."

Zee nodded. She felt no sense of victory, only massive weariness and the urgent desire to move this tragedy to conclusion. As the final cruelty, she must push him to act in the midst of his terrible grief. "I need your help," she said, holding his gaze. "Will you go with me to the police?"

He didn't answer. Immobile, he stared as if into the depths of hell. "All her life, Shandra's been a bit high-strung. Always been fixated on money. It only got worse after her mother's stroke. But I deserve the bigger blame. Same old story, too busy with my career to be the father she wanted." He ran fingers through his greasy hair. "She tried so hard to make me that."

Zee thought of all the photos in Shandra's sitting room. "Mister Bottmeyer."

He didn't seem to hear her. Outside, the storm had abated, but the old cabin creaked around them. He strained to speak, as if he had to pull loose the words lodged in his throat. "Trouble is, Shandra's adoration suffocates me. I thought she'd have her own life after she married, and finally leave me alone." He slammed the empty glass on the coffee table.

Zee jumped but didn't take her eyes from him.

"And now she plans to move back in?" His voice rose. "No. Even if she wasn't a . . . murderer, I can't *stand* the idea."

"Papa!"

Zee jerked her eyes in the direction of the strangled cry.

Bottmeyer whirled toward the door. "Shandra, honey."

"Don't *honey* me," Shandra screeched. Red blotches marred her creamy skin, and her perfectly cut curtain of blonde hair dripped down the soaked sleeves of her silken jacket. Sleeves that ended in shaking hands. Shaking hands that pointed a gun.

CHAPTER 39

Z EE FROZE IN THE SPINDLY CHAIR, unable to take her eyes from the gun in Shandra's dripping hands. Bottmeyer's mouth gaped.

His drenched daughter stomped into the cabin. "Everything I did was for *you*," she cried. She circled, closing on the arm of the couch where her father sat.

He turned in slow motion, following her. Behind him, rain blew in through the open door, spattering the old wooden floor.

Fury shook Shandra's body but didn't reach her stony eyes. She stopped a few feet from Zee's rickety dining chair, in a position where she could keep both her prey in sight. She flicked the gun barrel at Zee. "You stay where you are."

Her gaze shifted to her father. "McNeary ruined you, and I could've killed him right then." Her voice climbed and quivered. She paced between the door and the curtained window, but kept the weapon trained on Bottmeyer. "Later, I almost forgave him because he did me a favor, showed me the kind of man I was marrying, the kind of family that spawned him."

Zee shuddered at the venom in her tone.

Shandra halted. Closer to Zee, but out of reach. Her rage-blotched face softened. Her voice lost its manic edge and became childlike, wheedling. "You were struggling, Papa, and suddenly I saw how it could all work."

Bottmeyer stared, his mouth slack, and said nothing. Sodden leaves gusted in from the porch.

Shandra appeared to wait for a response. When none came, her jaw hardened. Her fingers tightened on the weapon.

Zee started in the chair. "What are you doing with a gun?" she blurted, then mentally kicked herself for asking such a stupid question.

The socialite's laugh chilled Zee's marrow. "I bought it for protection. And power." She bored icy eyes into Zee's. "Ever shoot a gun? It's fabulous. Whenever I couldn't stand Henry, I'd imagine snuggling the barrel against his shiny, sweaty, worthless head while he slept and—bang." She jerked the firearm, mimicking the shot.

Zee's heart threatened to beat its way out of her chest.

"Got'cha." Shandra laughed again. "I can see why Papa likes writing about violence."

Bottmeyer's Adam's apple bobbed in his scrawny neck. He licked his dry lips. "It's one thing to plan a murder for a book, but to actually do it? What's wrong with you?"

Shandra stiffened. "Nothing's wrong with *me*." She strode toward the shrunken man on the couch. The gun barrel dipped.

Zee kicked her mind past paralytic terror. She gauged the distance at no more than five feet. She could throw herself at the woman, knock her off balance. A corner of the listing coffee table stood in her way, but she might be able to dodge that. If Shandra squeezed the trigger, though, the bullet could fly anywhere. Pain stitched beneath Zee's scar.

Bottmeyer shot Zee a glance and leaned toward Shandra. "I meant what I said." His voice crawled from his throat, laden with disgust. "I've earned some blame, but sooner or later, everybody has to grow up. You didn't. You wouldn't." He tried to stand, wobbled, and fell heavily onto the cushions.

Eyes glued to the gun, Zee slid her foot back and braced herself to lunge.

Shandra stepped closer to her father.

He pushed his face in hers. "You're a, a succubus, stuck to me, draining my life."

Zee shifted her weight. The wobbly chair creaked.

Shandra whipped her head, backed a step, and swung the firearm toward Zee. She hissed through her teeth. "I said don't move."

Zee's muscles turned to water.

Shandra glanced at Bottmeyer. "Nice try, Papa." Derision dripped in her voice. "Guess you have a few brain cells that still function."

She leveled her scorn at Zee. "All I needed you to do was point the police in the right direction after they arrested Jim. Figured they'd listen to you after you helped them with that other case. But you didn't know when to stop." She sneered. "And you *still* got it wrong. You thought Papa killed him."

The accusation stung, but Zee held her tongue. Better if Shandra thought her dimwitted. Instead, Zee parroted Rico. "The police are going to figure this out."

Shandra ignored the comment. "What were you going to do here? Get Papa to confess?" The socialite's eyes, blue and soulless, drilled into her. "That's rich."

"Shandra, you *killed* a man." Bottmeyer choked out the words.

His daughter pivoted toward him, her face a mask of hatred. "Yes, Papa. I did. I *killed* him. For us. So we could be together."

She flung the words at her father like daggers. He recoiled as if they pinned him to the couch.

"Too late now. That plan won't work." With the back of her hand, Shandra wiped spittle from her lips. The maroon gloss bloodied her knuckles. "You let me marry that loathsome coward of a man, just so you could get me out of your life."

Zee wiped her palms on her rain-soaked pants. Her mind raced for a way to stop Shandra, but the woman remained several feet from both her and Bottmeyer. He sagged against the cushions, beaten.

Shandra surveyed the small, shabby room. A smile crept across her face.

Zee fought her rising panic. She must keep Bottmeyer's daughter talking. "Shandra, listen to me. Whatever you're thinking, it's not going to work. People know I'm here."

The socialite flicked her a contemptuous glance. "Not a problem." She backed toward the door and, keeping the gun trained on Zee, lifted her purse from the floor, and tossed it onto the couch. "Inside you'll find a bottle of sleeping pills. Take a couple, *Daadeee*." She drew the word out, mocking him. "Take half a dozen. They worked like a charm on poor, dear Henry."

Horror weakened Zee's knees. Poor, dear Henry never suspected the viper in his bed. She forced her mind from the thought. Sympathy could come later—if there was a later. "You can't run far enough, Shandra." She half-rose from her chair.

Shandra pointed the gun at Zee's chest. She made a show of flexing her trigger finger. "Sit down or I'll shoot you right now."

Zee's legs buckled, but when she sat, she chose the edge of the chair.

Shandra smirked. "I won't need to run. The pills are so Papa won't feel anything in the fire. Be nice and I might let you have a few."

Ice ran down the back of Zee's shirt. Horrified, she watched as Bottmeyer struggled to unscrew the cap.

"Push down and twist, Papa." Shandra barked a contemptuous laugh. "Sorry it's not a whiskey bottle."

The old man's unsteady hands worked the cap until it freed. He shook a pile of white tablets into his palm.

"Pete," Zee cried. "Don't!"

He turned defeated eyes to Zee. "Maybe it's better that my life ends now." He glanced toward his daughter, a dripping Fury holding a gun leveled at him. "I've lived too long as it is."

Before Zee could say another word, he popped the pills into his mouth, leaned down, and picked up the bourbon bottle. His watery eyes caught Zee's, not conquered but fierce, determined. In one smooth motion, he twisted and hurled the whiskey at Shandra.

Zee launched from her chair.

The bottle exploded against the wall as she slammed into Shandra. Zee's elbow cracked against the coffee table. Her arm spasmed, but she didn't need finesse, only blunt force. She got it.

She and Shandra thudded onto the floor. Stars imploded behind her eyes, but something hard and metal skittered across the rough planks.

Zee landed on top of the slender socialite, but momentum rolled her to the side. Before she could get clear, Shandra clamped her wrist, viselike, and wrenched her arm. Fire burst from her shoulder socket and seared across her collarbone.

Zee yelped. Shandra seemed to draw strength from the cry. She shoved Zee down, heaved her weight atop her, and pinned her chest to the floor. Zee twisted her head as burgundy lacquered nails stabbed at her eyes but tore her cheek. A river of pain streaked from ear to throat. Anger overrode shock. "Damn you!"

With her good arm, Zee punched hard at Shandra's face. Her fist landed in the soft throat tissue, and she felt a moment's triumph at the other woman's gasp. Taking advantage of the distraction, she grabbed Shandra's arm and rolled, thrusting her hip upward with all her might.

Shandra toppled.

Zee scrambled free. She scooted backward, kicking wildly. Agile as a panther, Shandra dodged her sluggish strikes. She sneered, derision in her ice-blue gaze.

Zee swiped stinging sweat from her eyes. *Damn Shandra and her skim-milk lattes.* She lashed out with her foot. Sandra grabbed it and twisted. Agony spiked through Zee's ankle. She howled despite herself.

Shandra grinned and launched her body, slamming Zee against the wooden frame on the back of the couch. Pain detonated in her injured shoulder. Her head smacked the boards. Bells clanged in her ears.

She gasped for air, but none came. Instead, sharp-nailed thumbs dug against her windpipe. She clawed at the tightening noose, trying to stave off the blackness at the edges of her vision. In the swirling darkness, a memory glimmered, something Fontina taught her.

Fighting dizziness and screams from her bruised, torn body, Zee stretched behind her neck. She fastened her hands around Shandra's little fingers and yanked them backward. An ear-splitting yowl sliced through the air. The lacquered talons came loose from her neck.

Zee gulped a draught of air and head-butted toward Shandra's face. Her attacker's nose gave with a satisfying crack. Shandra screeched and fell backward.

Zee shoved the shrieking socialite aside. She struggled to stand, to protect the vulnerable injured parts of her body. Her leaden limbs got her to her knees.

Shandra landed a kick hard below her ribs. Air burst from her lungs. Shandra kicked again. Zee's stomach squashed. Nausea ribboned through her gut.

Shandra laughed, a hyena braying, glorying in the kill. She rained savage blows, her leather-shod feet like pile drivers. White-hot blasts exploded from Zee's hip, her shoulder blade, her ribcage. She twisted to fend off the attacks, but she couldn't block them all.

Desperate, she tried to crawl out of reach. A kidney strike paralyzed her with shock waves. She collapsed onto the floor, broken glass biting into her forearms and palms, bourbon stinging in her wounds.

The assault stopped.

Her mind screamed frantic orders to move. Her spasming muscles could not comply. She lay on the floor, panting. Cool damp air washed over her, soothing, almost seductive. She drew strength from it and managed to roll onto her back on her bed of glass shards. It was the best she could do. At least, she could face whatever came next.

The air was full of labored breathing. Hers and Shandra's. Blood gushed from Shandra's nose. She swiped at it with the back of her hand and smeared it down the front of her blouse.

Like an apparition, she loomed over Zee's helpless supine form. A lake of ice spread in Zee's chest as she read the woman's intention.

Everything slowed. The cacophony of pain that battered her body, muted. Dreamlike, Shandra floated above her.

Zee's tortured mind objected. The body did not move like that. The body must obey the laws of physics.

Physics. From some remote crevice in her brain, an idea wriggled free. She searched with her fingers near her hip and closed around what she needed, then concentrated on lying still and marshalling her strength.

The malice in Shandra's eyes unnerved Zee, but she dared not look away. She tracked the upraised foot in her peripheral vision.

It demanded all Zee's will to gauge the moment and wait. It commanded all her physical strength to squirm aside at the last instant. Pain lanced through her ribs, but Shandra's stomp sliced past her, and its momentum as it missed its target threw the standing woman off balance.

Zee shot her arm out, grabbed Shandra's ankle, and jerked it toward her. With all the force she could muster, she slashed with the chunk of glass she'd hidden in her hand. She grit her teeth as she felt her weapon bite deep into flesh. Batted back queasiness at the blood that slicked her fingers. Closed her ears to Shandra's primal scream.

Shoving aside any thought of hesitation, Zee struck again with the jagged shard. She fought her instinctive recoil at the resistance of skin and muscle, then released the juddering limb and scrambled free.

Shandra's shrieks flooded the cabin with pain, terror, and fury. "You fucking bitch!"

Zee dragged herself to her knees. Her chest heaved. Sharp pangs splintered across her ribs. A hammer beat behind her eyes.

The wounded woman lay near the open cabin door. Spewing invective, she crawled to the wall and pushed her body to a sitting position against it. Her wounds left a crimson trail that glistened on the floorboards.

Panting, Zee backed to spread the distance between them. She scanned for the firearm.

"I have the gun." Bottmeyer's voice croaked from the direction of the couch.

Zee sagged with relief. Then swiveled toward him in a moment of doubt. Whose side was he on?

He directed his grim stare, and the weapon, toward his daughter.

Braced against the wall, Shandra glared back. Sweat and blood streaked her elegant features as she hunched over her ravaged leg. Defiance flared in her eyes, and she jutted her chin despite the tears that dripped from it.

"It's over, Shandra," Zee said. And to Bottmeyer, "I'll call the police. Keep her covered."

"I know how to keep a cornered animal trapped." He clenched his jaw with such ferocity she feared it might break, but she had no time for comforting yet. Hampered by her twisted ankle, she hobbled toward her purse. She righted the spindly overturned chair.

Behind her, a voice rose. "Zee-zee!"

Fontina.

Zee whirled. Her friend stood just inside the door.

"No!" Zee cried.

Shandra had pushed herself upright. She lashed an arm across Fontina's chest. Against her throat, she pressed the broken neck of the whiskey bottle. She hissed. "Drop the gun, *Daddy.*"

CHAPTER 40

Her bleeding leg braced against the open cabin door, Shandra tightened her grasp on Fontina. She pressed the jagged neck of the bourbon bottle hard against her captive's throat. "You," she spat at Zee, "sit."

Zee obeyed, dropping into the spindly chair. She hurt all over, but her injured ankle throbbed all the way to her knee. Seated, she could exert more control over her body, though she was careful to hide that from Shandra.

"Papa," Shandra coated the word in ice. "Drop. The. Gun." She pricked Fontina's copper skin. A bead of blood welled. Zee tasted it in her own mouth. She forced down boiling rage.

From his perch on the couch, the old man jutted his chin. "Why should I? You'll kill us anyway. In fact," he raised the barrel to his temple, "I'll expedite the process."

"Don't!" Zee cried.

His finger tightened on the trigger.

Her glance fell on the coffee table. With her good leg, she kicked hard at the edge. It bashed against his shins.

"Son of a—" He grabbed at his leg.

Zee threw herself across the flimsy table. One end splintered and collapsed. She slid toward Bottmeyer, batting at his scrawny arm. A shot exploded. Fire burst in her shoulder as she plowed into him.

The gun flew from his upraised hand.

A thought pushed through the freight train roaring in her brain. If she could get the weapon, she'd have a chance.

Ignoring the screams from her battered body, she lunged for the drifting gray metal. Her fingers closed around the handle. Slipped. Juggled. She landed amid the debris of the ruined table, clutching the barrel. Heart pounding, she rolled onto her back and switched her grip. She swept the room.

Bottmeyer slumped against the cushions. She couldn't see anyone else, couldn't hear, either, above the din in her tortured ears. She forced herself to flip onto her protesting ribcage. Blind and deaf, she edged along the side of the couch and peered around the corner.

Shandra sprawled face down on the floor. Fontina bent over her, a boot planted between the socialite's shoulder blades.

"I got this." Fontina's muffled voice barely penetrated.

Blood from Shandra's calf saturated her silk trousers. She shifted. Fontina resettled her foot.

Zee let her head drop onto her hands, then jerked as her forehead brushed cold steel. She'd never fired a gun. She needed to get rid of it before she hurt someone.

She levered herself to her feet. A bright flare fanned across the room, followed by another, and another. Headlights, shining through the ragged curtain. Relief weakened her knees, and she sagged against the thinly upholstered arm of the couch.

"Check her father," Fontina said.

Bottmeyer's chest heaved. Zee touched his bony shoulder. "You okay?"

In the wash of light, he turned dazed eyes on her. "I think I missed."

EYES CLOSED, HUDDLED ON THE COUCH, Zee let *home* lap at her ears. A comforting purr vibrated from the nest of blankets in her lap. Its bass note underscored the clink of ice, the rustle of plastic wrap, and the low murmurs of Fontina and Rico in the kitchen. Through the open balcony doors, the post-midnight breeze brought the low hoot of a barred owl.

The disparate parts of Zee's body had coalesced into one dull ache, periodically pierced by an arrow of pain, a spasm of fire, or an anvil dropping on her head. Sometime during the visit to the emergency room, her mind spun off its hinges and refused to produce anything but static. Fontina saved her, answering the nurse's questions.

Zee shifted her weight. A barbed twinge forked through her separated shoulder. From her burrow, Candy lifted her head, blinked yellow eyes, and then snuggled deeper. Zee shivered and clutched the blanket closer. The feline's usual furnace failed to thaw the trauma-induced chattering in her limbs.

Rico pressed a tumbler of scotch into her hand. "Drink this. I swear it will help." He passed another to Fontina, then reclaimed his spot next to Zee.

She dared a cautious sip. The liquid burned down her throat and landed in a pool of flame in her belly. "Not bad," she croaked. "Hope I have some stomach lining when I'm finished."

Rico's grin softened into an affectionate smile. Tension eased from his eyes. He glanced toward Fontina. "Good stuff. Thank Emilio."

"For all this too," whispered Zee. She gestured to the plate of cheeses, olives, and nuts.

"I will." Fontina palmed a handful of almonds and sat back in the overstuffed chair. "He thinks of these things."

Zee swallowed more scotch, coughed, and regretted it. Pain spidered through her abused ribs.

Rico caught her eyes. "Want to go to bed?" His gaze held only concern, though a flush spread beneath the nubby shadow on his jaw.

She proffered a smile, quickly aborted. Her flesh stung where Shandra's nails ripped. "Can't sleep yet." A giggle bubbled from her lips. "I need a bedtime story."

His dark brows arched over the rim of his glass.

Fontina set her untouched scotch on the side table and laced her fingers in her lap. "Once upon a time, there were two friends,"— she smiled at Rico—"*three* friends who confronted a mystery. And despite their bumbling, they managed to solve it."

"Stop it," Zee said. "It hurts to laugh."

"Nut graph then," said Rico.

Fontina raised her brows.

"It's news lingo for summary," Zee explained. "Like we use angel on a pinhead."

Rico chuckled. "One of these days I'll learn all *your* codes." He turned toward Zee and found her eyes. "Key question: why was the knife in the lake? Answer: because the police *had* to find it. Shandra planned to leave it in McNeary's office, but Hawethorne's arrival prevented that. And she couldn't take the time to dispose of it in the dumpster."

A shudder rippled through Zee at the memory of her noxious excursion. "I'm never getting anywhere near the inside of a dumpster again."

"Good," said Rico. "Searching it was foolish, and dangerous."

Zee chuckled. "True, but you should've seen the poor cop who had to frisk me. And sweet Burger Boy." She let another silken sip of scotch trickle down her throat, then extended an unsteady hand toward the plate.

Rico touched her forearm. "Let me. You stay warm." He tucked the soft fabric around her shoulders. Her next shiver had nothing to do with her chill and everything to do with the glow that danced in his ridiculously blue eyes and the electricity that sparked from his fingertips. He cupped her hand in his, a cradle that heated her arm all the way to her elbow.

"Cheese?" he said.

She nodded.

"Gouda okay?"

"That would be gooo-dah." She snickered.

He sent her a sideways grin and leaned toward the coffee table. His fingers lingered over the plate. "I could feed you." His eyes twinkled.

"Gimme." She stuck out her palm, giggled again. He was right, the scotch slid down more smoothly with every swallow. "You forget; I'm a mean fighter."

"Yeah, I like that about you." He smiled, teeth gleaming against dusky skin, crinkled eyes sparkling. "As you wish." He surrendered the creamy square.

Zee stifled a grin, though smiling didn't hurt as much anymore.

"Be right back." Fontina's quiet voice penetrated the warm cocoon. "Going to get napkins." She rose from the armchair, trailing luminescent ethereal fibers.

Zee blinked. She must be hallucinating from painkillers . . . alcohol . . . shock . . . all of the above. She turned to Rico and melted toward his soft radiance.

Some part of her clamored to slam the brakes before reality abandoned her. Another part urged her to go ahead, yield to this alternate world.

Her hand must have listened to the clamor. She found the cheese in her mouth. Its initial firmness gave way to velvety texture that smoothed itself over her tongue. Sweetness laced with hints of caramel and nuts triggered exultations from her taste buds. Such a tiny package for a universe of flavors.

She opened her eyes. Her heart felt a pang of regret at Rico's fading aura. Her mind grabbed the chance to latch onto normalcy. "How did you know where to find me?"

Fontina, no longer trailing tendrils of light, laid napkins on the table. "I got your message, and your conclusions made sense. But I wondered whether her father helped her plan it. Either way, I wanted you nowhere near either of them. I called Rico, but I was halfway down the freeway when he called me back."

"I agreed we needed to get to you, but on *my* way," Rico shot a reproachful glance at Fontina, "I called Bernstow. Turns out he had his own questions. Been searching for a witness. Hoping someone saw who dropped the knife in the lake. And, he found one, an old lady walking her dog."

"Mary," Zee murmured. A sharp-eyed, invisible old woman. Zee resolved to find her and thank her, buy Louisa some dog treats.

Rico sipped his scotch. "The witness described Shandra. Said the same lady put the note on your car."

The note she never gave to Bernstow. Zee hid her face behind the whiskey glass. When she'd mapped her way to the truth earlier in her apartment, it was Shandra's lie about why she wrote it that changed her perspective.

Rico leaned closer. "I gotta know. How'd you figure it out before the cops?"

An upsurge of tears tightened Zee's throat. He wasn't humoring her. He sincerely wanted to know. She swallowed a tiny bit of her drink. "To begin with, there were all those clues that she was totally freaking nuts."

"To say the least," he said.

"The break came when you told me Henry had trouble sleeping, but he slept for nine hours that night. Struck me as convenient."

"Me, too, but it was irrelevant," Rico said. "He was out of the house when McNeary was murdered."

"That's what Shandra wanted me to believe," said Zee. "She said her maid told her he'd gone to the office, but that was impossible." Zee straightened. Muffled pain stitched her side, easy to ignore. "Henry told the police it was Margaret's day off."

Rico nodded. "A typical trap criminals fall into, adding an extra detail. Bernstow should've caught that. Still . . ." He tapped his fingers against the side of his tumbler. "Slim basis for going to Bottmeyer's cabin."

"That was the beginning," Zee said. "The lie that made me question everything and led me to the note. I was sure at the time that Shandra lied about why she wrote it. I asked myself why she would want to point me toward money as a motive. From there, the whole plot unraveled." She raised pleading eyes to Rico. "Don't taunt Bernstow about it, okay?"

"I'll protect your delicate relationship." He patted her hand. "But you didn't have the note when you confronted Shandra's father."

Zee started, then realized Rico thought she'd given Bernstow the incriminating piece of paper. She averted her gaze. She would find another time to confess.

"The last piece was the knife," she said. "Henry wasn't a hunter, you said so. Why would he own an expensive, high-end hunting knife? Then I remembered that Bottmeyer said he used to hunt with McNeary." She glanced at Fontina. "I had a gut feeling that Shandra's father held the key to the whole thing."

Rico shook his head. "Good thing your instinct was right. You can't always trust it."

"It's been right a few times during this case," Zee said. "It sent me on my 'church-lady' visit to Shandra."

Blush darkened Rico's cheeks.

Zee smiled to let him know she forgave his mockery.

Rico clinked his glass to hers. "Good job." They drank in tandem. "Karl's going to find it hard to reject this story. You will write it, right?"

Zee nodded, her chest warming from more than whiskey.

"More news," said Rico. "The police arrested Paselly in connection with the death of James Hawethorne."

Zee sucked in a breath. She'd been right about that, too.

"His sister turned him in." Rico laid his hand on her undamaged cheek. "You won't need to worry about him anymore."

She swallowed scotch. The burning cleared Hawethorne's dead face from her mind, but another thought intruded. "Did he try to kill Angelica Street, too?"

"Don't know." Kindness softened his voice. "Bernstow's got his teeth in him now. He'll find out." He brushed a curl from her cheek. "Please try not to worry."

Easier said than done.

He flashed a mischievous grin. "From what Bottmeyer said, we missed one hell of a girl fight."

It was clearly a ploy to redirect her focus. A little awkward, but she appreciated it. "Guys. All alike." She rolled her eyes and discovered her sockets hurt. "How is the total freaking nutcase?"

"She'll recover." Bitterness tinged Fontina's voice. "If she had done . . ."

The visceral memory ambushed Zee, sharpening the aches in her body. Her lightheartedness evaporated. "Fools rush in," she murmured.

Rico slipped fingertips beneath her quivering chin. "You did great."

She soaked in courage along with his heat and managed a smile. "At least I didn't get shot this time, though I damn near fired that gun when I tried to grab it from Bottmeyer."

"My fault." Fontina's eyes glistened. "I always tell you to heed your intuition, but I overrode mine. If not, I'd have noticed Shandra before she had that piece of glass at my throat."

Zee's hand fluttered to the soft flesh of her own throat. "I've never been so scared." She swallowed. "I'd never forgive myself if—"

"Over and gone."

Fontina's soft assertion anchored Zee in the safety of her living room, but an unsettling thought pricked her. Fontina had jumped in her car, rushed to Zee's rescue, and arrived at exactly the wrong time, upending Zee's victory. Precisely what Zee had feared Rico would do. Yet she accepted Fontina's behavior and resisted Rico's.

"Drachma?" Fontina queried.

Zee decided to ponder the dilemma later. "Wish I'd seen what you did to disable Shandra."

"Credit goes to you and Pete. You distracted her." Fontina gestured with her arm. "A simple leg sweep and pin."

"I need more of your self-defense classes." Zee grimaced. "And fewer pastries. For a pampered socialite, that damn psycho was a vicious fighter."

"From the look of her, you held your own." Pride glimmered in Rico's eyes.

"She didn't take into account your tenacity," said Fontina with a grin.

"Tenacity." Zee laughed. "I like that word better than some I've heard."

Rico chuckled. "I'll remember your preference."

Fontina's smile faded. She moved to sit beside Zee, enfolding Zee's hand with both of hers. "Your heart is always in the right place, Zee-zee. You could have ignored Hawethorne, more than once. And, although your moves were not always entirely well-thought-out, you put yourself in danger to help Henry and protect Bottmeyer."

Everything she'd been through balled itself up and crashed down on Zee. It all could have gone so wrong. She stroked Candy's ears. "Maybe I should try thinking with my head instead of my heart."

Fontina wrapped her in a gentle hug. "Don't you dare. Your head can lie, but your heart always tells the truth."

Hot tears built behind Zee's eyes. "Thanks, big sister."

Fontina gathered her shawl around her shoulders. "This big sister has a class in way too few hours. I'll see myself out." She touched Rico's shoulder. "Take care of her."

As Fontina's footsteps faded, warmth from her embrace lingered, balm for Zee's soul.

Rico brushed her wet cheeks with his thumb as the door clicked shut. "I know you're fully capable, but let me help you right now."

Zee wriggled free of the blanket tent, careful not to upend Candy. "Rico, I—"

He covered her fluttering hand with his. "Once you're settled, I'll go."

She lifted her arm. Her shoulder winced a warning. She ignored it and burrowed her fingers in his hair. "Don't."

He locked his eyes with hers. "What are you doing?"

"Stay."

He touched the tender junction at her jaw, then brought his hand to rest on the back of her neck. "I want to. You don't know how much I want to. But I can't. You're too vulnerable."

She caressed his chin. "I'm physically wrecked. Highly emotional. And very possibly drunk." She brushed a finger across his lips. "And I know what I want."

He curled his fingers around hers. "You're ready to face your ghosts?"

His gaze scoured her. She wished she knew the answer. She settled for the truth of the moment. "Nothing worthwhile comes easily."

He snaked one arm around her shoulders, slipped the other beneath her knees, and lifted her from the couch. "Let's get you to bed." He cradled her to his chest. "I'll sleep on the futon. We can talk in the morning, when we're both thinking more clearly."

She nestled to him and inhaled the scent of leather and motor oil, citrus and woods. "My head says sleep on the futon if you must, but my heart . . ." She met his parted lips.

Terri Maue has been in love with words for as long as she can remember. Even today, she's still awed by the fact that little black marks on a sheet of paper have the power to fill her mind with images, ideas, and emotions.

Many of Terri's interests find their way into her stories. She holds a first-degree black belt in TaeKwon Do, much to her surprise, as she dislikes violence and never expected to enjoy kicking, punching, and breaking bricks. She is intrigued by psychic phenomena and all forms of spirituality, believing that everyone has access to realms beyond the physical and can enter altered states of consciousness—without drugs. Like her protagonist, she loves food, especially pastry. Fortunately, her husband, Eddie, is a good cook.

Terri is a member of Sisters in Crime, Mystery Writers of America, and several local writers groups. She and Eddie are Ohio transplants who now live in Las Vegas, Nevada. Visit her on her website terrimaue.com to find out what she has in store next for Zee, Rico, and Fontina in the not-so-sleepy town of Valerian, Ohio.

Printed in the USA
CPSIA information can be obtained
at www.ICGtesting.com
BVHW031926080823
668343BV00006B/19